THE TEMPORAL DETECTIVES!
SERIES 1

By STEPHEN JOHN WILLIAMS

Based on the original internet adventure series: "The amazing adventures of Jericho Tibbs!" by Stephen J. Williams writing as 'William Alexander Stephens.' SERIES 1 contains TWELVE selected episodes from SEASON 1 of those internet-based adventures from 2017/18. **THIS IS THE FIRST BOOK IN THE SERIES.**

NOTES:
[1] **Front Cover:** the original photograph is from **'ISTOCK' – 916399712 – 612x612** and is used under License by the author.
[2] For other illustration credits, please see page 403 for details.

"Dedicated with thanks to Jennifer O'Donnell and Peter Goldie."

VISIT 'THE TEMPORAL DETECTIVES' WEBSITE, SCAN THIS CODE:

Or type: https://temporaldetectives.blogspot.com

 # SERIES 1: THE EPISODES.

EPISODE 1: "THE MAN WHO DIED IN THE FUTURE TO SAVE HIS PAST."
START PAGE: 9.

MISSION SUMMARY:
"Old Arthur Smith jumps into the road and saves the life of a young child but is killed. He finds Mr. Tibbs on his case because he doesn't exist! Jericho's team can find no trace of the old man and it appears that 'old Arthur Smith' is not who he says, his real story is violent and steeped in black magic from the dreadful days of Nazi Germany - Is a Minion of the 'Dark Prince' involved?"

NOTES: This episode was the 'pilot' of the series and is slightly shorter in length than most subsequent episodes.

 **ALCOHOL, VIOLENCE, STRONG LANGUAGE & NAZI'S!**

EPISODE 2: "THE DUNMORE WITCH TRIALS."
START PAGE: 30.

MISSION SUMMARY:
"A young woman in Medieval England is accused of witchcraft; apparently she has visions of the future which come true. But the King's special Herald; Sir Henry Barfield [the younger] believes she could prove useful for the King's wars with France and Scotland - her gift could change the current Human Timeline and Mr. Tibbs must investigate; but who does the girl really serve?"

NOTES:
[1] Contains references to 'witchcraft'.
[2] This is a special **Extended** Edition.

ALCOHOL, SEXUAL REFERENCES, VIOLENCE [Including graphic descriptions of torture and death] STRONG LANGUAGE.

EPISODE 3: "THE GHOSTS AND MISS JESSICA MARTIN."
START PAGE: 60.

MISSION SUMMARY:

"London 1940 - The Blitz - Mr. Tibbs investigates a strange 'apparition' which has appeared on the streets of war-torn London during the German bombing of the East End. But is distracted by the curious case of young Jessica Martin and the RAF pilot who has just crashed his Spitfire on wasteland to avoid coming down on nearby houses; the two should never have met but they did!"

NOTES: It is – partly – based on a true historical incident.

TRIGGER WARNING ALCOHOL, VIOLENCE [Including graphic descriptions of war deaths] STRONG LANGUAGE & MILD HORROR.

EPISODE 4: "DR. ALEXANDER HARRIS AND HIS BATTLE WITH GOD."
START PAGE: 83.

MISSION SUMMARY:

"A Medical Officer on the Western Front receives a visit from Mr. Tibbs - Someone is saving lives of the dead and the Human Time-Line could be seriously threatened. It's the eve of the Battle of the Somme [July 1st, 1916] and Jericho, with his team, are in the trenches on the day before the bloodiest battle in British Military History. Now posing as foreign diplomats and reporters, the team investigates Casualty Clearing Station No.21 and the strange Doctor Alexander Harris."

NOTES: It is – partly – based on a true historical incident.

TRIGGER WARNING ALCOHOL, VIOLENCE, STRONG LANGUAGE & MILD HORROR.

EPISODE 5: "THE IMPOSSIBLE FILMS OF MISS STOCKYARD CANNING."
START PAGE: 109.

MISSION SUMMARY:
"Mr. Jericho Tibbs investigates newly discovered films from the Edwardian era, which were recovered from a derelict London shop's basement, and they appear to show the impossible: Napoleon on the march, the Battle of Agincourt, Romans and King Henry VIII - is there a 'Time-traveler' operating in the early 20th Century who is collecting a record of their travels?"

NOTES: It is – partly – based on a true incident.

TRIGGER WARNING ALCOHOL, VIOLENCE [Including graphic description of Demonic assault] STRONG LANGUAGE & MILD HORROR.

EPISODE 6: "BETRAYAL AT GETTYSBURG."
START PAGE: 139.

MISSION SUMMARY:
"Someone or something is trying to change the outcome of the American Civil War and Mr. Tibbs must prevent the Time-Line from being altered; so, it's back to 1863 and the forthcoming Battle of Gettysburg. Jericho must discover the plot and who's behind it and quickly, for he also knows that someone is about to betray the temporal detectives - is it a spy, time-traveler or something more sinister?"

NOTES:
[1] Contains language that is relevant for the time period but is now considered offensive. It contains 'censored' dialogue.
[2] It is – partly – based on a true historical incident.
[3] This is a special **Extended** Edition.

TRIGGER WARNING ALCOHOL, VIOLENCE, SEXUAL REFERENCES, STRONG LANGUAGE [including racial slurs] & MILD HORROR.

EPISODE 7: "HOBBS ABBEY AND THE DEVIL'S GRAVEYARD."
START PAGE: 178.

MISSION SUMMARY:

"In the summer of 1970, a small team of student archaeologists have a field trip for ten days to the ruins of Hobbs Abbey - a ancient place steeped in legends and tales of the paranormal: mostly about the Devil and his demons. Local folklore has whispered for centuries, that the Monk's of Hobbs Abbey were always specially selected; to guard a terrible secret hidden about the Abbey grounds. But this summer is special: It is the 666th Anniversary of the Abbey's founding and has something sinister come to celebrate?"

NOTES: Contains references to witchcraft & Demonic activity.

TRIGGER WARNING ALCOHOL, VIOLENCE, STRONG SEXUAL REFERENCES, STRONG LANGUAGE & MILD HORROR.

EPISODE 8: "CORDLESS, CORDLESS & FRASER (SOLICITORS)."
START PAGE: 203.

MISSION SUMMARY:

"The established family solicitors of Cordless, Cordless & Fraser have existed in the heart of Edinburgh's old city for over 200 years. In the summer of 1980, the young Clerk who looks after the basement archives of the firm, informs the Senior partner; Sir David Fraser, that it's time to deliver the old document pouch to the address marked upon it - except the pouch was lodged with the Solicitors way back in 1780, to be delivered on its Bicentennial year! - Mr. Tibbs is now on the case."

NOTES:
[1] Names have been changed to protect the innocent!
[2] This is a special **Extended** Edition.

TRIGGER WARNING ALCOHOL, VIOLENCE, STRONG SEXUAL REFERENCES [including sexual assault] STRONG LANGUAGE & MILD HORROR.

EPISODE 9: "PHARAOH AMENHOTEPH V AND THE MIRROR OF TIME."
START PAGE: 241.

MISSION SUMMARY:

"Pharaoh Amenhotep V's magician has been ordered to investigate a strange mirror that appears to show alternative versions of the future - apparently, the mirror was robbed from an ancient tomb which belonged to the legendary magician; Tha, who is said to have received it from the God Thoth himself. But the King is known as the 'Dark Pharaoh' and plans to use the device for his own benefit and alter the destiny of his ancient Empire - Mr. Tibbs is dispatched to protect the current Time-Line from change."

NOTES: This is a special **Extended** Edition.

TRIGGER WARNING ALCOHOL, VIOLENCE, STRONG SEXUAL REFERENCES [including sexual assault] STRONG LANGUAGE & MILD HORROR.

EPISODE 10: "THE DEVIL'S CIRCUS."
START PAGE: 280.

MISSION SUMMARY:

"Damian Coffin is the Ringmaster of 'Circus Diablo' who tour late Victorian Britain, but this is no entertainment for families as they perform only for the ultra wealthy and the powerful. Only the morally corrupt and sexually deviant are their Patrons - and some of them are prepared to pay their Soul for a very special performance; 'The Dance of the Black Queen'. Mr. Tibbs is back in 1889, in the East End of London; because the Devil's Circus has come to town!"

NOTES: This episode was the 'Seasonal Special' for Series 1 [online at website] and was written with humour to the fore!

TRIGGER WARNING ALCOHOL, COMICAL VIOLENCE, SEXUAL REFERENCES, STRONG LANGUAGE & MILD HORROR.

EPISODE 11: "GHOSTS IN THE DEVIL'S GARDEN OF THE DAMNED."
START PAGE: 323.

MISSION SUMMARY:

"There has been an error in the 'Dispatch Department' [They keep the records of deaths] and Mr. Jericho Tibbs must find and bring back Patrick 'Bends' McGill from the dead of the Underworld, despite being a man of evil disposition, he must be returned to the Dimension of the living. This will involve a dangerous trip to a part of Hell colloquially known as the 'Devil's Garden' - where the Dark Prince rules!"

NOTES: Contains scenes which may distress more sensitive readers!

TRIGGER WARNING ALCOHOL, VIOLENCE, SOME SEXUAL REFERENCES, STRONG LANGUAGE & MILD HORROR.

EPISODE 12: "THE GALLOWS TREE HOTEL MYSTERY."
START PAGE: 363.

MISSION SUMMARY:

"In the early summer of 1999, Anne and Kent Murphy are excited - and dreading it a little - that work on the new restaurant extension for their hotel; 'The Gallows Tree' is underway. But contractors excavating in the old gardens have hit a problem; they have discovered the remains of ancient dungeons, complete with graveyard. Now work has halted while Archaeologists from Rutland University check out the uncovered ruins. Mr. Tibbs is on scene because two souls have gone missing from the current human timeline..."

NOTES: Contains language that is relevant for the time period but is now considered offensive.

TRIGGER WARNING ALCOHOL, VIOLENCE, SEXUAL REFERENCES, STRONG LANGUAGE & MILD HORROR.

DISCLAIMER FOR ALL WORKS BY THE AUTHOR:

"All incidents and dialogue, and all characters with the exception of some well-known historical figures, are products of the author's imagination and are not to be construed as real. Where real-life historical figures appear, the situations, incidents, and dialogues concerning those persons are entirely fictional and are not intended to depict actual events or to change the entirely fictional nature of the work. In all other respects, any resemblance to actual persons, living or dead, events, or locales is entirely coincidental."

CAUTION:

"SOME OF THESE EPISODES CONTAIN VERY STRONG LANGUAGE, VIOLENCE, HORROR AND SEXUAL REFERENCES. Some are RECOMMENDED suitable for persons aged 15+ years only."

PLEASE REMEMBER: ALL STORIES ARE RATED

   OR   

AGE 15+ ONLY   **AGE 12+ ONLY.**

AVERAGE READING TIMES: between 30 to 45 minutes [approx.]

EPISODE 1: "THE MAN WHO DIED IN THE FUTURE TO SAVE HIS PAST."

MISSION SUMMARY:
"Old Arthur Smith jumps into the road and saves the life of a young child but is killed. He finds Mr. Tibbs on his case because he doesn't exist! Jericho's team can find no trace of the old man and it appears that 'old Arthur Smith' is not who he says, his real story is violent and steeped in black magic from the dreadful days of Nazi Germany; Is a Minion of the 'Dark Prince' involved?"

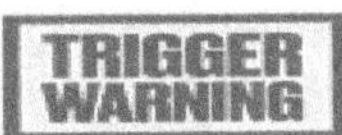 **ALCOHOL, VIOLENCE, STRONG LANGUAGE & NAZI'S!**

 **AGE 12+ ONLY.**    **30 Minutes reading time.**

1. DEATH ON A SUNNY AFTERNOON.

The shocked passer-byes, local residents and motorists had formed a large broken circle about the vehicle. It's engine now silent, door hanging open, windscreen glass scattered about the wet oily road, coloured a vivid red from released blood.

Some turned away from the awful scene to watch the Ambulance arrive, the crew decamping at speed, following a sturdy young firewoman who was shouting and gesturing at the vehicle, where three of her colleagues, sweating and cursing, had managed to jack the front of the shattered vehicle up, just enough for one to crawl under.

"She's alive! Sweet Jesus, she's alive!" He shouted with real emotion in his voice, the little girl gripped his hands and gently he pulled her from the clinging arms of the old man, who's still body appeared to have become one with the metal; flesh and steel seemed indistinguishable. The road was covered with oil, screen-wash, and radiator fluid, liquids from the dead engine and puddles of bright red blood from the dead old man, who now seemed to have vanished as a human; becoming one with the iron and liquid.

Whilst the crowd cheered and clapped, the ambulance-man wrapped the shocked little girl in a blanket and placed her on the stretcher, her sobbing mother, almost staggering with a mixture of disbelief and sheer joy, gripped her tightly and thanked everyone from God to St. Christopher.

Then she saw the broken legs protruding from the wreck and whispered: "Oh God, thank you for him, thank you, thank you......"

The mother and daughter were taken to the ambulance as the fire officer and the young constable exchanged glances. "Dead." The fireman said simply, and the constable nodded – the old man was gone - his life over in seconds, terminated by a foolish young driver, speeding down a quiet residential road who only the saw the child running after her ball when she was in front of him. Then, the figure jumping from the kerbside, the bright coloured plastic shopping bags falling from his hands, then the old man before the car, wrapping the child into his arms.

The driver kept repeating that the old man turned and looked at him, as if he knew he couldn't run or turn away. The old man knew he was dead before the vehicle crushed the life from his body with screaming tyres, bending steel, snapping plastic, shattering glass and then, a terrible silence for an eternity. By nightfall, the scene was now quiet while methodical Police Officers made notes, measured skid marks and had photographs taken.

They believed the road could be open again, in just a few hours. The old man's body had been removed to the local morgue and enquiries were in hand to try and identify him. They had little to go on, he carried no wallet, just a few pound coins and other loose change, a couple of keys on a 'Bugs Bunny' keyring and a rolled up, blood-soaked copy of the local paper.

None of the witnesses or local residents that gave statements professed to know him, though a couple of pensioners had stated that they had seen him about the place, but never had spoken to him. The Traffic Police Inspector sighed; this one could be a real problem and the media was all over the case, upon hearing how the old man died, they wanted to proclaim their hero in tomorrow's edition, and they wanted answers now.

He walked back to his car and pulled a packet of humbugs from his pocket, sometimes, just sometimes, he really wanted a cigarette again – humbugs really didn't have the same effect - after viewing something like this.

2. THE COLLECTOR AND THE DETECTIVES.

The old man sat down on the steps of the local hall and watched the scene unfold before him, the happy child, the speeding car, the little red ball bouncing from the kerb into the road, the plastic carrier bags thrown down, and the sudden and brutal transformation from life to death on a beautiful sunny afternoon.

He looked up at the tall young man, who smiled at him and said; "Hello Solomon, I'm Herbert, but nearly everyone calls me 'Herbie' – well, except the boss, she always calls me Herbert. I'm sorry Solomon, but I can't take you, I've put a call in for a Temporal Detective to attend. You see, I have the little girl in my Soul ledger for today; not you. Yes, this is all wrong my friend. Your name was in my Ledger, but for October 1942, not today!" He spoke softly and then slapped the small black book shut with an amused look upon his face. "You see Solomon, you should have been collected many years ago - but your Soul failed to show up!" Herbert added and stopped smiling.

"I don't understand, I am dead, am I not?" The old man spoke quietly and touched the young man's hand, he really didn't understand what had happened, but he knew he was dead, so how could he be sitting here, talking to this friendly young man, who dressed like an Edwardian Bookkeeper!

Herbert nodded and gripped the old man's hand; "You certainly are dead now Solomon!" There was a quiet glow of pure white light and that's when the young woman joined them, Solomon stood up and smiled at her, holding out his hand. She gripped it quite tightly for a woman he thought, and she nodded agreeably, with a wonderful big smile upon her pretty face.

"This is Temporal Detective Alex Cappanni." Herbert said quietly and folded his arms. "Hello Solomon!" She exclaimed with real affection in her soft voice and touched his shoulder; "Well Solomon, we really need to sort this one out, don't we!" She added and pushed her fingers through her long dark hair; "May I ask how you knew to be here today at this time? I've seen the record of this time and you are not present because you died in October 1942 and somehow, your Soul avoided collection."

The old man shrugged his shoulders; "I don't know what you're talking about. I saw the little girl run into the road after her red ball. I saw the speeding car and knew I had to do something." He looked the young woman up and down; she was a real beauty with pale skin, black hair and dark black eyes. Solomon stared at her large firm breasts, beneath her crisp white blouse and smiled. Her short dark skirt covered very little of her long slender legs; Detective Constable Alexandra Mary Cappanni was a real beauty - few men would disagree with that assessment - including the late Solomon Schmidt.

Alex folded her arms and sighed; Solomon was not hiding his appreciation of her figure by any means; "Bloody men, still the same despite being dead." She said under her breath. Then her mirror buzzed, and she pulled it from her handbag; it was a Senior Time Controller. Alex answered the call with some politeness and concern; Senior Time Controllers just didn't call up temporal detective constables every day.

Alex listened quietly and then replied; "Yes Sir, I do appreciate and understand that. Team 74 has been allocated the Mission. Yes, that's right Sir; Inspector Jericho Tibbs. Yes. Thank you, Sir." She closed the mirror and looked at Solomon; saving the little girl will have major ramifications for the current Human Timeline.

There was a soft flash of white light and Solomon greeted the new person who had arrived, Temporal Detective Inspector Jericho Tibbs. He was about six feet tall and slender, dressed in a dark three-piece suite with black boots and a black frock coat. He wore a black bowler hat on the back of his head. Solomon commented on how smart he looked. Jericho just smiled and shook his hand, introducing himself.

The Detective stepped back and took a good look at Solomon; "Why did you jump out and save the girl? She was fated to die today and now your actions could seriously jeopardise the future history of Humanity." Jericho rubbed his chin and waited for Solomon to reply. He just shrugged his shoulders; "I dreamt it you see, the little girl, the red ball, the car, I saw it all and knew I had to do something."

"You are already dead Solomon, you died in 1942. But your soul was not collected; so how did you get to 1990?" The Detective tapped his mirror; "The dead do not dream, and they certainly don't pop up some 48 years later; alive and kicking without something being terribly wrong."

"I have dealt with several cases similar to your own; people that appeared in the wrong time and place, in the future or the past and did or attempted to change the Current Timeline." Jericho sighed and glanced at Alex, who was checking her mirror. He turned back to Solomon and asked quietly; "Where were you for 48 years?"

Solomon looked at his feet and folded his arms; "I'm a Janitor at the Town Hall and I don't really know what you're saying, I was walking back from the shops and suddenly realised that my dream was unfolding before my eyes." He placed both hands on his sides and glanced at Alex's breasts again.

"OK, what did you buy at the shops; what was in your shopping bags Solomon?" Alex asked with a diminishing smile and clasped her elegant hands together; Solomon could see her glistening silver fingernails and slender fingers, wrapped around her 'mirror'.

"I don't know, I can't remember what I bought. The accident must have swept it from my memory, sorry." Solomon muttered, gripping his hands together.

There was a silence for a few seconds between them. "You have changed the Human Timeline and not for the best - the Timeline must be restored so I think we need to investigate further." Jericho finally spoke and pulled his mirror out.

The Collector watched as the two Temporal Detectives and Mr. Solomon Schmidt simply vanished. Herbert the Collector whispered; "Good luck my friend." He opened his Soul-ledger and noticed that the old man's entry had been replaced by a single line; '147733 - 3 - 2013 TIBBS.' The matter was now in the hands of Temporal Detectives. He sighed and checked the next collection; May 18th, 1671, and a certain Ivan Smirnoff, who was currently being tortured to death in a Moscow prison. He was eighteen years old and had been accused of stealing chickens from a local landowner. Herbie was to collect his soul and make sure it was processed.

No living humans had seen Solomon's soul talking with the Collector or the temporal detectives and no human time had passed during the conversations.

3. THE LIGHTHOUSE ON HEAVEN'S EDGE BAY.

The lighthouse was still and looked quite peaceful in the late evening sunshine and haze, the waves of an almost calm sea slapped against the rocks below and several seagulls dived and swooped in the light blue sky in strange silence. Far beyond Heaven's Edge Bay, Arthur/Solomon could see the three masts of a large sailing ship, under full sail, heading north towards the horizon.

The loose gravel of the pathway crunched and shifted under his boots as he followed Mr. Tibbs towards the Lighthouse, which seemed to grow at their approach. Detective Cappanni gestured towards the imposing building and spoke directly to Solomon; "The lighthouse was built and commissioned in the 1870's, but the crew of three Keepers was removed in the 1980's when the place was automated. Now it's the home of Mr. Tibbs and the local office of the Temporal Detection Directorate. Just out of interest, the current year is 1901 and it always remains that year because the passing of human time doesn't matter here."

Solomon adjusted his tight collar and shielding his eyes from the bright sun with his hand asked; "but if it's 1901, the Keepers would still be here?" He said and saw Mr. Tibbs glance over his shoulder and noticed the look that passed between him and Detective Cappanni, who answered, "That's very clever Solomon and well reasoned, but there are no human Keepers presently here that can see or hear us. Our entire existence here is happening in a millisecond, we operate on God's time - not human time – so we're invisible to them."

Solomon nodded; "And God's seconds are a lot longer than ours!" and smiled. Mr. Tibbs stopped walking and turned slightly, looking at Solomon with an odd expression; "Quite so, we could exist here for a century and only a few seconds would have passed in God's time: the humans who inhabit the lighthouse will never see or hear us, we're on a very different frequency to them." Mr. Tibbs turned his back and started to walk to the lighthouse again.

Detective Cappanni whispered to Solomon; "That's not quite right, in the year 2026 a family moved into the lighthouse, and it became a family home. The couple was wealthy, they refurbished the place. But they had a young daughter; Emma, who was about six years old - she could see and hear us. We all had little chats with her; she seemed so lonely with no other children to play with. Even Mr. Tibbs played catch with her!"

Solomon laughed quietly to himself and asked; "What became of the little girl?"

Alex sighed and smiled; "When she grew up, she wrote a bestselling book about her ghostly friends from past times, and it became a hit moving picture called 'The Ghosts of Heaven's Edge Bay.' I understand Mr. Tibbs had some explaining to Angel Margret, but nothing came of it." Detective Cappanni grinned, then shouted out; "Hello Mr. Harris!" she waved to the impressive figure who had appeared in the doorway of the lighthouse.

Harris was a big man, well over six feet in height and clearly knew his way around a gym, he was dressed immaculately in a three-piece suit with polished shoes and clean white gloves. When you looked at Mr. Harris you were always impressed.

"That's Mr. Harris, he's the Butler here, A fine man and very loyal to Mr. Tibbs." Alex smiled at Harris and received a slight bow in return. "His wife; Cleo is the Housekeeper and cook, her food is totally delicious." The group had reached the black, front double doors of the lighthouse, now held open by Harris, and Mr. Tibbs gestured them to enter.

"Mrs. Harris will serve dinner at seven thirty-five Sir." Harris
spoke quietly to Mr. Tibbs and took Alex Cappanni's coat.
Solomon then realised the inside of the lighthouse was huge,
with a grand entrance and staircase, complete with rooms
coming off the main hall - he shook his head in disbelief; "I see
that the Laws of Physics don't apply in God's time either."

That's when he saw the nervous looking young man in an ill-
fitting suit, by the staircase, gripping a brown folder and smiling.
"That's Acting Detective Owen Jones; he's already been working
on your case Solomon." Alex stated, watching the look of
surprise pass over Solomon's face; "I know he doesn't look much
like a Detective, but he has a very sharp mind and I think he's
waiting to see Mr. Tibbs."

Harris ushered the small group into the front reception room and
served whisky and brandy; for those wanting it. Alex Cappanni
sipped a small brandy with great elegance and Solomon sat
upright in one of the large leather chairs clutching his whisky
class. Young Owen Jones also took a whisky and much to
Solomon's surprise downed it in one and received a fresh class
from the ever-attentive Mr. Harris. "That's better, it tastes far
nicer here than amongst the living." Owen smiled directly at
Solomon and raised his glass, adding; "Here's to the dead; who
know and to the living; who think they know."

Solomon raised his glass to return the salutation and sipped the
whisky very slowly. He could see Mr. Tibbs, relaxing in a similar
chair, but this one was worn about the arms and back cushion -
he wondered about the hours Tibbs must have spent in the chair,
thinking about his latest case?

That's when he noticed the big black cat sprawled on the carpet,
moving in its sleep before the fireplace. "That's Mr. Parker; he's
been around here for years; I think he arrived with the stones
and cement." Owen chuckled and sipped his whisky. "I noticed
one of the three small cottages had smoke coming from its
chimney, who else lives on this little piece of rock?" Solomon
asked, peering through the small window of the reception room.

"John lives there." Owen said simply and received a re-fill from
Mr. Harris. Alex nodded towards the window; "John is a recluse
and has been for many years, he and Mr. Tibbs are good friends.
He has an incredible knowledge of human history and the human

condition." Then another joined the group, following Mr. Harris into the room and accepting a large brandy glass from him. It was Jericho's deputy, Temporal Detective Sergeant Wilson Franklyn, just back from the land of the living. Solomon was impressed; Wilson Franklyn was equal in statue to Mr. Harris and dressed in an orange and white 1970's suit with wide flared trousers. Wilson had an 'Afro' hair style that could hide several bird nests and sideburns that easily could be mistaken as hedgerows!

The big man sipped his brandy and smiled broadly; "Alex my baby! Little Lady Alex!" He bent down and kissed Alex on the forehead; "Hell girl, sweet Jesus, you're hotter than the Devil's hair tongs!" He dropped into the chair opposite Solomon and pulled a brown folder from his jacket and placed it on the small coffee table at his side. "Beauty and brains in one neat package!" He added grinning and then poured the brandy down his neck in one hit.

Solomon said quietly to Owen; "Why did Mr. Franklyn call Miss Alex: Lady Alex?"

Owen smiled and gestured towards Alex; "That's because she is a real Lady; Detective Alex was married to an Italian Count [that's the equivalent of an Earl in British aristocracy] she was the 23rd Countess of Cappanni. She was married to Henri, the 16th Count and her son Philippe was the 17th Count of Cappanni and her descendants are still Counts there."

Solomon nodded to Wilson Franklyn who was talking to Mr. Tibbs and asked Owen; "Now he is some character, was he a footballer?" Owen actually laughed out loud and shook his head; "The sergeant was actually a real detective in the seventies New York Police Department, so he knows his way around an investigation." Owen swallowed down his whisky and stood up because Mr. Harris had announced lunch and the group filed into the dining room, welcomed by the smell of hot food and the House Maid, Miss Ruth Hall. She grinned at Owen, and he shyly smiled back and nervously fiddled with his tie; like he normally did when she smiled at him.

4. DINNER.

Ruth showed everyone to their seats, except Mr. Tibbs, who sat at the table head and nodded to Mr. Harris that dinner could proceed. Ruth filled the wine glasses and topped up the water pitchers; she gave a shy smile to Owen who grinned back and nervously adjusted his napkin.

Young Ruth quite liked Owen and he certainly liked her; they exchanged glances again and Ruth started to serve the soup from the tureen that Mr. Harris carried. Ruth glanced - again – at Owen; she sighed. He must have looked quite a sight in the monk's habit, striding around the grounds of the ancient and beautiful Moorland Monastery, administering to the poor and needy, in medieval Yorkshire.

"This soup is excellent; vegetable is my favourite." Solomon commented, dipping his spoon back into the bowl and then caught the attention of Mr. Tibbs, who sat with his chin placed on the back of his hands, and Solomon lowered his spoon and said quietly; "What is it Mr. Tibbs?"

Mr. Tibbs tapped the two brown folders by his soup bowl; "We have a small problem Solomon and I wonder if you could help us a little on this one?" Mr. Tibbs nodded to Owen, who wiped his mouth and placed the soup spoon on his napkin.

"It appears that 'Old Solomon Schmidt didn't actually exist in 1990, as one of the living. I mean, there are several 'Solomon Schmidt's' in the Soul Ledgers for that time. But you're not any of them. No living human, at the time, could remember you and even your work colleagues at the Town Hall could not recall you; no one knew the Janitor Solomon Schmidt."

Owen picked up his water pitcher and filled his glass adding; "I saw the body in the morgue, it was badly damaged, and the Police could find no identity papers on you. Your fingerprints came back unknown and the new DNA tests [for 1990] revealed you were originally from Germany or Denmark." Owen sipped his water and continued to eat his soup.

Wilson Franklyn coughed and spoke quietly; "That's where it gets really interesting Solomon; there was a German family who were Jewish and seven recorded members perished in Dachau and were collected the very same day. The family name was 'Schmidt' and we cannot find any other soul collected that could be linked to them; except you."

Wilson smiled slightly and added; "There was one soul missing from that extended family group and it has been missing for nearly forty-eight years, that's you isn't it Solomon?"

Solomon said nothing, but looked down at the table cloth.

Lady Cappanni lowered her spoon and lifted her wine glass, but didn't drink from it; "The little girl was in Herbert's Soul Ledger for that very time and date. She was to have no descendants and yet by the year 2100, no-less that ninety such souls exist and here's the worse part: over seventy of those souls belong to the 'Dark Side'."

Wilson Franklyn tapped the table and pointed to Solomon; "That sweet little girl grew up to be a practicing Satanist and Black Witch, her influence has spread through the generations she created and recruited solders for the 'Dark Prince'. Her life was supposed to end that day and you prevented it. Yet you have no real history in that time period, we cannot find a living human who actually knew you. There are lots of 'Solomon Schmidt's' in the Soul Ledgers, and all have been collected; save one; that's you." Wilson leaned back in his chair and watched Solomon carefully, repeating; "You're not one of them." Shrugging his shoulders, Wilson swallowed down his drink and placed the class upon the table.

"Your body lay in the local morgue for nearly three months before the Newspapers pulled a collection together to give you a big funeral; and guess what?" Owen said, then dropped his napkin on the table and smiled at Solomon.

"I don't know about any of this." Solomon said simply; his appetite for the soup gone. Owen folded his arms and nodded; "Not one relative turned up for the ceremony - nobody, not a single soul. No-one had a clue about who the hell you were!"

Solomon sat in silence with a little smile upon his face. Mr. Tibbs leaned back in his dinning chair and said, "You see that's the problem Solomon. You don't exist - but you were there! - Changing human history."

5. CONFESSIONS OF A LOST SOUL.

Solomon lifted his glass and sipped some wine, his eyes never left Mr. Tibbs who was now leaning forward on the table, his soup bowel pushed to one side and his right hand lay upon the two folders – the other hand appeared out of sight beneath the dark wood table.

There was silence for a while and the group exchanged glances between themselves until Solomon coughed quietly and spoke, looking down at the clean white tablecloth; "I really didn't have any choice in the matter Mr. Tibbs." He looked up and all could see the tears that rolled down the pained expression upon his pale face. He coughed again and choked back the tears, wiping his face with the napkin.

"Please continue Solomon." Alex said gently and placed her wine glass upon the table. Mr. Tibbs lent back in his chair with no expression upon his face. "Yes, please carry on with your story Solomon." He said and nodded to Owen who produced his little black notebook from his jacket pocket; "Owen will record all you have to say."

Solomon took a deep breath and gripped his trembling hands together, he looked about the Dining Room and then his eyes rested upon Mr. Tibbs who sat hand on chin, ready to listen.

"I first met the strange old man in a back street of our little town one wet night. I was panting with fear, running from several Nazi thugs who really wanted to beat me with clubs and sticks because I had taken off the 'Star of David' from my jacket – it had worked before, but not that night; one of the younger boys had recognized me and called out my name with real hatred and anger: "Fuck! It's Solomon Schmidt! The slimy Jewish pig is trying to pass himself off as a real German!" They came after me and I knew my fate if they caught me; I ran like the wind, looking for a place to hide, I ran down a little alley way and to my utter horror found it was a dead end. I was trapped and when I turned, the group had appeared in the entrance; they were laughing and shouting, and I knew I was dead. As they approached, I was begging and screaming for my life; I pissed myself with fear and that seemed to edge them on. They surrounded me and the beating started. I tried rolling myself into a small ball; but I could still feel the blows."

Solomon used the napkin to wipe his face again and with a trembling hand sipped some more wine. "What year was this?"

Mr. Tibbs asked; again, with no emotion showing on his face.

"It was October 1942, I think. I was only seventeen at the time and living alone in a single room, within a tenement slum in the new Jewish Ghetto. I had left the Ghetto to buy or trade for food, that's why I took off the Star. It had worked before and I had passed unnoticed, until that boy recognized me. I had been friends with his older brother until he was killed in the invasion of Poland. I had no family; my parents were both dead – they died in a typhoid outbreak in 1938 - which left me alone. Any family I had was very distant and I knew none of them. But I made my living by singing in café's and clubs. Everyone said I had the voice of an angel; a real gift from God."

Solomon slumped back in his chair, the emotion of the memories he had invoked overcame him for a short time and he sat head in hands until Mr. Tibbs spoke again; "The strange old man, what happened with him?"

Solomon sat bolt upright and wiped his face again, he took a deep breath and swallowed down his wine; having his glass topped up by Mr. Harris who was standing just behind Solomon's chair. He looked directly at Mr. Tibbs and quietly continued his story;

"I was lying on the filthy wet road covered in rain and my own piss and blood. I just wanted it to end; the pain and terror to go away. I prayed to God so hard. Then the beating stopped, I could hear them whispering and swearing; they were backing away from me and suddenly, they started to run, and I watched them disappear from the alley, throwing down their sticks and clubs. I turned my head and wiped blood from my eyes and face; that's when I saw him standing over me. The old man was dressed like a doctor from the last century and carried a silver and wood walking stick with a Boar's head handle. He wiped his glasses with a white hankie and offered it, telling me to clean myself up."

"Such a strangely dressed old man would have been known around a small district in those days. An eccentric figure like him would have been subject to rumour and gossip surely?" asked Alex. "What had you heard about him?" She added, sipping her wine and adjusting the chair.

Solomon ran his fingers through his short hair and breathing deeply, whispered; "if I knew then, what I know about him now; I would have wished the fucking Nazi's had beaten me to death."

6. THE DEVIL'S PROFESSOR.

There was silence in the Dining room and Mr. Tibbs said simply; "Please tell us about the strange old man." Solomon looked up at the ceiling and then back to Mr. Tibbs. He continued;

"I had heard of him; the stories, the gossip, the rumours – the fear. But I just dismissed them as rubbish, I was a stupid young man whose life he had just saved, and I was so very grateful. He cleaned me up, dressed my wounds and gave me vodka to ease the pain. He had rooms above the Italian Laundry in Hindenburgstrassa. The place was filled with strange antiques, books, and manuscripts. He told me that he was a Professor of Mathematics' and once had worked with Albert Einstein, but his real passion was the supernatural. I should have run screaming from there, but the Police were everywhere; looking for the stupid young Jew who had defied the Nazi's and so I was trapped. Just like in that damn alley – except this was worse; far worse."

Solomon slumped in his chair and struggled to speak; the emotion of those memories swept over him, and he sobbed for some minutes, until Alex pushed a fresh glass of wine into his hands, and he swallowed it down. Composing himself yet again, Solomon continued his story.

"I could not leave the apartment and the old man worked on me to join in his little experiment. After hiding for almost a week in sheer fear of discovery and transportation to a concentration camp, I agreed to help him – God have mercy on me, but I had no choice. He practised Black Magic and admitted to being a minion of the Devil and for a small sacrifice; I could escape from this hell hole and live in freedom and peace, in a place of my choosing. Totally desperate; I agreed."

Solomon struggled to sit straight and finished his wine slowly. Then shrugging his shoulders in a sign of capitulation, he finished the story;

"The old man was Professor Wolfgang Leitcher, who admitted that he had been born in Saxony, in the year 1764 and thus he

*was actually 178 years old and had been granted certain powers
by the Devil himself. He used them to spirit me away to the year
1990 and a quiet town in England. But upon arrival, I found that
I had aged to match the year; I was an old man of 65. I knew he
had allowed that to happen; to ensure that I carried out his plan.
If I wanted to return to my Country and my youth; I had to die in
the future to save it."*

"What was his plan?" Mr. Tibbs asked quietly, now concerned
about what had taken place – little wonder 'old Solomon Schmidt'
didn't exist in 1990 because he should have died in 1942 and
been collected then. This was a 'lost' soul and involved with a
powerful minion of the Dark One, Jericho knew he needed to
proceed with caution now.

"It was to save a little girl who was important to his Master; I
don't know why she is; sorry."

"The purpose of all this must be to allow one of her descendants
to be born; so that they can serve him. But that person must be
really important to the Dark Prince; why?" Alex spoke directly to
Mr. Tibbs, who sat with a grim expression upon his face.

A few seconds in total silence passed and Jericho rose from his
chair and said quietly; "For what some people call an Antichrist,
but we call a Dark Angel in human form."

Jericho turned to Solomon and explained that; by mutual
agreement, both dark and light angels were forbidden to enter
the realm of mortal man. But the 'Dark Prince' did try to sneak
one through, now and again by having it born to a mortal
woman. Such a creature could easily destroy the careful balance
struck between light and dark forces - the result would be
Armageddon - he further explained that was the reason, for using
humans to police the Timeline; it reduced the chance that light
and dark angels could meet and clash; hence Temporal
Detectives, Collectors, Guardians and Knights were all once
human.

"I need to report this matter to Angel Margret." He said simply
and excused himself from the room, where the meal continued in
relative silence. Solomon ate nothing; he just sat quietly, staring
at the fireplace.

---

7. NAZI GERMANY.

Jericho finished talking to Angel Margret and returned to the Dining Room where the sad Solomon Schmidt sat at the table, head in hands. "Wilson and Owen, you get back to the incident with the child and make sure that she meets her departure on time; Herbie the Collector will be in attendance to scoop her up. Meanwhile, Alex and I are heading for Germany to ensure that young Mr. Solomon Schmidt meets the correct time and date of his scheduled departure." Jericho spoke with some authority and Owen with Wilson following headed for the 'Light-Room' and prepared to jump to 1990.

"Solomon; are you ready?" Alex asked the young man, who raised his head and nodded; "Does this mean I have to be killed on that morning? – I don't think that I can face that Miss." Jericho patted his shoulder and said quietly;"It's necessary to have you collected at your true point of departure and that means those bastards will have to kill you. You won't feel anything; it will be like watching a film clip, the Collector will do his job and your soul will be processed correctly."

"What about the Professor?" Solomon asked nervously; "I really don't want to meet him again." Jericho and Alex smiled, she spoke quietly; "Mr. Tibbs and I will be there and we will deal with Wolfgang – if he shows up – so don't be concerned by him."

The three made their way to the 'Light-Room' and simply walked into the bright light and they were gone.

Jericho wrapped his long dark coat about himself and adjusted his hat, glancing across at Alex who was adjusting her scarf as the snow flurries swept about the odd looking pair. They made their way down NebrisskiStrazza towards the little back alley where they knew 'Arthur Smith/Solomon Schmidt' would have just run into. Young Solomon let the tears run down his face – he was home again, and the emotion swelled up and overcame him. He staggered a little and when Alex placed her hand upon his arm, he straightened up and whispered; "I can do this."

"I should have guessed it would be snowing, it is October after all." Alex called out, her boots crunching upon the hardened snow as they approached the alley entrance. Jericho gestured towards the group of boys and young men running into the alleyway.

They wore Nazi armbands and carried clubs and sticks – they were hunting Jews and screaming with delight - they had one cornered.

"That's them." Solomon fell to his knees in the snow and started to pray. Both Jericho and Alex placed a hand upon his shoulders and watched the gang enter the alleyway.

The living humans could not see or hear the pair of Temporal Detectives [if they didn't wish it so] and thus, the Time-Sequence played itself out according to the record already in existence.

Alex and Jericho watched without emotion as the seventeen-year-old boy was beaten to death before their eyes. Professor Wolfgang Leitcher did not make an appearance and the gang, panting and sweating from their exertions made their way from the dirty little alley in high spirits.

"Some of them are Dutch!" Alex sounded quite astonished as the group passed by; "Yes, Dutch Nazi's, probably worse than the real thing." Jericho commented whilst examining the young Solomon Schmidt's battered corpse, slowly being covered by quite heavy snow. That's when Alex saw the young man standing by the shop doorway; it was Herbert; the Collector. He was tapping his 'Soul Ledger' against the up turned palm of his right hand.

"Hello Miss Alex, I see he's shown up this time." Herbert pointed to the snow-covered body and shrugged his shoulders. Alex turned to Jericho, who stepped away from the body and consulted his mirror, saying; "Please check your ledger, Herbert; who should have been collected here?"

The Collector snapped open his book and read the name out loud; "Solomon Schmidt." He said simply and closed the little notebook. Jericho was now ruffling through the pockets of the dead man and pulled some bloodstained papers from its coat pocket. "Solomon Schmidt's Identity card and a 'Star of David' piece of fabric." He muttered and exchanged looks with Alex, who pulled a little mirror from her bag and started to read what had appeared, whilst Jericho fumbled about the dead boy's neck, pulling a small silver locket into the dull sunshine.

Mr. Tibbs read the inscription out to Alex: "Rachel Bullmann

1941." He held open the locket and both admired the girl's very pretty face. "She must be a sweetheart, she's very pretty. Alex commented and Jericho nodded towards the little mirror she held; "What's on file?"

8. SOLOMON SCHMIDT'S DEPARTURE - AGAIN.

"Solomon Schmidt was born in Berlin in 1925 and murdered in October 1942 by a group of Nazi supporters; his body has no known burial place." Alex looked down at the corpse, now face upwards and covered with a dusting of snow. She knelt down and gently brushed the white ice and blood splatter's from the face; her hankie quickly becoming sodden with blood. But she continued to clean the face and stood up, tossing the hankie away and smiled at Mr. Tibbs; "This corpse is definitely Solomon Schmidt, and we now have his soul here, so the timeline should now be healed. Wilson and Owen should report that to us."

Jericho nodded his agreement and spoke directly to Solomon; "The Collector will take you before the Duty Death Angel who will review your human existence and decide what happens next – I have made a full report about your co-operation with us - take care of him Herbert; get the boy home safe."

The Collector smiled at young Solomon; "Well its better late than never." The pair disappeared from the street and Mr. Tibbs smiled and pulled his coat shut; "Back to the office Alexandra." He and Alex produced their mirrors, and the street was suddenly empty; apart from the still body of young Solomon Schmidt and a couple of curious skinny dogs.

From the derelict café on the corner emerged the old man; the Professor walked over to the body and violently kicked it several times, panting a little he cursed; "Fucking Jericho Tibbs, you will rue the day you fucked me up!"

Adjusting his coat and hat against the snow flurries and cold bitter wind, Wolfgang stepped back from the corpse and made his way home. He did not relish the forthcoming chat with Simon; the 'Dark Prince's' Minion – he didn't appreciate failure – but he would understand about bloody Jericho Tibbs interference.

Back in the drawing room of the lighthouse Mr. Tibbs sipped a hot coffee and flicked through two brown paper files. Alex was standing before the fireplace; warming her backside with the flames that jumped and flickered in the grate. They were both waiting for Wilson and Owen to return, so Alex accepted a glass of brandy from Harris and settled in a well upholstered chair by the fireplace with a copy of 'Treasure Island'.

Wilson came through the door, followed by Owen and both accepted whisky from Mr. Harris and Wilson said simply; "She's been collected Mr. Tibbs." He sipped his whisky and smiled at Alex who closed her book and continued relaxing in the chair.

"All her descendants have vanished from the Timeline, and it has returned to its original path." Owen added and raised his glass; "There was no strange old man to save her."

"Professor Wolfgang Leitcher's soul is still missing; he missed his departure date in 1805, which means he has not died yet or his soul is lost to the darkness because he has died outside his ordained time period. He is one of a number that have vanished without trace, some of them living centuries beyond their scheduled departure dates." Jericho paced the room quietly and stood before the large ornate mirror above the grand Fire-Place – it gave no reflection of him or the room in which it hung - he turned back to the others and added; "It can only be the work of the Dark Prince; His fingerprints are all over this case."

"Solomon will probably do a century in quarantine and then be released back into the Life-Cycle; he does have some good mitigating circumstances." Owen spoke quietly, placing his empty glass upon the coffee table, next to Alex's book.

"I love that story; it's one of my favourites." He told her with a big grin on his face.

Jericho smiled at the pair and gently goaded the spluttering fire with the poker and stared into the flames; "But who is the man behind the mask?" Jericho muttered to himself and wondered who Wolfgang Leitcher really was and what was the old man planning?

THE END

EPILOGUE:

"The current human timeline had been restored with the ordained death of the child in the traffic accident; none of her devil worshipping descendants existed now and Solomon Schmidt's soul was returned to the human life cycle. The mission was deemed a success."
SJW

CHARACTERS:

Solomon Schmidt had been returned to his correct departure date [date of death] and thus, his soul was collected and correctly processed. Angel Margret was sympathetic to his case, and he received no quarantine for his actions and was allowed to 'jump' to a new human lifecycle immediately.

Police Inspector Roy Gains attended many more horrific scenes at traffic accidents before he retired in 1997. He moved to Spain and lived out the remainder of his life in a quiet Spanish village near the sea. He died peacefully in 2004. His soul was collected and processed.

Fire Officer Karen De Weiss served in the fire service for another three years and left to run her late father's Sweet Shop in Blackpool. She and her partner; Gail had no children. She died from cancer in 2017. Her soul was collected and processed.

Sarah Taylor should never have survived the road accident that initially killed her saviour, Solomon Schmidt. Without his rescue, the original timeline played itself out and she was killed in that accident. All her descendants vanished from the timeline; they should never have existed. Her soul was collected and processed.

Richard Forbes, the young driver, was sentenced to five years in prison for 'causing death by dangerous driving' and was released after serving three and half years. He was to return to prison on several occasions during his short life. He was found dead in a Manchester 'squat' in 2001, apparently from a Heroin overdose. His soul was collected and processed.

Rachel Bullmann [Solomon's sweetheart in 1942] died in Bergen-Belsen Concentration Camp in 1943; she was seventeen years old at the time. Her soul was collected and processed.

Wolfgang Leitcher missed his departure date in 1805 and his soul is still missing to this day. Wolfgang is a persistent time offender and dedicated follower of the Dark Prince. He and Jericho Tibbs were to meet again on several occasions, and he was to appear in episodes where his presence in the 'background' is noted.

EPISODE 2: "THE DUNMORE WITCH TRIALS."

MISSION SUMMARY:

"A young woman in Medieval England is accused of witchcraft - apparently she has visions of the future which come true. But the King's special Herald; Sir Henry Barfield [the younger] believes she could prove useful for the King's wars with France and Scotland - her gift could change the current Human Timeline and Mr. Tibbs must investigate; but who does the girl really serve?"

 **ALCOHOL, SEXUAL REFERENCES, VIOLENCE [Including graphic descriptions of torture and death] STRONG LANGUAGE.**

AGE 15+ ONLY.  **45 Minutes reading time.**

1. NOT GOOD NEWS

Lord Arthur Osborne sat at his grand table with both hands placed upon his head of grey hair, eyes closed and breathed several times quite deeply; "Damnation and plague!" He muttered and then looked up at Alwyn, his Welsh sergeant-at-arms and shook his head, then slumped back into the large chair.

Alwyn shifted his feet and gripped his helmet as he swung it - gently from side to side – his other hand was fixed tightly on the hilt of his sword. He really had not wished to inform his master of such events. Alwyn knew what would happen; if word spread of the story and it reached the wrong ears in the High Church.

"They will send a fucking witch-finder to my villages! Do you know what that will mean?" Lord Arthur rose slowly from his chair and walked to the fireplace. He stood staring at the flames for some moments, remembering what he had witnessed as a younger man nearly twenty years ago. Sometimes, as he watched the fire flickering in its grate, he could still see, hear and smell that terrible day.

The screaming young girl dragged to her funeral pyre - but still alive. Arthur had watched as they chained her to the stake, sobbing hysterically and asking what she had done wrong. Then calling for her mother and father; she was calling for mercy, begging for God's mercy'

But none heard her plea, and the fire was started. The flames grew quickly from the wood and brush piled about the base of the stake and the girl was soon coughing from the thick smoke, between screams, as the flames crept up her legs with increasing ferocity, then the guards threw fresh timber upon the fire.

The roaring flames burst open her skin, her eyes now black and burnt, she was plunged into darkness, and she could scream no more. The heat was shriveling her long dark hair and her flesh was melting; then her stomach came away, tumbling from her twitching body' smoking and hissing, it dropped into the roaring fire.

He had turned away after that, but the noise behind him seemed to make everything worse. Mistress Alice Hornside had died at the stake; aged fourteen, found guilty of 'witchcraft'. It still made the old Knight shudder to this day. Now another two girls stand accused of the same practice – and both from a village under his Stewardship. His master, The Earl of Whitestock, was a stupidly pious man who believed every word that poured from the pulpit; he had already given nearly a quarter of his land to the bloodsucking church authorities, in the desperate hope of buying Indulgences for his sins. Lord Arthur spat into the fire and slammed his hands together and sighed.

The first girl accused was Mistress Ruth Blacksmith [nee Humblestone] was seventeen and had been married only a few months to the Blacksmith's son. A dull, silly little thing whose only ambition in life was to bake the perfect pie – but she kept an unguarded tongue and upset the wrong people in the village, especially other women. Probably only guilty of being an idiot who didn't know when to shut her mouth; Lord Arthur allowed himself a smile over that.

But the other girl was a different matter; Mistress Mary Whitefoot was an intelligent and clever young girl, probably not more that fifteen years old and considered the beauty of the village. She could read and write – just like her mother had done so. That damn Priest, Father Richard had been hanging about the Whitefoot's farm for some time, with little excuse, until he found a couple of books in a language he couldn't read and some strange objects he could not understand, in Mary's room; the prick immediately shouted; "The Devil's work!"

Then of course, the dreams or visions that came upon the young girl at certain times. The last one, about a donkey found dead on the Church steps had come true; two weeks after prophesied. Then Old man Sommer's collapse and death on the road to York and the Raven's picking at his dead flesh; another true vision.

Little wonder the Priest had called the girl out as a witch – the fucking ignorant bastard! But Lord Arthur could not see the girl go the stake – he had made a blood promise to her mother at the child's birth - to protect her and her incredible gift; as did old Henry Barfield

He sipped some wine and offered a goblet to Alwyn, who downed it in one swig and wiped his mouth – wine had never been more needed! Lord Arthur gripped Alwyn by the shoulder and smiled; "Take a couple of men and gallop hard and fast to Barfield castle and ask Sir Henry Barfield to come here; with some haste. I and his father have history; he will not refuse such a request."

Alwyn nodded, then bowed and departed swiftly for Barfield castle and an audience with the King's Special Herald. Old Lord Barfield and Lord Arthur had fought together in the King's French war and again, when subduing Scottish raiders in the war of the Boarder's. It is said they owed each other, their lives more than once; they were 'blood brothers' in the real sense of the term and very close old friends.

Sir Henry Barfield, old Lord Barfield's son and heir, was the King's 'Special Herald' and one of the King's most trusted men. In later times, his role would have many titles; but all concerned matters of intelligence and information for the Government of the time – in this century - the King was that government.

Lord Arthur called for his house Steward; Peter and told him to make haste to the jail, where the two girls had been incarcerated, in chains. The message to the Jailer was simple; no torture – yet. He gave Peter some coins for the Jailer's troubles and obedience, then sat before the fire and planned.

2. THE BARFIELDS.

Alwyn and his companions reached the castle, late the following morning and upon being recognized, were immediately admitted and granted audience with Old Lord Henry Barfield and his son.

Old Henry Barfield sat upon a stool in the antechamber to the Great Hall and rubbed his crippled hand gently; the fingers were bending like a claw and in winter months: decidedly painful. "Not much use on the King's battlefield's now or to squeeze a buxom wench's tit." He spoke softly to his son and chuckled. Young Henry smiled at his father and sipped wine, watching Alwyn and his men bowing low as they entered the chamber.

Both men were silent as Alwyn outlined the message from his master, when he finished speaking Old Henry Barfield sat quietly for a further few minutes, then asked; "Lord Arthur is sure that the second accused is Mary Whitefoot the younger?"

Alwyn nodded, wiping the sweat and dirt of the road from his face with a rag; "Yes my Lord, it's the younger girl of that name. I understand she's named after her dead mother."

Old Henry Barfield shifted his weight and young Henry helped his father rise from the stool and limp to the warmth of the fireplace. He could see the strange look upon his father's face, and he whispered; "Who is this girl and what is she to us and Lord Arthur?" Old Henry never noticed the insincerity in his son's voice; young Henry knew Mary Whitefoot better than his father could ever imagine.

Old Henry patted his son's shoulder and smiled; "Get these men some food and drink; they have ridden hard all night and part of the morning. Let them catch some sleep before you return with them."

Young Henry nodded and gave the order to servants, who scattered to fetch food and bedding for the guests. Before Alwyn left the chamber, old Henry asked him one last question: he knew about the accused, but who were the accusers?

"For Mistress Humblestone, its Fletcher, who runs the 'Bear and Dog' tavern; and for Mistress Whitefoot....." Alwyn hesitated to take a breath and then finished; "The Priest, Father Richard." He saw the expression change on both the Henry's faces.

"That sniveling little piece of dog shit!" Old Henry muttered; "He that thinks so well of himself and knows donkey crap about God and life!" He slumped back down on the stool and tapped his son's shoulder; "The Tavern owner can be dealt with, but the Priest must be handled carefully – he has the bishop's ear - and they are both dangerous imbeciles!"

Young Henry was surprised by the priest being named as Mary's accuser but did not show it. "What is that silly bastard playing at?" He whispered and stared at the fire burning in the ornate grate. Young Henry dismissed Alwyn and his companions and when the chamber was empty, apart from his father, he pulled up a stool and sat near old Henry, who gripped his shoulder tightly with his good hand and placed his mouth close to his son's ear. "The girl must be saved. I will not allow the master's gift to be burnt by ignorant fools. You must save her and bring her to safely, for her visions come true – just like her mother and down the generations of Whitefoot women; but always and only, the first-born daughter receives the gift."

Old Henry straightened and smiled; "Her mother was a beauty, a real beauty. Arthur and I attended her deathbed and promised to protect the child – always. We owed her that, for all she gave us." He rose slowly and swayed a little, as the memories flooded back. He glanced at young Henry and wondered about confessing to him that Mary Whitefoot's mother was also his blood mother - not the late Lady Alice, who gave old Henry nothing but a cold bed and cold sex to match.

"I can still see her running through the woods, barefoot, hair

streaming and laughing. She told Arthur and me many things –
some good and some bad. But what she imparted to us gave me
this castle and Arthur's Manor and estates. When we joined the
old King's army, we were just soldiers of no note, two years later
we were Knights!" He grinned, folding his arms around himself as
the wonderful days of his past appeared before him.

Old Henry had no idea that his son knew far more about young
Mary Whitefoot that he could ever imagine. The pair had been
lovers on many occasions and young Henry was surprised that
Mary had not become with child. He knew that his father had
fathered two bastard children by maid servants over the years -
despite his age; both by force it was rumoured. 'Like father, like
son' he thought and smiled.

Old Henry turned and whispered closely again to his son's ear:
"Imagine the King's Herald coming into information about the
hereafter; the future. What favours and riches will a grateful King
heap upon such a man?"

"I understand fully Father." Young Henry said simply and helped
the old man to the Great Hall for warmth and food, then set
about preparations for the ride to Lord Arthur's Manor. In the
solitude of his private chambers, Henry collected a bag of silver
and gold pieces and from the secret place, he recovered the
book. No bigger than a sword hilt and bound in dark leather, he
hid the book in his secret pocket and knew that, if it was ever
found; torture and the gallows; if he was lucky!

3. JOHN NORMAN AND THE PRIEST.

Henry had sent his trusted servant; Fieldsman, to fetch John
Norman from the tavern, where he had rooms and board. He
would have need of John's skill and loyalty in this matter – the
man hardly spoke - but then his bow and dagger did the talking
for him.

A small, but powerful man, John Norman had no love for the
Church, Priests or Bishop's; he despised them all. He was well
travelled for a man of his times; it was said that he crossed the
Holy lands and received instruction from various Arab mystics
and Teachers. The rumour was that the Church had accused his
young wife of being a Heretic. She was Muslim by birth but had
converted to marry him. That mattered not to the Church

official's and the corrupt Magistrate; they found her guilty, and she was burnt to death in the town square.

John Norman walked away from that town of fanatic's and disappeared. But not before killing the two priests and the Magistrate that pronounced the deadly verdict. That was some years ago, and the incident had turned into legend and rumour; a story recounted in Tavern's and around campfires. John had also changed for the stories; he was now almost a giant with red eyes, who could crush a skull with one hand, so he now passed totally unnoticed amongst the villages and towns.

He had found shelter and protection with the Barfield's, and he repaid their kindness with total loyalty. You did not cross John Norman unless you meant to kill him because he would kill you any way he could. He took council from only three people; Lord Arthur Osborne and Lord Henry Barfield – and by blood default - Young Henry.

That afternoon, Young Sir Henry, John Norman, Alwyn and his companions, with six other men at arms, left Barfield Castle for the Witch Trials at Dunmore village. Some distance behind the group, which was disappearing into the forest, rode a single horseman; he raised an arm to old Henry in salute and vanished into the thick foliage, only notable because of his size and a beautiful, but deadly, black hilted sword that hung at his side. Old Lord Barfield watched the departure with some satisfaction and hoped that interfering bastard Jericho Tibbs didn't stumble upon the story of the Dunmore Witches and show up. He flexed both hands and gripped his wine goblet; that fucking idiot Father Richard was a liability now and their future together must now come to an end; despite their past.

He had heard from the crone, Meg the washerwoman, [one of his informants in the village] all about the Priest's pursuit of young Mary and her steadfast refusal to have anything to do with him. "Hell has no fury like a lovesick bastard who has been spurned." He whispered and sipped his wine, now convinced he had made the right decision about the Priest.

He sat before the fire and cursed. The loss of his little notebook weighed upon his mind; someone had discovered its hiding place and stole the book. He hoped that the thieving bastard would not understand what it contained. If it had fallen into wrong hands, then it could bring big trouble to the Barfield's dynasty he was creating. He had arranged the marriage of his only son and heir - with the King's permission - to Lady Katherine Talport; who was from a landed and wealthy family. "The fucking start of something great and my master will be pleased." He said openly and then looked around; but the chamber was empty.

Old Henry Barfield suddenly jumped to his feet and gave a little dance, with the infirmities of his apparent old age fell away and he laughed out loud. He thought about the young kitchen maid with big breasts and smiled; the stupid little bitch will share his bed; willing or not and headed for the kitchens.

Father Richard sorted through the dirty coins and counted four pence in total; he was happy with that. He could give two pennies to Mistress Gwen for her Housekeeping [the Priest's cook/cleaner], send a whole penny to keep favour with Bishop Charles and spend the rest in Fletcher's tavern; maybe even have some entertainment with that young trollop Lizzy. He always did enjoy her strong thighs and soft mouth - despite the cost - but then, his parishioners did pay for that! He laughed softly and picked up his tankard.

He sipped his cider and reflected that it had been a good Sunday Mass collection and the evening looks even better. He smiled broadly to himself; and he had that little bitch in the jail – she can burn for her sins and love of the 'Dark Prince' - the irony of that made the priest chuckle loudly to himself, well; that's what she will officially die for and not for spitting in his face and refusing to fuck with him.

The priest relaxed in the high backed chair and found life was quite pleasant in the village of Dunmore and watched the sun set through the small window of his house, and at the silhouette of his church [St. James the lesser] against the fading sun. Father Richard heard something behind him and turned, placing his leather tankard down upon the rough wooden table.

He was already dead as his flaccid body slid from the chair and crumpled upon the dirty floor; through his throat was a thin metal skewer. His eyes were wide open, and his mouth contorted in a scream that was silent. The candle upon the table flickered and died too; from the draft caused by the door quietly shutting behind the assassin – the grubby four pennies lay untouched upon the table - and Jeb the Collector persuaded the shocked soul of the late Father Richard to go towards the light.

"I didn't even see him!" Father Richard spluttered and coughed as the Collector gripped his arm and spoke quietly; "You don't have to worry about any of that. I'll take you before the Duty death Angel and she will review your human time and decide what happens next."

Father Richard wiped his face with shaking hands and whispered; "There will be a judgment of me?" He asked and when the Collector nodded; he threw up his hands and shouted; "Oh God, please forgive me!" The Collector smiled to himself and knew that there would be little forgiveness from Angel Margret, for this man who liked little girls and boys and the pain and horror he had inflicted upon so many – there also was several murders to explain – of old men, women and even very young children.

The Collector already knew where the late Father Richard's soul was heading and he smiled broadly as they walked towards the door of Margret; the Duty Death Angel.

His body was found by Mistress Gwen when she returned from her daughters later that evening. Most of the village turned out upon her screams for help and many crowded in and around the Priests house to view the body. Big Harold [The Blacksmith] told his youngest son to fetch Lord Arthur Osborne and particularly his visitor; the Kings Special Herald – he would know how to handle this situation - the foul murder of a Priest in his own home.

Big Harold also knew that the Church authorities would send the Inquisition to investigate the priest's death, and it would be better for all concerned [mainly the villagers] that someone like the Kings Herald was on the scene. He glanced towards the old jail and crossed himself; the two girls were now likely to face the Inquisition and not just the local Magistrate and that would mean terrible torture before they reached the flames; the Inquisition found no-one 'Innocent'.

Sir Henry viewed the body and the scene of the killing with great interest and much trepidation; for like big Harold, he knew that the Inquisition would now be involved and the rescue of young Mistress Whitefoot had become urgent.

John Norman was searching the body on his orders as soldiers kept the villager's outside - apart from Mistress Gwen and her sister Alice; the two old women would prepare the Priest for burial - Mistress Alice had already fetched a clean sheet - for a shroud - from the Church laundry.

His body was placed upon the Church Alter and was stripped for washing and dressing in his burial sheet. That's when the two women called for Sir Henry with great urgency in their voices. Sir Henry stared down at the naked body of the late Priest and exchanged a knowing look with John Norman.

Across the priest's chest was tattooed a crude wolf's head: the symbol of the 'Wolf Border Reviver's tribe' – one of the worst raiders - along the Scottish/ English border. They robbed, raped and murdered for almost ten years before being smashed by the army of the Scottish King. Many had avoided the hangman and fled south to England – apparently 'Father Richard' had escaped by joining the Church - cleverly concealing his terrible past.

Sir Henry rubbed his chin and spoke softly to John Norman; "Maybe someone knew more about the damn priest than Father Richard suspected?"

John Norman nodded and pointed out three old wounds upon the dead priest; "They look like old sword wounds, cauterized by hot irons." But it was it was the mark about the neck that caught Sir Henry's eye; it was clear some kind of necklace had been worn there – for many years - by the colourisation of the skin in a smooth line.

"Why did the killer leave the coins but take the necklace, if robbery was the motive?" John Norman asked, and Sir Henry had no immediate answer - well, none that he would impart to John - for now. His hand ran about the collar of his shirt and touched the necklace that lay there. "Some bastard knows the worth of it and what it means." He whispered, but the pair were interrupted by Alwyn calling from the doorway; "My Lord, Edward the village Blacksmiths oldest son has disappeared!"

Sir Henry sighed and said quietly to John Norman; "The boy is married to Ruth, the other accused girl." They left the pair of old women to finish dressing the dead priest for his grave and stood in the warm evening sunshine. The villagers had gathered in small groups with the murder of Father Richard and the disappearance of the Blacksmith's son the major talking points. "It doesn't make sense John, the priest had not accused the Blacksmith's daughter-in-law – it was Fletcher, the tavern owner that did that – so why would the boy kill the priest?" Sir Henry walked slowly towards the jail with John Norman following, hand firmly on his sword hilt. Sir Henry told Alwyn to fetch the Blacksmith for questioning about his son.

4. THE JAIL.

Old John Floorcat unlocked the heavy door of the small jail and bowed towards Sir Henry; "This way my Lord. I've had orders to keep them chained and no visitors until your arrival." The only light was from old John's small lamp and a little barred window, high in the ceiling. "They have had some bread and cheese with a little beer. Lord Osborne paid for that." The smelly old cripple added with a toothless grin; he had enjoyed the morning - exposing his limp and diseased cock to the young girls and making them touch it for a drink of water.

Ruth lay on the muddy floor, which was covered with some straw, sobbing and whispering to herself, whilst Mary Whitefoot sat in the corner and said nothing. She looked up at Sir Henry and pushed her long dark hair back; but did not smile. "From the shouts and screams outside, I understand that the damn priest has finally encountered justice. Good." Mary slowly rose from the filthy floor and adjusted her dress and apron; as best as her chains allowed.

Sir Henry pressed close towards the cage and spoke softly: "Everything is being done; we need to get you out before the Inquisition arrives, but the killing of Father Richard hasn't helped."

Mary nodded and whispered with her voice full of fear; "The priest is still dangerous; make sure you place many heavy stones upon his corpse when buried and do not leave his body unattended before that. He was in league with some very evil people."

Sir Henry smiled, a little puzzled by her words; "Don't worry head and whispered again; "Be careful Sir Henry, the priest has never been what he seems, and he served a master who is dark and powerful. Remember; make sure his body is buried deep and weighed down with heavy stone." She then slumped back down upon the dirty floor and stared at Ruth, who had rolled into a ball and was groaning loudly. She knew that a minion of her master would seize the opportunity to re-animate the dead Priest - if given the chance - to bring a little terror to the followers of the so called 'one God'.

"That girl needs out of here before she loses what's left of her mind." John Norman gestured towards Ruth and sighed. He had seen enough of the Church's 'benevolence towards women – young and old – and the horrors they inflicted in the name of a loving Christ. Sir Henry turned to old John and asked about the priest's reputation in the village.

The old man grinned, showing yellow and missing teeth he wiped snot from his nose and chin with the sleeve of his grubby shirt and chuckled; "The priest loved that trollop Lizzy's tuppence [her vagina] more than the church!"

Sir Henry grunted and pushed a couple of silver sixpences into the old man's hand; "Make sure they get food, drink and blankets for the night or you'll be explaining to me or John Norman." Sir Henry smiled and the old man nodded; he knew John Norman's reputation for killing and young Henry had the ear of the King – the life of an old cripple counted for nothing - except to the old cripple himself! Sir Henry would be obeyed. He followed the pair from the cell and smiled - gripping the coins - still; he would make the girls show their tits and fanny's for the food. He almost laughed but held it back until the visitors were gone.

The pair left the jail and already Sir Henry had a plan in mind, but he needed to speak to Lord Osborne and that could be achieved over dinner at the Manor House. Alwyn pushed big Harold before him and Sir Henry learnt that no-one had seen Edward [Ruth's husband] since yesterday, but the Blacksmith informed him that the priest had received two visitors the day he accused Mary. They looked like soldiers; everyone thought they could be mercenaries as they spoke in Irish. It was known that the King was recruiting such men for his wars with France and Scotland. They had left the same afternoon on the York Road – their destination unknown – but appeared in a hurry.

"They were pagans!" The Blacksmith spat the words out, adding;

"Black hearted devil worshippers and the priest did nothing about them. They drank in Fletcher's tavern and enjoyed that trollop Lizzy for sixpence and the priest calls out two young girls instead of real evil. He and Fletcher were close; like snakes in the same hole!" Big Harold did not shield his words and Sir Henry and John Norman could hear the truth when spoken. The Blacksmith was allowed to return to his shop and continue the urgent and most needed repairs of the village scythes; the harvest was due.

A search for young Edward was ordered and Sir Henry retired to the Manor House for rest and food after standing soldiers at the Church doors to guard the priest's body – as Mary had insisted upon - Father Richard would be buried in his own Church yard the following noontime. Sir Henry now believed there was a real connection between the priest and Fletcher; it clearly centered on the accusations made against the girls by that pair – but why? – The priest had always appeared not to be that stupid. Fletcher was an old soldier who knew – exactly – what his words could do.

Fletcher would be brought before him tomorrow and the young whore Lizzy also will be questioned, particularly about the two Irish soldiers and their visit to the priest. "I bet it wasn't about converting to the true faith!" John Norman chuckled and like Sir Henry, retired for the night.

5. DEATH IN THE DARK WOODS.

"He died at the right time and place Mister Tibbs; except with no soul to collect." Yuri the Collector closed his Soul Ledger and smiled at Jericho and Owen. He stepped back from the mortal remains of young Edward Blacksmith and folded his arms.

Jericho looked down at the body, partly stripped with the skull crushed. The murdering thieves had taken everything of value including his boots and the little crucifix he wore about his neck, a gift from his late mother. "There are no traces of a Minion from the 'Dark Side' about, which means he had already traded his Soul."

Owen tapped his mirror; "Demon Ingress have reported that a demon's presence was reported here some two human years ago and that a young girl's soul was collected from a gathering of 'Devil Worshippers at that time." He looked quite grim and

Jericho asked him to continue. "Well, the collector reported that the young girl had been raped and murdered by five men and two women during a Black magic ritual. He called for detectives because there was a strong presence of a Minion detected."

Jericho looked up from his own mirror and nodded; "The demon was given two souls for his master; this boy's and one of the women; Mary Whitefoot. The 'Dark Prince' really looked after them." Jericho spoke with some contempt in his voice and looked about, adding; "They sold their souls cheaply, the boy for un-ending sexual stamina and attraction to women; the girl received the power of prophecy - just like her mother did when she sold hers - two generations of women, all devil followers for the same power."

Through the trees and dark foliage he could make out a small derelict tower at the edge of the woods. "What do we know about that place Owen?" He asked and Owen pulled his mirror out and read about 'Lepers Leap' – a small stone tower used by lepers as a refuge and sometimes as a place of suicide – over the years, several of the poor, suffering creatures had jumped to the relief of death from its dark walls. "It's also used for the Devil's rituals." Owen added and placed his mirror in a coat pocket.

"Can you think of a better place to worship the 'Dark One'?" Jericho sighed and nodded for Yuri to depart. They said goodbye to Yuri, who had handed the case of the missing soul over to the temporal Detectives and now continued to collect others.

"Where's the nearest human habitation?" Jericho also asked and Owen pointed south; "Some five miles down that dirt road is the village of Dunmore with some two hundred inhabitants in this year of 1371." He glanced down at his mirror and smiled; "It's famous for black magic, witches, Satan Worship and having very few deaths from the Black Plague, oh, and a little cake called the 'Dunmore Half Crown.'" Owen grinned, but Jericho rubbed his chin and thought hard.

"The village of Dunmore is ringing a bell in my head; why?" Jericho said quietly and Owen again consulted his mirror; "In this very year they held the famous 'Dunmore Witch Trials' during which, legend has it, the devil himself put in an appearance!" Owen laughed and then grinned broadly as the pair was joined by Alex and Wilson, having just returned from 17th Paris.

Jericho rubbed his chin again; "Owen, put in a call to Human Records and find the names of the other Devil Worshippers who were there, the night the girl was killed." He had read the report on the Priest's death, who had claimed to follow the Devil, but still possessed his soul when killed. "I think the dead priest may be the key to this; he apparently ran with the Devil's crowd - but kept a good grip on his own soul - interesting that." He smiled at Alex and Wilson; "What have you got Alexandra?"

Alex tapped her mirror and said quietly; "There was a breech in the Timeline for this place in the year 1342, two humans crossed over from 1997, it was a natural tear in the Time fabric. Inspector Stella Longstreet investigated, but nothing major changed from the original time settings. They must have hidden themselves quite well and no return has been shown yet." Then Alex hesitated; "The records have just been updated; someone crossed over to this year from Scotland in 1746. That was NOT a natural tear. Human records are tracing the object used and should be able to name the human; eventually."

Jericho nodded; "Well I think it's time for a little daytrip to Dunmore and say hello to the witches, devil worshippers and some well disguised Time-travelers!"

The small band of pilgrims who were travelling to York arrived in the village that afternoon; a wealthy merchant, his widowed sister and her young maid, a young Silversmith apprentice and a Christian Moor whose appearance frightened everyone except John Norman and Young Henry Barfield.

Young Ruth Hall was thoroughly enjoying the adventure; playing Lady Alex's maid and being able to chat with Owen for hours on the road. Wilson was dressed as a Christian Moor; a merchant of slaves and silks commissioned by the King of Castillo to trade with England. Owen was smartly dressed as a Silversmith's apprentice and was travelling to York Minister to represent his 'Master' at the trade fairs there.

Jericho really did look impressive, dressed in a Merchant's finery and riding a white mare, while Alex looked stunning, dressed up as a lady of quality and heading to York with her brother, to re-join their family after being widowed. The temporal detectives really did look the part! The Supplies Department had come up trumps; again.

Owen was driving the wagon with the body of young Edward blacksmith, wrapped tightly with rags and laid in the rear; amongst the luggage and trade fair items. Ruth sat next to him, watching the two black horses straining, as they progressed towards the village, over the muddy track that called itself the 'York Road'.

Alex was riding side-saddle upon her pony and chatting to her 'brother', whilst Wilson, astride a magnificent black stallion, was at the rear and keeping a close eye on the woods that surround the so-called 'York Road'. He had already told the others about the horseman in the woods; a dark clad figure that kept its distance from the travelling party - staying well back in the woods - but clearly keeping a close eye on them and the village.

The village was in uproar as the party arrived outside Fletcher's tavern and Jericho asked Fletcher what the commotion was all about, as he appeared bowing low, to welcome his unexpected guests.

"Never seen anything like it My Lord; the accused young witch Mary simply vanished from the jail, leaving her leg irons still locked together and a stout padlock, unbroken on her cell door!" He gripped Jericho's reins and added; "The body of the murdered priest was stolen off the church alter and has disappeared, and the Blacksmith's young son has vanished."

Jericho asked for the boy's description and when Fletcher had detailed his looks; Jericho showed him the body they found by the old leper's Tower. Fletcher stared at the body without emotion and said, "I'll fetch his father; he'll want to thank you Sir, for bringing the boy home." Sarah, Fletcher's serving girl, showed the travelling party their rooms and bought food and drink.

It wasn't long before Sir Henry Barfield [the younger] and John Norman appeared at the tavern to look over the visitors. Everyone chatted politely and quietly, with Jericho buying them some drinks and inviting them to eat. But the pair said their thanks and departed; they were on the trail of the Priest's murderer and escaped witch; apparently.

Young Henry seemed most reluctant to part from Lady Alex and kissed her hand upon leaving. Owen sighed and whispered to

Wilson; "Another moth heads for the flame." They both chuckled, until they saw the look Alex gave the pair.

In a quiet corner of the almost empty tavern, Jericho and Alex consulted their mirrors regarding young Sir Henry Barfield and John Norman. Sir Henry [the younger] was shown as a Devil's follower and complicit in the murder and rape of two young girls, during black magic rituals. His birth was recorded in 1347 and his mother was the same mother as young Mary Whitefoot, who she birthed in 1356.

Jericho nodded; "So young Henry and Mary are brother and sister - yet Old Sir Henry presented the boy as a son by his wife Lady Alice - but not the girl - interesting that." The mirror also informed them, that John Norman was a certain William De Lancey - a former English knight - who had deserted his King and God; he now ran with the dark side.

But it was the lack of entries, for old Sir Henry that troubled Jericho; it normally indicated one thing; that he was a time-traveler himself. A discrete chat with Fletcher confirmed young Henry's birth some 24 years previously. "I think we may have found the time-traveler; his father." Jericho said quietly and both Alex and Wilson agreed. They would have to update Records, so that when he dies in this era; a collection can be scheduled. But they could find no record of a birth, in the name of Sir Henry Barfield; the older one. "Now that's a fucking big red flag; right there." Wilson muttered and Jericho took note of that.

Fletcher also confirmed that Sir Henry Senior took over the castle in 1350, as a reward for services to the King. Then Fletcher, quite unknowingly, told Jericho something very important; that his father [Fletcher's] had said that Henry Barfield had appeared in the village with a young woman - who was Mary Whitefoot's mother - in 1342. She was supposedly a widow and married a local farmer; George Whitefoot and birthed a baby boy some years later, followed by the girl. But apparently the boy had died as an infant. But Human records informed Jericho that at the time, it was claimed the boy died as an infant - there was no such dispatch [death] recorded - the child had actually lived; Jericho already knew the answer to that mystery.

Old Henry and Arthur became friends and allies; they pair went to war together and made their fortunes together. Now both rich and powerful, they kept a firm grip on the people and land they had been given by the King.

"I strongly suspect that Old Sir Henry is behind all this devil worship, and we know that the Whitefoot women all accepted the gift of prophecy from the 'Dark Prince'. So, old Henry probably came from 1997, with Mary's mother, as the other person who crossed over." Jericho muttered and sipped his ale quietly.

But their discussions were disturbed by Owen, suddenly standing and heading for the doorway and he didn't look happy; "The fucking Inquisition has arrived from York." Alex sadly shook her head; "That poor bloody girl." was all she said. Everyone agreed with her sentiment. But the girl's fate was really out of their hands.

They stood by the doorway and watched as several foot soldiers appeared, being led by a Knight in dull armour, bearing the crest of the Archbishop of York. Three wagons followed and more walking men - servants and bodyguards - of the Royal Magistrate who would hear the case against young Mistress Blacksmith and the Witch finder; Father William of Doncaster Abbey.

Jericho turned away and sat back down; "That bastard Father William has butchered over a dozen innocent women and girls. He has a place waiting in quarantine for him already." Fletcher appeared looking anxious and afraid; "I'm sorry my Lord, but I must have your rooms for the Arch-Bishops men. I'm so sorry my Lord." He handed back the coins that Jericho had paid him earlier; he couldn't apologize enough.

Jericho smiled; "The Ladies can sleep in the wagon, whilst I and my companions can find our own beds - we're use to sleeping where we can - if necessary." He slapped Fletcher on the shoulder and gave him a silver sixpence for his troubles, which was greatly appreciated.

Alex watched him walk away and sipped her beer; "There's something about that man I do not like." Owen nodded; he knew Alex was good judge of men's characters and she seldom got it wrong.

The little party of 'Merchants' left the tavern and returned to their wagon and horses. They watched the Royal Magistrate striding into Lord Osborne's Manor house and the Witch finder headed straight for the jail with two big, evil looking servants. They also watched the gathering villagers bowing at the pair and crossing themselves. "All we need now is for the Dark Prince to drop by and join in the fun." Wilson whispered to Alex and made himself scarce - they would be drawn to the big African like bees to honey - so no point in drawing too much unwanted attention to the Temporal Detectives, but little wonder John Norman had also departed.

6. TORTURE AND THE DEVIL'S VISIT.

After a rough night sleeping in the wagon, Alex and her 'maid' young Ruth were washing up in the tavern; the girls were chatting about Jericho and the boys sleeping under the wagon, particularly the snoring that came from Wilson, when they heard the first screams.

They both went outside and realised that the screaming was coming from the jail; they stood horrified as one of the Witch finders men appeared at the jail's doorway and emptied a basin of bloody water onto the ground and went back inside. The screaming continued until midday and then stopped.

Most of the village had gathered outside the jail in almost silence, Jericho and his team stood by the tavern talking in whispers, grim faced and feeling impotent. The Witch finder: Father William appeared with blood-stained sleeves rolled up and declared; "Mistress Blacksmith has confessed to witchcraft and carnal knowledge with Satan himself!"

The declaration was met with almost silence and many villagers simply walked away; the Blacksmith [still in mourning for his son] stood, arms folded, by the village well and said nothing. Those who had remained, now witnessed Mistress Blacksmith being taken before the Magistrate - this sight actually moved Alex and Ruth to tears - and they simply had to turn away. Two guards dragged the strangely quiet girl with ropes; she couldn't walk having had both feet broken and she had been whipped and branded with pokers. Mistress Blacksmith had been repeatedly raped and beaten for most of the night and finally confessed to whatever the Witch finder demanded.

The 'confession' was read aloud to the Magistrate, and he

announced the sentence; death by burning at the stake the following noon day. Those villagers that waited around for the verdict crossed themselves and went home. That night, the village was quiet as a graveyard. But the tavern was packed; with the magistrates and witch finders men celebrating with the young whore Lizzy doing quite a trade.

Owen reported to the team, what Human records had pulled up about the Devil Worshippers, who had killed and raped the young girl with the blacksmith's son and young Mary Whitefoot present. He spoke softly; "There were five men present; Old Henry Barfield and his son, Edward Blacksmith, Fletcher the Tavern owner and you will love this, that bastard; Father William; the so-called Witch Finder!"

Alex angrily interrupted; "What a fucking hypocritical lying bastard!" Everyone was surprised by her language, but not her reaction to the news. Owen nodded and continued; "The other woman present was none other than Ruth Blacksmith's mother; Elizabeth Humblestone! - Now that is some interesting combination - considering Fletcher called out her daughter, who was the wife of another member of the group."

"Maybe Ruth didn't want any part, in what her husband and mother indulged in. A free-for-all orgy normally takes place after such an initiation." Jericho said without any emotion. "She could have been a real danger to the group and to end any fears of being revealed, they had Fletcher call her out as a witch - her so called husband had already taken two other girls as mistresses - her mother would have endured the sacrifice of her daughter for the good of the group and keep in service to her master; the 'Dark Prince."

Wilson sighed; "What they didn't count on was Father Richard calling out Mary in revenge for being spurned by the girl - he saw the opportunity of Ruth's arrest - to gain his revenge on Mary." Everyone agreed with the deductions made and watched the wood being piled up around the stake; that had been set up in the Market square. "We have to help her." Alex said simply. But Jericho didn't answer; he was deep in thought. It was going to be a difficult night for Alex; her and Jericho had been invited to dinner with Lord Arthur Osbourne who was hosting the Royal Magistrate and that evil bastard; Father William. Sir Henry Barfield [the younger] had not returned from the hunt for the

Priest's murders - the two Irish mercenaries were now suspected - after the body of the Blacksmith's son had been found by the old tower.

Father William praised the Lady Alex for her apparent submissive quietness at the dinner table; "Your sister knows that a woman's place is beneath the command of men, and I respect and admire her quiet manner." He informed Jericho as they sipped wine and ate roast boar. Jericho really was impressed with Alex; he was actually a little amazed that she managed to control her tongue and temper with the priest. But she did, smiling on cue and saying, 'thank you Father' when necessary.

"I cannot understand how, as you say Father, that the devil freed his witch-slave Mary Whitefoot from the jail and yet, left behind the other girl who has now confessed to being a witch?" Jericho made a puzzled look and swallowed down his wine and was refilled immediately. The Priest nodded and smiled; "You're a simple merchant Master Tibbs; you don't understand the wiles of the evil one."

Jericho smiled and kicked Alex gently under the table; a signal to put a lid on whatever she wanted to say. Alex also smiled; "Father, what do you think happened to the body of the poor priest; Father Richard?" The Priest nodded and picked roast boar from his yellowing teeth; "Father Richard's body was probably taken by the escaped witch and those who aided her; so, he wouldn't receive a proper Christian burial; a little insult to our Father in Heaven." He crossed himself and the Magistrate said, "Amen."

Lord Osbourne's steward approached his master and whispered into his ear; that made his lordship smile and he announced that Lord Henry Barfield had arrived with more men to help in the apprehension of the witch and her followers. Jericho and Alex exchanged glances; the 'Time-traveler' had decided to put in an appearance.

They all rose as old Lord Henry Barfield made his dramatic appearance in the chamber, cloak flowing behind, wearing his armour and accompanied by two Knights; Sir Robert and Sir William. He stopped and stared at Jericho and Alex - the look upon his face was priceless - Lord Henry Barfield was actually Wolfgang Leitcher! [See Episode: **'The man who died in the**

future to save his past.']

There was silence for several long seconds and then 'Sir Henry' exploded; he drew his sword and shouted; "For God sake Arthur, its fucking Jericho Tibbs and that fucking bitch from Cappanni!" That's when he noticed the shocked faces of the Royal magistrate and the Witch finder. Father William rose slowly with real fear upon his face; "That's fucking Jericho Tibbs and his harlot?" He stepped back, knocking over his chair and drew his dagger; "Kill them!" was all Lord Henry shouted and with some really quick thinking added; "He is the devil himself and the bitch is a Dark Lady who has birthed his minions!"

With all swords raised against them, Jericho said quietly to Alex, as they backed against the fireplace; "Time to go." Jericho operated the little red circle on his mirror which would recall everyone to the lighthouse. They vanished in an instance, taking Wilson, Owen and Ruth with them; wherever they were.

The story spread quickly around the village by servants of Lord Osbourne who had actually witnessed the Devil and his Harlot disappears into thin air. The magistrate, running from the house screaming, didn't help diffuse the situation.

The little gang of Devil Worshippers gathered in the Church and planned their next move, knowing that temporal detectives were on their case. Their leader Lord Henry cursed his luck and wondered how that bastard Jericho had found out about them.

But he had some pretty demanding, immediate problems to deal with; the villagers were in full riot; tearing the place to pieces, searching in fear and terror for the devil and his minions. But someone had kept his head amongst the riot and burning; he killed the guard on the jail and carried away Mistress Blacksmith.

Several villagers claimed to have seen the dead priest; Father Richard wandering around the village, complete with shroud and loose head; from having his throat cut. He apparently stole a horse and disappeared up the York Road taking the hysterical whore Lizzy with him.

7. BOTH SIDES NOW AND BLACK SWORD.

Sir Henry [the younger] and his men had camped by the Leper's

Tower and word was brought to them of the happenings in the village of Dunmore. Wrapped coarsely in blood marked blankets were the bodies of the two Irish mercenaries; they had caught them near the Doncaster crossroads and the two chose to fight; they were cut down by cross bows and finished off with axes.

Sir Henry knew he had the right men - the murdered Blacksmith's boy's personal items - and clothes were found amongst their processions. He also knew that they had nothing to do with the witches disappearance; that was John Norman and him but could be blamed for spiriting her away and they had seen her turn into a black raven and fly away - well, that would be the story reported - the dead men really couldn't deny what was apparently said by them; before they died!

Already, the pair [John Norman and Mary] would have put some serious miles between themselves and Dunmore on the fresh horses they had been given. From his secret pocket, Sir Henry pulled the little book out and snapped it open, to the page he had previously marked. By the feeble lamp light, he read about the witch trials and knew something had gone wrong; the history of the time had changed and not in the best interests of his master; The Dark Prince.

Young Henry knew what he had to do and made arrangements to disappear. Everyone was glad to be back at the lighthouse and the prospect of good food, showers and real beds was overwhelming, especially for young Ruth. She rushed straight to the bathroom to shower and use a proper toilet! Everyone was relaxed and enjoying dinner, especially since they had a very popular guest; Guardian Oscar De Vere was always pleased to receive a dinner invitation from his old colleagues. He had been Jericho's Temporal Detective Sergeant before Detective Constable Wilson had been promoted and a certain Lady Alex was the Temporal Trainee [the position Owen now holds]. He had always felt totally accepted by his friends and colleagues, of Jericho's team and the staff of the lighthouse.

Mr. Harris kept his wine glass full and actually did have a soft spot for the little man and was pleased that he had been promoted to a Guardian of God; the fact he was a dwarf made no difference to anyone!

The biggest laugh was Jericho's story about having to explain to

Angel Margret about being the devil that actually made an appearance in 1371. Alex wasn't too happy about being known as a harlot of the devil and spawning his scaly children. But she did see the funny side of the story. Jericho tapped his wine class with a fork and called the dinner/briefing to order; "Well some of us [indicating Alex and himself] have seen both sides now." That caused a few chuckles and he continued; "Owen will bring us up to date with the case of the Dunmore witches and its devil worshipping friends."

Owen coughed and smiled at young Ruth, who piled more chicken pieces upon his plate and then did the same for Oscar. "Sir Henry Barfield [Senior] was indeed our old adversary; Wolfgang Leitcher. He fled the time period as soon as we left - he simply couldn't explain how he knew Jericho was the devil - without giving himself away. That also meant that young Henry had to disappear, and the Barfield castle and lands were confiscated by the King [Edward III]. Lord Osbourne was exiled from England and apparently, he disappeared to Scotland with a few loyal supporters - nothing more is known of him - until his soul was collected in 1379. It was placed in quarantine and has made no comments about the incident." Owen sipped some wine and took a mouthful of chicken and continued:

"We know that John Norman a.k.a. Sir William De Lacey married young Mary Whitefoot and settled in Pontefract, becoming a Farrier to the Kings Warden who held the great castle there. He died in 1380 - no soul collected, of course - and nothing is known of Mary, her soul hasn't been collected and is still shown as 'Missing'. Mistress Ruth, the Blacksmith's daughter-in-law died of her injuries, late summer 1371 and her soul was collected and processed. The man who rescued her, a certain Alexander McIves is known to us all - he likes to be known as 'Black Sword' because of his Spanish Blade - and has travelled through many time periods and is still missing to this day. There's a full and comprehensive report on his persistent breeches of the Time-Line available - it makes really interesting reading - his last reported sighting was in 1746, in Scotland. It goes without saying that his soul is missing." Owen sipped his wine; "Young Henry changed his name and became a paid mercenary for the King of Spain; he died in some Spanish Monastery of wounds, received during a minor skirmish on the French border in 1382 and his soul was never collected. His secret book [stolen from his father] was never recovered; it was believed to describe future events and is a wanted item by Angel Margret." Owen finished his meal and smiled broadly as Ruth fetched his pudding.

Jericho added; "But McIves is a most intriguing individual; we know that he doesn't work directly for the 'Dark Prince' and is actually quite chivalrous. But he was in the pay of Lord Henry [Senior] and at his command, followed young Henry to Dunmore. I believe he killed the evil Father Richard for the terrible suffering he inflicted upon many young children, and he rescued the Mistress Ruth because she was just an innocent young girl. But obviously she died, her injuries even beyond his fabled medical skills. He was also known as a 'Healer' in many of these early time periods. As I say, quite an enigma - for a time-traveler - he is of course, like Wolfgang Leitcher, not ageing in any of the time periods he appears in. So, he must keep moving on or he would be noticed for that alone." Jericho raised his class and said quietly; "To God, the chivalrous and seeing both sides now!"

Everyone stood and raised their classes. Young Ruth whispered to Owen; "Chivalrous like you." Owen just grinned broadly and sipped his wine. Alex turned to Jericho and asked; "Have you ever met this 'Black Sword' and who is he really?"

Jericho swallowed his wine and sat down; "Oh yes, a couple of times. He's a big strapping fellow and I believe in he was a Spanish Knight who actually rode with the famous 'El Cid', before he discovered time travel. Later, it appears he became a doctor, in one time period he stayed." Jericho smiled and finished his wine. Yes, he knew Alexander McIves really well; little wonder he kept away from the village after seeing Jericho and his team there.

But he had left Jericho a little something. Wilson asked Owen what happened to that bastard Father William, the Witch finder. "He died of dysentery at Nottingham Abbey in 1379 and there was no soul to collect. But the Collector was on the ball and Inspector Yuri Kassim was called; he checked the body with Records and found that Father William was in fact; Roland Gates, who had crossed over from 2001, where he was on the run from the FBI, suspected of several gruesome, sexual murders." Owen continued: "He was also a Satanist and had found a tear in the time fabric, in an Arizona Cemetery that was locked to 1353. He joined the Church and becoming a Witch finder must have seemed to be heaven sent." Owen pushed the brown paper file to one side and added; "Fletcher [who accused the Blacksmith's daughter-in-law] was in league with Father Richard/ They were old colleagues from the raids on the Scottish borders. That's also, were he obtained the money to buy the tavern - He was killed by soldiers during the riots that followed the devil's appearance and the 'Wolf's' tattoo was found on him too."

Alex asked Owen about the alleged sightings of Father Richard during the riots and Owen chuckled; "I think a minor demon may have borrowed the body, but seriously, the prostitute Elizabeth Cowhand's body was never recovered and of course, nor was her soul." He shrugged his shoulders and headed for his rooms to retire for the night.

Alex and Wilson showed Oscar out and also retired. Jericho sat quietly in his study; alone now that everyone had gone and turned the strange old necklace about in his fingers; he re-read the note that had accompanied it: *'Jericho; this was taken from Father Richard. It's the symbol of the Black Circle Brotherhood - where you find it, you will find the Devil and his minions. Regards; McIves.'*

Jericho sipped his final brandy of the night and held the necklace up; A black serpent with a small gold circle in its mouth. He had seen this symbol a few times during his tenor as a Temporal Detective and once, when he still resided among the living.

He gripped it tightly and closed his eyes; stopping any tears that wanted to fall. Jericho rose and extinguished the lamp and crossed the room to the grand mirror on the wall, above the fireplace. He whispered; "Elizabeth." The picture formed behind the glass. He touched it gently and hung his head in sorrow, quietly saying; "Things we cannot and must not change have taken my heart." He turned and walked away, and the picture faded. Jericho retired to bed; some good, but many dark things plagued his dreams and Jericho slept badly; like he normally did.

THE END

EPILOGUE:

"The incident in the medieval village of Dunmore, exposed the persistent time offender and Devil worshipper; Wolfgang Leitcher

CHARACTERS:

Lord Arthur Osbourne was exiled from England and disappeared to Scotland with a few loyal supporters - nothing more is known of him until his soul was collected in 1379. It was placed in quarantine and made no comments about the incident. He was returned to the Human Lifecycle in 1590.

Alwyn Jones, Lord Arthurs' loyal servant, remained with his master in exile. He married a local Scottish woman in 1373 and had several children. He died in 1398 and his soul was collected and processed. Some of his dependents remain living in Scotland to this day.

Ruth Blacksmith [Nee Humblestone] died of her injuries, late summer 1371 and her soul was collected and processed. She was just one of several women tortured and/or executed for witchcraft over the centuries at Dunmore.

Mary Whitefoot, who was an actual 'devotee' of the Dark Prince escaped any punishments and married John Norman, upon her death, she became a minion of her master and is now known as the female demon 'Maris' - not a particularly nice demon by all accounts. Her soul has never been recovered.

Father Richard, who was killed by Alexander McIves [Black Sword] for crimes in Scotland and the English Borders, had his soul collected and placed in quarantine. His crimes committed as a living human, were considered so bad that he remains locked away from the Human Lifecycle to this day.

Sir Henry Barfield, who was actually the time travelling minion of the Dark Prince known as Wolfgang Leitcher, simply disappeared from this time period and made several appearances in other times. He and Jericho have met many times over the centuries. His soul remains missing to this day.

Sir Henry Barfield [the Younger] changed his name and became a paid mercenary for the King of Spain; he died in some Spanish Monastery of wounds, received during a minor skirmish on the French border in 1382 and his soul was never collected. It remains missing to this day. The little book he carried - that contained future events - was never recovered. It is a most wanted item by the Temporal Detectives Department and its whereabouts remains unknown.

John Norman [Sir William De Lacey] married young Mary Whitefoot and settled in Pontefract, becoming Keeper of the Horses to the Kings Warden, who held the great castle there. He died in 1380. No soul was collected, and it remains missing to this day.

John Fletcher [the Tavern owner] was in league with Father Richard; they were old colleagues from the raids on the Scottish borders. That's also were he obtained the money to buy the tavern - He was killed by soldiers during the riots that followed the devil's appearance and the 'Wolf's' tattoo was found on him too. No soul was collected and remains missing to this day.

Harold Blacksmith - known as 'Big Harold' - survived the Dunmore riots and rebellion but had to move to another village. He died in 1384 and his soul was collected and processed. For some reason - known only to himself - blamed himself for the death of his son Edward. He died alone and miserable, immersed in his supposed guilt.

Edward Blacksmith found murdered by 'Leper's Tower' had been a 'devotee' of the Dark Prince. He had sold his sold for the gift of sexual attraction to women. No soul was collected, and he became a minor minion of his master. His current whereabouts are unknown.

John Floorcat [the Jailer at Dunmore] survived the riots and continued his employment as Jailer until his death in 1375. His soul was collected and placed in quarantine for various serious Acts, committed during this particular lifecycle, including child rape and murder. He was released from quarantine in 1824.

Father William [the Witchfinder] died of dysentery at Nottingham Abbey in 1379 and there was no soul to collect. His body was checked with Human Records, and it was found, that Father

William was in fact; Roland Gates, who had crossed over from 2001, where he was on the run from the FBI, suspected of several gruesome sexual murders. Since he died out of his own time, his soul is missing and remains so, to this day.

Elizabeth Cowhand [the Tavern harlot] who was dragged away by the minor demon 'Gassi' was never seen or heard of again. Her date of death is unknown, and her soul remains missing. It is recorded as 'LTDA' - lost to demonic activity - and her case is currently closed.

Lady Katherine Talport obviously never married young Henry Barfoot and the following year married Sir Peter Morgan - a Welsh Knight - and moved to North Wales. She died in childbirth the following year. Her soul was collected and processed.

Meg Goosefoot [the Washerwoman] who was an informant for old Sir Henry Barfoot/Wolfgang Leitcher managed to escape the village and the riots but died on the York Road some days later. Her soul was collected and processed.

Gwen Harrowfield - Father Richard's Housekeeper- survived the riots and eventually married one of the Arch-Bishop's soldiers and moved to York. She died in an outbreak of the plague in the city in 1376. Her soul was collected and processed.

Alice Caskett [Gwen's sister] was from a neighbouring village and escaped the riots. She had been married to that village's Fish merchant and had five children living from the eight she had birthed, over the years. She died peacefully in her bed - surrounded by her large family - in 1382. Her soul was collected and processed. She now works as a Collector.

Bishop Charles Monfort wasn't happy about the death of Father Richard and the happenings at Dunmore Village - nor was his boss - the Archbishop of York. He was removed from office and become the Abbot at Doncaster Abbey. He died there in 1375 and his soul was collected and processed.

Sarah Coggle - the serving maid at Fletcher's Tavern - was raped and killed during the riots. Her body was dumped at the 'Leper's Tower' and never recovered for burial. Her soul was collected and processed.

Alexander McIves [Black Sword] remains a soul out of his own time. He is on the 'Most Wanted List' for the Temporal Detectives Department. He and Jericho were to meet on several occasions. Jericho regards him as 'quite an enigma'. His soul remains missing to this day.

The village of Dunmore became a district of quite a large city by 2050. Its previous history of Devil worship and witchcraft has almost been lost by the passage of history and time. But there remains a small, but active cell of witches there to this day. It also remains famous for its local delicacy; the little cake called the 'Dunmore Half Crown'.

Barfield Castle has passed through many families hands over the centuries and currently is the ancestral home of the Hadden family; two members of which will become human agents for Mister Jericho Tibbs in the early 20th Century.

EPISODE 3: "THE GHOSTS AND MISS JESSICA MARTIN."

MISSION SUMMARY:

"London 1940 - The Blitz. - Mr. Tibbs investigates a strange 'apparition' which has appeared on the streets of war-torn London during the German bombing of the East End. But is distracted by the curious case of young Jessica Martin and the RAF pilot who has just crashed his Spitfire on wasteland to avoid coming down on nearby houses - the two should never have met but they did!"

 **ALCOHOL, VIOLENCE [Including graphic descriptions of war deaths] STRONG LANGUAGE & MILD HORROR.**

AGE 15+ ONLY.  **30 Minutes reading time.**

1. MISS JESSICA MARTIN.

Miss Jessica Martin ran quietly down the worn and broken steps from her front door and reached the old Iron Gate that lay to one side, before her mum shouted after her. She sighed loudly and adjusted the annoying Gas mask bag that hung off her shoulder and called back; "Bleedin' 'ell ma, I'm gonna miss the bleedin' bus at this rate!"

Her mother stood in the front doorway and waved the small brown paper bag; "I queued for an hour yesterday for that bloody cheese, so get back here and get your lunch... and I managed to get an apple for you!" Helen folded her arms over the long white apron that covered a drab dress which had seen better days. She shook her head in mock despair but smiled as Jessica sauntered back up the garden path and accepted her lunch with a big grin.

The bottom windows were boarded up and the house had clearly seen better days; but it was their home and Mister bleeding Hitler wasn't about to drive them out.

"I'll try and get back before ten, but it depends on those bleedin' buses. This new war timetable is bleedin' useless. I'd be better off on a flamin' pushbike!" Miss Jessica Martin gave her mum a little kiss on the cheek and with a wave, headed for the bus stop and the fifteen-minute journey to "Arnold Packer & Sons Ltd." Where young Jessica would work a late shift in the canteen, serving behind the works counter, cleaning tables, washing up and making endless cups of tea throughout the shift and all for 25 shillings a week, having left school just last month. She didn't like this shift because it meant travelling home in the 'Black-out', but at least no-one noticed her old worn clothes in the darkness.

Jessica had no real money to buy work clothes - she gave her mother all of last week's wages - just to pay the back rent. Charlie's home allowance that he sent monthly put food on the table and her father's maintenance Postal Orders had a nasty habit of not appearing on time. She still could not forgive her dad for running off with some posh speaking tart from the Co-Op Store last year, leaving them in real poverty.

She couldn't even afford to purchase the subsidized meals provided at work; hence the lunch bag. But she was very grateful that the factory provided its canteen staff with quite a nice uniform: Black dress, white blouse and floppy mop cap.

But no stockings, they were really expensive and already in short supply, so Jessica wore white ankle socks – like she always did to school - where she admitted to herself; that she learnt 'bog all' of any use. It was the skills that mum had taught her, which landed Jessica the factory job. She could cook really well and knew how to clean thoroughly, but most important of all; she could brew a cracking cup of tea! She pulled her worn brown coat about her and peered up at the two barrage balloons floating above the docks; she could see several others in the distance, all moving gently on their cables. "Fat lot of bleedin' good they'll do when Mister Hitler calls again with his bloody Luftwaffe." She laughed to herself and then thought about her brother; Charlie, now serving in the Royal Navy and wondered what he would think of the bombing over the last couple of days.

Jessica had heard that several families in Park Road and Green Avenue had been killed and the rescue people were still trying to dig out survivors. Her mum: Helen, said she knew one of the families and all four had been killed, trying to hide under the kitchen table.

Jessica stared up at the clear sky and thought she could see little dark spots heading away from the city towards the coast. "May as well try and use bleedin' catapults to bring the buggers down." She grinned broadly and remembered Charlie and the things he smashed with the catapult, which he always kept in his rear pocket. Jessica wondered if Charlie still had it; maybe he had packed it in his kit bag when he was posted to HMS Cornwall. The last letter mum had received hinted he was in South Africa, and Jessica really envied him the opportunity of real travel, the last place she had visited was bloody Southend-On-Sea – but it had been a real laugh – lots of ice-cream, paddling in the cold sea and a trip down the pier, where a gust of wind stole her hat.

Then she noticed the bus was already waiting and she ran to the stop, joining the queue of several women and one old man who was clutching a little black book and he appeared to smile directly at her; if about to speak. Glancing behind, she saw the young RAF Pilot emerging from Albert Road, still clutching his flying helmet and dusting himself down. He grinned at Jessica and started to walk towards the bus stop slowly, looking about and smiling.

The Conductor, Mavis, a big woman with wide smile and ill-fitting trousers shouted; "Three downstairs and three up top, come on, before Adolf clips your ticket for good!" The queue, with a little ripple of laughter, started to shuffle forward and Jessica cursed her luck, there were seven in the queue, and she was last – again. The women climbed onto the bus and the old man waited at the rear and waved his little book about, as if trying to attract someone's attention. He didn't actually get on the bus, but stood back.

2. AIR RAID.

Then the sirens screamed into action and Jessica looked up to see large dark spots appearing in the sky, someway in the distance; but heading for her.

"Oh flippin' hell!" She shouted and remembered there was a Public Shelter in nearby Christopher Street, by the Gaumont Theatre. She recalled the sandbagged entrance by the sign declaring the forthcoming feature; Errol Flynn in the 'Prince and the Pauper'. She ran quickly, clutching her lunch with the awful gas mask bag slapping against her bum, she glanced up to the see that the dark spots were indeed planes - lots of them -she shouted angrily to herself; "Where the 'ell are our fly boys?"

The first explosion made the ground tremble and a large white and orange flash filled the sky some streets away, then a dark grey spout appeared and she could smell burning. A second one followed close to the first and Jessica was now running full pelt into Christopher Street which was filled with screaming, frantic people pushing their way into the Shelter by any means.

Unable to pass through the wall of struggling people, she glanced behind her and could see the bus she was about to board on its side; ablaze. Two flaming figures struggled from the wreck and collapsed onto the roadway, she knew one was Mavis, the big, cheerful conductor; she didn't know the other woman and never would. The smell of burning flesh filled her nostrils and Jessica wanted to vomit. But with shaking legs, she again tried to push through the hysterical crowd until her arm was grabbed by the young man in the dirty RAF uniform; "You'll never get in there, there are too many bloody people!" He shouted and dragged her towards the large stone doorway of the library which was also heavily sandbagged.

"We'll stand a better chance in here!" He yelled above the noise of more explosions nearby. Jessica followed the young Pilot into the semi-darkness of the fortified doorway, and they crouched down in a corner as the terrible noise of dying people continued unabated outside. "For gaud sake; it's raining bleedin' bombs!"

Jessica whispered, then more explosions followed, and the ground appeared to move in ripples, one was close, causing sand and dirt to fly about the confined space. The young couple coughed loudly, and the Pilot shouted; "There are more of the bastards than usual, Herr Goering is after the docks and he really doesn't mind who he kills!"

Jessica realised she was crying and wiped her damp face with a shaking hand; "Where the 'ell are our flying boys?" She repeated with real anger in her voice and the young Pilot crouching next to her laughed; "Well, this one is really close Miss!" Jessica brushed away more tears and then chuckled; "Why you down here and not up there then mate?"

The young man offered her a clean white hankie and sighed; "I was but didn't see a sneaky jerry come up from below me – bang! – I ended up here with my crate in pieces." He smiled and dusted himself down again and pulled a packet of cigarettes from his pocket and lit one up, offering it to Jessica, who shook her head and fumbled in her coat pocket for a couple of humbugs she knew were hiding there.

The young couple sat nervously chatting in the semi-darkness, swapping backgrounds, and even laughing at each other's daft comments. The raid had lasted for about an hour and evening was moving in. Pilot Officer Daniel 'Danny' Hart had only qualified as a Pilot two months ago and had fought in one 'sortie' before; without any luck; he suffered instrument failure and had to return to the airfield. It had been his twenty-first birthday just two weeks ago. He grinned at Jessica and chuckled; "Most men get the key to the ruddy door at 21. I got a bloody big Spitfire and a bloody big war to match it!"

Unknown to the pair – and everyone else at the time – some five or six streets away, another couple were walking slowly through the carnage, looking about at the death and destruction.

Mr. Jericho Tibbs and Lady Alexandra Cappanni passed unnoticed by the rescue crews who were struggling to reach survivors buried in their own homes. The dead and dying suddenly appeared on nearly every street corner, placed outside shattered shops and homes, sometimes on a stretcher, but most under a dirty sheet or Fireman's coat. An elderly policeman was tying tags to bodies indicating which house they were from; the proper identity process would start later: for now, there was simply no time. A builders lorry stood by, and the bodies were placed on the open back, some covered – the worse ones – and driver tried to cover what he could of the others, to give them some kind dignity in death. The old man wiped his face several times as he covered the bodies of two young children with his own coat that he pulled off and gently placed down on the little broken bodies.

The rescue services struggled over broken roads, soaked by ruptured water pipes and fire hoses; frantically trying to reach buried survivors before the planes returned.

Jericho glanced towards a burning Newspaper shop; outside was a mangled bike and a grey canvas bag from which newspapers had spilled onto the road. Red streaks of blood directed his eyes to the shattered body of the child, torn apart by the bomb he couldn't see or escape. Alex commented on his wonderful mop of blond hair and then realised it was no longer connected to his head. She covered her mouth in horror and the pair hurried past the awful sight.

Night was now falling and there would be no relief from the horrors, as Germany would now be bombing at night, having suffered heavy losses in daytime raids. They passed a couple of Collectors with several souls in tow; one raised his hand and shouted, 'Hello Mr. Tibbs!' Both Jericho and Alex returned the greeting with Jericho muttering; "They're going to be busy for the next few years!" Alex nodded her agreement and they walked on.

"Perfect environment for the 'Dark One' to strike, don't you think?" He quietly asked Alex, who was staring up at the darkening sky, as more planes filled the air. Jericho sighed and glanced down at the report about the strange apparition that had recently appeared on the streets of London's East End; right in the middle of the Blitz.

He looked up and pointed towards Cuthbert Street; "Down there and his address is just minutes away. He should be able to give us a full update on the sightings; he's been part of my human team here for some time with his sister. You'll like her Alexandra: she intelligent, independent and strong minded." He then smiled, adding; "And just as beautiful, you'll have a real rival there when she joins the department!"

"Here they come again." Alex said simply and the pair slowly de-materialized from their human form – for now.

3. A GLIMPSE OF HELL.

They emerged from the battered doorway into the gathering gloom and simply could not believe the sight before them, burning buildings, rancid thick smoke and the screams of the trapped and dying. The Co-operative butcher's shop just opposite was no more than a blazing frame, then the roof collapsed with an explosion of debris and flame. It threw two charred bodies upon the broken road and Jessica screamed in real horror.

Danny took hold of her hand quite firmly and the pair ran towards the street corner; neither one looked back, as grey smoke covered the dreadful scene, and the night sky became a vivid mix of yellow and orange. East London was burning.

"We need to get to a tube station; they'll be back, and it won't be safe to stay on the street." Danny shouted as they ran past a blazing Fire-engine; some on the crew still sprawled around it or rather pieces of the crew were still laying beside it. Two Constables staggered past them; their uniforms in rags and both covered in black burn wounds. One was blind and trying to grip his colleagues arm, but the skin on his hands simply peeled away. He was crying and screaming swear words every few seconds. The pair disappeared around the street corner and his voice was still heard for some time before it stopped.

Danny and Jessica made their way over the broken roads and pavements, past the burning buildings, past the frantic rescue attempts and past the dead covered with sheets, curtains, coats and anything that could hide their torn and dismembered bodies.

Finally, they reached St. Mungus church and both climbed the wooden and wire fencing placed by the local council to keep people from entering the ruins; the church had been derelict since the end of the last war.

"They're coming back; we'll never make the tube station now!" Danny had yelled as bombs started falling in the distance. From the Dock area they saw vivid explosions and heard the sound of anti-aircraft fire.

They made their way through the old church and down the worn steps to the crypt; the ground rumbled as bombs fell across the roadway, lighting up the crypt door, which was already shattered into several pieces, and they scrambled in as the light of the bomb flashes faded, allowing the darkness to return.

Danny was digging into his trouser pockets and cussing quietly, but he found what he was searching for: his little flight torch. He snapped the light on and slowly passed it around the crypt. They saw broken stone coffins, smashed angels, and pieces of timber, roof tiles and where the wall had partially collapsed: an old mirror with yellowing glass. Danny stared at the mirror for a couple of minutes, but it was Jessica that answered the question he had asked himself.

"It must have been bricked up behind that old wall." She spoke quietly and nervously, pushed the last surviving humbug into her dry mouth. "But this church was built in Medieval Times; they must have bricked it up centuries ago – but why?" Danny whispered and pushed a hand over his face, then snapped the torch off.

They sat silently in the dark for a few minutes until Danny finished his cigarette and tapped Jessica's arm; "Do you know what's really odd about the old mirror?" Jessica pulled her knees up and wrapped her arms around them; "No." She said quietly.

Danny chuckled and with a very quiet voice said, "When I shone the torch on it, I didn't see the light reflected back." They both stared into the darkness at the outline of the collapsed wall and Danny slowly pulled the torch from his pocket and snapped it on. He pointed the torch beam directly at the mirror, his hand shaking a little.

The figure appeared to be standing behind the glass with hands pressed against the inside frame. Its bright green eyes were looking directly at them, and one hand appeared to beckon them with a little wave. Danny and Jessica had cleared the church ruins, the desolate graveyard and the wood & wire fence in probably under a minute – had this been an Olympic race - they would have won gold!

4. THE UNDERGROUND.

The pair didn't stop running until they reached the High Street and ran down the tube Station steps – two at a time. They found the East bound platform packed with people sheltering from the bombing. There was music playing and a small group of families were singing and passing bottles of beer amongst themselves. People were sleeping wherever they could squeeze in, and no-one seemed to mind the crush.

They sat on the stairway's steps and pressed up against the wall; still panting from their frantic dash, then started laughing and Danny gripped her hand tightly and smiled; "It was probably some old vagrant kipping down and we've scared the pee out of the poor old bugger!" Jessica grinned broadly and fumbled in her coat pockets; pulling her brown lunch bag out and peering inside; "Two cheese and tomato sandwiches, an apple and four broken digestive biscuits." She announced handing Danny a sandwich and a couple of biscuit pieces. "Can you cut the apple in 'aff?" She added.

Danny nodded and from his pocket; pulled a small penknife and cleaned the blade with his hankie. He reluctantly had to let go of her hand to accept the apple and deftly sliced it into two pieces. They ate quietly watching the crowd milling about the platform until a middle-aged women approached them clutching a photograph. "Excuse me young man, have you seen this boy?"

Danny smiled and took the picture; it was a boy of about twelve in jumper and short trousers, standing next to his bicycle. He had quite a mop of light coloured hair. He shook his head and passed the picture to Jessica who also hadn't seen the youngster.

The sad looking woman sighed; "He was earning an extra shilling by delivering the late edition papers, I walked with him to the shop, but then the bombing started. I lost him and I've been searching ever since." She looked about and saying a quiet 'thank you' to the pair, wandered off. Danny watched her go, trying to approach other people who appeared to ignore the woman. Then he saw her pass the photograph to a young girl in ambulance driver's uniform – who also shook her head – no, she hadn't seen him.

Danny watched the young ambulance woman looking about, no-one seemed to notice her – apart from the desperate mum - and....him and Jessica.

"At least me mum won't start worrying 'bout me until after ten, that's when me bleedin' shift would have finished at Arnold bleedin' Packer and Sons." Jessica finished her apple and wiped her mouth with her sleeve, which made Danny laugh and smile, he glanced down at his watch and frowned; "My bloody watch has stopped." He pulled it from his wrist and shook it a couple of times; "No, it's definitely broken, stopped at one thirty."

He pushed the watch into his breast pocket and tried to remember what he was doing at one thirty that may have broken the damn thing. Suddenly, he had a vision of the German plane coming up from below him; the wings spitting little bursts of flame, then, as he pulled the stick back to climb, he saw his watch: it showed one thirty.

"I can't remember escaping from the jerry fighter or bailing out." He whispered and rubbed his eyes and face. He recalled smoke in the cockpit and pulling frantically at the canopy, but nothing after that – nothing – until he saw Jessica by the bus stop and that strange old man in the bright black suit who smiled at him.

Wailing sirens snapped him from the strange thoughts that were filling his troubled head. "That's the bleedin' All Clear!" Jessica grabbed his arm and pair made their way from the station, the dark London streets was full of activity; ambulances and fire engines screamed past, army trucks rumbled by towing anti-aircraft guns and rescue squads were working in the rubble - sometimes calling for silence - as they tried to listen for the cries of the trapped.

A couple of Air Raid Wardens strode past them with dogs, who had little boots on their paws – that made Jessica giggle - Danny explained they were search dogs and the boots stopped their little paws from being injured by glass and sharp rubble, when they climbed around bombed buildings.

"They'll probably dock me a day's pay for not turning in for me shift; bleedin' tight gits." Jessica said with some sadness as they headed up Cuthbert Street and the long walk back home. That's where they came upon the mob outside Brick Lane Police Station, where a couple of Constables were on the steps allowing one or two people through at a time.

"Reporting missing relatives." Danny said quietly to Jessica, who nodded her agreement. A young Constable was standing a few yards from them, arms folded, and his helmet pushed back; he turned and smiled; "What happened to you, forgot where you parked it?" Danny looked puzzled for a moment, then laughed; "No, some bleeding jerry took it off me."

The Policeman smiled and gave a jaunty salute; "Some of them are reporting the 'Apparition' again – apparently, it's been seen near the tube Station - normally after closing time at the Royal Oak!" Showing a smile he walked off, and Danny realised he had seen the young Policeman before but couldn't think where.

5. ROYAL OAK.

Jessica pushed her arm through his and the pair walked past the noisy mob and into Bridge Street, where a little flash of light drew their attention to the Royal Oak's darkened doorway. "Put that bloody light out!" Someone yelled and received a two fingered salute from a hand pushed from the black-out curtains. Jessica laughed and then sounded quite puzzled; "I thought the old Royal Oak copped it last week, they must have done a good job to get it open again."

They exchanged glances and grinned; then headed for the pub entrance. The place was heaving with customers and the two barmaids were busy; Irene sipped a straight gin and slowly drew on her cigarette; she straightened her very tight blouse. She knew the punters loved catching an eyeful of her expansive breasts and the drinks and tips came quickly. Only last week she had made her wages again from the tips. Earning nearly six pounds instead of just three pounds & ten shillings; but then her jumper had not left much to the imagination!

She watched the young airman approach the bar, hands shuffling in his pockets for money, after seating the young girl in the quiet corner by the kitchen door. "A half of best and a lemonade please." He smiled at Irene, and she liked the look of this dark haired, handsome young man – and a bloody pilot as well – what more could a girl want.

Kath stubbed out her cigarette and sipped her tea – it was lukewarm now - but she swallowed it down and checked her appearance in the mirror; she may be in her early forties, but she could still hold her own against young tarts like Irene and she had one other advantage; she was the landlady of the Royal Oak! "Ask the girls age please Irene." She called over as she served two rowdy sailors and their 'lady friend' who could easily pass as their mother – Kath looked again - 'Christ, their bloody grandmother!' Then laughed to herself.

"The old lady probably entertained their fathers during the last war." She whispered to Irene who squealed with laughter; "The gorgeous young flyboy says the girl is 18 and does shift work at Arnold Packers, they're having a quick drink before she goes home and he has to get back to the bloody war!"

Kath smiled at the pair, sitting staring at each other in the quiet corner and sighed; "What a bleedin' time to fall in love; in the middle of a bloody war." Then another couple caught her eye as they approached the bar. She eased past Irene; "I'll get this pair."

"Hello Mr. Tibbs and it's lovely to see you again Lady Alex, here to see Harry?" Kath motioned to the rear stairs and added; "He's up there; in front of the fire."

Jericho and Alex climbed the small attic stairs with a flickering oil lamp for guidance and Jericho knocked gently on the brightly painted door – though the paint was old and flaking - A soft voice called for them to enter and Jericho pushed open the creaking door and they entered the poorly lit, but surprisingly warm little room. Alex could see flames in the fireplace and the slight smell of Lavender pervaded the atmosphere. The voice had come from a high-backed chair placed before the fire; she and Jericho slowly sat on the sofa opposite.

"Harry, I want you to meet Alexandra; one of my colleagues." Jericho turned to Alex and smiled; "This is Harry Hadden. He's been one of my agents here for more years than I wish to remember." The old man managed a smile and leaned forward to shake Alex's hand and she gripped it firmly; "Hello Harry, it's nice to finally meet you." She spoke quietly and knew that he had been a strapping, handsome young man in his prime, with a quick mind and was possibly, one of London's finest Police Detectives. Jericho had always considered him one of his best human agents; him and his sister Dorothy.

Alex already knew that Jericho had spoken to Angel Margret

about Harry joining the Temporal Detectives Department, after he completed his assignment here. But Jericho had remained silent about Dorothy and that puzzled Alex, considering how much he admired her skills. Still, the young woman's fate would become apparent when Jericho wished to reveal it.

There was a quiet knock and Kath appeared with a large tea tray; "I managed to get some bleedin' biscuits Harry – the queue stretched down bleedin' Garden Street – you would have thought they were waiting for flippin' steak and not Crawford's bloody custard creams!" They all thanked Kath who quickly returned to the bar – she had nearly a full house - and Irene wasn't the quickest barmaid in London.

Harry nibbled his biscuit and looked over his teacup at Alex but spoke to Jericho; "You should bring Alexandra here, back when the old King was on the throne [King Edward VII] I think she would love the East end of those days."

Jericho smiled and nodded, turning to Alex; "Harry was one of the youngest Detective Inspectors ever and that was in 1901. He and his sister Dorothy are my finest agents for the early 20th Century in England. You would love to meet Dorothy; I think you two would become very close friends." Harry agreed with that, and Alex poured him a refill – intrigued by the young woman that Jericho always spoke so highly of - Alex would have liked to hear more about her. But they had the mission to discuss.

6. OPERATION "SHEPHERD."

But Jericho switched the conversation to the reason for their visit; "How's operation 'Shepherd' going?" He asked Harry and settled back, sipping his tea.

Harry chuckled; "I love that name. Well, we must have rounded up at least a dozen or so in the last couple of days and Kath says we have nearly a full house again tonight."

Jericho nodded; Operation 'Shepherd' had been set up to catch lost Souls; humans killed in the bombing who didn't realise they had passed over, so quick and instant were their deaths. The Royal Oak pub had now become a portal for the Collectors seeking missing souls – and it was working - with the newly dead turning up to be greeted by their Collectors.

Jericho pointed out to Alex that the pub itself had been destroyed by enemy bombing and its occupants killed, including Harry, Kath, Irene and the young cellar boy; Paul. But now they were working for Angel Margret, who had resurrected the pub and its occupants for this little operation and the bewildered dead were turning up in growing numbers.

"Only the dead can see the pub and fellow dead people inside; the living just sees a derelict, burnt-out pub, destroyed by German bombs." Jericho finished his tea and enjoyed another biscuit. Harry chuckled and said to Alex; "Never thought I'd finish my days being blown up by bloody German's in my own bed!" They sat chatting about the 'old days' and Harry informed them about the latest sightings of the 'apparition', creeping about the dark and bloody streets of East London, probably on the prowl for vulnerable souls. But here was another knock at the door and Kath pushed her head around and spoke to Harry; "I think you should know that we have a nice young couple downstairs that's seen the 'Apparition' and they know where the bugger is hiding out!" Harry gave the thumbs up and Jericho placed his tea cup down and nodded to Alex; "I think we'll have a little chat with them before their Collector whips them away."

Kath smiled and sighed; "Be gentle with 'em Mr. Tibbs, they're very young and they've fallen in love, bless 'em." Alex glanced at Jericho and saw the look upon his face; "It's called romance Jericho; you should look it up." She chuckled to herself, but Jericho just grunted, and the pair said their farewell's to Harry and returned to the bar with Kath, who pointed the love-struck youngsters out.

Alex grinned and sighed loudly; "Oh yes, Jericho that young pair are in love," The couple sat talking very close and holding hands below the little table. Alex noticed that Jericho had a strange smile upon his face, as they walked over and introduced themselves to the bewildered pair.

It was quite easy to convince the young Pilot that he was in fact; dead. Danny already had an inkling that something was dreadfully wrong – he knew that he could not have survived the crash onto that wasteland - never mind wander around the streets; but how come Jessica could see and touch him?

Alex explained to the pair that they were both in fact; dead. Alex consulted her mirror and told Danny how he died – when she stated the time had been one-thirty - he nodded and showed them his watch. "I sort of guessed that I had been killed; I couldn't get the bloody canopy open to jump." He swallowed his beer in one gulp and smiled at Jessica; "Sorry sweetheart." Gripping her hand with both of his, the pair exchanged a really sad and haunting look. Alex turned to Jessica, who had small tears running down her cheeks, and informed the girl that she had died the previous night; when her house had been struck by a bomb, killing her and her mother, as they cowered in the small cellar. Somehow the pair had been missed by their Collector and both her and her mother's soul was listed as missing.

"We can get a Collector to the address and save your mum's soul before something terrible happens to it; especially with the 'apparition' stalking the streets." Alex added and patted Jessica's wet face, wiping away her falling tears.

"Can we stay together Mr. Tibbs?" Danny asked; "I mean we're both now dead, can we stay with each other please?" Alex glanced at Jericho; she already knew that their souls would go to new, separate lives as directed by the Duty Death Angel. Jessica also pleaded with Mr. Tibbs to stay with Danny and Alex could feel she was getting a little emotional herself over the pair.

But Jericho pointed out that Jessica had died before Danny and so they should never have met; well, not whilst alive anyway! That's when Alex drew Jericho's attention to the bar and a young man being refused service by Kath; both Danny and Jessica asked about the strange glow he seemed to radiate. "He's still alive and doesn't realise he has the ability to see and speak to the dead. Kath has told him to leave, and he'll get a shock, if he looks back at the pub and see's its true appearance." Jericho said, watching the confused young man wander from the Royal Oak, totally unaware of the 'supernatural' experience he was just involved in.

The young pair sat desolate and heartbroken at Mr. Tibbs words about their fate. Nevertheless, they both volunteered to show the temporal detectives where they had seen the 'apparition' and the little group left the pub, with Jericho and Alex saying goodbye to Kath and Irene. They watched as a couple of souls also departed, now with their Collectors.

When Alex looked back at the pub, as they walked towards Queen's square, it had returned to its derelict and burnt out state. The remains of the Royal Oak would be demolished after the war and a new office building erected on the site – less than a century later - no-one would even remember that the pub stood there, never mind the people who lived and died in her.

"That's the funny old man who was at the bus stop!" Danny exclaimed and Jessica nodded her agreement. George the Collector smiled and lifted his hat to Alex and spoke to Jericho; "Morning Mr. Tibbs, busy around here these days. I see you've caught up with a couple of lost ones." He indicated to Danny and Jessica and added; "They're not in my book [Soul Ledger] but I called it in when I saw them at the bus stop. I've never seen a time with so many lost ones." He then smiled again and shrugged his shoulders; "Well apart from that last world war."

He waved goodbye and headed into the Royal Oak, whilst the little group made their way to St. Mungus Church. Danny was explaining to Jericho about the mirror and how it must have been bricked up in the wall, when the church was built back in the fifteen hundreds.

Jericho pulled his mirror from a pocket and looked the church up. He turned to Alex, who was in deep conversation with Jessica, and said softly; "Doc Underhill's team dealt with the demon back in 1482 and the Guardian assigned to the case could only imprison the bugger in glass. The local human team managed to have the mirror bricked up in the Church wall. Why this wasn't followed up is a mystery because Doc did file a report to the Demonic Ingresses Department; someone cocked up." Jericho sighed and placed a call for a Duty Guardian to attend, but he also noticed that a copy of his request was forwarded to Angel Margret for information. Alex tapped his shoulder; "Why would Angel Margret be interested in minor demon ingress?"

Jericho admitted that he didn't know, and they reached the derelict church some minutes later – just in time for the sirens to start again - as German raiders began to appear overhead. Danny stuck up two fingers at the planes which made Jessica laugh and grip his arm. "Least the bastards can't hurt us anymore." He muttered and then fell silent, staring at the figure waiting for them in the churchyard.

7. THE DEMON AND THE KNIGHT.

"It's alright; that's Oscar. He's a Guardian." Alex said and waved to Oscar who raised his arm in salute. The little man was dressed in a smart three-piece suit with a bright red waistcoat and dark bowler hat, clutched in his hand was a plain wooden staff. He leaned upon the staff and grinned; "Hi Alex, you always look gorgeous; no matter what time you're in!" Alex just laughed and introduced Oscar to Danny and Jessica who seemed quite amazed that a Guardian of God was a dwarf....and African. "I thought they would be like medieval knights with shining armour and swords!" Danny exclaimed; then grinned and shook Oscar's outstretched hand and the little man held up his staff; "You can't go far wrong with the staff of Moses - ideal for most demons!"

"About the armour and swords, you're thinking about a Knight of God - they dress up like that - sometimes! It does look impressive." Oscar indicated to himself with a wide grin, adding; "It can be bit of a surprise, I know and can be bit of a bummer when it comes to romance; but apart from that it really doesn't matter my friends." He smiled at the pair and pulled a mirror from his jacket pocket and turned to Jericho; "Apparently the cleanup was never completed and so this naughty little demon was left trapped in the mirror, until the bloody bombing pulled down the church wall and let Kasha out. She's probably well pissed off after spending hundreds of human years stuck in a piece of glass!"

"Talk of the devil." Muttered Alex and pointed to the crypt doorway as the figure emerged into the moonlight – it was the demon known as Kasha – and she didn't look happy.

Jericho gripped Oscar by the arm and unsmiling spoke quietly to the little man; "She's a First Tier Demon now Oscar!" Jericho now realised why she had only been quarantined all those years ago - a Guardian would not have the power to compel such an entity back to Hell - only a Knight of God possessed that strength and authority.

"I think an urgent call to Demon Ingress is required here." Alex whispered and pulled Danny and Jessica to one side - uncollected souls such as they - would be easy prey for such a demon: easy prey indeed. "Get them away from here Alex and do it now!" Jericho ordered and Alex obeyed without question. She pulled the mirror from her skirts pocket and flipped it open. Alex, Danny and Jessica disappeared in an instant.

Oscar gripped his staff with both hands and whispered closely to Jericho; "You best get the fuck outa here Jericho; I'll hold her for long as I can. Now go!" Jericho reluctantly agreed and pulled his own mirror from his coat pocket and flipped it open. But a stunning flash of light illuminated the old churchyard and both he and Oscar shielded their eyes, they could hear the snarling of the demon, as she also realised what just happened.

Jericho sighed loudly with utter relief and Oscar lifted his hat and wiped his brow; James, a Knight of God stood before them - sword in hand. He turned to the pair and smiled; "I suggest you two make yourself scarce. Margret certainly had your back on this one Jericho!" As the pair disappeared, Jericho heard Oscar mutter; "Another little battle in the bloody war of good and evil." They appeared outside number 37 Kitchener Road or rather, what was left of the little house. Alex was standing amongst the rubble with Jessica - who was cuddling her mother with great relief and much love - and a certain Mr. Silas Copperbent; a very senior Time-Controller, who was scribbling in a large red notebook. The old man looked up and smiled broadly at the pair and bowed a little. "Hello Jericho; been having a spot of bother with a pesky little demon, have we?"

He nodded at Oscar, who raised his hat and then vanished - returning to his office; the Demon Ingress Department - to fill out his report for Angel Margret. Jericho shook his hand and grinned; "The cavalry arrived, literally in the nick of time; thanks to Angel Margret." Alex gripped his arm and smiled; "Mr. Copperbent has told me of your plan and I would never have believed, that under that crusty exterior, you were an old romantic!"

Jericho rolled his eyes; but did smile. "I've been called many things over the years, but never that." Alex had to smile; what was Jericho up to?

8. MR. JERICHO TIBBS; AN OLD ROMANTIC?

Silas tapped his notebook and pointed down the road; a gaggle of Rescue workers, soldiers, firemen and other assorted characters were heading towards them, followed by an ambulance which picked its way carefully over the torn and rubble strewn road. "The local rescue centre has just realised, that they didn't search the last two remaining houses in Kitchener Road, due to the German bombers quick return and will do so now." He turned to Alex and gestured towards the souls of Miss Jessica Martin and her mother; Mrs. Helen Martin and added; "They will dig out these two alive from the rubble, not badly injured but they will require conveyance to hospital in the ambulance - which also contains a slightly injured young pilot - who was just pulled from his crashed plane some minutes ago after a spectacular and quite miraculous, crash landing!"

Old Silas chuckled to himself and wondered how Jericho had pulled this off with Angel Margret; but then, everyone knew the Angel had quite a soft spot for her favourite Temporal Detective Inspector. The Angel had given her authority, for the minor changes to the current timeline to take place. Miss Martin and her mother would both survive the war as would a certain young pilot. What happens when the pair meet up in the ambulance lay with themselves; the gift of freewill and all that!

Alex had explained to the young couple and Jessica's mother that they would remember nothing about their time whilst dead and should they meet up again, neither would recognize the other. She also explained that Angel Margret had made the decision because the error lay with the Collections Department; the pair should have never met; but they did!

So it was decided to resurrect the pair and Jessica's mother [because Jessica was supposed to die with her in the basement of their house; together] and allow the timeline to run with its new settings. All other deaths would remain on record. Danny would crash his plane, but survive, with Jessica and Helen being pulled from their house also alive. With everything explained, Alex said a quite emotional farewell to Jessica and the pair hugged tightly for a few minutes and suddenly Jessica and Helen were gone. From the basement of the collapsed house could be heard groans and little, strained shouts for help.

Mr. Silas Copperbent [still grinning broadly] took his farewell of the two Temporal Detectives and returned to the time-line control room; also, to write up his report for Angel Margret.

Alex and Jericho watched as the rescue party set about freeing the two women from the ruins of their house; they worked with great joy and relief as a dedicated team and soon the pair were pulled from the debris. Jessica crying and swearing loudly; to be admonished by her mother, who hugged the girl constantly as they were placed into the ambulance. The young pilot offered cigarettes all round and he and Jessica sat talking about their respective ordeals, as the ambulance man slowly closed the doors and headed for the cab.

None of the living humans could obviously see the pair of smiling Temporal Detectives, standing amongst the rubble and in particular Alex who was already reading her mirror. She sighed loudly and smiled broadly; "A smashing war time romance that resulted in a marriage that lasted for nearly forty-eight years." Alex wiped a little tear away with her soft white hankie and gripped Jericho's arm; "They were so close, they both passed over within a few weeks of each other."

Jericho just nodded, but he did smile a little; "Best we get back to the lighthouse, Angel Margret will want a full report on this one - someone is in for an arse kicking over that bloody demon - she managed to steal 22 souls and they are not likely to be recovered."

The pair disappeared as the sirens started to wail; the night would bring more horror, fear and death to the battered streets of east London. The Collectors would be out in large numbers yet again. Jericho and Alex walked slowly towards the grand door of the lighthouse, where Mr. Harris was waiting to take coats and hats. He also informed them that Mr. Wilson and young Owen had returned from their mission to Revolutionary America of 1775 - with a successful conclusion to the trip - and most importantly, the dinner guest had arrived; James, a Knight of God had accepted Jericho's invitation for supper and drinks.

"No doubt James will regale us with his heroic battle with the Demon and drain my bar of Vodka." Jericho muttered and held up both hands in mock despair; but he did notice the smile upon Alex's face at that announcement - he also smiled - but said nothing further.

THE END

EPILOGUE:

"This mission was particularly difficult for the Team; it was only part successful. The defeat of the Demon Kasha was necessary and was accomplished. But the unscheduled meeting between Jessica & Danny should never have happened. Angel Margret had to concede that the Collections Department was at fault. The changes to the human Timeline were allowed to remain."
SJW.

CHARACTERS:

Miss Jessica Martin should have died - aged sixteen - in the early German bombing of London's east end in 1940. But, somehow, her soul was overlooked or missed by the collector. She should never have met Danny Hart - who had also been killed on the same day - but she did. Angel Margret accepted that the error lay with the Collections Department and gave authority for the current timeline to alter a little. Jessica was to live until 1984, when she passed away due to complications of Type 1 Diabetes's. Her soul was collected correctly this time and processed.

Mrs. Helen Martin, Jessica's mother, should have died with her daughter in the bombing and was also overlooked by the Collector. She survived the war and re-married in 1948. She died in 1962 in a road traffic accident whilst on holiday in Blackpool. Her soul was collected correctly this time and processed.

Flight Officer Daniel 'Danny' Hart survived the war despite being shot down once more; He had also been overlooked by his Collector in the confusion of mass deaths. He and Jessica married in 1942 and remained together until her death. He died just two months after her passing - many said it was through total grief at losing Jessica - his soul was collected properly this time and processed.

Miss Mavis Richards - the bus conductress - apparently had some kind of premonition of her death that morning; she had hugged her mother and two younger brothers closely, before leaving for work that fateful morning. She never usually showed that sort of emotion. Her soul was collected and processed.

Kasha - the Demon - wasn't happy about being stuck in the

mirror for nearly five hundred human years! But she had made up for lost time by stealing 22 souls before James - a Knight of God - drove her back to her master - the Dark Prince. She's still around today; stealing souls and creating mischief for the armies of the BOSS.

Kenneth Michaels - the young Reserve Policeman - had only been in the police for a few months when he fell victim to a German bomb on that fateful day. The blast blinded him, and he suffered major burns. He died in hospital some days later and the surgeon confided to his grieving mother, that death had been a 'blessed relief' for the young man. His soul was collected and processed.

Norman Gates - a Reserve Policeman - had died just hours after the bombing and his soul had wandered the streets until he was found by a passing collector. He had told the collector about the two other souls he had encountered: Jessica and Danny. His own soul was processed.

Mrs. Doris Kent - the mother searching for her missing son - didn't realise she was dead for some time, after being killed by the bomb that hit the small News & sweet shop, where her young son Clifford worked as a paper delivery boy. Clifford had also been killed there and his soul was collected. Doris's soul was collected as she left the Underground station, where she had encountered Jessica and Danny.

Miss Alice Pullman - London Ambulance Service - should never have been on duty that day, but had swapped with a colleague, who had just become a father and wanted to see his baby son. She was on her way to the station when the bombing started and was killed trying to get into the Underground Station. After Doris had spoken to her, she followed the woman up the stairs and found the collector waiting. Her soul was processed.

Mrs. Irene Wilson - Barmaid at the Royal Oak - was killed by the bomb that had struck the pub. Like Kath and Harry, she had agreed to take part in 'Operation Shepherd' and she worked gathering souls together until late 1940, when her soul was finally collected and processed. Angel Margret thanked her personally before sending her back into the human life cycle.

Mrs. Katherine Meadows; Land Lady of the Royal Oak and a human agent for Jericho Tibbs, had been killed in the bombing of

the pub and like Irene and Harry had agreed to take part in
'Operation Shepherd', which had been set up by Jericho; with
Angel Margret's approval and assistance. Her soul was finally
collected and processed in early 1941. She now works as a
Collector.

Harry Hadden - Owner of the Royal Oak - had been a human
agent for Jericho Tibbs for many years [with his sister Dorothy]
and ran 'Operation Shepherd' for Jericho. His soul was finally
collected in early 1941 and Angel Margret had no hesitation in
assigning Harry to Team 7 as a Trainee Temporal Detective. He
was to make Temporal Detective Inspector in just a short few
human years; quicker than even Jericho had achieved! He is
now considered one of the finest Detectives the Department has
and now heads Temporal Detective Team 52. He and Jericho are
close friends.

EPISODE 4: "DR. ALEXANDER HARRIS AND HIS BATTLE WITH GOD."

MISSION SUMMARY:

"A Medical Officer on the Western Front receives a visit from Mr. Tibbs; someone is saving lives of the dead and the Human Time-Line could be seriously threatened. It's the eve of the Battle of the Somme [July 1st, 1916] and Jericho, with his team, are in the trenches on the day before the bloodiest battle in British Military History. Now posing as foreign diplomats and reporters, the team investigates Casualty Clearing Station No.21 and the strange Doctor Alexander Harris."

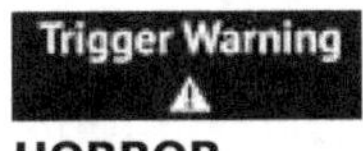

ALCOHOL, VIOLENCE, STRONG LANGUAGE & MILD HORROR.

 AGE 12+ ONLY.  30 Minutes reading time.

1. JERICHO GETS A NEW CASE.

Jericho and Wilson walked slowly down the bright corridor towards the Angel's office; both a little troubled about the summons from James, the Angel in charge of Collections, he didn't often call for Temporal Detectives directly. They were stopped by Rufus who slapped hands with Wilson and nodded a greeting to Mr. Tibbs. "You're gonna love this weird shit brother!"

Rufus exclaimed, pushing the dreadlocks from his grinning face; "Man, some dude is messing with the dying and its fucking up records: they are coming up short; big time!"

Rufus was the Senior Collector for one entire Century of human existence and one of the busiest; the 20th. He held a bunch of brown paper folders under his arm and shook his head, still grinning; "Three of my Collectors have reported that souls they were supposed to pick up, were still in their damn flesh suits!" Jericho and Wilson exchanged a puzzled look and Wilson asked; "How can that be man? Old man Death is always on top form when it comes to Dispatches!" Jericho nodded his agreement with Wilson's comments and smiled – Archangel Abraham who was in command of the Dispatch Department [responsible for scheduling human deaths] wouldn't appreciate being called 'Old Man Death'.

He had worked hard over the Millennia to give his department a new image; Even the old logo of the skeleton and scythe had been replaced with a bright white star and the names of his operatives had also been changed to 'Dispatchers' from the old title of 'Death Stalkers'. The Archangel believed that the changes would give his department a far friendlier appearance. Jericho chuckled to himself; I bet the living would disagree with that!

"It's happening in one place at the start of the century; slam bang in the middle of a fucking big war!" Rufus tapped gently on the door and added; "We're collecting loads every day and so far, nine souls have stayed firmly embedded in their fucking flesh suits and won't come out." He laughed loudly, flashing wonderful white teeth and threw back his head, the dreadlocks falling about his shoulders, adding; "Some dude is taking the piss and messing up our records and that isn't right."

Wilson grunted; "Which fucking big war is that; they had lot's in the century you cover Rufus." Jericho accepted a couple of files from Rufus but turned to Wilson; "The First World war or the Great War, as it was originally called before the Second World war dropped by. Basically, mass slaughter: it was the first real war of the Industrial Age and killing was now mechanized. The result was mass deaths; on a scale never seen before in human history."

"What's great about a war of mass killing and destruction?" Wilson asked and Jericho had to agree with him. Rufus tapped one of the brown paper files and said quietly; "We have nine souls still in their flesh suits and they were all soldiers who should have died. They were wounded in battle and should have passed over; it was scheduled. They were taken to...." He pulled open the file and then looked back up; "To Casualty Clearing Station No.21 - whatever that means - and every single one of them came into contact with one living human. Bit of a coincidence, eh?"

Jericho smiled; "I don't really believe in coincidence, what year are we talking about and who was it?" Rufus pulled open the file again and pointed to the page; "Same dude each time; a Doctor Alexander Harris and the same year: 1916."

"Well, I think we have enough already, to get authority for a little mission to that bloody piece of madness and check out this Doctor Harris character. But we'll need a doctor from that time period for advice on medical procedures and such. I think I know just the man." Jericho rubbed his chin and grinned, adding; "And it will make the girls happy."

Wilson gave Jericho a puzzled look, then shrugged his shoulders; "I don't expect I'll fit in back there." Jericho slapped him on the back; "You'll fit in like a glove; well, compared to our temporary new boy." Jericho chuckled; "I'll borrow him from Doc Underhill's team." Wilson caught on to what Jericho was saying and smiled; "Jesus Jericho, there won't be many of him around decent white folks back in 1916!" The sarcasm in his voice was obvious.

The door slid open in invitation for them to enter and the threesome walked quietly in and the door slowly closed behind them.

2. A NEW MEMBER OF THE TEAM - FOR NOW.

Jericho had called a team meeting and the crew assembled in the Drawing Room, well supplied with coffee and tea by the ever-attentive Mr. Harris. When everyone was seated, Jericho nodded to Owen who handed out a couple sheets of paper to each person. Alex quickly cast her eyes over the document and sighed loudly, she sipped her tea and spoke directly to Jericho; "Someone is saving lives of soldiers who should have died?"

"Yes. And messing up the current timeline by doing it; their souls were up for collection, my baby girl!" Wilson commented and stirred more sugar into his thick dark coffee. He turned to the new member of the team and added; "Our lady Alex has a soft spot for the living!" Then smiled and sipped his coffee with relish, while everyone chuckled at his comment – including Alex - who just smiled.

The 'new' team member he referred to was a Temporal Detective on loan from another team: 'Skyrise Young Mountain' was a strapping Apache Indian with dark hair and eyes; he resembled a Greek statue fitted out with a Seville Row suit and expensive shoes. In any age populated by female humans he would be considered a handsome man; a very handsome man.

"He's so bloody handsome, he's gorgeous!" Whispered young Ruth Hall who was peeking into the study with the Housekeeper Mrs. Harris; who chuckled and pointed out to young Ruth that men are not referred to as 'gorgeous'; but just 'handsome'. Ruth voiced her disagreement; "No, this one's gorgeous." Mrs. Harris gripped her arm and returned to the kitchen; taking the reluctant House Maid with her.

Alex studied the young man over her teacup and had to admit to herself that young Skyrise was quite a magnificent specimen of manhood. She watched him walk over to the table and place his coffee cup down. He moved like a big cat; with grace and poise that didn't match his size.

Had Alex heard young Ruth's comments, she would agree with her; totally.

Jericho called the meeting to order and explained the new forthcoming mission; "In late June of 1916 there is a war happening in Europe and the Collectors are out in force. But some have reported failures to collect certain souls because their lives have been saved and as Wilson pointed out, this is interfering with the Timeline and messing up Records. The Angel is not happy, and we've been tasked to investigate and bring this strange phenomenon to a close. I've borrowed Skyrise from Doc Underhill's team because he has special knowledge of this particular time period, especially this war."

Everyone glanced at Skyrise with the same thought; how the hell is an Apache Indian an expert on some European war?

Jericho Tibbs must have read their minds or their faces and chuckled loudly, slapping Skyrise on the shoulder; "People, Mr. Skyrise was one of some twenty thousand Native Americans who volunteered to serve their country in that war. He was in France, not at the time of this incident, but the following year after the United States joined the conflict in 1917. He volunteered as a Military Surgeon, so you see; he is superbly qualified to assist us."

Everyone sat in silence, a little ashamed at their ignorance of the person that stood smiling before them. "May I ask a personal question Doctor Skyrise and please be assured that I mean no offense by it." Alex rolled her teacup around in her hands and smiled at him. He nodded his agreement with no comment.

"How on earth did you end up a Military Surgeon in that racist time period, when other American's treated your people like bloody aliens in their own land?" Alex spoke softly, her voice betraying a little anger and amazement at the man's incredible achievement; why had she never heard of his exploits? Skyrise smiled; "Genetics Lady Alex, simple genetics." He clasped his hands together and explained to a very receptive audience how an Apache Indian was posted to France as a Military Surgeon;

"My father had an aptitude for medicine and the Christian brothers who visited his reservation saw his talent and arranged for him to receive Medical Training. But he proved such a good student they enrolled him in Medical School, paying for a scholarship and giving him a small allowance to survive on. He became one of the first Native American Doctors and a fine surgeon – but he was only allowed to treat other Native Americans, Mexicans, the Chinese and African Americans. He had no white patients. But he met my white mother, who was a doctor in her own right, and despite the opposition from both families they married. So, you see I was destined to be a doctor; whatever colour I was."

He laughed and continued; *"I practiced medicine on various reservations and quickly became proficient at gunshot wounds. My people had taken to alcohol and rifles; I was always busy. There were several mines staffed by the Mexican and Chinese settlers that used explosives; I became a regular visitor there too and finally when the war came, I found I was uniquely qualified to be a battlefield, Surgeon. After some opposition – mainly from the army commanders - I was accepted into the Army Medical Corp and went to France in late 1917."* He accepted another coffee from Mr. Harris and stood quietly by the fireplace, pulling a brown paper folder from his jacket pocket and glancing at the contents. Jericho addressed the meeting again; "Skyrise has a suspect in mind; it appears the nine souls that couldn't be collected all passed through this person's hands just before the Collectors arrived."

Skyrise nodded his agreement with Jericho's statement; "They all passed through a surgical unit located behind the Front-Line; No. 21 Casualty Clearing Station at Corbie, in the Somme Region and a Doctor called Captain Alexander Harris."

3. THE BIG PUSH.

"There's going to be a big push there and we should be able to spot what's happening, with so many casualties passing through it." Skyrise collected his papers and sipped his coffee. "What is a 'big push'?" queried Owen.

"It's a colloquialism for a big attack, you know; to push the Germans from Northern France." Skyrise did not smile and added; "There will be over a million casualties on both sides, by the time the insanity ends in the November of that year and they'll do it all again the following year, at another part of the line, with basically the same result."

"Were they fucking nuts?" Owen said with some amazement; "Maybe some were, but most were very brave men who believed they were saving their Country from enslavement." Skyrise replied and Jericho ordered everyone to the Light-Room. "The local human agent has made all the arrangements for our party to attend the Clearing Station as hosted diplomats." Jericho spoke, checking his mirror, then turned to Alex and Skyrise in particular; "Remember, my medical friends, this is a 'hands off' mission - don't get involved with the injured - Understand?"

They both nodded; reluctantly. Alex muttered something under her breath which made Skyrise smile; but passed unheard by Jericho. The Team headed for the light-room in silence, watched by Mr. Parker who jumped upon Jericho's armchair and settled down for a nap. Ruth, who was cleaning up glasses and cups, gave the big cat a stroke. Then looked up to see John in the doorway: "I'm afraid you just missed Mr. Tibbs; they have left already." Ruth told him, filling her tray with dirty glasses and cups.

"What year has he jumped too?" John asked quietly, running a hand through his dark beard, and staring at the floor. "1916." She said and headed for the kitchen, watching the reclusive John shuffle from the room and disappear.

"There's something about John. You can feel it." She told Mrs. Harris, as she washed glasses and cups in the deep sink. Cleo Harris just smiled; "He's a good man, a very good man." Ruth noticed the odd smile on Cleo's face; she always spoke highly of the strange man.

"I wonder how the team is getting on." Ruth said to herself, wiping down the draining board and peering through the kitchen window; watching John walking along the sea wall, head down and in silence; always on his own, she thought. He had few conversations with the people he resided with, except Jericho and Lady Alexandra. She watched him disappear from view, clutching a book from Jericho's collection. A very odd fellow, she mused and set about cleaning the kitchen table and chairs.

At first, the little group passed the soldiers practically unnoticed despite having an Apache Indian, an African American and even a woman – there were very few women here; in the support trenches that ran behind the Front line – and finally, a young boy trailing behind the group struggling with a wood and canvas stretcher. They were only challenged once; by a big Irish sergeant and his two men who were carrying the rum ration back to their unit in the Front line.

He saluted Captain Tibbs and asked directly about the Indian and the woman; Jericho explained that he was escorting an American Journalist; Mr. Mountain to Casualty Clearing station Number 21. He was doing a piece on the care of the wounded for the New York Times. The sergeant nodded and shook hands with Skyrise and mentioned that he was the first 'Yank' he had ever met. "Are they all that bloody big Sir?" He asked Jericho with a smile.

The big Sergeant clearly liked the look of Alex and voiced his disapproval of such a fine young woman being risked in the support trenches until Captain Tibbs pointed out that Lady Alex was a representative of the Italian Government [Allies of the British & French] and had to be afforded access to all areas for her report on medical care back to the Italian parliament. Jericho also spoke quietly into the Sergeants ear; "Apart from being a trained Nurse, she's the daughter of an Italian Count and Senior Government Minister; she takes bloody tea with Queen Mary!"

The sergeant whistled through his teeth and nodded, then pointed to Owen; "Is he underage Sir?" Jericho agreed and explained that Private Owen had enlisted whilst underage, so had been transferred to the Medical Corp as a Stretcher Bearer, to shield him from the horrors of war! The Sergeant laughed out loud at that and pointed the way to Casualty Clearing Station No. 21.

One of the younger Irish soldiers shook Wilson by the hand and admired the heavy camera that he carried effortlessly on his shoulder; "My brother George was a great portrait photographer in Wexford, he would love to see that bit of kit!" The young soldier wiped his face and stared down at his feet; "He caught one at Loo's last year with the Irish Brigade. Pity really, he was waiting for a transfer to the Army Photographic Unit, the letter turned up the day they buried him." Private O'Halloran wiped his face and smiled.

Wilson nodded; "It's a 'Speed Graphic', only made four years ago, she's manufactured by Graflex, in Rochester, New York. Certainly, is a good bit of kit, as you say." He replied and all three soldiers commented on his American accent.

"When the hell are you Yanks coming in?" The Sergeant asked Wilson directly and Wilson smiled; "Soon as our bloody President grows a backbone!"

That made the three Irish soldiers laugh loudly as they continued down the trench, waving and shouting 'bye' to the strange visitors who were passing through their world of constant death. Alex pushed her mirror back into her pocket after reading about the three young men they had just encountered. Owen caught the look upon her face and said quietly; "Do they make it?" Alex shook her head: negative. "They won't see tomorrow's sunset." She said simply and glanced back at the threesome disappearing into the growing darkness of night; still laughing and talking.

The little group passed on down the trench – Lady Alex received many 'wolf-whistles' and several shouts of: "WOW!" - She smiled and gave the men a little wave, which they cheered. "Just doing my little bit for morale." She whispered to Jericho who smiled broadly.

"We're looking for a trench called 'Oxford Street' that runs to the Dressing Station where we can grab an ambulance to the Casualty Clearing Station." Jericho called out as he led the group, in single file, through the damp trench, passing continuous lines of troops heading for the Front. Alex commented on how they joked and played about; "You would think they were trying to get into a football match and not a killing ground." She muttered to Jericho who suddenly pointed ahead; "There's the trench!"

The group stumbled across the broken floor of the trench and into 'Oxford Street'. They all could hear the continuous sound of the British barrage falling upon the German trenches. "It's been bombing the German lines for days and when it stops tomorrow; the poor bloody Brits will walk into hell because the wire won't be cut in many places and the German soldiers have survived in deep dugouts – thousands will be killed or wounded in just minutes - after the battle starts: a disaster, a bloody disaster." Skyrise shook his head with real sadness and the group continued down the trench in relative silence.

4. THE DRESSING STATION.

They found the Dressing Station as they rounded the next bend of the trench. Outside the dugout's entrance lay several stretchers' with bodies covered with dirty sheets. A young stretcher-bearer was pulling papers, cigarettes and personal items from a headless corpse and stuffing them in a heavy brown bag.

Private John Gates looked up from his gruesome task, pushed back his helmet and smiled; "Good morning, Sir." He gave a clumsy salute: his eyes fixed upon Alex and the Apache Indian; to say he was surprised would be a grand understatement. He gulped and wiped his brow, lifting up his tin hat which revealed a mop of thick black hair. Finally, he managed to stutter out; "Are they the party of foreign nobs Colonel Howes is expecting at No.21 Sir?"

Captain Tibbs smiled and nodded; "Two visitors from America and a diplomat from our Italian allies. Oh, and my soldier servant." Owen waved and grinned, whilst Alex noticed that the two boys must be the almost the same age; far too young for this hellhole she thought. Owen pointed towards a dozen dead men lying against a small stone wall. Two stretcher bearers were searching the bodies wearing gas masks and gloves. The bodies were bloated with horrific contorted faces. Owen spoke quietly to Skyrise; "What the fuck happened to those poor bastards?"

"Poison gas; If you're caught without a gas mask, it enters your lungs and produces a deadly foam - you would basically choke to death - like drowning without the need for any water." He looked quite grim and added; "The medic's have to wear masks and gloves when dealing with the dead bodies because the gas remains active on the clothes for some time afterwards - we learnt that little fact - the hard way." Owen saw the look on Skyrise's face and didn't ask any more questions of the big man.

"Mind your bleeding backs!" A panting corporal pushed past them, followed by two older soldiers carrying a stretcher with a young man groaning and swearing; laid upon it. His right arm was missing from the elbow down and was wrapped with a blood-soaked field dressing. His right leg was open from the thigh down and tied with his belt to prevent the blood spurting. They laid him down outside the entrance to the tent and corporal shouted in for help.

A tired looking young medic wandered out and knelt down next to the injured soldier; wiping his blood-stained hands with a rag. "He needs immediate removal to the Clearing Station; I can't do much for him here; except give the poor bugger some morphine."

Skyrise was about to interject, when he saw the look on Jericho's face and the little wave of his hand, simply indicating; back off. "The next ambulance is due in half hour." The medic muttered and started to examine the wounds more closely. Alex took a little breath; "He needs to go now private, and I mean now."

The young medic looked up and slightly smiled; "Sorry miss. But I can't produce ambulances out of my arse; so, he'll have to wait." He stood up and threw the blood-soaked cloth into the mud - he didn't smile - then disappeared back into the tent. The corporal muttered; "Bastard." quite softly and covered the groaning soldier with a piece of canvas and let him drink from his water bottle.

"He'll be dead long before that ambulance shows up." Skyrise spoke to Jericho, then added; "And this is a quiet day on the front; wait until tomorrow, when there will be thousands like that young man arriving here and even more laying in no-man's land with no chance of surviving their wounds."

The group stood around in relative silence until Alex said quietly to Jericho; "He's going to die without some proper medical attention. Skyrise and I can help him. Please, please let us do so - I'm willing to beg you if I have too - but please let us help him, please."

A grim faced Jericho simply said; no. Alex pulled up her dress a little and knelt down in the mud and stared up at Jericho; the tears in her eyes clear and obvious; "Please let us help him - please." The corporal and the two older soldiers couldn't actually believe what they were seeing, and they passed cigarettes between themselves in total silence.

Jericho folded his arms and sighed; quite deeply. Then looked down at the young soldier; groaning and swearing, his face white as snow; he was dying. Jericho held out his hand to Alex and slowly pulled her up. "You can have this one on me. But only this one not one more, do you understand?" He spoke softly into her ear with clear disappointment in his voice. He would have to square this with Angel Margret; later.

Alex and Skyrise rushed to the stretcher, yelling for the young medic to bring bandages, heavy dressings, and clean water. They worked on the boy for some minutes as everyone watched - a little crowd had gathered - finally, they pulled away from the stretcher with smiles of real satisfaction upon their faces.

The young medic nodded to Jericho; "I've seen a lot of doctors and surgeons working on the men and those two are about the best I've seen in a long time." He spoke with real respect in his voice. "Why the hell aren't they in uniform?" He added, lighting up a 'Woodbine' cigarette.

Jericho explained quietly that one was from a neutral country and the other was a diplomat from an allied country. They shouldn't be doing anything like it - but they had done so - he shrugged his shoulders and walked away; unsmiling.

Wilson grinned at Skyrise and whispered; "I told you that our lady Alex has a soft spot for the living!" They both chuckled, watching Alex wiping blood from her hands and dress. But a thin sergeant appeared and barked orders at the young private; to fetch Lt. Kenning who was to host the visiting party. He looked like a young version of Lord Kitchener, sporting a huge dark moustache and mad eyes. He introduced himself to Jericho with a salute and apologised that the roads were so choked with troops and supplies that they would leave tomorrow morning at seven. The 'guests' would be accommodated overnight in the ruins of a small farmhouse.

"It's quite comfortable Sir – very few rats - the lady can wash up there, I'll arrange for some warm water for her and get some hot meals for your people." He announced, saluted again and shouted fresh orders at the hapless young private to help with any equipment the visitors may have. Thus, Jericho and his team settled down for the night, with the British barrage as bedtime music in the distance.

Alex lay against the wall with a rough blanket wrapped around her. Owen was brewing tea and handed Alex a cup of hot sweet tea. "Well, did he make it? I saw you checking your mirror." He eased himself down next to her and sipped from his cup. Alex nodded; "Young Patrick O'Rook - aged nineteen from Limerick - will survive his wounds and despite losing a leg and part of his arm, will marry his childhood sweetheart and live until 1955. They didn't have any children and his widow - Katherine - died in 1961. He was a good man by all accounts; respected and much loved by family and friends. He managed to have a good and worthwhile life despite his injuries."

Owen smiled and then said quietly; "I still think a little apology to Jericho is in order; I mean, for putting him on the spot like that." Alex leaned back against the wall; "You're probably right Owen. I'll speak to him now." Alex, still in the blanket, wandered outside the little ruined cottage and found Jericho watching the flashes of the guns, arms folded and in quite a sombre mood. She slipped her arm through his and just nodded. Jericho smiled. The pair both knew that such apologies weren't needed between true friends and colleagues. They both stood watching the gun flashes.

5. CLEARING STATION NO.21

The following morning was clear and warm. After a light breakfast of porridge, bacon, egg and funny tasting tea, Lt. Kenning organised for two staff cars to carry the visitors to Casualty Clearing Station Number 21.

Owen asked Skyrise why the tea tasted so strange and was told that chlorine was used to keep the water fresh and that tainted the flavour, Owen seemed quite anxious; "Christ! don't they use that stuff in poisonous gas?" Everyone chuckled and gathered by the two cars in the warm morning sunshine, where Jericho gave a final briefing to his group.

The two Vauxhall D-Type's had their engines cranked by their drivers and the party split between the vehicles; Jericho, Alex and Lt. Kenning pulled away in the first car to leave; driven by a fat private with bad teeth who grinned constantly at Alex. The second car had the thin Sergeant, Skyrise, Wilson and Owen aboard; their driver was a tall man who appeared to be quite old for a soldier, but he certainly could drive. He admitted to Wilson that he was 61 years old and had been a Chauffeur to some Lord and Lady in Yorkshire, but decided to do 'his bit', so he lied about his age and joined up; only to be a bloody 'chauffeur' to officers now!

As the little convoy pulled away from the front, Jericho and Alex looked behind them and realized that the British barrage had stopped, for some moments there was a strange quietness and then an odd sound could be faintly heard.

"Tac, Tac, Tac." Skyrise whispered and Wilson asked him what that means, Skyrise sighed and wiped his brow; "German machine guns killing thousands of young men." He sat hands clasped in his lap; head bowed and said nothing more until they reached Casualty Clearing Station No.21.

As the visitor's convoy arrived at the clearing station, which was placed in the abandoned school at La Neauville; they saw that behind them came a long stream of ambulances, Lorries and carts. They could hear a bell tolling and the station seemed to burst into activity as nurses and orderly's started to gather by the large iron gates of the school complex. A very tall officer strode to the head of the crowd and shouted orders as he pulled his jacket off and handed it to a young nurse – he was organizing the station to take casualties – many casualties.

"That's him; Captain Harris." Skyrise said, jumping from the car with Wilson and Owen. "Can we help?" Skyrise shouted and helped Alex from the other car. Harris stared at Skyrise and shouted; "Yes, stay out the bloody way!"

6. THE MAN AND THE HOUR.

Col. Howes greeted the little group of visitors briefly; they, of course, understood the urgency of the situation; with mass numbers of wounded and dying men to attend. He was particularly surprised when both Alex and Skyrise offered their help and even more so when he discovered that Alex was a Nurse [Alex is, of course, a fully trained doctor. But playing a nurse as part of her cover on this mission] and Skyrise was a Native-American Surgeon – So it was explained - that was the reason why the Newspaper sent him, and the Italian Government had dispatched Lady Alex.

But Captain Harris displayed real reluctance to accept the assistance of either of them. That was noted by everyone in the group. Wilson spoke softly to Jericho; "I see he doesn't want us around. I wonder why that is?" Jericho just nodded in reply and the group was shown their quarters by a young Trainee Nurse; Rachel Goldman, who seemed fascinated by Alex and Skyrise – who admitted that she had never encountered an Apache Indian - apart from those in her young brother's novels about the American Wild West and she definitely liked what she saw!

The young nurse seemed in awe of Alex and kept calling her; 'My lady.' Alex told her on several occasions to call her just 'Alex'. But there really was no time for long introductions as the wounded started to arrive in large numbers. Col. Howes announced that a hospital train would arrive that evening to collect the most seriously wounded [but could be moved], for transfer to both civilian and military hospitals in the cities.

A tall, dark haired Staff Nurse stopped the group as they walked and stared at Alex; "Don't I know you?" She asked with great hesitation in her voice and then half smiled; "Its Alex, Doctor Alex Featherstone, isn't it?" Alex glanced at her teammates and shook her head; "No, I think your mistaken Staff. Right first name but wrong about everything else." Deliberately making her Italian accent clear - Alex smiled and the group moved on – with her colleagues looking a little puzzled by the incident; except Jericho.

But everyone could hear the Staff Nurse speaking to a couple of her friends [other nurses] in the quiet corridor; "You could knock me down with a feather, I would swear on my mother's grave that is Alex Featherstone. She and I served together at Whitechapel Hospital at the turn of the century. Her father was a senior surgeon there, I thought she would be at least; a qualified Doctor by now, but if it's her, she doesn't appear to have aged a single day since I last saw her and...."

The woman's voice faded as they reached the Doctors rest room and were served tea and sandwiches. Wilson stood close to Alex and whispered; "How does some lady in 1916 know you, when you died in 1801, in Italy?" He smiled a little, when Alex answered, "Well, because she doesn't and is wrong. Merely has me mistaken for someone else." Wilson shrugged his shoulders and said, "O.K. that's fine by me; mistaken identity, eh?" He grinned; "Anything you say baby girl!"

Alex directly asked Colonel Howes how she and Skyrise can be of assistance. But Jericho reluctantly pulled both Alex and Skyrise to one side and reminded them of their mission here and if both assisted in saving lives of men who would probably die from lack of immediate medical care, they would have some explaining to the Angel - like he already had to do so – he didn't smile. Skyrise accepted the reprimand with good grace, but Alex just folded her arms and said nothing. Wilson smiled and gripped Skyrise by the arm and the pair set about helping the Stretcher-bearers carry the casualties in. Young Owen was already busy doing the same and Alex volunteered to make endless cups of tea, whilst Jericho kept a close eye on Captain Harris.

7. MADE BEFORE ITS TIME.

In a quiet spell that evening, the group rendezvoused by the old boiler house of the school and talked softly about the day's events. They all had mugs of tea and cheese sandwiches, they all stood; except Alex; Wilson had found her an old armchair to doss in and she accepted it gratefully; she had been on her feet since arriving here.

That's when Skyrise waved them into relative silence; something had caught his sharp eyes. "Over there, where the ambulances and trucks are parked." He didn't point and everyone casually cast their eyes in that direction.

It was Captain Harris with an Orderly and one of the vehicle mechanics. The orderly was pushing a sack barrow which contained something obviously heavy and was covered in a dull, green sheet. The mechanic was wiping his greasy hands and saying that it had been fixed. Jericho caught some of the conversation as they passed by - 'Wires, Copper conductors and fuses' were mentioned - and the threesome disappeared towards the surgical unit at a good pace.

Jericho motioned to Skyrise to make a discrete call on the Captain and find out what was under the sheet. Skyrise smiled and made for the surgical unit in a casual manner; finishing his tea and sandwich's as he walked. That's when he heard the little bell being rung - indicating an emergency within the Surgical unit - so he increased his pace and arrived outside Operating Room 4 in time to see Captain Harris and the strange contraption being wheeled into the room, which had another Doctor and two nurses already waiting.

Skyrise placed himself by the small window in the door and watched carefully at the frantic actions of the medical staff, gathered around the patient on the operating table. He was very surprised to see sparks flying about and suddenly he realised that there was an elderly lady standing in the corner of the room. Jericho had now joined him, and pair realised that the nice old lady was Kate, a collector. She looked over to them and shrugged her shoulders, they watched her close the 'Soul Ledger' she was holding and disappear.

They walked from the building and found Kate waiting for them at the old boiler house and the conversation amongst the group was quite lively. "She was about to scoop up the young soldiers soul, when bang! - There were sparks and a strange smell - and the soul was firmly back into its flesh suit!" Wilson shook his head but smiled.

"He's using some kind of early defibrillator and restarting the heart. Little wonder the Records department is coming up short; such a machine didn't appear until the 1930's." Skyrise spoke softly and with a little admiration in his voice.

Jericho rubbed his chin and looked back to the hospital building; "Owen, pull the good Captains record and find out, if there has been any breeches of the time-line where he has been found." Owen nodded and pulled his mirror out and sat on the table edge, sipping his lukewarm tea.

"Maybe he's just invented the damn thing twenty years before anyone else thought of it." Alex finished her tea and stretched loosely in the evening sunshine and really wanted to soak her poor feet. Jericho shook his head; "If that's the case; why wasn't such machines in use immediately after the war? How come the first official use of such a device, doesn't appear until the 1930's?"

"Good point." Muttered Skyrise and they said farewell to Kate, who wandered off to the General ward to pick up a couple of young men who had just died in their sleep. No one had noticed that the pair were bleeding internally; caused by a nearby shell burst as the they were caught by machine gun fire.

"If he came up with it by a natural process or idea, then we could have a 'Mandela Effect' on our hands and that means changes to the current time-line which were unexpected - like saving the lives of hundreds of soldiers and later - it could run into thousands; every one changing the time-line and maybe not for the best." Jericho finished his now cold tea with a grimace and added; "If not, we need to find out who told him and it would have to be someone from the future - an illegal time-traveler – who wants to change history."

Owen pushed his mirror back into a uniform pocket and sighed; "Sorry Jericho, there's nothing really of interest - but our good Doctor doesn't survive the war - he gets killed in a few months and his soul was collected correctly. I'm still waiting on possible time breeches near him."

Jericho grunted his thanks and with their refreshments finished, the little group made their way back to the organized chaos and horrors of the casualty clearing station.

8. COLLECTORS EVERYWHERE.

Alex had the delightful job of emptying bed pans, which she completed without a single moan; that seemed to amaze young nurse Rachel Goldman, who normally would be tasked the job. "You're a fine lady, you shouldn't be doing this." She informed Alex as they emptied several ripe bed pans together. But Alex just laughed; "Believe me Rachel; I've done worse than this in the service of God." Rachel didn't quite understand that, but she still smiled.

The conversation turned to Captain Harris and unsurprisingly, Nurse Rachel was full of praise; "He works long hours, he really cares for the boys, and he actually treats us nurses with some respect - not like some of the other doctors - they really think we're their personal slaves." The girls stacked the clean pans, covering each with a cloth and Rachel continued; "He really fights for the boys, he often says that's it's a battle between him and God."

Rachel fell silent as Sister Isabella passed by, on her way to the General ward, but she stopped by the Sluice Room door and smiled at Alex; "I wonder if you can assist me, Lady Cappanni." She asked and Alex nodded; "Of course Sister, how may I help/"

After thoroughly cleaning and disinfecting her hands and arms, she joined the sister walking towards the ward. "We have a couple of your countrymen in the General Surgical Ward; they were airman on some kind of special mission but were shot down nearby - along with a couple of our planes [English] - our boys didn't make it. They are quite shot up and Doctor Marks doesn't believe they will make it." She pushed open the doors and Alex followed her in the large, crowded room, packed with beds, men and nurses.

An orderly pushed a trolley past carrying a body covered by a blood-soaked sheet; the sister stopped and the read the brown tag; "Peter, make sure Doctor Davis knows about the captain - he knew the man's brother - they were at school together." The young orderly nodded and wheeled the dead man away. Alex watched as the late Captain of Engineers departed with Kasim, his collector, who waved and smiled. Sister Isabella Edwards, who obviously could not see or hear the departing pair, pointed forward and walked on.

"As I was saying Lady Cappanni, the two Italian pilots won't be here much longer, and we really need to know who they are; their identity papers were blood soaked and burnt. We really need to know their names or unit; anything that may identify them. But both are lapsing in and out of unconsciousness and rambling in Italian. Do you think you can get some details for us?"

Alex nodded, and the pair arrived at the first bed; closed off by some drab-coloured curtains and the sister pulled back the flap and went in, Alex followed and was a little taken back by the sight. The young pilot was covered with wet sheets and lay upon a rubber mat; "He has major burns from the crash and is in great pain despite the morphine doses. I think death will bring welcome relief for the poor boy." The Sister whispered and picked up the clipboard and wrote a couple of words and checked her fob watch, adding; "It's almost time for another morphine shot; this is very unpleasant for all of us."

Alex pulled up the single rough chair that stood in the corner and sat by the boys head and started to speak to him in Italian. The sister was joined by Nurse Patricia Kelly who carried a needle and morphine vial on a little covered tray. The boy started to speak slowly, in broken little sentences punctuated by deep groans; Alex grabbed up the clipboard and with half a pencil, started to write on the blank rear of the form. Nurse Patricia had prepared his dose and Alex took the needle from her; "I'll do it." She said simply - the look of relief on the young nurse's face was obvious - and the sister told her to go and help elsewhere.

Alex administered the injection, and the boy made no noise; except to whisper in Italian. Alex stood up and handed the clipboard back to Sister Isabella; "His name is Roberto Russo, he is nineteen years of age and asks if he can see his mother to say goodbye." Alex walked quietly through the curtains; she was quite amazed that she had stopped the tears from showing. She swallowed hard and folded her arms, staring at the enormous amount of suffering in just this little ward and thought about the hundreds of other wards along the front - both sides of the trenches - each one full of Roberto Russo's; "Where's the other boy?" She asked the sister.

The sister pointed over to another set of curtains and the pair walked in silence to them. They were stopped by Doctor Marks,

who emerged from the curtains and shook his head; "His gone."
That was all he said and walked away. Only Alex could see the
young woman with the late Captain Luca Ricci as they
disappeared into the light.

"I think a cup of tea is in order." Sister Isabella gripped Alex by
the arm and took her to the sister's small office outside the ward.
"If ever you decide to return to a proper job, one for which you
are more than obviously qualified, let me know. True nurses are
hard to find; even in the middle of a bloody, God forsaken war."
The pair of women sat drinking tea quietly, until the sister was
called back to her never-ending duties - Alex accompanied her -
rolling up her sleeves and putting on a clean apron. "Fuck it."
Was all she muttered.

More wounded were arriving every few minutes and Alex noticed
several strangers wandering amongst the growing numbers of
injured and dying men; clutching little black books and no-one
but Alex could see them; a couple silently nodded their greeting
and continued to collect souls.

9. STAND DOWN.

Jericho called the team together by the boiler house and shared a
very good bottle of brandy with them. It was such good quality
that no-one poured any into their tea but drank it straight. Alex
greatly appreciated it after the day she had, working the wards
with Sister Isabella, who Alex respected as a woman and a
superb nurse. She had little idea that the good sister was singing
her praises to Colonel Howes and the senior doctors of the unit.

Owen stared towards the growing lines of dead soldiers – under
rough sheets and blankets – being laid in the old School's tennis
court. Skyrise tapped his shoulder and said quietly; "This is only
the first day of battle in just one surgical unit. In a few hours the
tennis court will be full, and they'll have to lay them wherever
they can find a space. The burials won't start until tomorrow.
After the Graves Registration boys turn up." He sipped his tea
soaked with brandy and added; "Their families won't be told for
some days yet."

Everyone relaxed a little and sipped their much-appreciated
brandy, Jericho informed his team that they were standing down;
the mission was over. Alex asked him; "What's happened, what

have you found out?" Jericho smiled a little and explained; "It appears that our good doctor has pre-empted the device's invention by almost twenty years, but historically, doesn't receive any acknowledgement for it. The damn thing gets reinvented in the 1930's."

Alex sipped her brandy and asked quietly;"Why doesn't he get any recognition for it?" Jericho placed the empty brandy bottle near Alex's thread bare armchair and sighed; "The good Doctor and some members of the medical staff here are killed, when the hospital ship; the SS Galeka strikes a mine in October of this year. He takes all knowledge of the device with him and the only other two people, who knew how it worked, were with him, on that ill-fated ship."

Jericho had made arrangements for his team to depart Casualty Clearing Station Number 21 in the morning; informing Colonel Howes that they had gathered all the information they needed for the respective Governments and news agencies that had asked. Strangely enough, the Colonel told Jericho that they would be missed; especially Lady Alex and Skyrise, who he praised for their assistance and help. Jericho nodded his appreciation of the thanks and praise. He knew now, why Angel Margret had messaged him [via his mirror] that she wished to see the entire team when they returned from the mission - straight away - in fact.

"Shit!" was all he muttered as he walked back to their ramshackle quarters of tents and outbuildings. In the distance he could hear the guns; the battle of the Somme was continuing and would struggle on until the November of this year. Leaving over 400,000 British casualties and would achieve no real break-through of the German front. The bloody murderous war would continue for another two years yet and result in casualties counted in their millions.

The final outcome of the war - to end all wars - would be round two in twenty year's time with the rise of Hitler and the Nazi party. World War II would eclipse the First World War in death and destruction and again; change the world entirely.

Jericho dropped onto his bunk and loosened his collar, pulling his old hipflask from his tunic pocket and sipped the contents slowly. The oil lamp flickered and cast a weak, yellow glow about

the small room. He tried to sleep a little - but it wouldn't come
and he sat up on the bunk and reached for his hip flask - again.

"Could I have a word please sir, I mean, since your still awake."
Staff Nurse Alice Hadden pushed the curtain aside - which served
as some sort of door - and stood in the doorway. Jericho had, of
course, recognised her in the corridor when she stopped Alex.
Alice was married to his best human agent for this particular time
period; The Metropolitan Police Detective Inspector Harry
Hadden. Jericho nodded and said, yes softly and rose from the
bed, turning up the lamp.

"I don't know what's going on sir, but Lady Alex Cappanni IS
Doctor Alex Featherstone. She doesn't appear to have aged a
day, since I last saw her. But I'm not mistaken about it sir. So,
I'm assuming she's sort of undercover. My husband is a detective
and he's told me about such adventures. Just let her know that
I'm so glad she is alive. My God, she was so missed when she
vanished back in 1901. Nobody knew what had happened to her
- please ask Alex to contact me when her jobs are over - we were
not just working colleagues, but good friends. I always suspected
that good looking Italian had something to do with her
disappearance - her Italian is now excellent! - I'm so glad to see
her again; alive and well. Please tell her that. Thank you, sir."

Jericho nodded, but said nothing and Alice Hadden walked quietly
away. He placed both hands on his head and slumped back on
the creaking bed; "Shit!" was all he whispered; then he thought
about the coming enquiry into the two detectives actions; they
had clearly defied direct orders not to interfere and the Angel
wanted to know why. He would, of course, support his team and
would have to materialize some cracking excuses, to get them off
the hook!

Jericho tried to sleep - again with little success - but the brandy
in his hipflask certainly helped and he tossed and turned until
morning.

10. DEPARTURE.

The two cars were cranked over, engines now running noisily
with the drivers standing by, with open doors. Jericho and his
team took their leave of the staff and climbed aboard. Captain
Harris and Colonel Howes waved them off. As they pulled away,

Alex could see Staff Nurse Alice Hadden give a little wave and smile broadly. Alex waved back and brushed a small tear from her face - noticed only by Jericho - who gripped her hand and said nothing.

Skyrise stared back at the disappearing hospital and grunted; "I'll be here properly in just under a year and even that I now know what I'm in for, I'll still be glad that I came." Jericho knew that Skyrise Young Mountain would be killed by enemy bombing, on a dirt road just outside Amiens, within months of arriving in France. He tapped the big man's shoulder and smiled.

"Who were the others from the unit that died on that ship?" Alex whispered to Jericho, and he handed her the hipflask. "Doctor Reginald Marks; Harris had trained him to use the device and he was making plans to produce the machine but died before anything was done." Alex sipped some brandy and asked; "The other one?"

Jericho sighed and took a swig from his flask; "The luck of war, she swapped assignments with the sister that should have sailed, but the women's child was very ill and the mother obviously wanted to stay close. So, Sister Isabella Edwards volunteered to take her place and drowned - trapped in the surgical unit with a couple of orderlies - when the ship went under. Sorry."

He then told Alex and Skyrise about Angel Margret's message, and both didn't seem to care; "So we get demoted to Collectors for a century or so." Skyrise chuckled and Alex had to smile. Jericho just shook his head and but smiled a little, then thought about Alice Hadden and wondered who she would tell about her meeting with Alex, who she realised, had not aged a day. Jericho glanced at the beautiful young woman sitting next to him and knew that there was more to Alex than anyone could really know; perhaps save him.

The mission had achieved what it was dispatched for; they had discovered the truth behind the missing souls and Angel Margret had allowed the changes to stand. "Just a little piece of the 'Mandela' effect', that should pass un-noticed by most living humans." Owen had muttered to Wilson, who agreed with his young colleague. The small convoy continued down the rough road and Alex smiled, thinking about Alice Hadden. Then she remembered about what she had read on her mirror about Alice.

Such knowledge of future events wasn't always for the best.

The guns continued to sound in the distance and the cars pulled over for a few minutes to allow a stream of ambulances and trucks to pass - carrying more wounded to casualty Clearing Station Number 21 – and it's totally dedicated staff. "God help the poor buggers." The driver said and lit a cigarette, whilst Alex muttered; "But he won't; free will and all that."

THE END

EPILOGUE:

"it was a relief for the Team 74 to discover that Doctor Harris had invented his amazing machine on his own incentive, nearly thirty years before it was 'invented' - again. All the souls that he had prevented from being collected were allowed to remain in the current human timeline. Angel Margret decided that was acceptable and correct."
SJW

CHARACTERS:

Skyrise Young Mountain or Doctor. S. Mountains had joined the American Army Medical Corps and arrived in France in August 1917. He was killed by enemy bombing, on a dirt road just outside Amiens, within months of arriving in France. His soul was collected and he now - obviously - works as a Temporal Detective Constable on 'Doc' Silas Underhill's team.

Sergeant John Liam Connerly [Irish Brigade - Front Line trench] went 'over the top' the following morning at 7.30am - he was dead by 7.33am. He was 27 years old. His soul was collected and processed.

Private Frederick O'Halloran [Irish Brigade - Front Line trench] went 'over the top' the following morning at 7.30am - he was dead by 7.36am. He was 22 years old. His soul was collected and processed.

Lt. Paul Kenning [Dressing Station] survived the war, despite being wounded twice. He was discharged from the army in March 1919 and left Britain for Canada, where he worked in local

Newspapers. He was killed in a railway accident outside Montreal in 1931. His soul was collected and processed.

Private Patrick O'Rook [wounded soldier - Dressing Station] survived his wounds despite losing a leg and part of his arm. He married his childhood sweetheart and lived until 1955. They didn't have any children and his widow - Katherine - died in 1961. His soul was collected and processed.

Private David Richards [the Driver] had signed on to fight, despite being 61 years old! He remained an Officer's Chauffer throughout the war. He died in 1919 from the 'Spanish Influenza' and his soul was collected and processed.

Doctor Alexander Harris [Casualty Clearing Station 21] was never credited with his discovery that could have saved many lives over the subsequent years. He was drowned on SS Galeka, when that Hospital ship sank in October 1916. His soul was collected and processed. He now works as a Collector.

Private John Gates [Stretcher-bearer - Dressing Station]] was actually under-age for the army - he was fifteen - but a big lad for his age. The Military authorities allowed him to stay serving, as a Stretcher-Bearer. He was killed at Passchendaele in November 1917; he was sixteen. His soul was collected and processed.

Private William Soames [Medical Orderly - Dressing Station] was killed the following day by a British shell that dropped short; several wounded men, he was attending, were also killed at the time. His soul was collected and processed.

Colonel Wilberforce Howes [Casualty Clearing Station 21] survived the war and returned to Manchester City Infirmary in 1919 as Chief Surgeon. He remained at the hospital until he retired in 1929. He was killed in 1941 during the 'black-out' - a car ran into him as he walked to the train station - after visiting his sister's home. His soul was collected and processed.

Nurse Rachel Goldman [Casualty Clearing Station 21] survived the war and returned home to Bradford, where she married a local coal merchant and had four children. Unfortunately, the fourth child came with complications and Rachel died. She was 31 years old. Her soul was collected and processed.

Staff Nurse Alice Hadden [Casualty Clearing Station 21] was married to Jericho's Human Agent for the early 20th Century; Police Inspector Harry Hadden. She alleges that Lady Alexandra Cappanni is really Doctor Alexandra Featherstone - a doctor at Whitechapel hospital in 1901 - who vanished without trace that year. Jericho never reported these matters up his chain of command. Alice died in 1922 from stomach cancer. Her soul was collected and processed.

Sister Isabella Edwards [Casualty Clearing Station 21] was on the ill-fated SS Galeka, after she volunteered to take a colleagues place and drowned - trapped in the surgical unit with a couple of orderlies - when the ship went under. Her soul was collected and processed.

Doctor Reginald Marks [Casualty Clearing Station 21] was killed when the SS Galeka sank in October 1916; he had been trained by Dr. Harris to use the machine. The secret died with those two men: on that ship. His soul was collected and processed.

Nurse Patricia Kelly [Casualty Clearing Station 21] survived the war and left Britain for a new life in America. She married well and died a wealthy widow in 1938 with her three children and eleven grandchildren at her side. Her soul was collected and processed.

Flight Officer Roberto Russo [Italian Pilot - Casualty Clearing Station 21] was nineteen years old when he died of his wounds at casualty Clearing Station 21. There was a problem with this young man in that, the Italian Military had no knowledge of him! His and Captain Ricci's mission on the Western Front was unknown to the Italian Authorities. There was no soul to collect and Temporal Inspector Stella Longstreet has been assigned the case; there is no resolution yet.

Captain Luca Ricci [Italian Pilot - Casualty Clearing Station 21] died of his wounds and his soul was collected and processed. But it appears that the Italian Authorities [at the time] had no idea of the captain's mission on the Western front! He was supposed to be on compassionate leave in his hometown of Rome. It remains a mystery to this day.

EPISODE 5: "THE IMPOSSIBLE FILMS OF MISS STOCKYARD CANNING."

MISSION SUMMARY:
"Mr. Jericho Tibbs investigates newly discovered films from the Edwardian era, which were recovered from a derelict London shop's basement, and they appear to show the impossible: Napoleon on the march, the Battle of Agincourt, Romans and King Henry VIII. Is there a 'Time-traveler' operating in the early 20th Century who is collecting a record of their travels? "

 **ALCOHOL, VIOLENCE [Including graphic description of Demonic assault] STRONG LANGUAGE & MILD HORROR.**

 **AGE 15+ ONLY.** **30 Minutes reading time.**

1. OLD FILMS.

Jericho was reading the New York Times, relaxed in his favourite armchair by the fireplace. He sipped whisky and smiled to himself; the paper was dated June 16, 1933, with President Roosevelt opening his 'New Deal' recovery program, signing bank, rail, and industry bills and initiating farm aid. "One for the history books." He muttered, looking up as the door opened into his study.

"I see you're up to date with all the modern events!" Alex flopped into the chair opposite and smiled broadly – she knew that Jericho made a point of reading old newspapers - looking for anything reported that could be considered 'out of the ordinary'. "I think you may want to read this interesting little article that I found in a copy of the London Times, just a few days ago." Alex added, pulling the newspaper from her handbag, and dropping it on Jericho's lap.

Jericho picked it up slowly and glanced at the page Alex had opened the paper at. He quickly placed down his glass and read the article with great interest. It appears that four old film canisters had been found in the basement of a derelict shop in London, during building refurbishment and the films apparently date from the early Edwardian era – well, the actual rolls of films were made at that time - but for their content; that was really something else.

Jericho read that the films had been forwarded to the British Film Institute for study and restoration. Experts had concluded that the film reels were genuine, from around 1903/4 and they could even identify the make and model of the camera that was used; also, from the early period of the Edwardian era.

But they were totally at a loss to explain the actual film content of all four films. One apparently showed Napoleon Bonaparte on the march with his troops in Belgium: in 1814. Another apparently covered the battle of Agincourt which took place in 1415, whilst the remaining two films showed Roman Galleys unloading soldiers and supplies from a Thames River landing stage in 19 BC and the final film purported to show a young King Henry VIII at a party in 1510; apparently held at a Tudor Hampton Court Palace.

All films held impossible content and the experts decided that these reels were very early 'movies' and they were catalogued as such. But there was one dissenting voice against this neat conclusion; a 'conspiracy theory' writer called Hoagy Treadwell had published several articles on various conspiracy websites, claiming they were in fact; genuine!

Alex pointed out to Jericho, that Mr. Treadwell had quite a compelling argument for their authenticity and she tapped that part of the article which quoted Mr. Treadwell's evidence - Jericho read that part with real interest – it was quite compelling actually.

"I like the quote from Professor Marks, the BFI's restoration expert; 'They appear totally genuine, but are completely impossible!' - Jericho nodded and rubbed his chin - adding; "Little wonder they classified them as early 'movies' or historical drama documentaries."

"Treadwell makes some superb points; especially the fact, that the four films needed hundreds of extras, hundreds of costumes, and serious money just to stage them. He also points out that the film's maker [whose name appeared on the faded canister labels] a 'Miss Stockyard Canning' has never been heard of in the Film and Photography industry; back then or even now; well not until these films were discovered!" She smiled broadly, especially when Mr. Harris arrived with a tray of tea.

Alex accepted a cup from the ever attentive Mr. Harris, adding; "Had such 'movies' really been staged in 1903 or 1904, there would be contemporary references all over the place; in papers, magazines and early books on the moving pictures industry – but there is absolutely nothing - Miss Canning would have been immortalized as one of the leading pioneers of the movie industry; particularly as a woman back then, but there is nothing about her or her films. Now that's a real enigma, don't you think?"

Jericho placed the paper on the coffee table and sipped his whisky; deep in thought. "Well, we can soon find out if they are real or just early movies. A trip to..." He picked up the paper and read the date: "Monday 5th July 2021."

"You intend that we travel to 2021 and view the evidence?" Alex sipped her tea and pushed back into her chair. Jericho nodded and said quietly; "We have met both Napoleon and King Henry – we will soon know - if they are just actors or the real thing." He smiled and lifted his glass adding; "We don't need the full team; yet."

2. UNPLEASANT MEMORIES.

Alex sighed; "Well, as long as we don't have to meet Henry Tudor again, I'll be quite happy to pay a visit to old London." That made

Jericho chuckle, when he recalled their trip to 1515, investigating the finding of a wristwatch in the crypt of Sir Edward Wallington, who had died in that year. His tomb had lain untouched for over five hundred years, but had been moved to allow for a new high speed railway link and when the coffin was opened; the mysterious item was discovered.

The pair had 'bumped' into the young King Henry at the funeral and if the King had his way; English [and world history] would have changed; not the best outcome for Temporal Detectives sworn to maintain the 'Time-Line' of humanity!

Alex actually blushed a little, when she remembered how the young King had pursued her around the small Kent town and simply wouldn't take no for an answer; he was totally besotted by her beauty and charm he even told her that he didn't mind that she was intelligent and educated!

"That could have been very embarrassing; trying to explain to Angel Margret how you became Queen of England and changed history." Jericho allowed himself another chuckle but dropped the subject when he saw the look upon Alex's face. Nevertheless, he smiled to himself and swallowed down the remains of the whisky as he recalled Napoleon had also taken a shine to Alex; but at least he took the hint that Alex was not interested in becoming his mistress or being made a Duchess for 'services' rendered!

Her husband; Count Henri Cappanni had been a very lucky man indeed to gain the love of such a woman Jericho mused and accepted a refill from Mr. Harris. Just for a moment, in his mind's eye; the face of Elizabeth appeared; smiling with her sharp blue eyes shining and her little mouth creasing into a wide grin. Her dark hair curled around her face, as if pushed by a gentle wind and Jericho reached out to push it away.

"Are you alright Jericho? "Asked Alex with a little concern in her voice, as she watched Jericho's hand pass through empty air. He snapped back from the beautiful daydream and smiled.

"I'll submit a report to Angel Margret and get Owen to look up the records for 'Miss Stockyard Canning' – which is a really unusual name for a woman - in the early 20th Century." Jericho tapped the glass with his finger and wondered why a Time traveler would film their visits and then hide the evidence away in some old shop's basement. He already knew one fact; that they must be from the early 20th Century because they used its technology – if they can travel through time - surely, they would have used some modern form of video recording and not a cumbersome and indiscreet camera from the early days of film?

Does this mean they only have the ability to travel backwards? Having just the means to jump backwards normally indicated a natural tear in the fabric of time and such a portal would only be locked to one specific time and place. But according to the newspaper, the films had been shot in four different eras'. If they proved to be genuine, then a very rare thing had occurred; a natural portal that allowed multiple journeys and that would make it a priority to find and close. Jericho recalled that he had only ever heard of two previous occasions with such a phenomenon and the Timeline had been in serious danger of change with both.

So it was agreed that Jericho and Alex would jump to 2021 and view the films which were apparently available on the 'Internet' at the time. A simple viewing would answer the really important question; was a time traveler operating in the early 20th century?

Mr. Parker emerged from beneath the coffee table and rubbed himself against Alex's ankle boots and received several strokes in return. "I see Owen has been grooming the cat again; he's fur is almost shinning." Alex commented and Jericho grunted in reply; his mind was elsewhere and seeing the cat with Alex; had bought back some unwanted memories of some dark days indeed.

3. LONDON; JULY 5th, 2021.

Jericho and Alex crossed the road when the little green man showed on the traffic light opposite. "I hate these time periods. I mean, after civilisation really ended in 1914. Look at this shit." He gestured towards the lines of vehicles waiting at the traffic lights. Alex chuckled; "I do see what you mean. I long for the quiet warm days of summer in Cappanni, watching over my children and reading in the shade. Simple days and simple pleasures; wonderful." Jericho nodded his agreement to that statement and pointed out the small shop on the corner; 'Ali & Dave's kebab and Internet café'. "We can view the films on the BFI's website in there." He fumbled about in his jacket pockets and found the thick brown envelope that contained a portion of money from this era. Both he and Alex were dressed for the period, wearing jackets and jeans in the warm sunshine. They both pulled on the mandatory face masks with Alex giggling about looking like Dick Turpin.

They wandered into the shop and booked half an hour on one of the three computers, which were located at the rear. They were the only people working on the computers and so they found the BFI site quickly. Alex moved the mouse about as Jericho pointed out the pages to visit. "This is quite good fun." She murmured.

Firstly, they viewed the two-minute film about King Henry VIII which purported to have been shot in 1510. They both went silent as the young King appeared, dancing with a very stern looking lady. "Shit." Was all Jericho said, it was indeed the King himself - the film was genuine – and that made Jericho grimace.

They viewed the other three films and commented that Napoleon had lost a little weight since they last saw him. Alex actually turned away from the battle scenes in the Agincourt film - being real they were not for the faint-hearted - with heads and limbs flying about the place.

But the Roman's landing on the Thames wharfs provided a little clue; it appears there were two camera's working the scene. Just for a few seconds, on the other bank of the river, you could make out two persons [one female; maybe] filming from across the river.

"That one is worth a closer look back at the Lighthouse." Alex commented to Jericho, but his smile had gone. They now had at least three people loose in the current human timeline. Alex downloaded the films onto her mirror and the pair left the shop. As they walked down the street, moving through the people on the pavement, Jericho said quietly to Alex; "We're being followed by those two men who were watching us in the shop." She nodded; "I know, they watched us the whole time and left when we did."

"I think they became particularly interested when I opened the envelope of money and paid for our time on the computer." Jericho jerked a thumb towards the alley entrance, which had appeared on their left. "Down there I think and home." He added, grinning. Alex glanced down the little alley and said softly; "They also saw what we were watching Jericho." He nodded his agreement with that and said, "Now!"

The two following were caught completely unaware as Alex and Jericho suddenly dived into the alley. They rushed forward, one pulling a hunting knife from under his jumper and the other; what appeared to be a large mobile phone.

They stood alone in the alley - their quarry had simply disappeared from a dead-end alley - with no doors and windows. The brick wall that closed the alley off was about ten feet in height, topped with wire; simply impossible to climb in the given time. They both stood in silence and the younger man cursed loudly and told his companion to hide the knife.

He lifted the black rectangular object to his face and tapped at the screen. The pair disappeared, leaving the alley quiet and empty. Standing in the entrance was a tall, dark haired young woman; she lowered the small, concealed hand camera and smiled; "We've Brice and Ellis on film now." She started to walk back to the dark van waiting on double yellow lines and her college, who stood with the side door slightly open. "Who the fuck was the other man and woman?" He asked and climbed in - she followed and the door slid shut - they sat studying the film being replayed and watched the four people disappear; apparently into thin air.

Special Agent Louise Sturdiski popped some chewing gum into her mouth and spoke softly in her southern American accent; "Whoever that couple is; if Brice & Ellis are after them, then they are of interest to us."

Her English companion sighed; "Are you sure that you and the rest of the NSA, are coming completely clean with us poor Brits about these time terrorists from the fucking future?" She grinned and shook her head; "Can't say Micky, even my bosses don't have the whole picture. This new pair used a totally different transportation device - it looks like a mirror - I definitely think they don't belong around here."

Micky slid his chair in front of the computer screen and tapped away, transferring the images from Louise's camera to their database. Louise sat at his shoulder, as she felt the van pull away and join the traffic. Micky said, "Fuck!" with real frustration and added; "Facial Recognition can find no trace on the unknown male, which is really fucking unusual, and the useless database has identified the woman as some Italian tart from the 1790's. Her painting is on-line in some old villa in Southern Italy!"

Louise told Micky to pull the details up and read with interest about Countess Alexandra Mary Cappanni who had died in 1801 at the age of 27 during a difficult and protracted childbirth – but the child had survived - Louise noted that the woman who had disappeared; was the spitting image of the long dead Countess.

"Maybe she's an ancestor of the Italian bird and inherited her genes and looks; totally." Micky offered in explanation. But Louise shook her head; "No, we would have her on the database and the software would have pulled her up and not her bloody ancestor."

"There's something wrong here Micky. The software is good; if it says that's the woman and 99% of the time, it is right then who the hell is she?" Louise sighed and slumped back in her seat as the van threaded through London traffic, heading back to the MI6 building. "Who the fuck are they and what are they doing here? We know that only the living from the future can travel back - the already dead [like the woman] cannot go anywhere - So how the hell did she get here?"

Micky shrugged his shoulders and grinned; "We're just getting what the pair viewed in that Internet café and its some old films from the English Edwardian era." He tapped his screen, and both watched the films playing on the BFI site. She and Micky exchanged concerned looks; "Why the fuck is everybody suddenly interested in these crappy old films?" Micky spoke quietly and Louise could offer no explanation; not yet anyway. They were exactly the same films that Brice & Ellis had watched in the café not twenty minutes earlier!

4. HOAGY TREADWELL - KING OF CONSPIRACY.

Wilson grabbed a whisky and eased himself down in his favourite armchair and smiled to himself. "Now that went bloody well." He muttered with some self satisfaction. He had passed the 'mock' Inspectors exam paper with flying colours! Owen joined him.

They were waiting in the study when Alex and Jericho returned to the lighthouse; he sipped a brandy and re-read the contents of the brown paper file. Wilson was sprawled in a very comfortable armchair and dozing. Alex smiled at Wilson and shook her head; "Hard day was it?" Owen chuckled; "His done bugger all except study for the Inspectors exam." Jericho stood by the fireplace and asked Owen what he had found out about the mysterious Miss Stockyard Canning.

Owen handed him the folder; "Well, surprisingly enough Miss Stockyard Canning did exist. Born in 1881 in New York City to a very rich cattle and mining family, her father named his only daughter after the stockyards that made him rich. But apparently, she always used her second name, Brice. She was into photography and the new moving pictures – she certainly had the money to indulge in whatever she wanted – daddy's favourite little girl wanted for nothing.

But she travelled to London in 1905 on some sort of photographic expedition with one of her brothers [she had four] and near Christmas that year simply vanished. A massive reward [for the time] was offered, but she never was found. The really interesting part is that according to Records; her soul is listed as missing to this day."

Wilson shifted and stood up, stretching, and bending; "So she could have lost her soul to some demon on the prowl, but Demon Ingress have no records of any demon at that time and place. Which means two other choices; she died in another time and so her soul was lost or she's still alive and moving through different time periods and simply hasn't died yet!"

Jericho nodded his agreement with that; "Well the films are genuine enough, so our Miss Stockyard must possess the ability to travel through any human time period. That makes her a priority to find and take possession of the time controlling device or close the natural portal she must be using."

Alex held up her mirror; "I think we need a closer look at those films, but I'll skip the Agincourt one thank you." Mr. Harris appeared and announced dinner, and everyone headed for the dining room.

Hoagy Treadwell wiped the sweat from his face with the sleeve of his shirt and sipped a little lukewarm coffee, staring at the pair sitting in front of him. His legs were shaking a little and his mouth was constantly dry – it wasn't everyday that two of God's temporal detectives appeared in your basement office - stopped time and insisted you answer their questions.

The big, powerful Black man in the seventies suit was pleasant enough, but Hoagy believed you wouldn't want to cross him. The strange boy dressed like a medieval monk, seemed harmless and he wrote everything down – missing nothing – not a word.

"That's it really, sir." Hoagy held up both hands and shrugged his shoulders; he had explained everything he had discovered about the films, Miss Stockyard Canning and her disappearance, including the part her fiancé, Professor Ellis Goodfield may have played in it. Despite their age differences, the pair had apparently fallen in love and ran away together. Hoagy nervously laughed; "I suppose not so where, but when!" The look he received from Wilson made him gulp and he hastily unlocked a bottom drawer on his desk.

He pulled a couple of photographs from a brown envelope and showed them to Wilson and Owen. One showed Miss Canning and her 'Fiancé' posing for their engagement in September 1905. "She's very pretty, isn't she?" Hoagy asked Wilson, but Owen chuckled; "Not a patch on our Alex."

The second apparently showed the pair on a ski holiday in Austria; next to a brand-new Land rover; the year was 1997. They had not aged a week. "I used facial recognition software, really good quality stuff and it matched the pair at 95% - which means, unless they're doppelgangers - the ski pair is this pair!" He tapped the engagement photo and grinned; he was a little more relaxed now. "They're using the married name of Wells; Mr. & Mrs. Ellis and Brice Wells." Hoagy clasped his hands together; "I knew I was right about bloody time-travelers, but I've not published any of that – yet."

Wilson nodded his thanks and rose to leave, with Owen pushing his notebook into the folds of his robes. Hoagy slowly eased from his chair and nervously gripped the desk; "You know about the strange stories that surround her father and the family?"

Wilson and Owen exchanged glances and sat back down." No,

but please enlighten us." Owen said quietly, pulling his notebook back out. Hoagy remained standing and wiped his face again; "Well, rumours at the time [1881] say that old man Canning never did have a daughter, but a very sickly son who died and he replaced the dead boy with a girl child – a changeling – because he always wanted a daughter and being so fucking rich; he got whatever he wanted. The rumours persisted for years, appearing in underground magazines and comics; they never surfaced again after she disappeared. The brother: Frederick, never went home and its rumoured he travelled to Germany and became a prominent member of the New Nazi party, when they formed in the 1920's. Apparently, he could speak fluent German and even fought for the Kaiser in the Great War. No one knows what became of him after the fall of Nazi Germany in 1945. His German name is not known."

Owen and Wilson thanked young Hoagy Treadwell and disappeared; turning time back on – Thus, the time they that had spent in the basement had not existed - Hoagy found himself sitting at his desk with no idea about what just happened or who had been talking to him. He stared at the photographs on his desk and wondered, why the hell am I looking at them?

5. HAMPTON COURT PALACE; AUGUST 3rd, 1510.

"Records confirm that Frederick George Canning's soul is also listed as missing; his mortal remains have never been discovered. But in the Nazi era, Germany had plenty of demons hanging about the place. So, anything could have happened to it." Owen closed the file and shifted in his armchair.

Jericho sat deep in thought and sighed loudly; "We all viewed the film about Henry VIII, and it was Wilson's sharp eyes that caught the Well's in attendance, suitability dressed for the period. But who was doing the filming? We definitely have another person loose in the Timeline, working in conjunction with them. But it does offer us a chance to confront the pair. She [Miss Stockyard Canning] made the silly mistake of writing the date upon the film canister; August 3rd, 1510. So, we know they will be there at that date and that's where we're headed!"

Alex was definitely not looking forward to 'bumping' into young Henry [he would be 19 at the time and had been King for a year] and muttered that she needed time to grow a beard! That did make the team chuckle and with some smiles, made the jump to England in 1510. Arrangements for the team to gain access to the Kings party had been made by Temporal Detective Inspector 'Doc' Silas Underhill's human agent for the time period; Sir Edward Wallington, who was part of the Kings entourage.

Sir Edward was tall for the age and must have been about forty years old, with a black beard and dark green eyes. For a noble man, he was noted as a scholar and deeply pious man, good to the poor. But he did have an unfair advantage over most at the Royal court; he actually knew that God did, indeed, exist!

Jericho, of course, didn't mention attending Sir Edward's funeral in just five years time or ask if he possessed an item from the 'Hereafter' - the wristwatch apparently found in his tomb some five hundred years later - that could wait for another time. He greeted the team, as they arrived at his apartments in Hampton Court Palace. He hugged Jericho like a long-lost son and did the same with Wilson and Owen. But for Alex, he bowed quite low and kissed her hand; "Old 'Doc' said you were a beauty beyond compare, a real English rose despite having married an Italian! You will light up the court like a thousand lamps!"

Alex thanked him for his compliments and adjusted her bosom, the bloody Tudor dress didn't hide them very well and she was quite uncomfortable in the damn thing. "Bloody corsets are stiff and unyielding." She muttered as they walked to the party. The little group was stopped by Royal guards at the entrance to the Kings public apartments.

Sir Edward introduced them to the Captain of the Guards – who simply couldn't take his eyes off Alex – Lord Jericho Tibbs and his sister were cousins of his, from their lands in Northumberland. The big African was Lord Tibbs loyal and faithful travelling Steward and the boy; Lord Tibb's ward; the son of an old friend who had died and left the boy in his charge. Well, that was the cover story anyway.

The captain bowed low to them all and allowed them to enter; after discreetly asking Sir Edward if his Lordship's sister was married or promised, Sir Edward pointed out that the Lady Alexandra was indeed a widow. That produced a huge smile on the captains face as he watched her sweep majestically into the chamber and then crossed himself, for possession of such a woman he would march into hell itself; naked and armed with just a spoon! He knew that his pounding heart was the lady's to command, he also knew that such a great lady would not look at him twice.

Captain Arthur Churchill sighed and drove the wonderful thoughts from his mind and got on with his duties, as more guests appeared. "One day my family will be great enough to claim such a woman." He whispered to himself, for he harboured ambitions to rise high in the army of the king and even the nobility.

Jericho's little diversion was working [the 'diversion' being Alex!] no-one really noticed him or Owen or even Wilson – a big African man should have evoked a great deal of conversation and questions at Henry's Court, despite Queen Katherine having an African Trumpeter on her staff. But all eyes were firmly on the stunning Lady of Cappanni.

This allowed Jericho and the team to wander about the packed party goers, looking for their quarry and they found the Well's in a quiet corner, complete with camera and tripod. "How the fuck did they manage to smuggle that bloody great thing in here un-noticed?" Owen asked; a little amazed.

Sir Edward supplied the answer; "An incense machine that the so-called Professor invented, you crank the handle, and it produces a lasting scent. The Lord Chamberlain inspected the device himself and was so impressed by the smells it apparently produced, allowed it to be used at this party."

"I strongly suspect that a couple tins of air freshener have been sprayed about." Wilson grunted and that made Owen chuckle. Alex grinned; "A very useful device in an age where nobody bathed regularly or changed their clothes often."

"Well, we've found the missing pair, but whom or where is the third person?" Jericho glanced about; on the film, the Well's had been briefly caught dancing at the rear of the party – together - so who had operated the camera?

Again Sir Edward supplied the answer; though unknowingly; "That skinny lad over there, who can be no older than your boy, is their servant; he's called John Goodfield." Wilson discreetly pulled his mirror and studied it for some moments. "That's the professor's son from his first wife. They divorced in 1899 and John stayed with his father."

"Quite the family business; this time travelling lark." Alex spoke softly and indicated quietly to Jericho that the Lord Chamberlain was approaching; it transpires that he and Sir Edward were old friends. Wilson, looking decidedly anxious, pushed the mirror back into his robes; "There's something else you should know Jericho; Professor Ellis Goodfield died in 1904 and his soul was collected quite correctly. But he died alone, during a hiking accident in the hills of North Wales. It appears that his family had no idea about his passing. They thought he was just missing because he's body was snatched from the valley he fell into and its whereabouts are still unknown."

Everyone stared at the very much alive professor, operating the camera and talking to his wife. There was silence until the Lord Chamberlain appeared and gripped his old friends arm; "I have a surprise for you Edward; it was the least I could do for an old friend and colleague." Sir Edward smiled broadly and introduced everyone, but again it was Alex that caught the old man's eye. He smiled and kissed her hand; "You are a widow lady?" He asked and positively grinned when she replied, yes.

"What is your surprise, Roger?" Sir Edward asked and that pulled the old man's attention away from Alex. The Lord Chamberlain patted his shoulder; "I have arranged for your cousin to be presented to the King. I told his Majesty that Lord Tibbs and his widowed sister have travelled from the far North to pledge fidelity and service to their new King. That will stand them, and you, in good stead with the young England [Henry]."

"Merde!" Alex uttered under her breath and both Wilson and Owen allowed themselves a little chuckle at that. Jericho managed to stop his smile being seen by Alex and he also passed, un-noticed by anyone, the little glass orb to Wilson, who nodded his understanding of what Jericho wanted.

The Lord Chamberlain escorted Sir Edward, Jericho and Lady Alexandra through the throng of party guests and they came before the King, resplendent upon a gilded seat of ermine and gold. Queen Katherine sat upon a similar seat some feet away from the King, surrounded by several grim-faced ladies-in-waiting. The Queen was unsmiling, having only recently birthed a

still-born girl; she clearly wasn't in a party mood – and it showed
- but the young King would soon be.

6. DANCING, DEMONS AND DEADLY DECEIT.

Henry sat slumped in his chair – unsmiling - as the Lord
Chamberlain approached; bowing low and the King indicated he
should speak. "Your majesty, may I have your leave to present a
loyal noble Lord from the far North who wishes to pledge his
service and loyalty to his new King. Lord Jericho Tibbs is
accompanied by his sister, a young, widowed lady from the
Italian state of Cappanni." The King nodded and looked up as
Jericho and Alex approached – there were many little gasps from
the gathered Court - at the beauty, which had suddenly appeared
amongst them.

The King sat upright and adjusted his tunic, a broad smile
appearing upon his face, which didn't go un-noticed by his
Minsters and high nobles. Lord Jericho knelt on one knee and
lowered his head; "My King, I bring my families love and loyalty
to their rightful Majesty and pledge their fidelity and strength to
England's sun, which surely eclipses anything that our European
cousins may hold dear and which, I say, casts them to dark
shadows of envy and despair, for the sun is now firmly resident
in England's glorious land; my heart and sword are yours"

The chamber erupted in applause and shouts of "YES!" The King
waved for silence; "Well noble Lord, how the good people of the
North view their new King?" and indicated for Jericho to stand,
his eyes falling again upon Alex. Jericho smiled; "Your majesty,
like me they stand firmly behind their King and the few miserable
wretches that don't, will stand firmly in front of my sword!"

The chamber again exploded with cheers and applause. The King
clearly appreciated the young Lords words, and he thanked
Jericho; saying that any such noble who wished to serve his King
is welcome, especially one so eloquent; he turned to Alex who
had curtsied quite low; "Do you, our beautiful English rose have
the same sentiments?"

Alex rose and smiled; "My King, I was born in fair England and
have travelled in many parts of the world, but none had the very
sun to call their own and my heart belongs where my sun
resides." She curtsied again to massive, appreciative applause

and shouts of "English Rose!" The King rose from his seat and gestured her to come near, taking hold of her hand, he said simply; "Lets us dance sweet lady." That caused a ripple of astonishment to roll about the chamber; normally all the King's dance partners were known and vetted in advance and Henry had simply thrown Court protocol out the window!

The Lord Chamberlain slipped between Sir Edward and Jericho and whispered; "The King has not smiled or danced in weeks; but our lady Alexandra has made the sun rise again – thank God!"

Wilson tapped Jericho on the shoulder; "Our friends have flown the coup, Owen is tracking them like the bloodhound he is." Wilson pushed the orb into Jericho's hand, and both could see the red streaks creeping about its circumference. He added; "I've put the call in for a Guardian. Oscar is on his way."

"Well, that explains how they are moving about the Time-Line, but I wonder if Miss Stockyard knows of this deadly deception?" Jericho spoke softly, watching the King dance with Alex – again. Sir Edward suddenly bowed quite low, making Jericho and Wilson do the same. The Lord Chamberlain spluttered out the introductions; "This is Lord Tibbs your grace." The Duke of Norfolk bowed a little and smiled; "Your sister is a rare beauty, clearly educated and intelligent. What was her late husband's rank?"

Jericho knew that the duke was the second most powerful man in the Kingdom and a close advisor of the young King – and its biggest schemer - for power and position. "Her husband had the equivalent rank, in Italy, that an Earl has here, your grace; Lady Alexandra is a Countess by marriage."

The Duke actually smiled at that revelation and exchanged looks with his companion; the Earl of Durham. The pair was known to be as close as a two headed snake – and just as cunning and power hungry – they both exchanged a happy smile.

"Does she have children Lord Tibbs – living children?" He asked and Jericho knew exactly what was on the good Duke's mind. He smiled broadly; "My sister has three living children; two strapping sons and a daughter who is said to be her only rival in beauty." He bowed quite low and really did struggle to stop smiling. "She has never miscarried a child or had one born already with the angels." He added for good measure; that should buy time to wrap this little case up – as a diversion - Alexandra was second to none!

The Duke and Earl took their leave, deep in whispered conversation and Sir Edward turned to Jericho and smiled; "Those two would have the Spanish Queen put aside and an English woman upon the throne – preferably one they could control - Your sister has the rank that would be more than acceptable for a future English Queen and if the Spanish Queen loses any more children of the King, they will act."

Jericho nodded and decided it was time to confront the demon masquerading as the professor and return Miss Stockyard Canning to the early 20th Century. But first, he had better extricate Alexandra from the clutches of a besotted young Henry!

Wilson had already departed to join Owen on the trail of the time travelling threesome and Jericho knew that Alex and he should do the same. That's when he saw Oscar standing by the main entrance, the little man was period dressed but still carried his staff of office. Most of the partygoers thought he was part of the entertainment!

They nodded to each other, and Jericho slipped through the throng of guests and edged next to Alex; "Time to depart." He whispered and when Henry turned to speak to a persistent court official, wanting a decision, they made for the doors and disappeared into the night, with Oscar following closely.

7. GALLIONS REACH TAVERN, EAST LONDON.

The sprawling tavern was well known and favoured by peasant and prince alike, situated on the Thames at the east end of London. Many customers came by rowboat; propelled by 'Ferrymen' like Robert Eel, in whose boat the team found themselves. He pulled the oars with some strength and watched his passengers closely - he was convinced that they were from some theatre or circus - a big African, a dwarf, a very comely wench dressed like a Lady and two pretend Lords, possibility with false swords and jewels sewn into their cloth. But the strange boy escaped him and why did he keep looking into a bloody little mirror: the whole length of the trip from Hampton Palace?

The little lamps attached to the bow and stern of his stout boat cast weak light upon the dark river. But on the approach to the tavern, there were several large braziers ablaze with yellowing light and the team could see many people thronging about the large establishment.

"Don't fall in the water; you wouldn't need to drown to die in that stuff." Wilson chuckled and unobserved, checked the orb; little red streaks indicated the presence of a minor demon in the vicinity. He nodded to Jericho, who just smiled in return.

As the boat reached an old and fragile looking wooden wharf, Owen pulled his companions close and spoke softly; "I followed the three buggers in there and made enquiries with a couple of barmaids - that cost me tuppence - Apparently the Well's and their servant have taken rooms in the rear. It appears young John Goodfield has gained a taste for the whores that abound the place and in the week that they have been here, has become a very regular customer and a very generous patron by what the girls told me."

Sir Edward paid the Ferryman a generous fee of thrupence [three pence] which was a full penny more than the regulations called for. Robert Eel smiled broadly and kissed the coins; "God bless you master." Wilson helped Alex from the boat and received a strange look from the Ferryman, a mix of surprise and a little anger. Sir Edward cautioned Wilson very quietly; "Don't ever touch a white Lady, not even to help her. A mob would form pretty quickly over such an incident." He patted Wilson on the shoulder and smiled, adding; "But you can do what you like with the baggage [whores] and no-one would care."

Everyone looked about; the place was packed with all types and different classes of Tudor society. Soldiers, fishermen, apprentices, tradesmen, shopkeepers, and even well-dressed gentry mixed with the pimps and whores. Several merchants were selling hot chestnuts, stuffed pigeons, baked dormouse, cooked eels, oysters and salted fish garnished with herbs. Small chunks of hot bread with cheese and raw onion were best sellers.

The sound of music and singing rose and fell from the tavern as the strange looking group entered - but they only drew the odd curious look - as a tavern servant found them a rough wooden table and several equally rough chairs. Sir Edwards tipped the ugly young man who possessed broken teeth and lacked a couple of dirty fingers. He also paid a farthing for Alex to have a cushion placed on her chair.

The boy stared at Alex with wide eyes and open mouth as he pocketed the coins; "Sweet master, what a fucking piece of cake!" The look from Sir Edward made the boy lower his eyes and quickly disappear. They sat closely together, talking softly and Alex noticed that all her companions kept a hand upon their sword hilts. She smiled and patted her right thigh; pressed into her stocking top was a slim little dagger - just in case!

Even Jericho was a little surprised when a young barmaid appeared with several tankards of ale, carried with great skill and dexterity - but that wasn't the surprise - she was bare breasted with her nipples painted with rouge and wore nothing but a thick, short black apron that covered very little.

She grinned and set the tankards down and Sir Edward gave her a few coins for the beer and another for herself. "Thank you, sweet master." She said softly and walked away showing her pale bare arse to all. It had several red hand marks upon the cheeks. The tavern owner knew how to keep his girls in order.

Alex sipped her warm beer and smiled at Owen; "Bet you didn't see that every day in the Monastery." Everyone laughed as he went a little red in the cheeks. "I've already seen the like. Maggie [pointing to the departing barmaid] told me about the Well's." He spluttered, spilling a little frothy beer. Jericho called the strange meeting to order and outlined the plan to his colleagues.

8. WHEN PLANS GO ASTRAY.

Sir Edward spoke briefly with Connor Saltfeet - the part owner of the tavern - who was serving behind the rough bar and keeping a close eye on all monies taken. Some silver coins exchanged hands, to Connor's delight. He was told that the strange group were all agents of the Lord Chamberlain, and they were here in disguise, to apprehend some clever and cunning enemies of the young King, but quietly and without commotion.

"We want no alarm, nothing to raise a mob that may snatch the King's enemies away from lawful custody and before they can be questioned. We'll have no lynching here - the King wants his justice to be seen." Sir Edward was actually quite convincing - Jericho was impressed - no wonder old 'Doc' Underhill spoke so highly of him.

Connor expressed his admiration at their 'disguises'; especially the one dressed as a woman! "I would have ball'd that in an instance, he makes a fine wench." Sir Edward simply nodded and whispered to Jericho that all was ready - the tavern owner believed Alex was, in fact, a boy in the King's service - as no woman would ever be employed in such a role.

Jericho and Wilson were first through the door; swords drawn, followed by Oscar and Owen, Alex followed up and kept watch for anyone entering the small corridor, which lead to the rooms that the Well's had rented. Sir Edward stayed by her side - sword drawn.

Suddenly, she heard Jericho calling for her and Sir Edward; they dashed to the rooms and found Wilson trying to stop the blood coming from several large scratches upon the body of Miss Stockyard Canning, who was naked upon the floor, half covered by a sheet.

Alex ripped strips of cotton from her petticoats and attempted to stop the blood oozing from the deep lacerations; "Sweet Jesus, she looks like she has been savaged by some wild animal!" Exclaimed Owen and held his sword ready. Jericho made a quick decision when Alex yelled that Miss Canning was still alive; "Take her back to 1905 and get medical assistance straight away - Owen go with them - Now!" The three disappeared in an instance.

Oscar shook his head; "The bastard has gone Jericho." He replaced his orb back into his tunic and looked about the room. The camera and tripod lay broken upon the blood splattered floor and then Sir Edward noticed the strange, black rectangular box on the chair. He picked it up and showed Jericho.

Jericho grunted, it appeared broken; like it had been dropped upon concrete and so pulled it open with his dagger - it contained nothing - a fake time controller.

He knew now that Miss Stockyard Canning had been deceived, he tapped the useless box and pictured the scene; somehow the

'Controller' had broken against something hard and Miss Stockyard could now see the deception.

She probably confronted the 'Professor' and the beast had turned nasty. "Where's the young boy?" Wilson said with some concern. Jericho pushed open the door to the adjoining room and stood back from the dreadful scene; the young man and woman had been butchered; there was no other word for it.

The two naked bodies had been thrown about the bed and floor; the girls throat was badly torn, and her head hung loose upon her shoulders, a breast had been ripped off and her stomach lay open. The boy had very little face left, and one leg lay almost severed, pressed against his upper arm.

Butchered really didn't describe the terrible scene. Oscar joined Jericho in the doorway and ran a hand over his face; "Kesbo." He said simply and gripped his staff with both hands. "What do you mean?" Jericho muttered, unable to pull his eyes away from the horror. "Kesbo, the demon that did this - it has his mark all over - he's been under the Guardian's radar for a while now. We all wondered what the little fucker was up to, well, now we know." Oscar sighed and returned to Sir Edward who was almost sick but composed himself.

"I think we best get the fuck outa here." Wilson muttered, gathering up the camera and Jericho nodded his agreement, but remembered that Sir Edward was of this time.

"Go Jericho, I'll be fine. Connor can call the guard and I'll make up some story about a wolf man or something these people will believe - just go my friend – and catch the beast that did this." Jericho gripped his hand tightly but said nothing. Sir Edward watched as Jericho, Wilson and Oscar vanished. He returned quietly to the bar and told Connor to fetch the city guard, explaining someone had already dispatched one of the King's enemies and the unlucky, poor whore that just happened to be with him; they didn't want to leave any witnesses.

A very tired Jericho and Wilson made their way to the lighthouse, and both slumped into armchairs with large brandies. Jericho attempted to call Alex on her mirror without any luck. But then his mirror began to vibrate and bleep - an incoming call - he snatched it up and found, with some relief, that Owen was calling

9. JERICHO'S REVELATION.

Jericho stood by the fireplace and sipped his brandy, Alex and Owen should return at any moment. Wilson was at the Records office with Oscar, looking up the Demon known as 'Kesbo' and collating missing souls from the time and dates of those old films.

The soul of young John Goodfield was missing; but that didn't surprise Jericho - the boy had died out of his own time - the young woman who had died with him; a certain Mistress Mary Chapel, her soul was also missing. He chalked that one up to the demon.

Alex pushed open the study door and collected a large brandy from the tray, as she slumped into an armchair by the fire. Owen followed and also helped himself to a large brandy. He smiled at Jericho; "Well at least her soul was collected correctly. Alex delayed the Collector - it was old Charlie Le Beeoff by the way - until she questioned Miss Stockyard Canning, or should I say...."

Alex stopped him there and took up the story; "The injuries were just too much despite getting her to Whitechapel Hospital, Stockyard passed away a few minutes after arrival there. A savage death like that would have been suspicious to the Doctors, so Owen contacted the human Agent for that time and place, and he dealt with them."

"Inspector Harry Hadden - he's one of my best - that was a very smart move, Alex; very smart." Jericho was well pleased with his team's performance, especially Alexandra's. She nodded her thanks and continued: "That's when we found out that Miss Stockyard Canning was actually Mr. Stockyard Canning. The Collector - old Charlie - was on scene quite quickly, but I managed to question Stockyard. The story is a little odd, so here goes."

Owen dropped onto the sofa opposite and sipped his brandy. Jericho remained standing; arms folded. They listened intently to Alex's story.

"Apparently he was the fifth son of the Canning's, and his parents really wanted a girl. So, his father, an arrogant, selfish bastard had the boy raised as a girl. He didn't really know what or who he was - until he encountered Professor Goodfield who seduced the boy and for the first time in his/her short life felt; 'normal'. That was her words and she wanted to identify as a woman, so I'll run with her wishes. The Professor had convinced her that he possessed a machine to travel through time; so, with his son John in tow, the pair jumped through different era's with Stockyard filming their travels. She said it was 'bloody fantastic' at first, but then a big crack appeared; John had noticed that a lot of mysterious and sometimes horrifying deaths seem to be following them in each of the different time periods, that they appeared in." Alex sipped her brandy and Mr. Harris refilled her class, Jericho also accepted another from the big man.

"Finally, it came to a head by accident. At the Gallions Reach Tavern Stockyard accidently dropped the supposed 'controller' and it broke open. She realised that something else was doing the time travel and she confronted the professor. The rest we knew already. After attacking her, he turned on the boy and the young prostitute; killing them both and stealing her soul - young John's is probably lost in the darkness of real death - poor little sod."

Jericho said nothing but swallowed down his brandy and allowed Mr. Harris to refill him - yet again - as Wilson appeared and also accepted a drink. "62 missing in just the eras we know they visited from the four time periods that appeared in those films." Wilson looked quite grim and knocked back his whisky in one hit. "Oscar has gone on its trail with his friend; Guardian Emma Bateman. Angel Margret wants the bastard."

"Shit!" Owen muttered and finished his drink. "What now boss?" He asked Jericho, who stood in silence, gently rubbing his chin - deep in thought. Finally, Jericho looked up: "What have we overlooked my friends and it's staring us in the bloody face?"

Everyone exchanged bemused looks with each other and finally Owen asked; "What have we overlooked boss?" Jericho actually allowed himself a little smile; "Stockyard and John Goodfield were killed in 1510, AFTER filming good King Harry and the only party left, that we know, had knowledge about the films, was the demon. So, who the fuck hid those old films in the shop basement? Remember, the film about Henry was in the basement, who the hell put it there? Both Stockyard and John were dead and our friend the demon certainly wouldn't bother."Wilson grunted his agreement; "When I grabbed the camera, the film was gone. Someone had already taken the King Henry film and must have placed it with the others in the basement." He accepted a refill from Mr. Harris and tapped the class gently with a finger; thinking.

"But no-one, except the demon had the power to travel through time. So how did the film get back to Edwardian London and into the shop basement, if the demon didn't take it?" Alex held both hands up, adding; "Remember the bloody time controller was a fake!"

Jericho walked over to the grand mirror hanging above the fireplace and said quietly; "Play the scene from where the temporal detectives leave the internet café."

The mirror flickered into life, and everyone sat forward to view. They watched as the two men followed Jericho and Alex down the busy street and into the alley, where they vanished. They sat in silence as Stockyard supposedly operated the time controlling device and also vanished with her companion.

"Have a real close look at the second man." Jericho said and sat down in his favourite armchair and cradled his drink with both hands. The scene was replayed again, and he sat sipping his brandy, waiting for an answer.

"If Stockyard had already been murdered by the demon in 1510, how the hell could she have followed us from the café. Where, you remember, we viewed the films just released to the public domain. It can't have been Stockyard." Alex had reasoned it out and Jericho was again impressed.

"Play on." He said simply to the mirror and they continued to watch and saw Special Agent Louise Sturdiski leave the entrance of the alley and return to her British colleague, MI5 Agent Michael Shannon, waiting by the black van.

"In this particular time period; the early 21st Century, some Governments are investigating instances of 'Time-travel' which they perceive to be a threat to their National Security and they have caught, only on camera thankfully, quite a few temporal detectives passing through; including us!" He jabbed a finger at Alexandra, then himself. Everybody chuckled at that as Alex held up her hands and said, "Guilty."

"The most worrying thing is; they have apparently caught others coming from the future - in growing numbers - to their century and the 20th. But that's for another day." Jericho suddenly produced the fake time controller and told the mirror to zoom in on the controller held by Stockyard Canning. Everyone rose from their chairs and gathered about the mirror. They all agreed - it was indeed the fake controller - but it showed damage around the edges; just like when Jericho first picked it up in the rooms at the rear of Gallions Reach Tavern.

Alex started to chuckle and smiled in amazement at Jericho's incredible detective abilities; "How the hell did you catch on to this?" She asked, shaking her head. Everyone now knew that this was filmed after Stockyard's death and after the controller had been damaged.

Jericho grinned broadly; "Well, it was a certain, mad conspiracy theorist that actually solved the case for us." He tossed the fake time controller to Owen and allowed himself a small chuckle. "The man with the knife is indeed our demon friend masquerading as Professor Goodfield. But the young man, who believes he's operating a time controlling device, is certainly not Stockyard - she's already dead - but is so like Stockyard, we accepted it was her; just like those living detectives did in the van. That lovely young agent says, 'Brice and Ellis.' They fell for the deception, as we did, to our shame."

"Who the hell is it then?" Owen asked, staring closely at the frozen image. Jericho tapped the screen and sighed; "Frederick George Canning."

10. IN PURSUIT OF EVIL.

"Obergruppenführer Fredrick Von Cannell was a high-ranking Nazi, who disappeared just before the fall of Berlin in 1945. His filthy bloodstained hands can be found in murder degrees to various concentration camps during the Nazi period. He's probably, personally responsible for the deaths of thousands of innocent men, women and children. He was never brought to justice because he apparently vanished off the face of the Earth or so it seemed. We know the bastard as Frederick George Canning, and we now know where he has been hiding; in time." Jericho pointed to the smiling Nazi on the mirror's screen and then pulled up Frederick Canning; they were the same man.

"Owen, unknowingly, hit the nail on the head when he made the comment; 'in the Nazi era, Germany had plenty of demons hanging about the place', he was so right. I strongly suspect that one was 'Kesbo' and of course, Frederick knew it well and had been its real partner since 1905. Had his sister not discovered the deception, Stockyard would have probably been involved with the Nazi's as well - though I hope - she had the strength to turn away, but we'll never know now." Jericho continued, stopping only to take a bite from his sandwich; cheese and cucumber; a favourite.

Mrs. Harris had supplied the team with well earned sandwiches as the briefing continued - they couldn't stop for dinner; much to Wilson's and Owen's regret. "If I had actually listened to Alexandra, we would have been on to this earlier." He smiled at Alex, who looked quite puzzled. "What the hell did I say?" She asked and everyone chuckled.

"You said we should view the Roman era film again because of the two people seen filming on the river's other bank - one man and one female; possibly." Jericho pointed to the mirror and the scene was replayed - in real close up - and everyone nodded their agreement; it was Stockyard and her brother Frederick.

"John and his supposed father was actually doing the filming and again captured Stockyard - just like in the King Henry film and if we closely view the other two films, we'll find her in them too; she was a real time tourist!" Jericho allowed himself a little chuckle and then turned serious.

"I believe that Frederick was the person who hid the films in the old basement, despite him following the demon for all it could offer him; he still had some kind of feeling for his younger brother/sister and wanted to keep the films. The demon wouldn't actually mind, because of the sheer number of souls the evil bastard had access to, following the murdering Frederick about a war-torn Europe." Jericho showed a picture of the old shop as it appeared in 1905.

"Canning's Photographic and Portrait Studio." He said simply. "He simply couldn't return to retrieve the films because of two bloody great world wars and Britain and Germany were absolute enemies in both. I'm sure that at the end of the Second World War, when Frederick was of no further use to it; the demon disposed of him too."

"The body was never found because the demon finished him off in another time period and of course, there would be no collector to recover the soul." Wilson concluded, nodding his agreement with all Jericho had said.

"I hope Oscar and his companion find the bastard and kill it." Alex said quietly and everyone was a little surprised to hear the Lady swear; but they all laughed about it.

"In the pursuit of evil, there really can be no prisoners." Jericho whispered and the meeting broke up, with Mr. Harris appearing and informing Jericho that 'little Ivan' had arrived with a dispatch from Angel Margret. Jericho collected the file and sat in his armchair, sipping a brandy.

"Anything interesting?" queried Owen, warming his backside by the fire. Jericho looked up and smiled; "Fancy a trip to old Gettysburg?"

THE END

EPILOGUE:

"This mission was quite difficult for Team 74; it discovered that over sixty souls had been lost or stolen due to time travelling activities of the Demon Kesbo, who remains at large. It also spawned no less than three other Temporal Detective investigations and showed that human authorities knew about the activities of the Temporal Department. It really could not be described as a 'success' for that Department."
SJW.

CHARACTERS:

Hoagy Treadwell continued to run his 'conspiracy' website for many years and rather surprisingly, on several occasions, got it right. He made a small living through advertisements on his site and could be called a recluse. He was found dead at Christmas in 2033 and no soul was collected. Temporal Detective Inspector Ali Khan and Team 59 have been assigned the case; there is currently no resolution.

Sir Edward Wallington, the human agent for this time and place, contracted the feared 'sweating sickness' which was rampant at the time. He died in 1515 and his soul was collected and processed. His mortal remains and tomb was subject of a Temporal Investigation, when a small wristwatch was discovered in his tomb in 2022. It was being removed to make way for a new high speed railway link. That case awaits resolution and is being investigated by Inspector Jericho Tibbs and Team 74.

Special Agent Louise Sturdiski (NSA) returned to the USA and continued to work for the National Security Agency until her early death; she was killed in a traffic accident by a drunk driver. Her soul was collected and processed. She is currently working as a Collector but has applied to join the Temporal Detective Department.

Stockyard Brice Goodfield [nee Canning] was lucky, in that Alex and Owen managed to return her to Edwardian times before she succumbed to her terrible injuries. This allowed her soul to be collected and processed. It was quarantined until 2100.

Michael Shannon, A British MI6 agent [Special Intelligence Service - SIS] remained in the department for several years and was part of the highly secret section that watched invading 'time-travelers'. He soon realised that many of the persons he saw and recorded, where something far more than time- travelers. They were, of course, Temporal Detectives passing through on missions. Unfortunately, he accidently drowns whilst on a family holiday in Australia. His soul was collected and processed.

Frederick George Canning [Obergruppenführer Fredrick Von Cannell] was probably terminated by the demon, at the end of the Second World War, when he was of no longer use to the creature. No soul has been collected and the whereabouts of his death remains a mystery - but it was not within in his ordained 'Life-cycle' and so - as a human out of his own time; his soul was lost. Temporal Detective Inspector 'Doc' Silas Underhill has been assigned his case - it currently remains unresolved.

Professor Ellis Goodfield [Kesbo the Demon] managed to steal over sixty souls with the help of his 'wife' and 'son'. The Demon Ingress Department [Intelligence Service Section] reports that he was last sighted in Afghanistan in the year 1899.

Captain Arthur Churchill, part of the King's bodyguard, liked to drink and was caught up in a tavern brawl in the King Lud tavern and was accidently struck with a sword. He survived the wound, but within days was seriously ill. The small wound had become infected. His arm had to be amputated, but that didn't save him. The sepsis had spread through his body, and he died - in agony - in 1518. His soul was collected and processed.

Lord Herbert, the Lord Chamberlain, died in 1526 and his soul was collected and processed.

Thomas Howard, 2nd Duke of Norfolk, died in 1524 at over 80 years of age, which was good for the time period. His soul was collected and processed.

Robert Eel, the 'ferryman' rowed the river for some nine years and was well respected for his quiet and pleasant manners. Unfortunately, he contracted the feared 'sweating sickness' in 1515 and died within days of falling ill; his soul was collected and processed.

Connor Saltfeet was the part owner of the 'Galleon's Reach' tavern and kept good order in the pub. A violent man by nature, he was easily provoked and whilst beating one of the girls for a minor infringement one night, used far too much force and accidently killed her. The city watch went after him, and he was caught in a Whitechapel brothel. He was hung on St. Martin's Day 1512. His soul was collected and processed.

John Goodfield had spent much time at Boarding School, so didn't really know his father. The demon 'Kesbo' was able to fool him easily. He was brutally killed by the demon, when Stockyard realised what was happening and confronted 'Kesbo'. He was a human out of his own time and so; his soul is lost.

Mary Chapel was the common prostitute killed with John Goodfield at the Gallion's Reach tavern; she was seventeen at the time. Her soul is missing, and the file is marked; LTDA - Lost To Demonic Activity.

Special appearance by King Henry VIII, as himself.

The KING died in 1547 and was succeeded by his feeble son; Edward VI who was just a boy. Unfortunately, the young boy died in 1553 (aged 15 years). The Tudor dynasty he worked so hard to maintain expired with the death of his daughter; Elizabeth I in 1603. History remembers him, mainly for his numerous wives and the creation of the English Church - which was and remains - independent of Rome. His soul was collected and processed.

EPISODE 6: "BETRAYAL AT GETTYSBURG."

MISSION SUMMARY:
"Someone or something is trying to change the outcome of the American Civil War and Mr. Tibbs must prevent the Time-Line from being altered; so it's back to 1863 and the forthcoming Battle of Gettysburg. Jericho must discover the plot and who's behind it and quickly, for he also knows that someone is about to betray the temporal detectives - is it a spy, time-traveler or something more sinister?"

NOTES: This episode contains language [relevant for the time period] that may be considered offensive in these 'enlightened' times. Nevertheless, History cannot and should not be sanitized, in any way. But this episode does contain censored dialogue.

ALCOHOL, VIOLENCE, SEXUAL REFERENCES, STRONG LANGUAGE [including racial slurs] & MILD HORROR.

AGE 15+ ONLY.   **45 Minutes reading time.**

1. THE SECRET LOST AT GETTYSBURG.
The rebel picket found the body slumped against a small tree; the young man had been stabbed through the stomach and still clutched his pistol in a dirty, gloved hand. The old sergeant prodded the corpse with his rifle and wiped his face with his free hand. "Fresh, only could have been dead a couple of hours." The

young corporal coughed and pointed to the body; "His been run through with a fuckin' sword I'd say, look at the gap on that cut." A couple of other soldiers stared down at the dead man and one scratched his head; "He's got a cocked pistol in his hand ready to shoot, yet someone got so close that he could run a fuckin' sword through him; that don't make sense!"

The sergeant examined the pistol; it had not been fired. One name came to mind: 'Black sword'. That's when the old man noticed the dead man's other hand; the remains of a torn piece of paper was still tightly held in his fingers. He pulled it gently from the dead fingers and pushed on his spectacles to read.

"Looks like a piece from some map." He turned the fragment about in his hand and could make out just one place name: 'Gettysburg - 1863'. He stared down at the young dead man and told his Corporal to search the body thoroughly. "I think he could 'ave been riding for the damn Yankee's." The corporal grunted and started through the man's pockets and even searched his hat and boots.

The old sergeant looked about; whoever killed him had probably taken his horse - you couldn't get far around these parts without a horse - Far in the distance he could make out a figure on horseback. He pulled a small brass telescope from his canvas sack and focused on the figure. "God damn it, he's lookin' back at me with a damn scope!" He exclaimed and lowered the telescope; "Some fella in a yellow dust coat, but he has only one horse with him."

"Look see Sergeant; this was stashed in a hidden pocket, sewn into his shirt." The young corporal held out a small silver, rectangular box with a black glass front and the sergeant took it carefully, turning it in his hands. "Ain't never seen anythin' like this before." He muttered and struggled to open it. He stared at the inside, as the box was now in a couple of pieces. "What fuckin' useless shit is this!" He laughed and threw the broken box onto the mud and grass.

"Yankee Calvary coming' fast up the road!" One of the pickets waved his hat from the thick bushes on the opposite side of the road and everyone dashed into the relative safety of the woods, to watch the Yankee Calvary patrol ride past.

"Whoever killed that young fella must 'ave robbed him sarge, didn't have a plugged nickel on him." The young corporal shouldered his rifle and fell in behind his colleagues, for the long walk back to the rebel encampment. The old sergeant nodded and rubbed the fragment of paper between his fingers; he had never seen paper like it and he had spent seventeen years working the presses for the main newspaper at Richmond, before joining the colours and fighting in the army of North Virginia under General Robert E. Lee.

"Strange paper and an even stranger little useless box." He muttered to himself and wondered why the notorious character 'Black sword' had killed the young fella - but then - he didn't have another horse when spotted by the picket; strange stuff indeed.

He had heard a couple of rumours about the fella in the yellow dust coat from some boys in the 22nd. Apparently, he had killed two men over Greenbrier way with a fucking sword - a fucking black sword - before they even managed to pull their god damn pistols out!

He chuckled to himself and pushed the paper fragment into his pocket. He would report all that his picket had found to Captain Joe 'Shamrock' Delaney and so he headed for the captains tent. He stared about the growing city of tents, horses, wagons and men - if many more arrive - then a great big battle is in the offering here.

He spat and wiped his mouth and beard and told his men to rest and get some grub on. The old sergeant made his way to Captain Delaney's tent, clutching the fragment of strange paper. He passed the two strangers leaving the good captain's tent; they nodded and raised their hats and started to talk quietly with each other. The sergeant laughed; the men called the pair 'Too tall and way short."

They were apparently 'whisky drummers' trying to sell their stuff to the officers in the army; probably to both God damn sides! Still, they claimed to be English and so they were 'neutrals' in this bloody war and could visit any side they wanted and sell their whisky to whoever they wanted. It was a very good war for some people, the sergeant mused as he arrived at the captains tent. He shouted out his name and stood outside until Captain

Delaney called him in. The captain was a big, powerful Irish man who came from Virginia and sported a black beard to match his hair and eyes. He was sitting on a rough wooden chair with his boots off, rubbing his feet with whisky and cold water. He took a couple of swigs from the same bottle that he had applied to his feet and coughed.

The sergeant pulled open the tent flap and stepped in; he saluted and stood in silence. Delaney looked up and didn't smile; "What you got for me Frank?" The old sergeant recounted the events of the patrol; the dead body, the piece of strange paper, a Yankee cavalry patrol and that strange fellow who carried an old black sword. Captain Delaney stood and leaned upon the small desk that was cluttered with personal objects and maps.

The sergeant actually jumped when the captain swept everything from the table with one hand - except the whisky bottle - and cussed loudly. He grabbed up the bottle and took a long hard swig and cursed some more. Finally, he composed himself and straightened his open tunic. "The bastard in the yellow dust coat killed the boy?" he asked the old soldier with clear anger in his voice. The sergeant nodded that 'Black Sword' must have done so; how many cowboys and ranch hands carry a fucking black sword?

The captain stared at the fragment of paper and cursed again. "Was any money found on him?" The sergeant said the boy had probably been robbed by whoever killed him. Delaney stared at the old sergeant with some suspicion, but then dismissed him and sent for young Lieutenant Tom Harvey - who he could trust - to inform the local Sheriff; he would pay the man a visit later, to discuss the death.

Alone in his tent, Captain Delaney sat nursing the whisky bottle and then slowly placed the whisky bottle upon the empty table and pulled his officer's truck from the rear of the tent and slowly opened the chest. He rummaged inside for a few seconds and pulled out a dark canvas bag and placed it on the table. Slowly he un-wrapped the bundle and ran a hand across the strange object that lay before him.

His thoughts were interrupted by a shout outside his tent; "Sir, the scout Mister Sage is here!" Delaney covered the object up and slumped in his chair. The scout pushed his way in and unbuttoned his long dark dust coat, the two white pearl handled pistols, hanging from each hip were immediately noticeable. The scout folded his arms and stared at the whisky bottle; he said nothing for now.

"That bastard McIves has killed young Benny and probably has the map." He held up the fragment and then handed Mister Sage the whisky bottle. "Sorry to hear that Joe, I know you liked the boy." Sage took a swig and wiped his mouth, then slapped his dust covered hat against his leg. "It's gonna break his mothers heart when I tell her." Delaney muttered and accepted the bottle back.

"Those two fuckwits I hired with that money you gave me, to kill McIves let him get too close despite all what I told them." Sage grunted and added; "They won't make that mistake again; he killed the pair without getting a scratch." Delaney sighed and placed a hand upon the hilt of his Sabre; "If I ever catch up with that bastard, we'll see how good he is with a sword."

Sage nodded and pulled a half-smoked cigar from his coat and placed it in his mouth. Delaney tossed him a large match and Sage struck it against his boot and lit his cigar. "Worse new I'm afraid; that other bastard Jericho Tibbs is on his way here." Delaney groaned and ran several fingers through his beard. "Can you get another copy of that damn map before the fight starts?"

Sage blew smoke from his mouth and nodded; "Yep, but how do we get it here in secret, under that fucker's Tibbs nose; his bound to know about me if McIves is on the scene." Delaney leaned back on his wobbly chair and half smiled; "Just get the map to her and she'll do the rest." Sage actually chuckled, then picked up the whisky bottle again; "Don't leave this around Joe; those other two retards don't have a clue. You won't be able to buy a bottle like this for another couple of years here in the States."

Delaney nodded and accepted the bottle back and placed it in his officer's chest. "No money was found on his body, so McIves must have the money we arranged to pay that slimy little rat for his information. See that he gets what's due to him."

The scout pushed his hat back on and said softly; "That will be a pleasure." He turned and left the captain alone. Sage would

make sure that the little rat and his dirty whore of a girlfriend
would get what's coming to them. He chuckled and glanced back
at the tent, then walked over to Major Canter's HQ located in a
small seed barn, by the little stream. Sage chuckled; the Major
was a known misogynist and a terrible racist - he also didn't mind
killing off the battlefield - a perfect choice.

2. MRS. PHILADELPHIA HAZZARD.

The four riders skirted the little ridge and headed into the quiet
green valley; ahead lay a small farmhouse and outbuildings with
a solitary horse tied outside. "That's Clem Hazzard's place."
Jericho said simply and spurred his mount forward. Wilson looked
awkward on his horse; riding horse's wasn't his strong point. "We
could have hired a carriage in Gettysburg for the price of these
four beasts." He muttered, holding tightly onto the reins.

Jericho smiled at the big man; "Didn't have many horses in the
NYPD then?"

Wilson nodded; "Not near me. Damn beasts, all hair and teeth;
reminds me of my damn Mother-in-law!" That made Jericho
laugh, and the little group headed for the farmstead that stood
out against the small mountains which made up the background.

Owen was a natural horseman and guided his mount with a light
touch and clear skill. "I first rode a pony when I was five. Riding
was the one real thing that I missed about home when Father
sent me to the Monastery." He spoke to Alex who was riding
'side-saddle' with equal skill and balance.

"I really have difficulty envisioning you as a Monk Owen; you
definitely don't have a Monk's attributes." Alex said softly and
then saw the woman's figure standing upon the farmhouse's
wooden porch, arms folded across her clean white apron, she
raised a hand in greeting and Jericho waved back; "That's
Philadelphia; Clem's wife."

The little group pulled up at the farmhouse and dismounted, well
Wilson didn't quite dismount, he sort of slid from the horse and
managed to land on both feet. He growled at Owen, when he
gave the big man a little applause.

Owen helped Alex from her saddle whilst Jericho dropped from his mount and handed his reins to Owen, who tied the horses together at the hitch post and then joined the others in the farmhouse. Mrs. Philadelphia Hazzard welcomed her visitors with fresh brewed coffee, biscuits and gravy. They sat at the large dining table, eating and chatting. Philadelphia had been a Temporal Agent for Jericho for some years, joining her husband Clement after they married, who had been working for Mr. Tibbs since his teen years.

Wilson was mopping up his breakfast with gusto and thanked Philadelphia, he had not tasted such good biscuits and gravy since he was a boy and stayed at his grandmother's a couple of times a week. He sat back and grinned; "That makes the damn horse-ride worthwhile!"

Everyone laughed and then the door swung open, and Philadelphia's other guest sauntered into the Dining Room. Jericho and Alex recognised him at once; it was 'Strange-ways Stevens' a well-known train and bank robber who had worked for Jericho on a casual basis over the years. "My guts are giving me gripes and that's the second damn visit to the thunder box in an hour." He moaned and slowly sat down; Philadelphia handed him a black coffee, stirring a large spoonful of sugar into the cup.

"You're not gonna like what I'm about to say Jericho, but you need to know about a strange pair hanging around that blue-belly Army of the Potomac, the one under that General Meade. They stick out like tits on a bull. Apparently, they are English Whisky Drummers, looking to sell their wares. But they aren't right, as I was telling Phil here, they talk real strange and don't know shit about anything. But it's what I caught a glimpse of that will scratch your interest." Strange-ways leaned back in the chair and sipped his coffee.

"It was a small, dark rectangular box with a class front that had tiny pictures or drawings on – it fits in your hand and Strange-ways says the little fat one of the pair was whispering into it. The tall skinny one kept looking about while he did it." Philadelphia topped up Owen and Wilson's coffee cups and sat down. Jericho rubbed his chin and sat back; thinking.

Owen looked quite puzzled by that; "How could they use a mobile phone here; there's no satellites or towers to carry the signals and who the hell would they call?" Wilson nodded his agreement at that statement, but Jericho made no comment and only Alex caught the strange look upon his face.

"I take it you know that the Reb army under 'Granny Lee' is about thirty miles south of us, heading north. The Blue-bellies are about the same distance south heading north in pursuit. The Reb's have been using the Mountains to screen their movements. The pair should meet up tomorrow somewhere near Gettysburg and that is gonna be a dandy of a fight!" Strange ways laughed to himself and drained his coffee cup, looking for a refill.

Jericho turned to his team; "About six weeks ago in this time, there was a breach of the Timeline, and it wasn't a natural hit. Two humans' crossed over from the year 2018. Doc Underhill and his team investigated and found nothing. There have been no changes to the current Timeline, so the pair has kept a very efficient 'Low Profile' here – until now - I suspect. But just a few months ago a breech occurred, and someone crossed over from 2016 - why are time travelers arriving here in force, at this time and place? "

"The battle." Alex said quietly, adding "They were going to try and change the outcome of the most important battle of the American Civil war; but how?"

"Don't forget your old friend - McIves was reported in this year some months ago - is that another coincidence?" Wilson sat back and sipped his coffee, but Jericho just nodded and finished his breakfast.

"I ain't told you the best bit yet, Jericho." Strange ways accepted more coffee from Philadelphia and some fruit cake to help ease his growling stomach; "Them strange pair have been seen hanging around with an actor, who we know works for General Longstreet; he commands the reb's First Corps under old 'Granny Lee'. The actor was the bugger that warned the reb's about the Yankee's movements – he has the ear and confidence of Jim Longstreet - so what if them pair from the hereafter, get the damn actor to rat out the Yankee's plan's and change what the South intends to do here?"

Jericho nodded and smiled; but said nothing in reply. He glanced across at Alex and she took up the conversation. Alex sipped her coffee; "Where's Clem, Philly?"

Philadelphia sat back down and gripped her cup with both hands;
"He's over at the Mercy Hospital; old Doc Hogan is down with the
fever again, so he has to help out." Alex placed her cup upon the
table and smiled; Clem Hazzard could never turn his back on a
cry for help!

Jericho considered what he had heard and pushed his hands
through his dark wavy hair and sat back in the rough chair;
Doctor Clement Hazzard was a man of principle – that's what
Jericho liked and admired about the man – and that hospital will
surely need all the Doctors and Surgeons it can get hold of, in
the next few days.

"I'll catch up with Clem when we ride to Gettysburg; is there
anything you want us to deliver Philly?" Jericho leaned forward
and drained his cup. The others knew that was a signal to finish
their late breakfasts and get ready to saddle up again. Wilson
groaned to himself, his arse and thighs were already feeling the
effects of the short ride from their 'Jump Point' and he really
didn't relish another couple of hours on the back of that damn
horse.

Philadelphia smiled and rose up quickly from her chair and
smoothed down her apron; "There is indeed Jericho; I'll fetch
them from the kitchen." Philly had prepared two apple pies; one
for her husband who adored apple pie and another for Jericho's
team. The thought of her apple pie produced a smile on Wilson's
face and he volunteered to look after the pies. Owen commented
that he would also look after the pies, particularly from Wilson!

3. THE BOARDING HOUSE.

Old Strange way's muttered that he was never given pies; by
anyone, never mind Philadelphia. But cheered up when Philly told
him he could finish up the biscuits and gravy. Then Jericho took
Strangways to one side and gave him some instructions and
several silver Dollars, which put an even bigger smile upon his
face. The foursome stated their goodbyes and mounted up,
heading down the rough road to Gettysburg.

"We'll get rooms at old Ma Crabb's boarding house, just on the
outside of the town; the Rebel army will occupy the town
tomorrow and we'll be away from it there." Jericho informed Alex
as the group rode towards the North Gettysburg turnpike with

some determination. In the distance, behind them, they could see blue figures and many horses: the Federal Army was on the move too.

It was Wilson's sharp eye that caught the figure trailing some miles behind them, but keeping ahead of the Federal Army, a lone horseman with a distinctive bright yellow dust coat. "He's been behind us since we left the Hazzard's place." Wilson told Jericho, but the group didn't slow or change course and reached the boarding house a couple of hours later. They could see the figure in the distance, and it vanished beyond small woodland: heading south.

"Heading towards blue or grey?" Wilson grinned and they dismounted; Owen walked the horse's towards the Boarding House's Livery stable, tossing a silver dollar in the air that Jericho had given him to pay the stable boy. They walked into the lobby of the house and were greeted by old Ma Crabb's eldest daughter, Victoria. A sour faced spinster in her late thirties with dark greasy hair and missing teeth. She didn't smile when she looked up from her paperwork on the front desk.

"You'll have to keep your n****r outside; Negro servants sleep in the stables loft room." She said simply and gestured towards the door; "We only charge two bits for that." She added and again pointed towards the door; "Go on boy, just follow the damn horses." Before Wilson could comment, Jericho tugged gently on his sleeve and nodded towards the door; "You knew to expect this."

But Alex was having none of 'this': "Mister Wilson is a free man and entitled to respect and proper treatment when he's paying for a room here!" She tapped the desk gently with her hand and added quietly; "He's name is MISTER Wilson Franklyn for your register."

Miss Victoria Crabb actually smiled and folded her arms, nodding her head she muttered; "You don't say Missy!" Standing in the doorway to the kitchen was another woman; tall and thin, wearing a drab grey dress and watching the row develop between Victoria and the beautiful young lady. Smiling, she was clutching a handful of old books that Ma Crabb had given her for the school.

Miss Lillian then noticed the young man standing next to the lovely lady and her smile vanished; "Fucking Jericho Tibbs." She whispered to herself and wondered where young Benny was.

Samuel, Ma Crabb's grandson ran past her and through the kitchen door towards the yard, all excited. His aunt (Victoria) had sent him to fetch Sheriff Rook, to the full-blown argument happening in Reception.

Miss Lillian sighed and followed the boy through the kitchen and into the street. Young Samuel was already pushing through the doors of the Sheriff's office, shouting. Miss Lillian stood quietly in the street, as several Union Troopers rode past the dry goods store behind her. She knew that the battle was only a day away now and nothing must interfere with the plan. She would tell Rook to tread carefully in his dealings with that bastard Tibbs.

It was with some relief to her that Jacob 'pudding' Davis wandered from the Jail with Samuel next to him. Sheriff Rook's deputy was fat, useless, and avoided any kind of confrontations - if he could - she would be able to manipulate him easily. Miss Lillian called Jacob and Samuel over and spoke quietly to the sweating deputy who constantly wiped his face and neck in the late sunshine.

Apparently the good Sheriff was in the Mayor's Office, being briefed about the two enormous armies that were converging on the town - along with the entire town council. They were clearly trying to avoid any panic setting in - most hoped that the Union army would occupy the town before the rebels and confine the fighting to the fields and roads around Gettysburg. Lillian chuckled at that; some hope!

Suitably 'advised' by Miss Lillian, the reluctant Jacob headed for the reception area, hitching up his wide trousers and nervously adjusting the badge that hung from his dirty white shirt; stained with sweat and food debris. She watched him go and headed for the rear of the undertaker's, where Troy and Dauphin would be waiting with the wagon and for her instructions. But all she could think of was Benny.

The loft above the barn was quite large and packed with hay; Wilson and Jericho were still chuckling to themselves as they laid blankets out and prepared to settle in for the night. "Well, you told old sour face straight baby girl!" Wilson smiled broadly and eased his sore back down upon the hay and laughed to himself – again. "Fancy not knowing what 'racist' means." He turned to Jericho and whispered; "But she certainly knew what 'white trash' meant!" Jericho grinned and sighed, pulling the blanket about his shoulders. Old Ma Crabb had intervened before the row at the front desk actually required the local Sheriff being called. His useless deputy: Jacob had done nothing really - except stare at Alex and wipe his fat face – It could have been the worst outcome possible for a team of temporal Detectives trying to keep a low profile!

But old Ma Crabb settled the matter: for a dollar they could all sleep in the hay loft. "Sorry boy's, I sort of lost my head a little there." Alex explained and pulled bits of straw from her hair and skirts. But the rest of the team rejected her apology with some humour; "I think the best bits were frustrated old spinster and pea-brained." Owen said quietly and chuckled loudly.

"Let's get some sleep people; we have a long day tomorrow." Jericho said and still smiling, curled up in his rough blanket. "White trash was my favourite part." He softly added and drifted off to sleep. In the street below the loft's big window, a lone horseman pulled his bright yellow dust coat off and watched the lamp light flickering through the glass and also smiled. He rattled the little black drawstring bag which contained ten silver Yankee dollars: apparently a down payment for some murder.

4. ASSISTANCE FROM A STRANGE PLACE.

Alex suddenly sat up and rubbed her eyes gently. She looked about the hay loft and wondered why she had woken up; it was still dark. The lamp was casting a dull yellow light about the place, and she could smell something sweet. Jericho also stirred and sat up, as something dropped from his chest into the hay, he pushed about and pulled up a small black drawstring bag, wrapped in a piece of paper, held by a length of green string.

Wilson leaned upon his elbows and nodded to the bag Jericho held up; "That sounds like coins rattling." Jericho opened the handwritten note carefully and held it by the lamp. The look upon his face was priceless; he coughed and shook his head in disbelief.

"What does it say?" Owen asked, yawing and stretching - he was used to being aroused from sleep in the middle of night; life in the monastery had seen to that. "I almost started praying again." He chuckled to himself, kneeling in the soft hay. Everyone looked at Alex as she held the single red rose up for all to see. "Where does anyone get a fresh cut English rose in the middle of America in 1863?" She asked with real bewilderment in her voice, adding; "I found it next to my bag." which she was using as a makeshift pillow.

Jericho tossed the bag a couple of times, and everyone heard the coins it contained; "Ten silver dollars paid to a certain 'Black eyed Benny' for a little murder." He spoke softly and pushed the bag into his coat pocket.

"Murder of who?" Wilson asked and Jericho smiled a little; "Me." He said simply.

Alex accepted the note from Jericho and read it aloud;*"Jericho, I believe someone paid 'Black eyed Benny' - a new young killer, ten silver dollars to end your time here. You won't be able to question Benny's soul - he was originally from 2016! When I encountered him, he was a carrying a torn map of Gettysburg and Ma Crabb's boarding house was marked on it. I suspect someone knows you and why your here. Go carefully. McIves."*

There was silence for a few seconds and Jericho started to chuckle, taking the note from Alex and placing it with the money bag. "Bloody McIves!" He muttered and slumped back into the hay and consulted his small fob watch, which was set to local time, it showed 4.45 am.

"The sun will be up in an hour." He looked through the large window and could see the flickering of several blazing torches. Wilson wandered to the window and peered out; "Looks like a couple of Sheriff Deputies are bringing a body slung over a horse." He turned and smiled at Jericho; "Young 'Black eyed Benny' I would assume."

"Why would he help us. McIves I mean?" Owen asked, pulling bits of straw from his hair and jacket. Jericho didn't answer, but sat thoughtfully rubbing his chin, wondering what McIves was doing here in 1863 and more importantly; who else knows that temporal detectives are on scene?

Jericho looked up and could see his three colleagues grouped around the hayloft window, watching Sheriff Theodore Rook's men unloading the body outside the jail, which was directly opposite the stables. "They are telling the Sheriff that rebel troops are camped just a few miles from here. But no rebel cavalry has been seen and that's strange apparently." Owen called back to Jericho, still brushing himself down from the straw.

"No cavalry, did you say no cavalry?" Jericho asked and pulled his mirror from the depths of his frock coat pockets. Own walked back over and helped Alex brush down her coat; "Yeah, they seemed to be fascinated that the rebels have no real cavalry with them." Jericho read, then re-read his mirror and nodded to himself. That could well be the answer to why there were repeated breeches to the timeline, here at this period and place.

A thought crept into his head and Jericho had a very strong feeling he could be on the right line of thinking here; the rebel cavalry arrived too late to really influence the outcome of the battle; a defeat for the rebels. What if someone managed to get the rebel cavalry here nice and early? Would that be enough to change the result? Who could do that? Or was he missing something else?

5. THE PIE THAT CHANGED EVERYTHING.

The team took breakfast at Brady's eating house on South Street and rather strangely - to Jericho and his team - none of the early morning patrons objected to Wilson sitting at the table with his white friends. They had told the owner; Tom Brady, that they were reporters from the Citizens Compiler Newspaper, based in Washington DC, and was covering the exploits of the Union Army.

The large camera, tripod and film cases carried by Wilson and Owen drew attention, with many amazed that a black man could take photographs, but they were truly amazed when told that Alex was a reporter working for that title. Some really didn't like that and just stared at her.

One dissenting patron paid his bill and left muttering; "N****rs and women working together, what the fuck next?" Tom Brady half smiled and almost apologised to them for the man's comments; "That's Billy Logan; he and his family are dirt farmers who fled Carolina at the start of the war - they didn't want to fight for anyone - rebels or union. He's all mouth; don't pay any mind to him."

But one man did pay some attention to the little group of strangers; Sheriff Theodore Rook finished up his plate and sipped his coffee, watching Jericho and his team carefully over his cup. He threw a couple of bits on the table and wiped his face with a napkin. Standing, he looked down at his fat and already sweating deputy; "I'm gonna have words with them strangers from the east; stay here."

He walked slowly to their table, scatter gun slung over his shoulder. Sheriff Rook was in his early forties and a former cattle man who had fallen on hard times before he was elected Sheriff - after he shot dead two outlaws, trying to rob the local post office. He was known as fair, but hard. You didn't mess with Rook unless you were prepared to pull your pistol and use it.

Jericho rose slowly from his chair and held out his hand; "Good morning, Sheriff, my colleagues and I are getting some breakfast before we head to the union camp. We're reporters from..." But Jericho never finished his greeting, Sheriff Rook waved his hand aside; "I heard tell who you people are. Old ma Crabb's grandson painted a pretty picture 'bout what occurred at his grandma's boarding house."

The table went silent, except for Owen deliberately slurping his coffee and Alex stared at the big man, who was wearing a bright red waistcoat with a silver star pinned to it. The sheriff wiped his face with a gaudy yellow hankie and blew his nose. "I hear tell that this pretty little thing told Victoria, in no uncertain terms, what she thought of her."

Jericho coughed slightly and nodded.

"Well, you being reporters and the like, I'm sure old Ma Crabb wouldn't want her name plastered across the Northern papers, so I'll leave it at that. I got damn two huge armies sitting on my porch and a young fella killed with a damn sword to sort. Just keep your noses clean, that's all I ask."

He turned to go but stopped and spoke to Jericho again; "You reporters like to stick your snouts in people's business, don't you?" he didn't wait for Jericho to reply, adding; "Never mind the Rebels or Yankee's, you should speak to Miss Lillian, the school ma'am. She'll tell you a story to curdle your milk and that's a fact. You'll find her place next to the schoolhouse on the Old Turner's Pike. She ain't been here long, but she knows her stuff alright." He actually chuckled and wandered out the cafe, with his deputy in tow.

The group finished their breakfast and made their way back to the stables in relative silence. They passed a couple of black labourers, loading a wagon, who stopped and raised their hats to Alex and Wilson.

"Word spreads quickly. We need to be really careful now; especially you and Wilson." Jericho spoke softly to Alex, adding; "Whatever our feelings are about the people of this period, we must complete the mission. Can you imagine the future if the South win this battle?" Alex nodded, but said nothing, thinking what on earth the local schoolteacher knew, that would interest reporters, here to cover the union army. They quickly saddled the horses and that's when Wilson noticed the open saddlebag, he peered inside and shouted to Owen; "Someone has lifted a pie!"

Owen and Alex joined him and agreed that one pie had gone. "It's the one with Clem's name on - thankfully." Wilson said with some humour. But Owen pointed down to a large stack of straw and quietly said; "There's a ragged old boot sticking out and I think there's a bloody leg attached to it."

Wilson kicked the boot and told the owner to stand up - he had actually drawn his revolver. But a skinny boy emerged from the bale of hay, armed only with an empty pie dish. He had a well-worn confederate infantry uniform hung about him; at least a couple of sizes too large. Alex sighed; the boy was even younger than Owen; a deserter from the army now camped a few miles away.

He was shaking, and Alex slowly took the pie dish from him; "Put it down Wilson, he has no gun and he's just a boy." That's when she saw the piece of paper stuck to the pie dish and prised it from the still sticky bottom.

Jericho quietly accepted the paper from Alex, who was giving the boy water from her canteen. "Since when did America in 1863 have laminated paper?" Wilson asked with some apparent sarcasm in his voice. The paper was unfolded in silence and Jericho held it up for his team to see; it was the battle plan showing the first day of fighting at Gettysburg - a laminated photocopy taken from a very famous book of the battle - printed in 1986.

Jericho pushed the map into his coat; "Can you imagine if this map fell into Rebel hands - it would change the outcome of the battle - the war and world history in one foul blow."

"I don't want to state the obvious, but what the fuck was the map doing hidden in Clem Hazzard's apple pie?" Owen gave the boy some biscuits he had saved from breakfast and added; "There's only one person that could have placed it under the pie and why the hell would she do that?"

Jericho pulled the money bag from his coat pocket that McIves had left with him and tossed it in the air a couple of times, the coins rattling together; "These are the same ten silver dollar coins that I gave 'Strange ways' Stevens' yesterday and where did we last see him?"

"At Philadelphia's place." Owen said and sighed; "And that's where the pie came from."

"We've been played for suckers Jericho." Wilson sat on an upturned crate and shook his head with some sadness. The young deserter raised a bandaged hand nervously; "Do you mean doc Hazzard?" Alex nodded and the boy waved his injured hand about; "He fixed my hand up, a couple of days ago before I decided that the army wasn't for me. He's two friends gave him whisky for free and said that Captain Delaney would get the prize, when young black eyes turned up."

"Doc Hazzard was drinking with a confederate captain and two whisky drummers, is that what your saying?" Jericho asked the boy directly, who nodded yes vigorously, adding: "He said the south was about to rise again. I didn't understand that Sir, we ain't down yet!"

Alex saw the expression change on Jericho's face and that

puzzled her; "What's up Jericho?" She asked quietly and Jericho pulled her aside and whispered; "Oh yes, we've been played for suckers - but nothing is always what it seems." He actually grinned and tossed the boy a couple of silver dollars; "Get yourself some clothes that won't draw the attention of your Adjutant Generals men. Best you get out of the city on the quick. Go now!"

The boy pocketed the coins and profusely thanking everyone, disappeared through the rear door of the stables. Alex folded her arms and smiled at Jericho; "What have you just worked out; I see it on your face." Jericho shrugged his shoulders; "We best join that young boy and get out the city too." They left the stables and mounted up, heading out to the foothills.

6. THE GUNPOWDER PLOT.

It was Wilson who spotted the schoolhouse and a shabby timber-built bungalow standing some yards away. There was a single horse wagon tied up outside and Owen pointed out, that the two labourers who raised their hats to Alex and Wilson, had been loading the same wagon back in Gettysburg.

"They must have been collecting some supplies for Miss Lillian." He said and then noticed that the wagon was deep in the dirt. "It's certainly loaded with something heavy."

Jericho waved his group towards the buildings, and they tied their horses outside. "I can hear something; like a woman moaning." Owen lifted his hat and wiped his face. Jericho and Alex walked to the side window of the bungalow and peered through the dirty glass, whilst Owen and Wilson checked the wagon. Alex actually put her hand over her mouth to stop amazed laughter from blurting out.

Jericho just shook his head and smiled a little; Miss Lillian, a skinny thirty-year-old 'respectable', white schoolteacher was quite naked - apart from her ankle boots - sandwiched between the two black labourers, who oddly enough, were also stark naked, apart from their boots. She was now moaning loudly and shouting; that the boys should fuck her harder. Especially the one in her bum!

Alex and Jericho turned away and chuckled, as Wilson and Owen

Alex and Jericho turned away and chuckled, as Wilson and Owen approached - they were both grim faced - Wilson jerked a thumb towards the wagon; "You had better see what's under that canvas sheet Jericho." He asked Alex about what had made her laugh. She pointed to the window; "You best take a look." Alex giggled a little more, which intrigued Wilson and Owen, who both went straight to the window.

Alex and Jericho walked to the wagon and pulled the filthy canvas tarpaulin open a little and peered in. Jericho rubbed his chin and said quietly to Alex; "What the hell would a schoolteacher want with ten barrels of gunpowder; there's enough there to blow up a small town." They were joined by Wilson and Owen, laughing and wiping their faces; "That's one old white spinster that don't mind coloured folk!" Wilson managed to say between chuckles. Owen said nothing; he was still a bit shocked at what he had seen. Finally, he turned to Wilson and asked; "How is it possible....I mean doing it with two men at the same time?"

Alex patted Wilson on the shoulder and between giggles said; "We'll leave you to explain that one to our resident novice monk." They returned to their horses and rode a small distance from the settlement and dismounted. Jericho and the team concealed themselves in a clump of trees. They passed a brandy bottle amongst themselves and waited. It was about half an hour later that the two men emerged from the bungalow and climbed aboard the wagon.

They headed it south along Old Turner's Pike and their singing could be faintly heard. "There, at the rear of the bungalow." Owen suddenly rose from the trees and pointed down to the settlement. From the rear of the bungalow came a single rider; it was Miss Lillian, and she was following the wagon at a distance. "In this time and place, a white woman just being seen alone with black men could get her lynched." Jericho said grimly and they mounted up and followed the little convoy.

It stopped outside a small grey stone-built farmhouse and the two men jumped from the wagon and pulled back the tarpaulin. That's when Jericho and his team spotted the group of riders coming into the farmyard from the south lane.

Watching from a small ridge, Jericho pulled his mirror and

scanned the buildings and yards. "There doesn't appear to be anyone in the building - no wait - there's two men inside with shovels and crowbars!" His team was concealed by the ridge they hid behind but could see down into the small farm. "What the fuck are they doing?" Whispered Owen and then he gripped Jericho's arm; "Jericho, according to my mirror we're on Seminary Ridge; along the Chambersburg Pike and that's seems an important place during the forthcoming battle - my mirror has called it up - this house belongs to an old, widowed lady: Mary Thompson."

Jericho was watching the five riders dismounting and greeting Miss Lillian, who had now joined the group. "Well Sheriff Rook and his large deputy are two of them, who's the other three men?" Alex whispered to Jericho who suddenly sat up and asked Owen to repeat what he had just said; which he did.

Jericho wiped his face and pointed down to the house; "This house belongs to the widow Thompson and during the battle, it was the Headquarters of the Confederate Army of North Virginia. General Robert E. Lee will direct his army from here." Everyone sat in silence as they watched the barrels of gunpowder being unloaded. Large white grain sacks - empty - were also removed from the wagon by the two men and handed over to Sheriff Rook.

Wilson grunted; "Look there, those two men. One is tall and skinny and the other is short and fat. Do you think they are our whisky drummers?" Jericho nodded, he now had a pretty good idea of the plan was and it certainly wasn't about changing the outcome of the battle; the North will win here.

"They're filling the sacks with powder; very carefully, I must say." Alex spoke softly and realised she needed to pee. Muttering her excuses, headed for a thick clump of bushes to relieve herself. "Who is that fifth man?" Puzzled Owen and Wilson shook his head; "Dunno, but he's a big lad and carrying two pistols; a gunfighter?"

Their thoughts we interrupted by a stifled scream from Alex, who ran back from the bushes in some haste. She was still trying to pull down her dress and petticoats; so, everyone gained a glimpse of her thighs as she struggled with her clothes. "Now that's a pleasant treat." Murmured Wilson, grinning. "I've just pissed on a dead man!" She yelped and the group made their way to the clump of bushes, moving quickly, but keeping low.

It was the young confederate deserter, laying face up in the wet dirt - half concealed by loose branches and leaves - in one hand was an old, large 'Navy' pistol, the other lay across his open stomach. The intestines had spilled out and lay sprawled down his legs. There were several silver coins scattered about his body. "He must have been killed only a few hours ago, probably just after he left us." Alex said quietly, now recovered from the shock; her medical training had kicked in. She knelt down and examined the open wound. It was finely sliced, but deep.

She rose slowly; "He was killed with a large knife or maybe...." Wilson interrupted; "or a bloody sword and we know who carries one of those." They exchanged glances with the same thought; why would McIves kill the boy? Owen rubbed his face; "How the fuck does McIves do that?" He waved a hand at the boy; "I mean get so close to someone with a cocked pistol and kill them with a fucking sword, without being shot?"

No-one could answer that - not even Jericho - "Well it means that McIves has been here. But before the gunpowder turned up and why was he here?" Jericho pointed to the dead boy. "I had suspected that he was a 'plant', to foster suspicion against Clem Hazzard. The scrap piece of paper could easily have been placed in the pie tin after the pie was removed. Apparently eaten by the boy and left for us to find. Then that odd comment for a soldier deserting the Confederate army, do you remember it: "He [Clem Hazzard] said the south was about to rise again. I didn't understand that Sir, we ain't down yet!" Not the talk of someone about to walk away from the cause. I suspect that someone is playing a very clever game with us."

"Let's get to Clem Hazzard's place for now." Jericho added, staring down at the boy. He then spoke to Owen; "Call up Dispatches and find which Collector attended this dispatch [death] and find out what he said." They quietly returned to their horses and set off for Clem Hazzard's home

7. STUCK IN A BIG BATTLE.

They had crossed a small dirt road, between thin trees and broken fencing, when the first bullet struck a tree next to where

Owen was standing; adjusting the girth of his horse. Everyone fell from their horses and crawled into the tree's for cover as bullets started to slap into trees and bushes around them.

Wilson found some large stones to hide his bulk behind and was joined by Alex. "Who the fuck is doing all the shooting!" She shouted and bullets ricocheted off the stones and hit the bushes nearby. "Bloody rebels - lots of them - down by that old died up creek bed and they're coming this way." Wilson flipped onto his back and checked his pistol, then saw Jericho gesturing at them. He and Owen were hunkered down amongst some thick bushes - the ground around them kicked up - as bullets hit the dirt.

Wilson reached into his pocket and pulled out his vibrating mirror; it was Jericho calling; "No arguments - jump now. You really cannot become a prisoner of these people. Get to Clem's place when you jump back; you may need another horse. They seem to have all ran off." Wilson was about to argue about leaving, when Alex slapped his arm; "Get the fuck out of here; you know what these bastards will do to a captured Black man!"

Reluctantly he nodded his agreement and activated the mirror; he was gone in an instant and she snuggled closer to the rocks. Alex could see several armed men approaching the trees where they were sheltering; two carried rebel flags and one was clearly an officer; he carried a sword and was actually wearing a proper grey uniform.

Jericho yelled across to Alex; "Pull your skirts up and use your petticoat as a white flag!" The bullets were now flying thick as flies, so Alex grabbed up her dress and pulled down her frilly white petticoat, exposing her long legs and thighs. Owen groaned and shouted to Jericho; "Wilson won't be happy at missing that treat!" Jericho just shook his head and then noticed the firing had stopped - then he saw why - Alex was waving her white petticoat above her head, with her dress still pulled up!

"Clever boss; No man is going to shoot that." Owen actually grinned and with Jericho, rose from the bushes, hands in air. Alex was decent again, when they joined her with the Confederate Officer and a small group of soldiers; all very interested in introducing themselves to Alex. But the officer waved them away and spoke directly to Jericho; "Miss Alexandra tells me you are reporters from the Citizens Compiler Newspaper, based in Washington DC, covering the fighting here. I had heard tell from the town, that there were some nosey Yankee reporters hanging about the place."

"That's us Sir; we're covering the war for our readers up North. But we appear to have lost our cameraman and our damn horses. You can't miss him - a big coloured man - who's a freeman and well spoken." Jericho removed his hat and wiped his brow; "As I say Sir, he's a free born man of colour."

The officer just grunted; "If he's a n****r - then he's a slave. I don't go for any of this 'freeman' shit; he's contraband," The officer pushed his sword back into its scabbard and called over for the sergeant. Jericho was impressed that Alex kept her tongue firmly in her mouth; especially with the look she gave the rebel officer.

"Grab a couple of boys and take these Yankee reporters to Captain Delaney; he'll know what to do with them." The officer lifted his hat to Alex and re-joined his men, who were forming up in the dried Creek Bed. Jericho watched as the officer spoke to two men and they joined the sergeant. The old sergeant shouldered his musket and with the two scruffy men - one had no shoes - ordered the reporters to follow him; with hands on heads.

"That name rings a bell." Whispered Owen to Jericho and Alex; "Wasn't that the name of the rebel captain that the deserter mentioned, I mean the one talking to Clem Hazzard?" Jericho nodded; yes. But was watching the quiet conversation between the two men, one had pulled a coin out and tossed it in the air. Jericho turned to Alex and said quietly; "I don't think they're taking us to their captain. I think we will never make the rebel encampment." She nodded her agreement; "We need to reach our mirrors; how do we do that with our hands up?" She whispered, then clearly heard one of the soldiers laughing about 'going first'.

Jericho and Alex exchanged glances; "Distraction time....and press that button as quickly as you can." Alex sighed and suddenly broke step, groaning and grabbing her ankle; she slid to the dirt, moaning about her ankle. The shoeless soldier pointed his musket - with bayonet attached - straight at her; "Get up you Yankee trollop." He said quietly.

Alex babbled on about her ankle and pointed to it, as she pulled
her skirt right up - not forgetting she had removed her petticoat
earlier - The soldier was getting a first class, close up look at
what was on offer. He lowered the musket a little and smiled.
The other soldier pushed him shouting; "I won the fucking toss,
she's mine first."

The sergeant pushed between the two but said nothing as the
roar of cannon drowned out any thinking or speaking. The ground
was moving with shell fire, with dirt thrown up several feet into
the air; the noise was unbearable. There was no time to do
anything except find cover.

Jericho grabbed Alex and together they fell down a small incline
and scrambled for a horseshoe shaped group of rocks and dived
in. "Where's Owen?" Alex shouted above the noise of the
bombardment. Jericho didn't know and could now see lines of
blue soldiers appearing; hundreds of them.

"The bloody battle has started!" He shouted and added; "We
appear to be in the middle of a bloody big battle, and I mean a
big battle!" He pulled his mirror out and jabbed at the emergency
icon; he, Alex and Owen were returned instantly to outside the
lighthouse.

"They're all dead. The soldiers that were escorting us, they were
caught by the cannon fire. I saw it happen; bloody awful." Owen
was brushing dirt from his clothes, and he still looked a little
shocked by what he had just witnessed. Alex gave him her
hipflask and wiped his face with a hankie. It had little splatters of
blood from the three soldiers. "There wasn't much left of them."
He whispered to Alex and took a big swig from the hipflask.

"Wilson's calling." Jericho muttered and answered his mirror,
after a few minutes he looked up; "Well, Wilson has made
contact with Clem, and we must return at once."

8. THAT'S NOT HISTORY.

From a small group of trees, Jericho, Alex and Owen sat and
watched the sky. It was filled with whistling cannon fire and
screaming of shells, as both armies clashed in the fields and
roads of Gettysburg. Owen was keeping an eye on the small dirt
road which lay behind the trees; "Nothing yet." He wiped sweat

from his face with a gaudy red hankie and grinned at Alex; "Poor old Wilson missed the best bit - you'll have to hitch up your skirts again - so that he doesn't feel left out." He chuckled and checked his mirror.

Alex simply ignored him and spoke to Jericho; "I did wonder why old Sheriff Rook took the trouble to tell us about Miss Lillian and her supposed strange story that we would be interested in." Jericho nodded; "Well he couldn't really tell us directly that the lady was involved in a gunpowder plot to blow up the rebel HQ. What intrigues me is who told the conspirators, that the rebels would use the widow Thompson's house during the battle; that type of knowledge could only have come from time-travelers." Alex had to agree with that and wondered when Wilson would turn up with the wagon, she didn't wait long. "They're here." Owen rose from the damp dirt and brushed his trousers down. Alex did the same with her dress and straightened her bonnet. Jericho gestured towards the approaching wagon and keeping low, they quickly departed the trees for the dirt road.

They were clad to see Wilson and watched with great interest as Jericho and Clem Hazzard stood under a large tree and discussed some matters, for several minutes. Finally, they walked back towards the wagon. Alex whispered to Owen; "I'd love to have been a fly on that tree."They joined Wilson; climbing aboard the canvas covered wagon, on which someone had painted - in black tar - 'Hospital' on both sides. A single brown horse with a saddle was tied behind it with bulging saddlebags. Clem helped Alex aboard and she smiled to herself, as Clem Hazzard kissed her hand and asked her about being a female doctor; he was good looking and charming.

Philadelphia was a lucky lady, she mused and asked Clem about the full saddlebags. "Medical supplies, I think I may need them." He explained with a smile. Wilson slapped the reins and the horses pulled away. Owen was impressed; the big man knew how to drive a two-horse wagon. Wilson spoke quietly with Jericho; "Sheriff Rook has no great love for the Yankee's, but he doesn't think much of the Confederates either. He found out about the gunpowder plot from 'Strange ways Stevens', who got drunk one night whilst playing poker with the sheriff and his brother-in-law; he blabbered out every detail. Luckily Sheriff Rook didn't pay any attention to his talk about 'small & tall' being time travelers."

Jericho nodded; "Why Miss Lillian?" Wilson smiled at that comment; "Pillow talk. It appears that the respectable School Ma'am really does like cock. 'Small & Tall' serviced her – together - she became part of their plan to blow up General Lee. It was her that told 'Strange ways' of the plot - he was yet another lover - and introduced him to 'small & tall'. Apparently, it was him who told 'small & tall' about a certain Jericho Tibbs; for money. So they arranged for one of their number [Black eyed Benny] to knock you off; when you arrived. 'Strange ways' would give them the nod."

"Bastard traitor." Muttered Owen and then smiled; "Fancy old Miss Lillian being a sexually liberated woman long before it was invented." Jericho turned round; "Say that again." Owen shrugged his shoulders and repeated what he had said. Alex smiled at Jericho; "You have that annoyingly 'I know' look on your face."

Jericho just smiled and pulled his mirror out. "Why didn't the Sheriff arrest the fuckers; if he knew about the plot?" Owen asked and passed his hipflask round the little group. Clem Hazzard answered that one;" When the Sheriff had obtained all the details, he wondered who to call. But who could he call? The Northern Army wouldn't be exactly unhappy if General Robert E. Lee disappeared in a puff of smoke. The Confederates? He doesn't hold with their principles, and he already had a run-in with Captain Delaney over the death of 'Black eyed Benny'. So he did some exemplary police work for an ex-cattleman; he infiltrated the group to find out more."

Jericho rubbed his chin; "Clem, what was the 'run in' between Captain Delaney and the Sheriff over the dead gunman?" Clem waved away the offered hip-flask - he didn't touch alcohol - and settled back in the jolting wagon; "He wanted the Sheriff to raise a posse and get after McIves, he really wasn't happy about the death of 'Black eyed Benny'. I saw the reason when the Sheriff had me examine the boy's body. The Sheriff refused his request point blank; he wasn't about to take out a group of armed men, when they were surrounded by two enormous trigger-happy armies."

Alex sipped at the hipflask; ""What was the reason you saw?" She asked Clem and passed the hipflask to Wilson. Clem sighed; "It was realised by everyone who saw the body; the family resemblance between the two - Delaney and Benny - was really obvious, two peas' in a pod." Jericho looked up from his mirror. "Delaney is of this time; he's a known historical figure. But we know that Benny was from 2016, he had to be a descendant of the captain." Jericho looked out the wagon, you could still see cannon fire and hear fighting in the distance; tomorrow would be the second day of battle.

He turned back to his team; "Miss Lillian Scott is the key to all this." and returned to his mirror. Everyone exchanged glances and Alex just had to ask; "How so Jericho?"

Jericho smiled; "Miss Scott hails from Delaware and probably breached the timeline in 2016 with our nasty little friend Benny; who is her oldest son by the way. Young Benny Scott was on the run for murder in 2016 and his darling mother knew the best place to hide him and where, he would be useful to her plans. None of them counted on McIves appearing on the scene."

"How did you get onto her?" Wilson sounded a little amazed and Jericho jerked a thumb at Owen; "He told me." Everyone stared at Owen who simply shrugged his shoulders; "What the hell did I say?" he asked. Jericho chuckled; "You said, 'Fancy old Miss Lillian being a sexually liberated woman long before it was invented' - and of course -remember, the Sheriff stated that she hadn't been around here long. I looked her up and found she wasn't from this time."

He pushed his mirror back into his coat pocket; "According to Human Records, she was born in 1975, got married, had three children and guess who was the oldest?" He smiled at his team; "All three children were not by her estranged husband and that poor sap is a teacher of History and surprise, surprise, he is an indirect descendant of the Confederate General James Longstreet, who, if her plan went right, would be standing next to General Lee, when the bloody house disappears in a big explosion."

"Holy fucking shit, she wanted to bump off her estranged husband before he was even fucking born!" Owen exclaimed; "Now that's one way to get away with murder." Alex smiled; "And it would not affect the outcome of the battle and thus the North would still win the civil war, would it not?"

"What is now of equal importance, to us anyway, is finding how Miss Lillian and her murdering brat managed to jump through time and arrive here." Jericho turned to Clem, adding: "Any ideas on that would be welcome." Clem leaned back against the side of the wagon and blew his nose into a clean white hankie. "Delaney has a strange object stored in his travelling chest. I heard from his young soldier servant whose hand I fixed up, that he keeps it hidden. But the boy caught sight of it once when cleaning up in his tent. I don't know if this makes sense to any of you, but it was a human skull made of glass - beautiful but strange."

Jericho sighed; "A 'Da Vinci skull' - there were seven originally - I know we have recovered three, but there is still four out there and this must be one of them. They are 'free time portals' and they can take a living human to any place in history, provided you have a key to fix the time you want to visit."

Wilson coughed and waved a hand about; "They are named after the great man himself because it's suspected that he used one. But they have a big drawback; you must have another object from the time you wish to visit, so logically, they can only take you backwards in history. After all, few living humans possess stuff from the future."

"Miss Lillian's husband was well into history and may have possessed relics from his ancestor from this time. All she had to do was match it with a 'Da Vinci' skull and she's away." Owen reasoned and sipped a little brandy.

Jericho turned again to Clem; "Best tell them about the messenger pies." and chuckled. "When I was called to cover old Doc Hogan, Miss Lillian was the one who conveyed the request. Being a kindly lady - apparently - she stayed with Philly and helped her bake some pies. She placed another copy of the map under the cooked pie that Philly was going to send to me. What she didn't realise was that Philly helped me with my assignments from Jericho and Philly caught on. So, Philly placed a message under your pie; you just didn't eat the damn thing quickly enough!"

Owen folded his arms; "Why put the map in your dish, if you were loyal to Jericho, that doesn't make sense?" Alex had to nod her agreement with that.

Clem chuckled; "Miss Lillian knew that she, Captain Delaney and old Doc Hogan would be enjoying the pie after our dinner together and she would be serving the meal. She could retrieve the new map, without any danger of her being caught with it, and pass it onto Delaney, who was her direct ancestor and whose descendant - according to Jericho's search of Human Records - was her lover and father of her first child; that bastard 'Black eyed Benny'."

He grinned and held up his hands; "She also had the delicious irony, that dumb Temporal Detectives would be responsible for delivering the map that would change the battle. It didn't matter if the great general Lee and Longstreet were killed. Any of the other Confederate generals could, following a bloody map like that, turn the battle, if necessary. But there was a huge fly in their pudding, and they had to deal with that." Clem looked at Jericho, who took up the story:

"She had to get rid of her husband's ancestor by killing Longstreet, but she still needed the North to win because somehow, Delaney must survive the war and produce descendants; her being one of them. Had the North lost here, the war would have dragged on for another four years with the North still winning in the end. The good Captain Delaney would have had a very, almost certain chance of being killed in the much longer conflict. I checked with the Senior Time Controller about the alternative time-line, that extended war would have produced and there is no Miss Lillian Scott of Delaware." Jericho smiled and accepted the hipflask from Owen.

"Now you don't read about this in the bloody history books." Chuckled Owen, but Alex voiced her concerns; "Who are 'small & tall' and what the hell are they trying to achieve? Wilson coughed; "Never mind them; who was the bloody big fly in their pudding?"

Clem smiled and spoke softly; "'Black eyed Benny' had taken ten silver dollars off Delaney to kill Jericho, but I met up with McIves; he was passing through to Washington on matters that he didn't talk about. I told him what Delaney had arranged with Benny about Jericho's murder and he muttered that he had a debt to pay to Jericho and said he would deal with it and he did. He became a big fly in their pudding because that could wreck their plans, if Jericho was still around."

"Now for small, tall and Miss Lillian." Muttered Jericho, as the widow's Thompson's house came into view - the confederates had not occupied it yet. Union forces were encamped there - for the moment - Doctor Clem Hazzard unfurled the Union Flag and Flew it from the 'hospital' wagon.

9. ONE MOMENT IN TIME.

The Union picket watched the wagon approach quite carefully; this was a quiet sector of the battle - at the moment - but they wouldn't take any chances. They raised their muskets and shouted for the wagon to stop.

Jericho and Clem jumped from the wagon and walked slowly to the soldiers. Wilson turned to the others and grinned; "Our boss is a clever old bugger; just watch."

Alex and Owen smiled as the soldiers saluted Jericho and called for their officer. "What the fuck!" Owen seemed quite amazed by this turn of events. Alex just shook her head and smiled. The wagon was waved forward, and the picket soldiers raised their hats to Alex with shouts of; "Welcome Ma'am!"

They met the officer some way from the farmhouse - just in case - The officer carefully checked the badges and papers shown to him by Jericho and Clem. "I'd heard that General Meade had set up such a group and called it 'Military Intelligence', but never thought I'd meet any of them!" The officer smiled and listened intently, as Jericho outlined the dastardly rebel plan to blow up General Meade, while he stayed at the farmhouse. He immediately ordered a search of the farmhouse - a very quiet and careful search - and was absolutely astonished to find the bags of gunpowder beneath the floorboards.

Jericho also advised him to search on the small ridge; because there was the body of brave and committed confederate soldier, who had been hiding, ready to set the explosives off. Clem admitted that one of their operatives had already dealt with him, finishing him quietly; with no shooting to raise the alarm.

A corporal from the Union picket found the body and signaled its finding from the ridge. They watched as the barrels were removed and the officer shook Jericho and Clem's hands vigorously. They celebrated by passing a brandy bottle amongst themselves; the young officer really enjoyed that, and he got to chat with Alex for some minutes; giving her his card and telling her to look him up, next time she was in Boston. They said their farewells and the wagon passed down The Chambersburg Pike towards the Union Army positions. That's when Wilson spotted the solitary horseman approaching; you couldn't really miss him; he was wearing a vivid yellow dust coat. "McIves." Alex whispered to Owen and the wagon pulled up.

McIves wiped dirt from his face and grinned broadly at Jericho and raised his hat to Alex. "So, you managed to dodge murder, execution and being blown up." McInes spoke to Jericho, who shook his hand. "What do you know of the pair called 'Too Tall and Way small'?" Jericho asked. McIves chuckled; "Sheriff Rook went after them after the explosives were discovered and thus he now has a free hand to deal with everything. He was a little astonished, that they escaped from him, despite being surrounded in a livery stable. He couldn't believe that they just vanished. All I know about that strange pair is that were from Scotland - originally - and they had some kind of connection with Captain Delaney."

Jericho sighed; he really wanted to catch up with that pair, but he asked about Miss Lillian. McIves's expression changed; "She and 'Strange ways' were caught by rebel troops just north of the town. They were camped down for the night, when the rebels surprised them. That bloody idiot 'Strange ways' pulled his pistol and was shot about four times by musket fire. The rebels searched the wagon and found Miss Lillian with two coloured men - unfortunately in a state of undress - The rebels didn't show any mercy; they lynched the two coloured lads and then shot Miss Lillian; after tying her to a big tree." McIves wiped his face and accepted Alex's hipflask.

He continued; "At least they had the decency to bury them near 'Small Round top'. I heard it from a drunken Confederate soldier that the officer in charge; a certain Major Cantor hated women and coloured people in equal measure. Apparently, he took great pleasure in the killings." He swigged the hipflask and handed it back; thanking Alex.

Wilson interrupted and tapped his mirror; "A collector filed a report about collecting my two 'brothers' souls at the time, but, obviously, not Miss Lillian's. Here's the interesting bit; there was no collection listed for a 'Thomas Louis 'Strange ways' Stevens' at the time; he wasn't dead. Somehow, he survived a multiple shooting! His soul wasn't collected for another year; in August 1864 to be exact."

McIves grunted; "The devil looks after his own." He jerked a thumb behind him, adding; "The rebels are now approaching here fast. I understand that old granny Lee himself is moving his HQ this way; towards the widow Thompson's place."

Alex leaned forward in the wagon and asked Jericho about the Union picket still at the farmhouse. Jericho didn't smile; "The rebels take the place after some fighting. None of the Union picket survives that scrap. That's how come the history books, say nothing of the Gettysburg Gunpowder plot - there was no-one left alive to tell the story - it was just one moment in time that went unrecorded."

"But what about Sheriff Rook; he knew all about it." Owen asked a little puzzled. Jericho nodded and folded his arms; "The Sheriff and his deputy, who were present at the farmhouse with the gunpowder, never told a soul about their involvement. They really didn't want the occupying Union forces to know that they thwarted a plot to blow up General Lee - they feared reprisals. But it didn't matter; just weeks after the battle, Rook and his over sized deputy were killed by renegade Union deserters, who were raiding the countryside around here. They took the story to their graves."Wilson leaned back on the wagon seat and rubbed his chin; "What about that gunfighter, we saw with the Sheriff at the unloading of the gunpowder; the fellow with two pistols?" Jericho shook his head; "History doesn't record his involvement; he must have stayed silent about the affair."

McIves had suddenly become interested in Wilson's words and asked him; "Was he a big man, with two white handled pistols; the handles pointing away from him?"

Wilson nodded. McIves sat up in his saddle; "Keep an eye out for him Jericho. Had you searched his travelling bags, you would have found a strange Aztec Statue. He used to be an bloody Archaeologist who went by the name of Doctor Sage Columbine. Sometime in the 1920's, he discovered the statute at some dig in Mexico; it's a free travel portal and he's been using it ever since. I've encountered him a couple of times in other eras. He's a strange dark character."

McIves expressed his goodbyes and disappeared down the road; heading towards the Union lines. Wilson turned to Alex; "And our friend would know all about objects that carry 'free time portals'. That bloody black sword is cursed with one." Alex agreed with Wilson's deduction; she had suspected it for some time. Then glanced at Jericho - deep in conversation with Clem Hazzard - and wondered why he hadn't dealt with the matter.

Everyone said farewell to Clem, who would take his horse into Gettysburg and offer his assistance to the Union Surgical Unit, now working there; with a wave, he disappeared towards the Union lines.

10. THE 'DA VINCI' SKULL.

Jericho told Wilson to head for the rebel lines, the back way! "You get everything I asked for?" Jericho asked Wilson, who nodded and told Owen to unwrap the canvas bundle under his seat. Owen pulled it through into the wagon and pulled it open. Alex just had to smile; "I take it we're going after that damn skull." Jericho chuckled; "Well, we can't leave the bloody thing laying around here, especially since Delaney knows what it's capable of."

By the time the 'hospital' wagon reached the rebel encampment, the team had acquired their new identities. Jericho was now a Surgeon in the Confederate Army with the rank of Captain; his uniform even had authentic looking blood stains and he smelt strongly of chloroform!

Owen was wearing an ill-fitting and shabby Confederate uniform complete with old boots and 'medical orderly' armband. Wilson was unchanged; he was the good 'Doctor's' Negro man servant and cook. He didn't have to dress up for that role. Miss Alexandra was now a Southern 'Belle' with blood-stained apron and her hair tied up - she was a certain Captain Joe 'Shamrock' Delaney's sister from Virginia - and had a pass from General James Longstreet to prove it!

They were stopped by several rebel soldiers guarding the dirt road into the camp and everyone was immediately impressed by Jericho's accent. He wearily explained to the sergeant, that he had to escort this lady to her brother on Jim Longstreet's orders, then make his way to the field hospital. He produced the pass and the sergeant examined it closely. But it was the skinny, younger man with pebble glasses that could actually read and agreed that was Longstreet's signature and the stamp was true. The sergeant called a young officer over to the group and explained about the pass. The young man bowed and lifted his hat to Alex and told her that he would personally escort her to her brother's tent. Owen helped Alex down and volunteered to carry her travelling case for her, which was gracefully received.

Jericho and Wilson would wait with the wagon, near the cookhouse tents for the pair's return. They reached Captain Delaney's tent a few minutes later and the officer said farewell - reluctantly - to Alex, kissing her hand and bowing.

Alex and Owen didn't waste any time searching the tent and pulled Delaney's travelling chest from under some horse blankets. Owen carefully opened the trunk and gently pulled the dark cloth back to reveal the eerie glass skull. "It's quite beautiful." Alex muttered and Owen carefully placed it into his canvas bag and covered it with a soft towel.

Alex pushed back the tent flap and stared about, then signalled Owen and the pair made for the Cookhouse tents, where several hundred men were starting to queue for their meals. Several cheered and waved at her; she returned a little lady-like wave and received even more cheers.

Jericho looked about and pressed the Travel App on his mirror and the team found themselves outside the lighthouse on a warm summer night. A three-mast sailing ship could be seen on the horizon. Alex noted that the time was 7.35pm; as it always was.

As they walked to the lighthouse, Owen suddenly remembered the assignment Jericho had given him regarding the dead confederate deserter and he pulled Alex to one side; "Should I bother to give Jericho the story, that the young dead deserter told Little Kate the Collector?" Alex shrugged her shoulders; "Seems a bit pointless now, but what was it?"

Owen sighed; "Well, he said that he was betrayed and the bugger with him pulled out a 'Bowie' knife and gutted him before he could use his pistol. They were on the ridge together; waiting for Miss Lillian and the wagon." Alex looked puzzled; "So McIves didn't kill him?"

Owen nodded; "Nah, he didn't. it was 'Strangways' that knifed him, came up from behind and gutted him like a fish - even with the pistol cocked - the boy never suspected that his companion would do such a thing - they were conspirators together.

'Strangways' dropped his money bag with all those silver dollars in, during the fight. He couldn't stop and pick them up because someone else had appeared." Owen started to walk to the lighthouse; arm in arm with Alex.

Alex remembered the coins scattered about the boy's body and no-one had questioned why they were there! She stopped; "So those coins were from Jericho, he gave 'Strange ways' them at the farmhouse. We should have guessed that 'Strange ways' had done the killing by the presence of those damn coins. We could have known about the two-timing rat earlier."

Owen nodded and continued with the story that the boy had recounted to the Collector; "The boy - whose name was Jacob Sanderson from Mississippi - had been working for Captain Delaney, posing as a deserter to infiltrate a nest of Union spies; that was us by the way. He was told to acquire the pie at all costs because the little dinner party, arranged for the delivery of the pie, had to be called off because they suspected Rook was on to them - especially after the row between Delaney and Rook over Benny. But hunger got the best of him and he ate the bloody thing and suddenly, we were onto him."

Jericho turned and gestured for Owen and Alex to catch up; dinner was roast lamb tonight. Alex said quietly; "What was he and 'Strange ways' doing on the ridge and who turned up after he had been killed?"

Owen gripped her arm and smiled, in that dumb manner that infuriated Wilson; "They were going to blow up the house after everyone had set the explosives and gone. Someone [the boy didn't know who] had paid 'Strange ways' to carry it out. He [Jacob] thought it was Captain Delaney because he turned up on the ridge after the boy was murdered. He couldn't see what the captain did because the Collector took his soul then. But the odd thing is, the captain didn't set the explosives off because we know that the ill-fated Union picket removed them later; now that's a strange twist, eh?"

Alex sighed; "Also, why didn't Delaney pick up the silver dollars and if 'Strange ways' was in collusion with him; why did he run off so fast that he didn't pick up the money? And what was Delaney going to do with that dam glass skull?" She believed that there was more to this mission than had been worked out and should Jericho hear about what Owen discovered; would it alter the results achieved by the team?

The captain must have returned to the farmhouse for some reason and why pay Steven's to blow up the damn place before anyone was even in it? Alex sighed and the thoughts swirled about her head. They followed Jericho and Wilson into the lighthouse, and she smiled to herself; there could be a very lively dinner conversation tonight!

THE END

EPILOGUE:

"Whilst there was little chance of the current human timeline being changed; if the plot to kill General Robert E. Lee had succeeded, there could, still have been many unwanted - and potentially dangerous - changes to the time line further down its length. On the balance of things, the mission was considered a success for Team 74."
SJW.

CHARACTERS:

Frank Turner, the Confederate Army Sergeant who found young Benny's body and the strange map [to him] was killed during 'Picket's Charge' on the last day of battle. His soul was collected and processed.

Joseph Francis 'Shamrock' Delaney, the Confederate Army Captain who was part of the plot to blow up the farmhouse, survived the war and married a local Doctor's daughter and settled down in Ridgeway, Maine. He had several children and died in 1881. He never mentioned or wrote about the Gunpowder plot. He was known to be a historical figure of that period and it was with great surprise, that no soul was collected. Inspector

Kate Zaskinsky of Team 44 has been tasked with the investigation: there is no resolution yet.

Sage Columbine, the Confederate Army Scout was a time-traveler from 1925 and his dealings with the Gunpowder plot remain a mystery. He is known to McIves [another time traveler] and his whereabouts - currently - are unknown. He remains a missing soul.

Doctor Clement Aaron Hazzard, Jericho's human agent for this time and place survived the war, but not his infidelity with a certain woman who had became the new teacher. Her husband found the pair in bed together and shot both dead. He was hanged for those murders despite a massive protest against the sentence. Clem's soul was collected and processed; his wife didn't attend the funeral.

Mrs. Philadelphia Hazzard, another of Jericho's human agents for the time and place continued to work for Jericho after her husband's unsavoury death. She remarried in 1869 and had three children. She died in 1884 and her soul was collected and processed. Jericho and Alex attended her funeral.

Thomas Louis 'Strangways' Stevens had been Jericho's part time human agent for the time and place. He had been shot in 1863 but survived for another year before succumbing to his injuries. Jericho himself attended the collection of his soul, but 'Strange ways' would say nothing about his actions during the Gettysburg Gunpowder plot. He was quarantined until 2150.

Alexander McIves is a persistent time-traveler and well known to Jericho and Team 74. He has habit of 'popping' up on some of Jericho's missions and even assisting them on occasion! He remains an elusive fugitive from the Temporal Detectives Department and his soul is still missing to this day.

Miss Victoria Crabb couldn't keep a civil tongue and in late spring 1868, she spoke the wrong words to the wrong man; a hard-faced ex-soldier from Richmond. He took great exception to what she said and that night, broke into her room. He tied up Miss Crabb and raped her quite brutally. The suspect fled the scene and was never captured - it was believed he had crossed into Mexico. Months later Victoria Crabb died in childbirth and her soul was collected and processed. The child survived and grew up in a

Catholic orphanage, becoming a Priest and working the missions in West Africa. He was a popular and much-loved padre.

Jacob 'pudding' Davis, Sheriff Rook's Deputy was killed, with the sheriff, just after the battle by Union Army deserters. His soul was collected and processed.

Lieutenant Tom Harvey - Confederate Army - never survived the battle. He was killed during 'Picket's Charge' on the last day of fighting. He was twenty years old. His soul was collected and processed.

Billy Logan - the unpleasant dirt farmer - new to the town, tried to flee with his family before the battle started; unfortunately, some renegade Union soldiers took pot shots at him and he was killed - shot off his horse - they robbed his wagon, stole the horses, and raped his young wife. His soul was collected and processed.

Troy and Dauphin Washington were two brothers who were slaves to the local Hardware merchant - the slave brothers were also Miss Lillian's lovers and they paid for that with their lives. Major Cantor hung the pair when he found them with her. Their souls were collected and processed.

Miss Lillian Scott's audacious plan to rid herself of her husband cost her dearly; her life and soul. She was a human who had died out of her own time and so; no soul was collected. It remains missing to this day.

Benjamin 'Black eyed Benny' Scott had jumped back to 1863 with his mother Lillian to avoid arrest for murder and assist in her plot to alter her estranged husband's fate. Unfortunately, he encountered 'Black Sword' and was killed. His soul was not collected, since he was a human out of his own time and remains missing to this day.

Thomas Arthur Brady, the café owner in Gettysburg, survived the war but died in a Dysentery outbreak in 1867. His soul was collected and processed.

Sheriff Theodore Rook took the story of the 'Gunpowder Plot' to his grave. He was killed by renegade Union soldiers who had deserted and were now raiding his district. For all his faults, he did try to do his job! His soul was collected and processed.

Jacob Sanderson - A Confederate Army Private was killed on the ridge after playing the deserter for Captain Delaney - he was sixteen years old. His soul was collected and processed.

Michael Edward Cantor, the Confederate Army Major who brutally executed Miss Lillian and the two slave brothers; Troy and Dauphin Washington, survived the war and became mayor of his local town and a senior member of the local KKK. He was known to have murdered over twenty coloured people in the troubled times following the civil war. He died at 73 surrounded by his children and grandchildren. His soul was collected and quarantined until 2600.

Peter Frederick Keppel, the young Union Army Lieutenant, who was killed when the Confederate Army took his position at the farmhouse, had his soul collected and processed. But several months after the battle, when his effects were returned to his grieving mother, she discovered his final letter written on that fatal day. He described the plot in detail and confided to his mother that at last; he had found the sort of woman that would do her son proud. His mother was so embittered with grief that she destroyed the letter in anger, thus the 'Betrayal at Gettysburg' never appeared in official history of the Civil War.

EPISODE 7: "HOBBS ABBEY AND THE DEVIL'S GRAVEYARD."

MISSION SUMMARY:
"In the summer of 1970, a small team of student archaeologists have a field trip for ten days to the ruins of Hobbs Abbey; a ancient place steeped in legends and tales of the paranormal; mostly about the Devil and his demons. Local folklore has whispered for centuries, that the Monk's of Hobbs Abbey were always specially selected; to guard a terrible secret hidden about the Abbey grounds. But this summer is special: It is the 666th Anniversary of the Abbey's founding and has something sinister come to celebrate?"

NOTES: This episode contains strong sexual references and references to witchcraft & Demonic activity.

**ALCOHOL, VIOLENCE, STRONG SEXUAL REFERENCES, STRONG LANGUAGE & MILD HORROR.**

**AGE 15+ ONLY.**   **30 Minutes reading time.**

1. CONVOY.
Clare started to brake slowly as the blue flashing lights appeared to grow larger in her extended; driver's side door mirror, [fitted because she was towing a caravan] and Dave peered out the passenger side window, but couldn't see past the drab, olive

coloured caravan. He called up the other two cars on the crackling 'walkie-talkie', telling them about the police vehicle.

"I think the bloody batteries need changing." Dave muttered and wondered where they could find a plug socket in the middle of nowhere. At least they had purchased extra batteries from the Army Surplus store in York before setting out.

Clare stopped on some gravel, which was thrown around a Farmer's padlocked gate and waited; "I'll bet ten shillings that the coppers think we're bloody gypsies!" Dave laughed and certainly wouldn't take that bet. He knew how the police liked to harass travelers and grunting, he managed to get the rusty passenger door open, then stepped out and now could see two Constables walking towards them.

Dave glanced up the tight country road and could see that the Professor and Doctor Shaw were making their way back to join them on foot. Clare joined him on the verge, clutching her little red Driving License and searching her crocheted, flowery handbag; "I know the bloody M.O.T. and Insurance is in here somewhere." She muttered, but Dave laughed;" You'll probably find a Dining table in that thing, you've got so much crap in there." The pair looked like a couple of hippies, but were dressed like most young people were; in this summer of 1970.

The two Policemen gave the pair a curious look; "They don't look much like bleeding Gypsies." The younger Policeman said quietly and pulled his little black notebook out and copied down the vehicle Registration plate.

The much older Policeman just nodded and pushed his cap back; "Bloody students." He said simply and sighed. Professor Theodore Hemmings now joined the little group and introduced himself to the officers, with a smile and handshakes. The two policemen listened with very little interest, as the Professor explained about the ten-day field trip for his Archaeological students, until he mentioned Hobbs Abbey Ruins. The older officer stopped the Professor in mid-sentence and didn't appear to be happy about them digging around the ruined Abbey.

"I've been around here all my life, born in Hempstead village, some ten miles down that road, and I wouldn't dig around those ruins for a gold-plated bed!" The old policeman shook his head and rubbed his chin as Dr. Shaw asked for the quickest way to the ruins. Constable Jones sighed and shrugged his shoulders; "You know the stories about that place and so it's on your own heads." He then gestured down a dark, leafy lane that forked left by the rusting bus stop.

"That's Bell's Lane, run down that for a couple miles and you'll come to Hobbs Wood. Beyond that lies the Abbey, There's good ground north of the ruins for your cars and the caravans. But if you take my advice, you'll head back home now and forget about all this." He advised with clear reluctance in his voice.

The Professor thanked the Constables, and everyone returned to their vehicles and the little convoy now headed down Bell's Lane towards the Abbey. The Morris 'Oxford' estate car bumped and swayed down the rough little lane and Clare gripped the wheel tightly, while Dave kept an eye on the little caravan, who was rolling like a ship at sea; "I bet Max loves all that bumping about, he had quite a hangover this morning." He grinned and pulled a packet of 'Players No.6' from his Safari shirt pocket and lit up a cigarette.

"He shouldn't be asleep in there; it's dangerous; what if we had an accident, that caravan would fold up like paper." Clare could see the brake lights coming on in front of her; "We must be there by now." She added, realising that the woods were unusually dark, with little of the late afternoon sunshine, filtering through the dense trees.

She actually shuddered a little; "I've got bloody goose-bumps, give us a fag Dave." The two cars and the Bedford J4 van driven by 'Little Mickey' formed a circle on the good ground and everyone started to unhitch the caravans and push them into shaded positions.

2. THE ABBEY RUINS.

The ruins of the old Abbey dominated the skyline, and it looked quite beautiful in the evening sunshine. Clare grabbed a couple of her cameras and snapped away, then slowly she lifted her eyes from the camera and stared across at the Abbey.

Dave caught the strange look upon her face and tapped her shoulder: "What's up?"

Clare lowered the camera and looked puzzled; "I thought I saw someone standing by that old wall – where the remains of that gateway are - but there's nothing there." Dave turned to Dr. Shaw and asked if she knew where the gateway went.

"Monk's old burial grounds." She replied and continued to unhitch the caravan from the Professor's Rover P7 car. Clare and Dave exchanged glances and then both chuckled. "We've been here bloody ten minutes and already seeing ghosts!" Clare smiled and replaced her cameras upon the car's rear seat, which was strewn with camera boxes, packets of film, lenses, bags of clothes and tinned food – not forgetting 'Jester' - Clare's large fat cat.

Dave peered in and shook his head; "Why did you bring the damn cat?" with some puzzlement in his voice. Clare sighed and reaching in, stroked the big cat gently; "My neighbours are on holiday in Scotland, and they normally take him when I do field trips, so he's having a field trip of his own this time!"

'Little Mickey' was dumping the digging gear, surveying equipment and canvas covers upon the ground, heaving them from the back of his van with little effort. Doctor Shaw was checking them over with a careful eye and penciling items in her little red notebook. The professor had lit his pipe and stood watching the last of the day's sunshine playing upon the Abbey ruins.

"That young copper said there was a pub down Gallows Lane that did good food in the evening, and it serves a decent pint of Guinness." Dave spoke with some enthusiasm, realising he hadn't eaten since the two fried egg sandwiches this morning. It was universally agreed that a trip to 'The King's Head' was a really great way to start the field trip.

Max had climbed from Clare's caravan and stood stretching and yawning; "I'll have a quick wash and brush up and be ready A.S.A.P." He grinned, and then asked Dave if he could lend him a couple of quid for the night, oh, and could he bum a couple of cigarettes also.

Maxwell Richard Alexander Victor Halls-Canton was the second son [the spare one] of the 9th Duke of Sommerton and looked and dressed like a penniless hippie. The fact was, Max normally didn't have a penny to his name for most of the month [until his father's allowance cheque cleared at the Bank] then he was flush and very generous to his mates for about a week. Then back to student poverty and handouts from friends. But the cheerful and helpful Max was well liked by all that met him, and he could certainly be described as 'a character.'

The group had piled into the now partially empty van and 'Little Mickey' took the happy crowd to the 'King's Head' for Sheppard's pie and Guinness. 'Little Mickey' always did the driving on pub and party runs simply because he was 'Tea-total' – he had never touched the stuff since - as a child, he watched his father disappear into bottles of whisky and emerge a monster; a big, abusive and violent monster.

The dark memories of his awful childhood would always appear in his mind and he would never touch alcohol. He towered over his friends and colleagues and was often referred to as 'The gentle giant'. He represented the University in wrestling and had been approached by several mangers and agencies to turn fully professional; but he wanted to complete his studies without too many distractions. Quiet spoken and cheerful; 'Little Mickey' was always well respected by those who encountered this big man.

3. UNEXPECTED VISITORS.

As the van pulled back onto the camp site, Dave pointed out the side door window; "Hey! There's torchlight in the ruins!" Everyone could see a yellowish white glow coming from the Abbey and Mickey pulled the van up by the caravan's and the van's headlights showed open door's, lights on and contents strewn about the grass.

"We've been fucking robbed!" Dave exclaimed and everyone emptied from the van with Clare running towards her caravan shouting; "I don't give a shit what they have nicked, as long as they didn't hurt Jester; I left him asleep on the bed!" Clare leaped through her open door and found the inside a complete mess; but a big fat cat sitting on the oven – safe and sound - She grabbed the cat and cuddled him. "The buggers don't appear to have taken anything; they even left this behind." The Professor held up a large brown envelope stuffed with Pound notes – the expense money for the trip - Max joined them and reported none of the dig's expensive equipment appears to be missing.

Clare wondered if it was local kids having a laugh at their expense, but it was little Mickey and Dr. Shaw's shouts that pulled them outside; they were coming back fast from the ruins; their torches swinging wildly in the dark.

The pair joined the group panting and shaking, finally Dr, Shaw gathered her wits together and spoke quietly with clear emotion in her voice; "Someone has dug up the old Monk's burial ground!" Everyone looked about and the Professor shook his head; "That's impossible; we've only been absent for a couple of hours." But Dr. Shaw insisted, and the entire group headed for the old Monk's burial ground and shone their torches over the graveyard. They stood in silence until Clare said quietly; "They look like mole hills."

Everyone could see the large mounts, about seven of them, at the Western edge of the cemetery and Max gripped Dave by the shoulder and said, "Moles burrow out of holes: But what the fuck burrowed out of these graves?" Everyone turned to him in silence and after a few seconds the Professor coughed nervously and lit his pipe; "No ghost stories please Max; let's go back and tidy up as best we can. In the morning we'll do a proper check to see if anything is missing and then we'll take a close look at this mess." He gestured towards the graveyard and the group walked back to the caravan's.

They could see and hear the motorbike approaching and grouped about the caravan's, as the big bike pulled up next to Clare's car. The rider jumped from his bike and pulled up the goggles; "What the hell happened here?" His soft Italian accent clearly apparent and Clare embraced him with some emotion; "I'm really glad to see you Rollo, someone trashed our caravan's but took nothing." She slipped her arm through his as he unbuttoned the old RAF Trench coat and shook hands with Max.

"They also trashed the old Monk's graveyard." Max said unsmiling, as the Professor clapped his hands together; "It's been quite a night, so let's get our heads down and start early in morning."

Everyone returned to their caravan's; except Mickey and Dave who crashed out in the van. Dr. Shaw was sharing with Clare and, of course, Jester the cat. Whilst Max and Rollo shared the smallest caravan; the Professor had one all to himself – he was a professor after all - and no-one else could fit in with all his books, maps and manuscripts. Not to mention the damn smell of his big pipe!

As lights went out amid shouts of 'goodnight', a quiet darkness descended upon Hobbs Abbey ruins. But deep within its fallen stones, broken gargoyles, silent Angels and empty doorways; something was moving.

4. A GRAVEYARD DEMON.

Jericho walked quietly over the broken earth, squatting down by the old Monk's burial ground wall and examined the heaps of soil thrown up. He glanced around and saw Alex a few paces behind. He had to chuckle; she clearly wasn't dressed for messing about in an old cemetery - late at night - but it did make him smile; Alex had a mini-dress on and a flowery white lace blouse. "Alexandra, if that skirt was much shorter, you would be wearing just a belt. But I do like the bright red Wellington boots." Jericho gestured to her footwear and just had to grin.

She stared at her boots and shrugged her shoulders; "I thought they were perfect for wandering around a graveyard in the middle of the night. If I fell into a bloody big hole; I could use them to signal for help!" Alex grinned broadly and joined Jericho peering into one of the holes.

After a few seconds, Jericho rubbed his chin and nodded to himself; "Ceebrus." He and Alex held their small torches over the hole. "What would bring such a Minion of the 'Dark one' to this place?" She asked looking about the ruins of the old Abbey. "It's not exactly a cornucopia of human souls ready for stealing." She added and looked towards the vehicles and caravan's parked north of the Abbey.

Jericho stood up and pointed to where Alex was looking; "Maybe someone there is the answer to our Demonic friends visit – Archaeological students from York University, here for a week or so." He looked back at the holes and muttered; "Ceebrus." Alex glanced back at the quiet caravan's and said, "Two of my descendants are among that group and one does have connections with the Church."

Jericho nodded and pulled a small glass orb from his coat pocket and held it out; he watched little red streaks appear around its circumference and sighed; "Quite a strong signal Alex – It's a Minion that could take Souls and Ceebrus fills the bill."

Alex nodded her agreement and shone her torch towards the Abbey ruins; "Quite beautiful, it must have been something special in its heyday; apart from when the devil dropped by." Jericho had to agree with that.

Then Alex tapped his arm and slowly backed into the shadows cast by the old wall; "There's someone watching from those tree's over there." Jericho also melted into the shadows, and both switched off their small torches. They could just make out the figure amongst a clump of bushes, it quickly moved away; backwards into the thick foliage and disappeared.

"It's human." Jericho whispered and relaxed a little. Alex agreed and pointed to the student's parking space; "They just opened a door on a caravan there, it must be one of them. Do you think they saw the torchlight?" "Probably; back to the office for now I think, we may have to ask for a Guardian on this one; if not a Knight." Jericho pulled his mirror out and the pair vanished.

5. DEAD MEN WALKING.

Father Rollo Cappanni gently pulled open the caravan door and eased himself inside, pulling off his jumper and loose boots, he lay on the small sofa that doubled as a bed and lit a cigarette. He smoked for some minutes before extinguishing it and then pulled his thick, red notebook from his discarded coat pocket and started to scribble notes with a half pencil.

Rollo had a pretty good idea that the Devil's Minion; Ceebrus was abroad and quite possibly, was using the Abbey for his own evil ends. Father Roland Cappanni worked for [in secret] a small department of the Vatican called 'The Prayer of Liberty' – he was an Exorcist and investigator of the Paranormal - that concerned the Church. Rollo had been dispatched to watch over the Abbey ruins during the excavations by the student Archaeologists; the place was well noted in Vatican records.

But he wondered who the young couple were and why are they poking about the Abbey ruins in the middle of the night; had they trashed the caravan's and for what purpose? Was it a warning?

The thoughts swamped his head, but no conclusions were reached because he fell asleep where he lay, clutching the precious notebook bound by a thick rubber band. He had a troubled and dark dream, and it was Max moving about the small room, that woke Rollo from his disturbing sleep. "Come on Rollo; Clare's knocked up some breakfast and we're invited!" Max was combing his long hair and smiling with anticipation of tea with bacon and eggs. Rollo blinked at the sunlight streaming through the large window and realised he had slept for nearly five hours. He coughed loudly and made for the small bathroom, telling Max that he would join him at Clare's caravan after he had a 'wash and brush up'.

Rollo stared at the face in the mirror and pulled two pill bottles from his shaving bag and unscrewed the lids slowly. Just six months left; that's all he had to go; six months and then a terrible end to suffer. He groaned loudly and pushed the pills into his mouth and swallowed hard. Six months was all that remained of the Priests life and the 'dark nights of the soul' plagued his thoughts constantly. He took several deep breaths and started to wash and shave without any enthusiasm; but he must keep up appearances for his kid stepsister: Clare, until he found the courage to tell her of his dreadful fate.

Max and Dave had settled in around the small table and tucked into bacon, eggs and beans with fresh tea and a slice of buttered bread. "Clare, if I could afford it, I would marry you tomorrow!" Max smiled broadly at her - she simply rolled her eyes in mock despair- and slapped eggs onto plates.

Dave laughed between mouthfuls and actually giggled; "Christ! You two should get married; you're the same class with both dads' aristocrats – what's your father Clare? - he's a bloody Count, isn't he?"

Clare shrugged her shoulders and sighed; "My father died when I was nine, my oldest stepbrother Henri is now the Count of Cappanni and I don't really know him. But Rollo and I are good friends; he's always been close to me, even after my parents divorced and mum and I came back to England to live."

"Talk of the good man and he will appear." Max smiled as Rollo appeared in the doorway and smiled broadly with a cheery; "Good morning, all!"

Rollo squeezed through the small door and was greeted by Clare who kissed him with a big smile; "Good morning big brother; tea or coffee?" She asked as the large priest eased into the seat next to Max. He asked for coffee and accepted a plate of bacon, eggs, beans and a large sausage, with two thick slices of bread; well buttered.

"You lucky bugger Rollo, your kid-sister looks after you alright. Mine wouldn't piss in my ear, even if my brains were on fire!" Dave wiped his plate with some bread and slurped his tea. That made Max chuckle, he knew Dave was right; his sister Ruth had no real love for her little brother and the pair hardly spoke. Max switched on the little transistor radio next to the sleeping cat on the end seat. Jester raised his head, yawned, then stretched and slipped back to sleep despite the pop music coming from the radio.

Everyone sat chatting, mainly about the coming dig, the strange behaviour of the old policeman and, of course, the caravan's being trashed; but nothing taken. Rollo offered cigarettes around and they were accepted by all except Clare. Max managed to 'bum' a couple of extra ones for later!

Rollo commented on the election of Mr. Ted Heath as Prime-Minister and Clare pointed out that Mr. Heath was one of just a handful of British Prime-Minister's that were bachelors. Dave [being a die hard Labour supporter] expressed his opinion that Heath was as sexually attractive as a "Toads arse" – So little wonder he was still single – even Clare chuckled at that; but the conversations were ended by the arrival of Professor Hemmings to brief them on the day's activities.

He told them that Doctor Shaw had gone to the village, to report the incident with the caravans, and pick up some more supplies. Little Mickey had volunteered to drive her. He accepted a welcome cup of tea from Clare and lit up his pipe which quickly cleared the small caravan, even Jester the cat shifted to the bedroom to continue his napping.

Rollo stood outside in the warm morning sunshine and smoked slowly, half listening to Dave and Max moaning about the Professors smelly pipe, when the radio news started playing on the transistor that Max had switched on. He held up his hand to silence the chatter and everyone listened to the news, including

Clare and the Professor. A dead body found in Catcall Lane was being investigated by Police; Dave rubbed his chin and pointed south of the Abbey; "I think Catcall Lane runs at the rear of the bloody abbey!" He shouted and everyone started to head for the Abbey ruins and the small road which lay behind it.

But the little group came to a stop as Mickey's van appeared from Bell's Lane, followed by a black Police van which in turn was followed by a dark blue Ford Zephyr Mark IV. "CID." Max said simply and Father Cappanni started to walk to the vehicles with the Professor. Clare gripped Max's arm and whispered; "You don't think the body and the raid on our caravan's are bloody connected?" Max nodded; "Yeah, and I bet the coppers think that too."

Little Mickey jumped from his van and walked over to Clare, Max and Dave, leaving the Professor, Dr. Shaw and Father Cappanni to speak to the two CID officers. "What's up big man?" Max asked quietly and the visibly shocked Mickey spoke quickly and softly.

They [him and Dr. Shaw] had been stopped by Police officers as they turned down Bell's Lane and questioned about the body lying in a small rainwater ditch, near the roadside. Apparently, the old Policeman had recognised the dead man as a local farmhand come poacher; who had been savagely attacked and killed; despite carrying a loaded shotgun!

"They think it could be some escaped wild animal; the poor bastard was torn up badly." Mickey added and accepted a cigarette from Dave, who wondered why the dead poacher hadn't given the unknown beast both barrels of his shotgun.

Wilson and Alex stood by the old wall of the Monk's burial ground and watched the police activity; "The Collector put the call in this morning – that poor bugger wasn't supposed to die for another three years - and of course; no Soul was found to collect." Wilson pushed the mirror back into his jacket pocket and folded his arms. Alex nodded and said softly; "Ceebrus."

6. HUNTING THE DEMON.

Oscar chuckled and took a swig from his hipflask: "Well, I've tangled with old Ceebrus a couple of times over the centuries, but never did discover where the bugger made his home." Oscar the Guardian gripped his staff and followed Alex and Wilson into the old Monk's cemetery. The little glass orb he held out immediately showed small red streaks. "He's about somewhere." Oscar muttered and then smiled, as Jericho and Owen appeared through the gateway and joined them at the edge of the cemetery.

Oscar greeted them both with real affection; Jericho had been his old temporal Inspector, when Oscar was a sergeant in the Temporal Directorate. "I've borrowed Inspector Ali's local human agent; he knows Ceebrus only too well and he'll assist us." Jericho informed the group and pushed his mirror into his coat pocket, adding; "We'll meet him at the gateway in the old South wall."

As the group headed for the south wall, Owen spoke softly to Alex and Wilson, about being privy to the conversation between their Jericho and Inspector Ali; regarding the local human agent. "He's well experienced in demonology, the 'Dark One' and most things supranational; well, supernatural to living humans anyway!" Wilson chuckled at that and jerked a thumb to towards the gateway; "Looks like he's here." Then smiled at Alex; "Could this be called a family reunion?"

Father Rollo Cappanni stood in the old gate way and watched the group of Temporal Detectives approach; he extinguished his cigarette and threw the butt down. Inspector Ali had told him about his ancestor; Lady Alexandra Mary Cappanni and he smiled, she was easily as beautiful as her portrait showed; the artist had certainly painted what he saw.

Jericho shook his hand firmly; "Do I call you father or Rollo?" He asked and Rollo just smiled; "Rollo will do nicely Mr. Tibbs." Jericho introduced his team and Rollo gripped Alex's hand and grinned; "You certainly are as beautiful as family legend always described. I can see a little of you in my kid sister Clare; she's considered very pretty."

Alex kissed him on both cheeks with real affection; "You certainly have inherited the male side of the family; it always produced big, strapping handsome boys and men. I am so pleased to meet you. I would love to meet Clare, but that would take some explaining I think!"

They both laughed, and Alex gripped his arm firmly; Yes, she could indeed see her oldest son Philippe in the big man. Same eyes, smile and same dedication to what he believed. Seeing Father Rollo bought back the unhappy thought that her all her children had been dead for many, many years. But she still smiled at the priest.

Rollo turned to Jericho; "I have researched the Abbey thoroughly. In pagan times this was a site for pagan rituals, including human sacrifice. The church, as usual, to show dominance over false gods raised a house of God here. But this Abbey was special. Local legend tells that the devil himself charged one of his minions; Ceebrus to watch over the old sacred ground. It is said that God sent a Knight to slay the beast and that he drove it underground." Father Rollo coughed into his hankie and Alex [being a doctor] knew that sign was bad; she had glimpsed fresh spots of blood on the cloth.

He continued; "The Abbey was supposedly built where this divine battle took place and to secure the ground for God - for good. But the devil is a cunning foe and he buried Ceebrus in a special place and made the promise to raise the creature when six hundred and sixty-six human years had passed. That anniversary came about this very year of our lord 1970." Everyone nodded; they now knew why Jericho had borrowed this priest from Inspector Ali's human team.

"It's also part of the reason; we have the legend of Saint George and the Dragon. That story is made up from various fights between Knights of God and the forces of darkness over the centuries." Owen added and Wilson patted him on the shoulder; "Spot on baby brother."

Rollo waved a hand at the Abbey ruins; "Over the centuries everyone believed that Ceebrus lay within the confines of the Abbey, but my research points to somewhere very different, simply because Ceebrus was worshipped as a pagan deity - a tree spirit - that 's what he's called in old manuscripts and texts."

"So where is the little bugger?" Oscar asked and gripped his Staff of Moses. Rollo smiled and turned a full half circle and pointed to Hobbs Wood; the ancient forest that was protected by law. "He's in there – somewhere - That's how come the poacher fell victim to him so easily. The man walked straight into his lair. That is the

Devils Graveyard." Everyone stared at Hobbs Wood; dark and foreboding.

"Then, that's where we have to go." Jericho looked quite grim and consulted his mirror. Rollo coughed again; "I think it would be very unwise to march into the demons lair, where it is fully prepared and waiting. There is a better way to tackle the monster I think." Father Rollo explained his plan to an astonished - and a little surprised - audience.

7. BLOOD SACRIFICE.

"You alright with this Alexandra?" Jericho asked – again - she smiled; "Well if it brings that bloody monster out into the open, then it has to be done." Wilson checked his orb and lowered himself behind the thick clump of bushes and watched the dark forest carefully; "No sign of the bastard; yet." He smiled broadly at Alex, as the group all hid behind the small trees and bushes. "You OK Alex?"

"I'm bloody stark naked under Jericho's frock coat, apart the flowers around my head. No, I'm not really alright, but if it lures him out, then it's worth it." Both Jericho and Wilson smiled broadly; Alex was one of a kind, brave and willing to face real danger, if needs demand it. Father Rollo flicked through his little notebook, reading with a small torch. "We'll start over there, by that old oak tree stump. We'll light a small fire and put lamps around it." He rummaged in his coat pockets and produced a dagger and a small gold chalice - he had borrowed that from the local church - but the old dagger was his own.

He also produced a small flute and blew a couple of notes, then coughed again. "Alex, dance around the tree stump with plenty of waving arms, like we practised this afternoon. I'll keep time with the flute." He produced a dead rabbit from his canvas bag which made Alex grimace, he smiled at her; "Blood is blood to a demon. That dead poacher had it in his bag and I sort of borrowed it from him." He slit open the dead animal and squeezed blood into the chalice; apologising to God as he did so.

Owen was sulking a little; he had been designated as 'back-up' and would be the only one carrying a mirror. He would locate a little away from the group, should things go badly wrong. "I won't be able to see the dance or anything interesting." He grumbled and Wilson slapped his back; "None of us can carry a mirror out there, so we have to depend on you, my little pervert. That beast can practically smell them and we've nowhere to hide the fuckers!"

"We won't be disturbed by the students. They have all gone to the pub in the next village. I told them I would watch the caravans and do some urgent letters to Rome. I gave Clare a couple of quid to buy some drinks. They won't be back till well after midnight."

"It may come as a shook to your kid sister to find her big brother - a priest - stark naked and performing pagan rituals in the middle of the night." Wilson chuckled and asked Owen the time. "Ten minutes to midnight." He said simply and made for his hiding place - reluctantly. Everyone looked at each other and Jericho grinned; "Well, let's get it done."

Oscar chuckled; "first time I've tackled a demon in the buff with only my staff for cover." The group of five then removed their coats and headed for the ancient tree stump. Alex was actually well surprised by Jericho's physic; he must work out in secret, she thought and then glanced at Wilson. Her eyes looked at one part of the big man and wouldn't look away; until Jericho started the fire.

"Bloody hell Wilson; have you a license for that?" She giggled and took up her position in front of the stump. Wilson just smiled and shrugged his shoulders; "My wife Rosie always said it was the best part of me." Alex had to agree with that; she had been one lucky woman!

Father Rollo set up the 'black alter' quickly, he looked up at the full moon and whispered; "Let's start, it's almost midnight." He started to play the flute, whilst Jericho, Wilson and Alex joined hands and began to dance slowly around the stump. Oscar held aloft the chaise and dagger. In monotonous tones he started to praise the 'Dark Prince'; reading from Father Rollo's little book by a small, flickering lamp.

Owen could see the figures a little by the light of the fire and cursed himself for not bringing binoculars! "I won't get a better chance to see Alex than now, and I fucked up." He whispered to himself and the suddenly saw the little orb starting to turn red.

"Sweet Jesus! It's fucking working!" He said aloud to himself and checked his mirror, his finger just above the emergency Travel App. From the dark edge of the ancient forest something was emerging; it was Ceebrus.

"Everyone kneel, but you keep on dancing Alex; remember he is a male demon, and you need to show him what's on offer." Father Rollo whispered, and everyone obeyed. Ceebrus was in human form, but with some scales on his legs and torso. He had the human body of an athlete and was nearly seven feet tall. He stood at the edge of the forest; watching Alex dance.

"A bloody demon with a six pack and looking like a young Apollo." She whispered to herself, as she squatted and turned on the damp grass, lifting her bum to him and wiggling it quite provocatively. "It's working; he's erected." Father Rollo spoke softly, between blowing on the little flute. "He wants her; he's accepted the gift."

Oscar had his staff close to his hand - covered with thick, smelly foliage to prevent Ceebrus from detecting its presence - as he knelt and watched carefully the approach of his old adversary; "You're in a for a surprise you little bastard." Ceebrus stopped some yards from the fire and everyone could now see him fully. If he was human, he would be a magnificent specimen with a handsome rugged face and dark black eyes. Most human women wouldn't think twice about jumping into bed with him. He watched as Alex rolled over onto her front and lifted her bum into the air, pulling the cheeks of her arse apart - as Father Rollo had suggested - Rollo knew that the demon simply wouldn't be able to resist an offer like that.

Ceebrus groaned loudly and pushed both hands through his long dark hair which was piled around his broad shoulders. He spoke in the ancient tongue, Aramaic. "I accept this woman as a gift to our Master and will take her fully. Place her upon the tree alter." He pulled the little golden loin cloth off, exposing his large erect penis. Jericho and Wilson lifted Alex and placed her face down upon the stump; she again lifted her bum to him.

The demon smiled and gripping his penis made for the stump slowly. "Now Oscar!" Was all Father Rollo shouted and threw the dagger into the torso of Ceebrus. He grabbed up his notebook and began to read aloud; the incantation for throwing demons back to hell. Oscar jumped over both the stump and Alex, his staff gripped in both hands.

"You're gonna get fucked old friend, but not the way you hoped!" Oscar shouted and the two squared up, whilst Wilson grabbed Alex and the pair ran for the little clump of tree's, where their clothes were and more importantly, their mirrors lay.

Father Rolland had never actually seen a demon and a Guardian of God fight - few living humans would had done so - It was violent and vicious, but Oscar had the upper hand; his staff had been supplied by the 'BOSS' [God] himself and the demon had no answer to it. Had the demon been a Tier One - the outcome would have been very different - only the Knights could tackle them and 'Dark Angels'. But Oscar was well up to this task and Ceebrus disappeared; back to his master to lick his wounds.

They joined Alex and Wilson back at the clump of trees and pulled on their coats. Owen joined them; grinning broadly; "Now that's what I call a job well done." He congratulated his colleagues but was disappointed that Alex had Jericho's coat firmly wrapped around her.

"It's not over yet, we need to find his lair whilst he licks his wounds and destroy it. He won't be able to return; ever." Father Rollo spoke quietly, and everyone nodded. "But that can wait until morning." He smiled and the victorious little group headed back to the caravans, where Jericho arranged to meet Father Rollo at the south gateway again, in the morning. Rollo fell into his caravan and swallowed down some whisky and drifted off to sleep - still partly dressed - on the small bed.

8. THE DEMON'S LAIR.

The team assembled by the old Monk's graveyard; just as the sun was rising and Jericho checked his mirror as everyone stood about chatting and sipping hot coffee from plastic cups. Oscar had returned to the Demon Ingress Office to fill out his report; but he did have an invitation to dinner. Wilson was teasing Owen about missing a naked Alex, while he hid in the bushes. Alex made the pair laugh, as she re-enacted some of the moves, she had to perform to lure the demon out.

She kept finding herself looking at Wilson; she couldn't get over the sight of his large penis - and that concerned her - and it wasn't even erect. She sipped her coffee and smiled at Wilson, then realised that she was flirting!

Father Rolland joined them, smoking and reading his notebook, he could not see that Clare, Max, Dave and Micky were all watching him from the North wall. They couldn't, of course, see the temporal detectives and were most concerned to see Father Rollo apparently talking to himself; complete with gestures and pointing!

Well, everyone except Clare was quite concerned. She just stood and stared in total silence. Max turned to Clare and sounded quite puzzled; "What the fuck is Rollo doing?" Dave sucked on his cigarette and coughed; "It looks like his having a conversation with himself - the poor old buggers finally gone mad - I put that down to too much celibacy."

Micky folded his arms and stared at the priest; "What's being famous got to do with it?" Everyone just laughed, except Clare and she turned to the others and spoke quietly; she would have a word with her brother - and she really did sound concerned - now. "He's been coughing a lot and I'd swear that I saw specks of blood on his hankie." She confided to Max. They watched as the priest made off towards to Hobbs Wood - deep in conversation with himself - apparently. "Come on Max." Clare said softly, and the pair set off for Hobbs Wood as well.

Father Rollo stopped by an ancient looking tree and started to pull away the undergrowth around its base; Wilson and Owen helped. Everyone was a little astonished to see the carving that was revealed, a dove. "Little bit of a joke by the 'Dark Prince's' minion; a dove - the symbol of peace covering the lair of a demon. I always thought that the dark bugger had a real sense of humour." Rollo muttered and they stood back; looking at the magnificent old tree.

Alex looked about and saw Clare and Max approaching; she smiled broadly; her descendant could pass as her sister!

Owen tapped Alex's shoulder; "Jesus Alex, she's certainly inherited a large chunk of your beauty." Wilson and Jericho nodded their agreement with that. Rollo turned and hastily pushed his notebook into the folds of his coat. "I'll deal with them; you know what is required." Jericho nodded and the team disappeared into the lair that was contained in the old tree. They found a stunning cavern with tapestries, pictures and priceless furniture; Ceebrus had lived well in his little lair, for centuries. Owen found a gold box containing many bones and Alex identified them; as all being from the little finger of numerous human hands; each finger from a separate human. Jericho closed the box slowly; "The little finger from each of the female sacrifices he was given. He fucked them and then killed them; no doubt they were souvenirs."

Owen, quite unintentionally, broke the grim mood; "Christ, why didn't the bugger just collect dirty panties, like normal men." Everyone chuckled and Wilson slapped him on the back; "Right up to your usual standard, my little perverted brother."

Alex stared at the gold box and shuddered at the thought; considering how she had danced to attract him. The terrible thought, of all the previous young girls and woman given up to the beast over the centuries, made her feel sick. She pulled her hipflask out and took a good swig. "Bastard." Was all she whispered. She straightened up and started to look around the demon's abode. That's when she noticed the ornate, gilded writing desk.

She rummaged through the papers scattered over the desk and pulled up a yellow parchment; it contained a list of names - written in blood - Alex called everyone over and they gathered around the desk. Jericho read the document carefully and did not smile at what he found. "It appears to be a current list of our friend's followers and some of them are interesting." He looked up and passed the sheet around. "A local policeman, a Magistrate, the fucking local Liberian; a Miss Ester Rands, two wealthy farmers, some girls from the local school - and their dad's - and...." Owen stopped speaking and showed it to Alex; "Isn't that the archaeologist running this dig?"

Alex nodded; Doctor Janet Shaw. Little wonder that Father Rollo had been dispatched by the Vatican to oversee the dig. Dr. Shaw would have made sure that nothing interfered or threatened her master - but she hadn't counted on Temporal Detectives being assigned to the case - and a Guardian of God turning up.

Wilson handed Alex another piece of paper and spoke solemnly;

"The date and time of another gift for the demon; to mark the 666th anniversary of the Abbey. Dr. Shaw wanted him to be very happy with the choice and she chooses her team here with great care." Alex stared at the paper; the human sacrifice was named as Miss Clare Cappanni. She swallowed hard; the date was tonight.

Wilson smiled; "Talk about going to the wire. The bugger must have wondered why the ceremony was a day early. If it had reservations about turning up to our little party, he soon forgot about them, when you offered your arse to him. Father Rollo was right; he simply couldn't refuse the chance to fuck it - most men or demons - couldn't resist that." He smiled again and joined Owen poking about the Gothic fireplace.

Jericho spoke directly to Alex; "I have no doubt that one of Doctor Shaw's devil worshipping friends trashed the caravan's; but what were they looking for? They had to trash all the caravans, but I suspect whatever they were after, was in Father Rollo's or the Professors caravan; but what?" He rubbed his chin and wondered what they were after. Still, it didn't really matter now that the demon was vanquished, and they had hard evidence against a cell of Devil Worshippers.

Owen called them over to the fireplace. Wilson had found what they were looking for; a small, ancient wooden chest and Jericho nodded that this was what they had come for; they left the ghastly place for the world of living humans.

Meanwhile, Clare and Max joined Father Rollo by the old tree and stared at the carving. But Clare had gone strangely quiet and gripped Max's arm. Rollo could see and sense that she was frightened. He gripped her shoulders and smiled; "It's just a Medieval carving Clare." But Clare shook her head; "I know..." She hesitated and pulled away from Max and whispered into her brother's ear. He was astonished, surprised and amazed at her soft words.

9. UNWANTED REVELATIONS.

"Who are they...I've seen the woman before; in a painting at Cappanni Palace." She spoke quietly and turned to Max; "Please let me and Rollo have a few minutes, in private please Max." He nodded and made for the edge of the old wood and waited. "You saw them, Clare?" Rollo sounded quite stunned by this revelation. Clare nodded; "The woman looks like our ancestor; Lady Alexandra Cappanni; the 'English Countess' as she was known. She died in 1801, so how the hell is she standing here!"

Rollo looked back to the tree; the Temporal Detectives had returned; Wilson was holding a moldy little wooden casket, no bigger that a cigarette case, gently in his big hands. "We have it." He said simply. Clare nervously whispered; "Rollo, are you going to introduce me to your strange new friends?"

Jericho smiled and removed his hat; "Good morning, Clare, I'm Jericho Tibbs and these people are all members of my team." He gestured to each in turn and introduced them to the young woman; he left Alex to last – deliberately - Clare managed a smile; "It's nice to meet, a quite famous ancestor - in the flesh, so as to speak - Lady Alexandra, I have read quite a bit about you and your husband; you were also my mum's favourite. A real character and a brave woman for the times you lived in."

Wilson and Owen exchanged a strange look; they both knew that 'Lady Alexandra' had been a Doctor in London; in 1901. They knew this was fact by the chance meeting of a certain Nurse Alice Hadden, when they investigated Doctor Alexander Harris in 1916, during the First World War. But neither made any comment on the matter; for now.

Rollo took the Detectives to one side as Alex and Clare chatted and asked to see the casket. Very carefully, he instructed Jericho to prise it open - no living human could open the casket - and survive. Finally, with great care, Jericho lifted the lid, and everyone stared at what lay inside; apparently wrapped in a piece of shriveled human skin.

"What the fuck is that?" Owen looked bewildered and Wilson said nothing but stared at the strange little thing. Jericho sighed; "It's a piece of the 'Dark Princes' fingernail; just a tiny shred of one of his fingernails and yet it was powerful enough to manifest a living demon, here in these woods for thousands of years. So just imagine what an entire fingernail could do?"

Rollo instructed that the casket should be consumed by fire and keep well away from it; whilst it burns. Clare gripped her brother's arm and asked to speak to him alone. Rollo knew it was time to impart his terrible secret to his young sister. The Temporal detectives said their goodbyes and left; Alex was a little emotional at leaving her descendants before they could have 'a proper chat' as she put it.

The team assembled in the Dining Room; Mrs. Harris had prepared the boys favourite; hot beef curry with all the trimmings. Alex sighed but did enjoy her meal - as she always did - Oscar was greeted warmly by his old colleagues and loved the curry, but not as much as the company he now enjoyed. The dinner conversation turned to Father Rollo and young Clare. Alex was a little sad to find that Father Rollo had passed over just four months later. But had already been accepted for training as a Temporal Detective. Wilson commented that Jericho had sung his praises to Angel Margret; so no-one should be surprised by that.

They all knew that Alex's descendant; Clare Cappanni possessed the powers of a 'Passer' - a human who can see and readily communicate with the dead." She definitely has the potential to join this department; when the time comes." Jericho announced as the pudding was served. Wilson turned to Alex and smiled; "Such power tends to run in families; anyone else in the Cappanni bloodline displayed such a gift?"

Alex ate her ice-cream slowly and unsmiling spoke quietly; "I would not call it a gift; more a curse." Jericho switched the conversation to the disposal of the casket, and everyone enjoyed their meal. Alex noticed Jericho kept glancing at her and asked him if anything was wrong. He simply smiled; "No Alexandra, nothing is wrong." But Alex had the feeling that was not true.

Having drinks in the study after dinner, Wilson made everyone laugh - including Alex - by showing his dance moves to attract demons. Oscar was almost crying with mirth and joined in. Owen, seeing that Alex was now happy and relaxed, decided to act upon the thoughts that had bothered him for so long, he joined Alex by the fireplace and spoke softly to her.

What he asked, made her laugh out loud and she tapped his face lightly; "I'll think about it." She managed to utter, between giggles. She smiled broadly at Wilson and some little erotic thoughts were pushed to the back of her mind; for now. She saw Jericho looking at her as he sipped his wine and spoke softly to Mr. Harris - she knew that he had uncovered her little secret –

but how long had he actually known and why no action?

Jericho smiled broadly at her and raised his glass; "Everyone, a little toast to our much respected and loved colleague Alexandra; The lady who will even dance stark naked, in a cold muddy field, to get the bloody job done!"

Everyone cheered at that statement and raised their glasses; "To Alex!" they shouted and started laughing - Alex felt much better and glanced at Jericho - she would really love to know his story and sipped her brandy quietly, as some really odd thoughts about the young man tumbled through her mind. Did she really have such feelings about him?

THE END

EPILOGUE:

"The mission was deemed a success; the team had driven the demon back to its master and removed its lair. Hobbs Abbey remains a major tourist attraction and many visitors love the guides tales about the supernatural legends that surround the place; little knowing that most are true!"
SJW.

CHARACTERS:

Clare Cappanni completed her course and became a professional Archaeologist for English Heritage. She left in 1976 and married David Granville Sebastian Halls-Canton - the 10th Duke of Sommerton and Max's elder brother! They remained married until her death from cancer; the same strain that killed her stepbrother, Roland in 1970. She left three children and two grandchildren. Her grandson Maxwell is currently the 12th Duke. Alex and Jericho attended the funeral. Her soul was collected and processed; she now works as a Collector.

Dave Williams never finished his Archaeology course at the University; he dropped out and became the drummer of the Rock band 'Stay Dead' and toured Europe and America for some years. He was found dead in a cheap New York hotel from a heroin overdose: he was 25. His younger sister didn't bother to attend the funeral. His soul was collected and processed.

Professor Theodore Hemmings continued to have many field trips over his years as Professor of Archaeology and wrote several books on the subject of English history. He retired from the University in 1983 and died in January 1992 after having a stroke. His soul was collected and processed.

Doctor Caroline Shaw resigned from the University and became a TV presenter; covering Archaeological digs around the UK for a local station. She remained a 'Devotee' of the Dark Prince and became the subject of an investigation by Team 62 and Temporal Inspector Dawn Daniels. She died in 1981 - in a strange car accident - and not surprisingly; there was no soul to collect. It remains missing to this day.

Michael O'Farrell - 'Little Mickey' - didn't complete his university course and dropped out: working as a farm hand for many years. Finally, he moved to Canada and became a recluse, living in the mountains. He simply disappeared from his log cabin and no trace of the 'big man' was ever found, including his soul. Temporal detective Inspector 'Doc' Underhill has been assigned the case; it remains unresolved to this day.

Maxwell Richard Alexander Victor Halls-Canton - Max - completed his course and became the Principal Archaeologist at a big Scottish University. He wrote many books on the subject and even fronted several TV shows on British Archaeology. He was made a professor at a very young age and travelled the world lecturing. He died at the grand age 0f 93, surrounded by his children and grandchildren. He had a very good life. His soul was collected and processed.

Constable Frederick Jones was an ardent follower of the Dark Prince and was the High priest of the local Devil Worshippers. it is known that he was involved in two ritualistic human sacrifices [murders] and had abused several young girls in the name of his 'Master'. One of the girl's father's took matters in his own hands, when his accusations against Jones were 'whitewashed': he stabbed the now retired Jones, several times. Jones died in 1992 and no soul was collected. Temporal Inspector Ali Khan and Team59 are assigned to the case.

Father Rollo Cappanni succumbed to his illness, just months after assisting Jericho and Team 74 at Hobbs Abbey. His stepsister Clare nursed him constantly through the last hard, awful days of his life. Jericho and Alex attended his funeral. His soul was collected and processed. He is now a Temporal Detective Trainee attached to Team 14.

Ceebrus - the Demon - never returned to Hobbs Abbey or his home in the Devil's graveyard. It is understood that he has become a 'Mentor' for new demons and enjoys the privileges afforded by his position, on the personal staff of the Dark Prince. He has been promoted to a Tier 1 Demon. But he and Team 74 were to meet again in strange and unexpected circumstances! [See the episodes "**Jericho Tibbs and the tablet of creation – Parts 1 & 2.**"]

EPISODE 8: "CORDLESS, CORDLESS & FRASER (SOLICITORS)."

MISSION SUMMARY:
"The established family solicitors of Cordless, Cordless & Fraser have existed in the heart of Edinburgh's old city for over 200 years. In the Summer of 1980, the young Clerk who looks after the basement archives of the firm, informs the Senior partner; Sir David Fraser, that it's time to deliver the old document pouch to the address marked upon it - except the pouch was lodged with the Solicitors way back in 1780, to be delivered on its Bicentennial year! Mr. Tibbs is now on the case."

NOTES: This episode contains a graphic description of a sexual assault.

 ALCOHOL, VIOLENCE, STRONG SEXUAL REFERENCES [including sexual assault] STRONG LANGUAGE & MILD HORROR.

 AGE 15+ ONLY. 45 Minutes reading time.

1. EDINBURGH CITY (LATE SEPTEMBER 1780)

The two horsemen entered through the old North gate amid little flurries of early winter snow. Several English soldiers manning the gate made no effort to stop or search the two rough old men;

they could see no weapons, and both were wearing breeches. Weapons and kilts had been banned after the battle of Culloden in 1746. There was talk that the ban would soon be lifted. But For now, it was still in force. The pair threaded through the busy traffic of people, horses and carriages looking for a specific street and set of offices. The taller one pointed down an alley and nodded. 'Cable Street' was their destination and they slowly passed down the narrow thoroughfare until stopping before a little wooden sign, hanging above a dark entrance, which declared: 'John Cordless - Solicitor'.

They exchanged smiles and dismounted, shaking snow from their long coats and the taller of the two old men, pulled a canvas sack from his saddle bag and patted it like a puppy dog. "John Cordless is young, hungry for business and won't ask too many questions." He grinned broadly, showing only a couple of remaining yellow teeth - most had been knocked out by an English musket; smashed into his face at the battle of Falkirk Muir. But Willy McKenzie knew that the injury he received had actually saved his life; simply because he missed the slaughter at Culloden Moor.

But old Danny Brown had fought on that dreadful Moor and lost an eye in the process. He escaped being shot by English soldiers, as he lay injured upon the battlefield - with nearly two thousand other dead and wounded Highlanders – by a woman's courage.

A woman camp follower called Edith Ross braved the bullets and bayonets of the English to drag him and her younger brother from that bloody field. Later that year he married the woman and had seven children by her - her young brother sadly died of his wounds - just days after the battle; he was sixteen.

The two battered old warriors stared at the sign hanging above their heads and nodded in agreement - they headed up the stairs to the office of young John Cordless - who greeted them with some enthusiasm, especially after they slapped the bag of Spanish Doubloon coins upon his desk; they would be worth thousands upon thousands of pounds today.

So impressed with his 'clients' was John Cordless, that he actually produced a bottle of whisky to seal the deal. With his eyes hardly leaving the sack of gold coins, they discussed what was required: Now that did make John sit up and take notice.

John Cordless sat sipping his whisky; watching the two old men throwing glass after glass of his precious whisky down their throats. Willy McKenzie leaned across John's polished [and quite empty] desk and pulled a large, leather document pouch from the canvas bag slung about his shoulders.

"You understand that no-one must open the pouch whilst it's in your care. That you'll care for it until it's delivered by hand to the addressee, who has been sewn onto the bag and it must be delivered on or after the day shown. This transaction between us and your company must remain totally confidential - we are paying you a good deal of money to EXACTLY carry out our instructions - Do you understand lad?"

John Cordless quietly accepted the bag which had little weight and nodded his agreement; he would draw up a contract, so that all the pair stipulated would be done under law. He stared at the address and coughed a little; "Wasn't Lord …."

Willy McKenzie stopped him in mid-sentence and smiled; "Aye, we know the good Laird [Lord] was hung by the English at Fort William, but this fellow will." Willy corrected himself and continued; "is a relative who will inherit his title."

John finished his whisky and scribbled more into his notebook and looked up to see Danny Brown refilling the glasses. "Well, I have everything I need except the date you wish the commission enacted." He lifted his glass in salute and again watched the two men empty the glasses in one swallow.

Willy grinned; "By enacted, you mean delivered?" Both old men exchanged a glance and John nodded. He picked up his quill and waited to write in his notebook. Danny wiped his mouth and nodded to the document pouch; "Your firm will deliver the pouch on 30th September nineteen hundred and eighty."

John started to write, but stopped suddenly; "Sorry Mr. Brown, but just for a second there, I thought you said nineteen hundred and eighty?"

Both men grinned and Willy McKenzie spoke softly; "Aye, you heard right lad, that's why your company has been given a big bag of Spanish gold; to pay for its rest in your hands until the year of our Lord nineteen hundred and eighty." Everyone sat in silence for some seconds until John Cordless, staring at the bag of gold coins [yet again!] spoke; "All what you wish will be done as you specify gentlemen." The three men shook hands upon the deal and John told them to return in three days and sign the contract, which he would draw up himself.

John stood at his small window and in the gathering gloom of snow and nightfall, watched the strange pair depart upon their plodding horses. They would stay at the 'Crown Hotel' until the contract was ready to be signed. John Cordless poured himself another – large – whisky and started to laugh. With such an amount of money, he could now marry young Mary and set up a fine and proper household for her. He would also spend some on the offices and employ more clerks; John Cordless Solicitors would be a law firm of note in Edinburgh, in Scotland and quite possibly, the British Empire. All because two crazy old men wanted a pouch delivered in the hereafter!

He walked back to his desk and picked up the pouch; "Well gentlemen, thank you for your trust and whilst a Cordless runs this company, your wishes will be adhered too." He chuckled to himself and placed the pouch into the small safe, which was hidden inside a large and imposing set of drawers.

Sipping his whisky, John picked up his notebook and read again, the date specified by the pair; Nineteen hundred and eighty. That was exactly two hundred years hence - two hundred years!

He sat thinking about the bags contents; how relevant could anything written [he assumed it contains papers because of the weight - or rather lack of it] in the year seventeen hundred and eighty would be two hundred years later?

Still, he pushed the little mound of gold coins about his desk, feeling each in his hands and fingers, grinning broadly. He lifted his glass and said quietly; "Well Mister Brown and McKenzie, none of us will surely be around when the bloody thing is delivered!" Laughing, he gathered up the coins and secured them in a leather bag, which he placed in his frock coat. Jauntily, he slapped his hat on and wound a scarf around his neck against the chill of the night. John Cordless walked home a happy man that night; and now a rich one!

2. EDINBURGH CITY (LATE SEPTEMBER 1980)

Young Peter Davidson pushed his bike against the black iron railings and secured it with a large padlock and chain. He pulled his trousers from his bright red socks and clutching his holdall, headed for the offices of Cordless, Cordless & Fraser where he held the grand title of 'Archives Manager' or filing clerk in the real world!

But today he had a task to fulfill that would take him, to the very high offices of the Senior Partner of the firm; Sir David Fraser. Today he would inform Mr. Fraser that the old document pouch, held under lock and key, for two hundred years should now be delivered. It had actually put a spring in his step and with a cheery 'God Morning!' to the Security Guard sitting with Liz, the receptionist [who he really fancied] made for his basement office.

Peter sat at his desk, eating a strawberry yogurt with a small plastic spoon, reading a photocopy of the original agreement - he wondered who Daniel Brown and William McKenzie really were. They gave their joint address [at the time] as "Prospect House, Inverness." He had actually looked it up with no success, going right back to the 1690's. But the address sewn onto the old document pouch, well, that was a different matter!

The phone ringing made him jump and spill yogurt on his trousers, he lifted the receiver carefully, wiping strawberry yogurt from his knees. It was Sir David's Secretary; Margret, informing him that he was required in Sir David's office - with the pouch - at exactly midday. He mumbled his agreement and slowly replaced the phone.

Peter's assistant had arrived and slumped into his chair, blowing his nose and coughing; "I'm sure that bitch I snogged last night has given me the chills." Carl wiped his face and grinned; "Today's the day my friend. After two hundred years of low paid, abused and bored filing clerks, you have been chosen, only you have the honour of delivering 'old crinkly' and getting your picture in the papers." He grinned broadly; "All the girls will think you're famous, you're bound to get laid once or twice!"

Peter just grunted; "Some fucking luck I don't think. SIR David will probably do the honour himself. I've already been summoned to his office at midday."

Carl shrugged his shoulders; "They probably know what's inside despite its remaining unsealed for all those bloody years, you've heard the legend about Sir David's Grandfather and Edinburgh Infirmary."

Peter nodded; he knew that story all too well. Sir David's grandfather. Sir Alistair Cordless, it was rumoured, had taken the pouch one night (in great secrecy) to an old friend at Edinburgh Infirmary and had it X-rayed. The legend tells that, all they could discover was the pouch contained several sheets of paper and what appeared to be a small ring. But it was just a story.

Peter sighed; "Pieces of paper are worth shit, unless they point to hidden treasure." He had also heard the legend of their founder's acquisition of old Spanish Gold - lots of it - apparently, because of the pouch.

"I dunno about that, look at the American Declaration of Independence; that little piece of paper changed the world." Carl pulled several files from his desk drawer and shuffled the contents about his desk. "After that fixed referendum; that's all we fucking need. A Scottish Declaration of Independence." Peter muttered and imagined himself dressed in a kilt, waving a broadsword at Mrs. bloody Thatcher! Peter could hear Carl laughing; "What the fuck are you doing mate?" Peter eased back into his chair after standing and waving his imaginary sword about; "Bloody Thatcher." He repeated to himself and smiled.

"You take that bird to 'Buster Browns' Saturday night?" Carl asked and threw a ball of screwed up paper at Peter, who grunted. The 'bird' Carl had mentioned was Liz the Receptionist and Peter still hadn't worked up the nerve to ask her out on Saturday night. "Maybe, maybe - I'll have to see." He said softly and the thought of Liz sitting naked behind her desk made the young man grin broadly.

Hamish, a young Junior Clerk from the third floor appeared in the doorway and jerked a thumb towards the ceiling; "The fucking press has turned up, there's a totally gorgeous tart reporter heading for Sir David's office with a cameraman. Jesus, she's all tits and long legs - fucking stunning." Peter and Carl exchanged looks; "Must be about 'old crinkly' - Sir David loves getting his name in the papers, he's a real tosser about publicity." Carl explained, looking over his shoulder and past Hamish in the doorway, who scratched his arse and added; "You on for 'Buster

Browns' Saturday night?" Both Carl and Peter nodded. "Fuck, I'll have to ask her now or be a fucking real lemon in front of these twats." Peter whispered, then sighed and chewed his pencil, then a wonderful idea came to him, and he shouted; "Yes!" punching a fist into the air. Carl and Hamish just chuckled; "What a knob." Hamish muttered and headed back upstairs, hoping to get another look at the reporter from the 'Scottish Record'.

Peter constantly looked at the office clock until it read eleven-thirty, then unlocked the wall key box and removed the old key for the basement safe. "Do you want me to make trumpet noses?" Carl giggled and stood, saluting.

Peter stuck up two fingers and headed for the safe. With 'old crinkly' tucked safely under his arm, Peter slipped quietly into Reception and waved Liz over to him. His 'brilliant' idea actually worked, he showed Liz the package and managed to turn the conversation around to Saturday night. A very happy filing clerk headed for Sir David's office; Liz had said: yes.

Peter was shown into the outer office of Sir David's by Margret and stood waiting. He stared through the clear glass partition and grinned broadly; 'What a fucking piece of skirt!' he said to himself. Peter simply couldn't take his eyes of the female reporter who sat upright in a small office chair, with Sir David standing over her. The reporter had a short skirt, well above her knee and a matching blue jacket. Her white blouse simply couldn't hide her magnificent breasts. She was scribing notes and smiling at Sir David. She was simply stunning; in all respects.

Peter actually groaned a little, when she crossed her legs which seemed to go on forever. "Best put your tongue back in your mouth and do try to stop dribbling." Margret smiled at Peter and carried a tray with coffee into the main office. That's when he bothered to look at the cameraman and was well surprised, a big black man in a smart suit with a couple of expensive looking camera's hanging around his neck. "Jesus, that's a big man. You don't get many of him around here." He spoke softly and straightened his tie, as Margret indicated to join them.

He gripped the old document pouch with both hands and glanced down at the address, which had been hand sewn onto one side. "How the fuck did those two know, that there would still be a Lord Falkirk two hundred years later and still living in Falkirk

Palace?" He whispered and smiling, walked with pretend purpose into the presence of Sir David and his gorgeous guest.

3. WAR OF THE WHITE ROSE (FEBRUARY 1985)

Jericho wrapped his coat around and pointed down the quiet street towards the well-built barricade; "There are several rebels manning it, they're armed and clever, so be really careful in how you act and speak." He cautioned his team, who stood amid the snow flurries and shared a hipflask of brandy amongst themselves.

Alex adjusted her little woolen bonnet and allowed her long dark hair to fall about her shoulders. She pulled down her short skirt again and straightened her coat. "They do know we're reporters and won't be trigger happy - will they?" Alex asked Jericho, who nodded and pushed his mirror back into the folds of his long coat. "Baby sister, no man in his right mind would shoot a piece of cake like you - keep your coat open and show them legs; you'll be safe as houses." Wilson chuckled and then added, as an afterthought; "And they may not shoot at us either; just in case they hit you!"

Jericho raised his hand; "Best American accents now people." He said and the little party, very slowly, started to head towards the wall of overturned vehicles, paving stones and shop doors.

They were challenged by two large, red-faced men with rifles and kilts. They were wearing old army uniforms, covered with thick dark trench coats and black berets - each with a little white rose attached. Jericho pointed to a large plastic card around his neck, hanging from a red tape; "Hello boys, we're the press team from CNN as arranged by your Captain Davidson." Even Wilson was impressed with his 'New York' accent and muttered; "You really do sound like a damn Yankee." Owen chuckled at that and whispered to Alex; "And he should know!" They all showed their Press cards and smiled; broadly.

The two men lowered their rifles and one called over his shoulder for Captain Davidson. A small gap was made, and the little group squeezed through, bending low, and found a busy street. Several old army vehicles were parked down one side, including a Red Cross ambulance and two jeeps: both flying the Scottish flag. There must have been thirty soldiers milling around including

several women, a couple were wearing Red Cross arm bands:
everyone seemed to stop and watch the reporters approach.

Alex received a couple of 'wolf-whistles' from two young soldiers
sitting on the tailgate of a lorry. She smiled and pulled her coat
around, as the snow seemed to be falling more quickly and
increasing in density. That's when she saw the tired looking
young Captain, emerge from a shattered shop doorway. She
gripped Jericho by the arm; "Shit! That young man knows me
and Wilson - he handed the pouch to his old boss back in 1980.
Change of role I think." She nodded to Wilson, who had also
recognised the former filing clerk.

"It's, good to meet you - Jerry Tibbs - CNN." Jericho held out his
hand, pulling the glove off. The captain gripped his hand firmly
and smiled. Alex could see that the young man had changed
some over the last five years; he seemed much older than his
true age; but his eyes were still bright.

Jericho introduced his team in a wonderful 'New York' accent;
Wilson his cameraman, Owen the production assistant and local
liaison was Alexandra, a reporter from a national paper, who was
assisting and guiding the team from New York. Captain Peter
Davidson of the SDF [Scottish Defence Force] smiled; "Hello
Miss, I do remember you and your cameraman from the day the
pouch was opened. I don't think any man could forget meeting
you or the big man." He indicated towards the shop doorway and
added; "Follow me. Colonel McIves has his HQ in the basement of
that shoe-shop; he's the one who authorised your Press visit.
Like you Alex, I'm local liaison."

The little group exchanged glances at the mention of 'McIves'. "Is
that Alexander McIves; from the Highlands?" Alex asked quietly
and saw the look upon Jericho's face when the captain replied
yes and did she know the Colonel?

"By reputation only." She muttered and the group followed the
captain into the shop doorway and descended some wooden
stairs into the basement which was lit by candles. Colonel McIves
was sitting at metal folding table, smoking a pipe and reading
various pieces of paper. The big man was in army uniform and
gripped a glass of whisky in one hand. The captain saluted and
introduced the group. The Colonel looked up and smiled broadly;
"Jerry Tibbs?" He said and stood, holding out his hand, telling the

captain to check the radio room for messages.

Nothing was said between them until the captain left, then McIves indicated for them to seat. Several fold-up chairs, stacked in a dirty corner, were pulled out and everyone was seated. The Colonel passed several plastic cups around and produced a bottle of whisky from the canvas bag at his feet. "Jerry Tibbs." He repeated softly and chuckled. Then he handed the bottle around with a quiet smile on his face.

There was a little silence as everyone filled their cups, then the Colonel scratched at his pipe with a small pen knife and refilled the bowl from a fat drawstring bag. He re-lit it slowly, peering over the top at Jericho. "I'm amazed that you let this slip by you Jericho, I'm sure Alex and Wilson reported back the contents of that pouch and what it could mean to the Scottish people; especially after that bent referendum that Thatcher concocted." He leaned back in his chair and puffed his pipe - smiling.

Jericho raised the plastic cup and shrugged; "Not my call McIves, I was running an errand for Angel Margret and the team were temporarily managed by Inspector Patrick O'Brien; who made the call, despite what Alexandra and Wilson reported. His decision has been called into question; that's why we're here."

"Ah, now I see. My faith in your abilities have been restored Jericho. But is your Mission to restore or damage limitation?" The Colonel sipped his whisky and placed his pipe down and shuffled some papers on his desk. Jericho sighed; "Neither really, our brief is to report the changes, so that Time-Control can run a few scenarios and see where it all ends up. Then the Boss will, apparently make the call himself."

"I think, we would all love to know how you did it McIves." Alex spoke softly and tapped her plastic cup with a finger; "We really would." The Colonel grinned and waved a hand into the air; "Jesus, I do love it when you use that Scottish accent, Alex; makes the hairs rise on the back of my neck." He offered the bottle around for refills and slumped back in his chair. "I can't take all the credit for it. The real brains behind it was a certain French ship's captain; a Monsignor Francis de Ville - late of his French's Majesty's navy - a fellow who hailed maybe, from 1766, so the story goes. He discovered that his father was a direct descendant of King Robert the Bruce! It appears that the Earl's of

Falkirk are the King's heirs and rightful Lord of the Clans." Owen coughed; "He's a missing soul Jericho; his departure date is logged at 1787 - he never appeared and is believed to have gained the ability to travel." Owen replaced his mirror in a coat pocket and refilled his cup, adding; "The only Scottish connection shown is that his mother; a certain Lady Alice MacKinnon was from Ayr. His father was a French merchant who traded with Scotland in the 1740's."

"That's not quite accurate Owen; his father was no French merchant, but the true King of Scotland." The Colonel smiled broadly; "All the proof needed was contained in that pouch - along with an incredible and iconic relic that tied everything up in nice fat ribbons." Jericho scratched his chin; "I don't understand that the current Pretender [1985] to the Scottish Throne is some German Duke I believe; a direct descent of the Stuart's."

"Had it not been for the pouch and its incredible contents, you would be right." The Colonel re-lit his pipe and tapped the desk gently, adding; "The pouch had evidence, that the original line of Scottish Kings from Robert the Bruce was still in existence and that dear Francis de Ville, had a better and totally legitimate claim to the old Scottish Throne. He was a direct and legitimate male descendant of King Robert. That sole fact changed everything. Scotland had a real Scottish King in the form of the Earl of Falkirk – Francis's direct descendant and heir."

"What was the relic that proved everything?" Wilson asked, quite intrigued and sipped his whisky. McIves chuckled; "Something that has been missing since 1329." He shifted on his chair and passed the whisky bottle around. "The pouch contained a simple gold ring inscribed with the word 'Fuimus', which was the Bruce clan motto. It was Robert the Bruce's coronation ring and had been missing for centuries. Experts examined the ring and declared it genuine. Then of course, there was the marriage contract between King David II [Robert the Bruce's son] and a certain Lady Mary Stratlain in 1363 and provisions for the King's son, another David, by that Lady. The Earl of Falkirk is his direct descendant and true King of Scotland by blood and Clan."

"I know my Scottish history is a little shaky, but wasn't King David married to Margaret Drummond who gave him no children?" Owen looked quite puzzled; his research was normally top-notch in these matters. McIves nodded his agreement and smiled - again; "Yes he did marry the woman; but in 1364. He desperately needed her family's support and so he simply hid his earlier marriage for political convenience and survival. It wasn't exactly uncommon in those days. Remember, in Scottish law, the earlier marriage would remain valid."

There was loud knocking at the door and a voice shouted; "An English patrol has been spotted east of the city Sir!" The Colonel jumped up, buttoning up his tunic and fixing his beret; "The captain will look after my guests until I return." He said to the young soldier who now appeared in the doorway - rifle in hand.

He patted Jericho on the shoulder and grinned; "Stay around Jerry and make yourself at home. I'm sure the great American public will love what you produce for CNN." He also winked and buckled his pistol belt on, disappearing up the staircase; shouting orders.

The group sat in silence for about a minute, considering what had been uncovered in that dark little cellar. "Shit, if that's all true, then Inspector O'Brien has made one of the greatest cock-ups in the history of the Temporal Department." Owen stated and shook his head, downing his whisky in one.

"No shit Sherlock." Muttered Wilson and slung the video camera back over his shoulder. Alex saw the concerned look on Jericho's face and whispered; "IF it is true, then surely the Boss will allow the new Time-Line to exist?" Jericho shook his head; "I don't really know, an independent Scottish Kingdom formed in the 1980's will cause major changes down the Timeline and could alter the history of humanity. Maybe not for the best either."

Jericho finished his whisky and eased from the uncomfortable little chair; "I think we need to take a closer look at this story." Alex replaced her mirror and looked quite grim; "People, the Time-Controller is holding this existence for twenty-four human hours. So, we only have one day to discover any truth about what's been discovered."

4. THE SIEGE OF EDINBURGH CASTLE.

Captain Davidson had found the team some reasonable accommodation in a looted town house, and they settled in. Alex found an armchair with a footrest and sat back, shoes off, massaging her feet. "If this snow gets any heavier, I'm going to need my wellingtons - these little ankle boots won't cope."

She noticed that Owen was staring at her feet with a little smile on his face. "I'd swear young Owen is turning into a pervert." Wilson declared and chuckled, having noticed where Owen was staring. Alex sighed; "Owen, they are just feet. I'm not rubbing my breasts or anything like that." Owen grinned; "I know, but it's the way you're doing it." She rolled her eyes and sighed; forcing the boy into the Monastic life, at a young age, had done him no favours.

Wilson wandered over to the damaged table placed by the window and poked the plate of sandwiches, which had been provided by a very pleasant young women in uniform, wearing a Red Cross armband. "There's cheese or corned beef and a big pot of tea." He picked up a cheese sandwich and took a massive bite, adding; "Hey, they're not bad." Alex stared at the plate and asked Owen why the girl had called them 'pieces'. Owen explained that was Scottish for a sandwich. She shrugged and picked up a cheese one; "Who wants tea?"

They didn't get time to finish their 'pieces' or even try some tea. Captain Davidson burst through the broken door
shouting: "They have broken our lines just south of the city and we've been ordered to reinforce the castle garrison; - the castle can never fall into English hands; that would be a disaster." A little calmer, he informed them that the unit was leaving immediately for the castle; and the reporters would be coming with them.

"What castle?" Wilson asked and Owen replied simply; "Edinburgh."

As they packed up the few items they carried, Owen spoke quietly to Jericho; "The papers and ring from that pouch are stored in the castle's archives, we won't get a better chance to examine then; given the time we have left." Jericho nodded his agreement, and the group quickly descended the stairs into the street which was in chaos; "You'll go in the ambulance. There's less chance that the bastards will shoot at it." Captain Davidson told them, and they jumped in, accompanied by the young female medic, who slammed the doors shut.

"There's serious fighting to the south of the city and casualties have to be taken to the castle infirmary now, they've over run the hospital we've been using." She didn't smile and adjusted her beret adding; "Still, the poor sods in that hospital will get much better treatment from the English surgeons than we could ever provide." Everyone gripped something as the ambulance pulled away at speed, driven by the other girl, who shouted back; "Hold on! It's gonna be a bumpy ride!"

The little convoy arrived at the castle just before midday; amid a heavy snowstorm and the sound of fighting could now, actually be heard in the distance. The young medic helped Alex down and pointed to a dark doorway; "Apparently there are a couple of small rooms put aside for us, the boys have one to themselves, but you have to share with me and Rosie." She indicated to the ambulance driver, who Wilson made laugh when he asked her; if she drove stock cars for a living.

Jericho gathered the team in the little dark room which was lit by two weak candles, stuck in egg cups. "There can be no better time to sneak around and get a look at the pouch's contents, everything is in chaos, and they won't pay too much attention to people already inside the castle. I've pulled up a map to the archives and where the pouch is stored." He tapped his mirror and checked the doorway; "Right, there's no time like the present, let's go!"

They carefully and quietly navigated the dark corridors, to the sound of gunfire and small explosions outside. "The castle is under siege." Owen said softly, lifting up his mirror to illuminate the way. They found the Lower West corridor and stairs down to the archives. The room containing the pouch was just around the next turn, but Owen stopped suddenly and snapped the light out. "A guard outside the door, sitting on a stool; he is armed." He whispered, adding; "Looks very young, probably stuck him down here because of that."

"I doubt he'll just let us wander in and read the damn thing." Wilson muttered, lowering the video camera down and wiping his face. But Jericho smiled and tapped Alex on the shoulder; "Over to you, I think." Alex didn't look impressed but tidied up her hair and straightened her short skirt, pulling the hem up a few more inches; then opened some more buttons on her blouse. "Run your mirror over each page." Owen spoke softly and grinned.

"I do know that." She muttered and took a few little breaths. Alex switched her mirror light on and said loudly; "Hello, is anyone there?" They heard the young soldier jump up, his stool falling to the floor. "Halt, who goes there?" He shouted - quite nervously - Owen glanced at Wilson and said, "Do you think he'll fall for the oldest trick in the book?" Wilson grinned; "With our girl? Hook, line and bloody sinker." They both nodded at that and even Jericho managed a smile.

Alex stepped around the corner with a big grin on her face, and with a little wave of her free hand, introduced herself. The remaining team waited in silence, but ready to spring if Alex needed assistance. They could hear a conversation but couldn't actually make out what was being said. But they all grinned at each other, when after a few minutes; they heard a heavy door being unlocked. They heard it close, and they edged round to find the stool on the floor. The guard and Alex were gone.

"Hook, line and bloody sinker." Wilson whispered and they stood outside the door, waiting. After a while Owen glanced down at his mirror; "It's been almost ten minutes." He sounded a little concerned. But the door creaked open, and Alex stepped through and smiled; "Mission almost complete. But the ring is not there, apparently the new Scottish King; Alexander, is wearing it." She pulled down her skirt to its original length and quickly buttoned her blouse up. "Come on, back to those dismal rooms." Jericho said and nodded to Alex; "Well done."

The team passed through the empty corridors and reached their 'dismal' rooms before anyone even realised; they had disappeared. "You were right about why the boy was guarding that door, Owen." Alex said, checking her mirror; "Colonel McIves told him, that it was one of the most important tasks in the castle and that, he could depend upon young Colin from Aberdeen."

Wilson shrugged his shoulders and seemed quite surprised; "So the black hearted git does have a conscious." He turned to her and smiled; "It didn't take you long to achieve what we needed." Alex waved the compliment away, saying softly; "He's not much older than Owen and I told him that I really needed to see the papers for my newspaper and that I would be grateful - very grateful indeed - and would do really anything to get my story. He caught on pretty quickly and I knew immediately that I would get my way." Wilson gave Alex a questioning look and said, "How grateful?"

Alex chuckled; "I slowly - very slowly - lifted my skirt so that he could have a good look at what's on offer and that done the trick. He had the door unlocked without a second thought." Owen actually groaned at the thought of that scene, which made Wilson and Jericho chuckle.

"He let me 'photograph' the papers because I promised him a little fun, when he came off duty in a couple of hours. But as down payment, I had to let feel round my bum, while I took the 'pictures'. He had very cold hands." Owen shook his head in a mix of frustration and disappointment that it wasn't his hands on Alex's bum. "I take it you won't keep that appointment?" Wilson muttered and Alex whispered; "I like men - real men - not boys. Sorry Owen." The look she gave Wilson didn't go unnoticed by the big man and he smiled to himself. Dancing naked around that dam tree stump did have it perks. Young Owen shrugged his shoulders and said quite sadly; "Lucky bastard."

Wilson passed around his hipflask and everyone enjoyed the brandy, whilst they waited for Human Records to analyze the papers. But loud sobbing from the room Alex shared with the medic's, drew her attention. Jericho indicated she should investigate, and Alex hurried out. It was some time before she returned - she had been clearly crying but was now quite composed. Wilson gripped her arm and asked what happened.

Alex drew a very heavy breath; "Young Rosie the ambulance driver went to help a badly wounded soldier and was caught by machine gun fire. She died instantly. Morag was quite distraught but pulled herself together and went back to work in the infirmary." They stood in silence for a few seconds, then Jericho said simply; "Brave girls." Everyone muttered their agreement with that.

Alex took a long swig from Wilson's flask and looked at their faces; "What's wrong?" She said slowly. Owen ran a hand over his face; "The papers are fake - made around the 1780's - but very good fakes." Alex stared at the floor and whispered with real emotion in her voice; "So young Rosie died for a bloody fake." She sighed deeply and sat slowly on a nearby chair; "For a bloody fake." She repeated; angrily.

"I wonder if McIves knows the papers are fake." Owen asked and sipped some brandy. Jericho grunted; "Our friend has been fighting other people's wars for centuries; I don't suppose he would care either way." Alex looked up from her chair and ran a hand through her long dark hair; "Thanks for reminding me about mercenaries; Young Colin told me that the Colonel intends to hold the castle, until a certain General Munroe arrives with the Scottish Northern Army - apparently in a couple of days - The army has many American volunteers, American descendants of Scots or Irish settlers. A lot of them have apparently served in the US forces and so they're professional soldiers; that could make a big difference to the rebellion."

Jericho nodded at that and eased himself onto a wobbly chair; "Now I understand why the English haven't used their heavy weapons on the Scots - planes and tanks - because of public opinion back in the states, which has large populations descended from Scotland and Ireland. Their President is a staunch supporter of the current Prime Minister, Mrs. Thatcher. But I bet, he has made it plain that such tactics would not be acceptable. The English are fighting a civil war with both arms tied behind their backs. Interesting that."

"You were always too clever for your own good." Colonel McIves stood in the doorway, unsmiling, with his arms folded. He placed a whisky bottle on an empty chair, with several decent looking glasses. He smiled at Alex; "A young, but very loyal trooper, has told me about your little visit to the archives and your promise. I'll be quite envious when he comes to collect his prize."

Alex smiled and shrugged her shoulders but said nothing. McIves chuckled; "I've given him a couple of hours off to spruce himself up and the keys to a VERY SPECIAL and lovely state bedroom. You should be undisturbed there. He'll be here shortly, so that you can keep your end of the bargain." He slowly unscrewed the whisky bottle and spoke directly to Jericho; "May I ask what you discovered by allowing our Alex to offer sexual favours to young men? Tut-Tut; very naughty!" He grinned and handed the bottle to Jericho.

Jericho accepted the open bottle and a glass from McIves and slowly poured whisky out. He sipped and spoke softly; "That this rebellion is based on lies - very well made lies - but lies, nevertheless." He raised the glass in salute. "Where does 'Black

Sword' stand, now he knows he's fighting for a lie; a lie that's killing people who should never have died yet and plunging his beloved, adopted country, into useless bloodshed?"

5. BLACK SWORD SURPRISES JERICHO.

McIves said nothing but indicated to the doorway; "May I introduce Monsignor Francis de Ville to you all." He said loudly and stood to one side. The little dark-haired Frenchman sauntered in and bowed; "So I finally meet the famed Temporal Detective Jericho Tibbs and his loyal foot soldiers." He bowed again to Alex; "You're as beautiful as I imagined. The young soldier is much privileged to be pleasured by you."

"Did the little shit run an advert on the TV about the archives visit?" Alex groaned, adding; "Does everyone bloody know?" Wilson shook his head and quietly showed Alex the little glass orb: it had turned red; completely.

They exchanged looks but said nothing; they were in the presence of a very powerful minion of the 'Dark One'. Wilson caught Jericho pushing his orb back into the folds of his long coat.

The group stood in silence as the Frenchman lifted a glass and sipped some whisky, he grinned at Jericho and pulled a small black jewel - no bigger that a thumb - from his jacket pocket. "You will discover, my friends that your mirrors will not work anymore. You now have no more power that a mortal human and completely at my command." Jericho stared at the gem and said quietly; "A Judas Stone." That's when three armed soldiers appeared in the doorway, including an excited looking young Colin from Aberdeen.

Owen pulled out his mirror and stared at the blank screen, each of the team checked their mirrors with the same result; they were offline. Jericho slowly pushed the mirror into the folds of his coat - he didn't smile but folded his arms and spoke quietly; "Only certain minions of the 'Dark One' can temporally close down a mirror." Monsignor Francis de Ville smiled; "And so I am; you may know me as Kiri." He whispered. Jericho's face did not betray the fear building inside; Kiri was a Tier One Demon. The only person, who could tackle him, in the human world of the living, would be a Knight of God. They really needed one; NOW.

Monsignor Francis de Ville pointed to Alex; "Young Colin, this lady will keep her promise to you - take her and enjoy yourself." Wilson and Owen jumped forward, but Alex shouted for them to stop. She took a heavy breath and said with no emotion in her voice; "He could easily kill you without breaking into a sweat. Stand down. Stand down I say." She walked to the doorway and didn't look back. She heard Wilson calling the Minion something very unpleasant and she half smiled; until Colin gripped her arm and walked her to a nearby staircase.

"The Colonel gave me the keys to the Old Queen's state bedroom, we'll be OK there." He sounded quite excited and took hold of her hand; "Best thing I ever did, letting you see the parchments. I've been told I can take all the time I need, so I want to do it a couple of times, understand?" Alex forced a smile at the boy; she could almost sense a change in his demeanour, and it wasn't a pleasant one. But then McIves words passed through her mind; 'to spruce himself up and the keys to a VERY SPECIAL and lovely state bedroom' was there a message there?

Was the infamous 'Black Sword' throwing her a lifeline? Can he really be trusted? Alex was quite distracted by Colonel McIves words. They arrived at the room in the old quarter of the castle and Colin nervously unlocked the door. Alex stepped in and stared about the room; it was quite stunning with a huge four poster bed covered with thick curtain in bright colours. There were many portraits and tapestries hanging on the walls.

"Well, this is absolutely stunning. I wouldn't mind this as my bedroom." Alex was impressed and then she realised she had 'young Colin from Aberdeen' to disappoint. "Women can change their mind at any time." She spoke quietly and turned around to speak to Colin about this 'agreement' But he was stark naked, holding his erection with both hands.

Alex sighed and folded her arms; "Colin, about this...." But she never finished her sentence. Colin walked straight up to her - grinning broadly and pushed his hand up her short skirt - his groping hand grabbed through her panties and touched her crotch. She slapped him so hard that he actually fell on the bed. He lay stunned and slowly rose, cursing. "You don't grab a woman like that - ever." She shouted at him and stared about the room. He was apologising and pleading with her to forgive him; when she spotted the mirror against the wall, opposite the window. "A Jerusalem Mirror!" She exclaimed and walked over and shook her head in relief. "You are a clever, cunning bugger McIves." She whispered and realised that 'Black Sword' must have decided previously, whose side he was on. With the bloody demon hanging about, he had to be really careful and clever.

Colin crept over and took hold of Alex by the waist from behind; forcing a hand into her blouse, taking a fierce hold on her left breast. It hurt. "You will keep your fucking promise!" He shouted Colin was bloody angry and frustrated; he was losing control and now tried to kiss her.

Well, Alex knew that the time for pleasantries was over. She turned slowly, with a lovely smile on her face and gently pulled his hand from her breast. "I think this should visit a better place." She guided it back up her skirt, staring into his eyes. He grinned and turned her to him, which she wanted; "That's more fucking like it; I'm going to fuck you like a fucking dog you bitch!" He spoke angrily, with a contorted smile, pushing his hand down into her panties and between her legs. He tried to push his tongue into her mouth, whispering; "So you fucking like it rough. Well, I'm gonna fuck your arse so hard, you won't sit straight for a week." He actually giggled and started to force his fingers into her. Alex was utterly calm and smiled. He never saw it coming.

'Young Colin from Aberdeen' was in such pain after Alex had smashed her knee straight into his testicles that he slid to the floor. He was suffering excruciating pain; he could not even cry, but just lay whimpering on the carpet, unable to breathe properly or speak.

"You turned out, not to be a very nice young man. But one of us, has certainly been fucked now" She muttered and straightened her blouse and adjusted her panties and then stared at the young man curled upon the floor; now sobbing. "By the way, the agreement is off," she said quietly and strode over to the mirror and stepped through.

She was in the Queen's bedchamber; in 1568. Luckily the place was empty, and she peered through the thick glass window to the late medieval streets of old Edinburgh. "Better view here and now than when I just came from." Chuckling with a little relief, she quickly pulled out her mirror and with some delight; saw it was online. Alex disappeared, before the Queen's Ladies-in-waiting arrived to prepare the bed for Her Majesty.

"It was the perfect decade for rebellion. Margret Thatcher was unpopular with her Poll Tax here, her attempts at smashing the Miners and selling state industries that were actually owned by the people. There were riots and strikes and Scotland had just been cheated out of Independence by a crooked referendum; so, the people thought. It was the best opportunity for a successful rebellion in over two hundred years." Monsignor Francis de Ville smiled and sipped his whisky.

"But for success, it had to start way back in 1780. With two old friends of mine and a very famous forger - at the time - who could recreate historically accurate documents. By the way, the ring is actually genuine. I took it from the Kings Body just hours after his death." Monsignor Francis de Ville sighed and walked to the door; "Goodbye Mister Jericho Tibbs. I will now take the place of that lucky young soldier. But I'm sure, that I will not be as pleasant with Lady Alex as the boy would have been. But he is quite a devoted follower of my Master; that's why I choose him to guard the door. I told the boy it was McIves idea." Laughing, he departed, and the door was slammed and bolted. The three sat in silence, Jericho checked his mirror again; it was still offline.

A 'Judas Stone' was a powerful weapon in the armoury of the 'Dark Prince's' 'minions. It basically disrupted communication between the forces of light and prevented travel between the dimensions of Time. They sat waiting in the darkness - the two miserable candles had long since died - All with one real concern on their minds; Alex.

A little stream of light started to appear through the doorway and they jumped up, as the old door swung slowly open. McIves stood in the doorway and gestured for them to come. "Quick lads, the fucking demon has gone after Alex." Wilson shouted something about ripping off a certain male appendage and stuffing it somewhere unpleasant. That's when they all stood still at the sight, standing in the corridor.

"Oh fucking shit." whispered McIves. He very slowly pulled his famous black sword, from the scabbard, that hung upon his back. Jericho checked his mirror; it was still offline. Monsignor Francis de Ville had reverted to his true form as the demon Kiri; a senior

Minion of the 'Dark Prince' and it wasn't happy. "Where is the bitch?" It hissed and rolled dark eyes about and licked its sharp teeth. "Where's the bitch?"" It repeated and crashed its tail against the corridor ceiling, bringing down plaster and age-old dirt. Jericho whispered to McIves; "Alexandra must have escaped." McIves smiled and lifted his sword slowly; "I knew she was clever enough to de-code my message about the 'Jerusalem Mirror'. She's jumped!"

"Not quite, I'm still here actually and I've brought an old friend." Everyone turned behind them and saw Alex standing in the doorway, hands on hips and not looking happy. "You see, you scaly bastard, you don't need working mirrors when you have one of these." She stepped aside and James - Knight of God - stood in the doorway, gripping his sword, he dropped his visor and said softly; "I think its best, you people wait in the Great Hall." Everyone disappeared at his command; you certainly didn't need a mirror with him around!

Jericho and his team surprised several sleeping soldiers; who jumped from chairs, sofas and tables as the group appeared in the middle of them. McIves slowly sheaved his sword and grinned broadly at Alex; "I hope you didn't hurt that horny young twat too much." He chuckled and started to speak to the amazed soldiers, who gathered around him.

Alex walked up to McIves and placed a smacker of a kiss upon his lips and stayed there for some time. Finally, she broke the kiss and smiled; "That's a little thank you for being a really clever git and staying true to who you really are. Gracias Rodrigo, eres verdaderamente un hombre de gran honor." 'Black Sword' nodded his head and stared into her eyes; "So you know."

Alex whispered; "Yes we know." There was silence between the two, until one of the young soldiers asked if he could have one as well and received it for sheer cheek alone!

"They're back on!" Owen exclaimed and held up his mirror and received a little admonishment from Jericho about showing a mirror near living humans. Wilson tapped Alex on the shoulder; "Glad to have you back with us, how's your new boyfriend?" Alex stuck up a single finger; but smiled.

6. HIGHLANDS OF SCOTLAND (1780)

Jericho lowered the small brass telescope and rubbed his face; large snow flurries slapped against his coat and hat, as they rose and fell with the wind. "There's a small farm about two miles south of our position; that's where we will head." He turned and spoke to his team, waiting behind him in single file along the rugged little ridge. Wilson muttered something; he just wanted off this damn horse, even for half hour.

Owen grinned; "Thighs playing up big man?" and received a two-finger salute in return; he knew that Wilson did not care for horses or horse riding. Alex shifted on her mount; happy she didn't have to ride side saddle. But she was showing a lot of her boots; considered a little bit shocking for a lady of quality in this year 1780. She had a black and white, fur trimmed coat, which covered down to her ankles. But was now cast behind her, covering the flanks of her horse. She had pulled the white fur hood, over her head and stared at the gathering snow clouds.

"Does it always snow in bloody Scotland?" She asked no-one in particular. Owen wiped snow from his face and pulled his bonnet down a little; "It does, if it's winter in the Highlands." Jericho waved the little group forward and they started to head out of the shallow valley, towards the thin column of grey smoke, coming from the house's chimney.

"At least they must have a bleeding fire on." Wilson commented, bundling his dark riding coat around his large frame. "And some whisky." Owen grunted, shaking his hipflask which was empty of brandy. "I might be able to get this refilled." He added, smiling a little at that thought. Wilson was chuckling to himself, and he turned to Alex, who was now aside of him. "Is that really true what our little pervert asked you?"

Owen groaned and slumped in his saddle. "Does every bugger know?" He said, not a happy young man. Wilson just smiled at him, but spoke to Alex; "Well, is it?" He certainly wasn't going to let the subject drop. It was too good an opportunity; to take the

rise out of his young colleague. Alex smiled at Owen and nodded.

That made Wilson's day and he laughed out loud - drawing a strange look from Jericho - who was consulting his mirror.

"I only meant that..." Owen said softly, but was interrupted by

Wilson; "You asked our lovely colleague and friend to show you her fanny because you've never seen one?" He laughed again, adding; "My God, I wish I had been there to hear that request." Alex stopped brushing snow from her arms and gloves; "Don't be mean Wilson, if poor young Owen has never seen a woman properly and then he's bound to be curious. Especially since that father of his dumped him in that bloody Monastery; at such a young age. He never got the chance to find out about girls or women." She grinned and spoke to Owen but winked at Wilson; "I'm still thinking about your request. I bet you couldn't ask anyone at Moorland Monastery!"

Owen sat bolt upright in his saddle and smiled broadly; "Christ Alex, are you really considering my request? I mean that would really help me cope." Wilson shook his head and smiled; "You're not serious Alex?" She spurred her horse forward and glanced over her shoulder at the pair. "If it really helps poor Owen to cope with his feelings, I just may have to do so." Then joined a very amused Jericho at the front, adding; "After all, what are friends for?"

"Now that's a real friend." Owen said to Wilson; "Not like some." Wilson just grunted and slapped his horse gently. "Come on you mangy beast." The team made the farmhouse, just as night was dropping and the temperature was following it down. Jericho dismounted and pointed to the barn; "The horses will be alright in there. I'll speak to the owners about us staying the night. I'm sure they will like some coins in payment. Times are hard around here after the rebellion was defeated in 1746."

Owen pointed his mirror down and activated its light. In the bright glow everyone could see the three bodies, half buried by the falling snow. Everyone drew their pistols and Alex dismounted and knelt down by the bodies. "Three men; all shot apparently." She lifted one arm of the nearest corpse and nodded; "They haven't been dead long and if I had to guess; I would say they were lined up and shot - by the way they fell - executed." Owen joined her and pushed about in the snow; "No weapons - if they had any." He then stood up and raised his hands nodding towards the barn.

Several British 'redcoat' soldiers were pointing their muskets at them - having emerged quietly from the barn - The Officer lifted his hat and bowed a little; "Please place your weapons upon the ground. You know that carrying weapons in Scotland is an offence and I would be most reluctant to shoot such a pretty lady and one that clearly is not squeamish about examining dead bodies. I find that fact alone intriguing." He replaced his pistol and pointed to the ground; "Very slowly now; no quick movements please."

Jericho, with raised hands, smiled and indicated to his coat pocket; "Lieutenant, I applaud you for your diligence to duty and your application of our laws, but please read the papers that I carry. Then we can all get inside out of this damn weather and have some whisky." The officer glanced at his sergeant; "They are English, fetch whatever is in his pocket." The sergeant walked slowly over and with his pistol still pointing at Jericho, reached in and pulled out [tied and sealed] a rolled parchment. He walked back to the officer and handed it over. A lamp was produced, and the young lieutenant slowly opened the document and read it with great interest for some minutes. "You recognise the signature and seal of the Lord Advocate Sir?" Jericho said softly, adding; "May we please lower our arms and replace our pistols?"

The lieutenant nodded; this strange little group were carrying a very powerful document signed by the Lord Advocate himself; Henry Dundas, 1st Viscount Melville and de-facto ruler of Scotland. "We're all his men - well, except the lady of course - she works for me." Jericho smiled as the soldiers shouldered their muskets at the sergeant's command. "Let's get inside and have some damn whisky." Jericho produced a black bottle of single malt and gestured to the door, adding; "May I have my instructions returned please - if all our officers are as diligent as you - we may need it more than once!"

Owen, with the help of a couple of soldiers, stabled the horses in the barn, where the 'redcoats' had made their beds. The officer's black mare was tied up with a pack mule. Jericho and the officer, with Alex and Wilson following pushed into the farmhouse, the sergeant came too, unloading his pack upon the floor and pulled a small pipe from his pocket and started to fill the bowl.

The officer pulled a chair close to the fire and indicated for Alex to sit and warm herself. She unbuttoned her coat and gracefully eased herself into the seat. Alex was wearing a low-cut bodice and her magnificent breasts were almost showing. She smiled at the young lieutenant as she accepted a glass of whisky from him.

"Another moth to the flame." Muttered Wilson and smiled, gripping his glass and sipping a most welcome drop of whisky. Jericho and the officer sat at the table, drinking and talking. Owen had returned and was placing more coal on the fire. He downed his whisky in one throw and refilled his - and the sergeants - glasses. The sergeant was from Yorkshire and he and Owen got on like a house on fire. He was veteran of the war in the American Colonies and liked his whisky. He was fascinated by Wilson's story; how he had served the crown in the America's [he was a free born man] and being loyal to the King. Had been driven from his home by the American rebels; he now worked for the Lord Advocate here in Scotland.

The sergeant admitted to Owen, that the lady travelling with them, was the best 'piece of skirt' he had seen in years and wondered about what services she performed for Mr. Tibbs, on behalf of the Lord Advocate. Owen just smiled and re-filled his glass. Alex leaned back in her seat and sipped her whisky, she had already noticed that the lieutenant kept throwing glances at her - despite his ongoing conversation with Jericho - she sighed and leaned forward, tapping an escaped piece of coal back into the fire with her boot; unintentionally giving the young man a real show of her magnificent breasts, barely constrained by her bodice. The look on his face priceless and he coughed a little, as he gulped down his whisky.

Alex was given the sole bedroom of the house, whilst Jericho's team and the officer [with the sergeant] bedded down in the living room. The night passed without further incident and over a breakfast of tea, bread, cheese and apples, Jericho briefed his team.

It appears that Willy McKenzie and Daniel Brown were known to the British authorities and had been incarcerated at Scone Castle on suspicion of treason to the crown. But they had produced a smart talking lawyer from Edinburgh and it looked like they would walk from the charges, free men. So, the decision was made; Jericho and his team would accompany the English patrol to Scone castle.

Finally, Alex asked the lieutenant about the three dead men and would they receive a decent Christian burial. He shrugged his shoulders; it appears they were caught with an old broadsword and a pistol that had seen better days. The youngest had the outlawed Scottish flag wrapped around his chest. The lieutenant's orders were clear and concise; they were shot where they stood as traitors to the crown. But just to salve Alex's conscious, he would have them buried and a prayer read over them - he didn't even know their names – he hadn't bothered to ask.

But he was intrigued how Alex knew about medicine and accepted her explanation about her father being a surgeon, who pandered to his daughter's strange fascination with all things medical. The lieutenant was greatly amused by Alex's comments regarding the future, where women would be allowed to practice as Licensed Doctors. "A wonderful dream Alex; but who would trust their health to a woman?" He chuckled and re-filled her glass with a big smile.

They set out for Castle Scone in light snow, but the fallen snow was quite deep - it had snowed all night - but the infantry seemed to cope well enough. Owen overheard a few ripe comments about Wilson riding a horse, when 'decent white men' had to 'fucking' walk. He didn't pass them onto Wilson; the big man was unhappy enough, having to ride the bloody horse in the first place!

The journey would take three days slogging through the snow and the highlight of the trek was finding a small village with a tavern. That made Alex very happy because the owner's wife was genuinely delighted to have a 'Lady of quality' under her roof. She even arranged for a hot bath to be provided and had Alex's travelling clothes cleaned. The hot water wasn't wasted on just bathing Alex; when she had soaked long enough and dressed properly, the tavern's serving girl was allowed to bath - apparently she needed it after servicing four of the soldiers in the small back room - kept aside for such fornication.

When the group left the next day, Jericho paid the tavern owner with silver coin and arranged for the soldiers to have beer and a hot breakfast taken to the stables where they were billeted. They actually gave their benefactor three cheers for that act of kindness; orchestrated by the happy sergeant. Alex gave the tavern owner's wife some silver coin too and they parted like old friends. The officer smiled and spoke quietly to Owen; "Working for the Lord Advocate must pay really well?" Owen nodded; "Mr.

TIbbs is his best servant; he ALWAYS gets the job done - regardless of what the task entails - he gets it done." The officer said nothing further, and the convoy headed out into the snow-covered hills.

Late the following afternoon, Castle Scone came into view across the river. Jericho saw through his telescope that several villages were clustered around its imposing walls. As they passed through its grand entrance, everyone saw the two decomposing men hanging from a wooden gibbet; both had small boards hung around their necks, which said simply: Traitor.

Owen whispered to Alex; "There seems to be a lot of them around here - still." Alex nodded and stared at the pitiful sight, slowing her mount to take a good look. She turned to Owen and said quietly; "I know they are quite ripe, but don't they look familiar?" Owen stared at the bodies hanging before the gates, which were being pulled open by several grunting soldiers and nodded slowly; "I think your right. Where have we met a tall skinny man and a short fat one together; before here?" The little convoy passed into the courtyard of the castle and the great gates were closed behind them.

7. CASTLE SCONE.

The garrison Commander; Captain Edward Sackville watched the patrol return with their 'guests' in tow, from the bay window of his office. He adjusted his wig and placed his large hat upon his head and checked his appearance in the long mirror that stood by the door. Sir Edward was in his late thirties and was a professional soldier; he had served now for almost twenty years and never advanced beyond the rank of Captain.

The reason was simple; he was a bad soldier and an even worse officer. Captain Sackville simply steered away from decision making; any decision making. His soldier servant often repeated the story about the captain and breakfast; he actually took several minutes to decide if he wanted one egg or two! He carefully positioned himself at the desk and moved his chair about; to achieve the best position to portray the air of authority; he needn't bothered; none of his officers or men really had any respect for him. He sat drumming his fingers upon the desk and sat bolt upright when there was a knock at his door. "Enter." He spoke, attempting to inject some authority into his weedy voice.

His clerk: Sergeant Robertson stuck his head around the door and informed him that Lt. Dunbar and those servants of the Lord Advocate were here.

Captain Sackville straightened himself and adjusted his hat - yet again. Lt. Dunbar entered, saluted and sat down without even being asked. Sackville said nothing about that slight to his rank. "The one called Mr. Tibbs is carrying the Token and Warrant of the Lord Advocate; he certainly seems to know what he's doing. They in pursuit of William McKenzie and Daniel Brown; that pair of fuckers, have apparently, been forging stuff they should have left well alone."

Sackville nodded and ensured that his jacket was fastened properly; he glanced enviously at the mirror, but his attention was drawn back to Lt. Dunbar when he mentioned the woman travelling with the Tibbs party. A real beauty according to his Lieutenant and being a vain man, he believed he could seduce the lady easily; he smiled so much that Lt. Dunbar actually asked him, if anything was wrong. He snapped back; "No."

He stood and paced by the fireplace for a minute or so, and he did not reproach the lieutenant about remaining seated when he rose from his chair. Whilst it, made it him a little angry, he said nothing; "Did you say William McKenzie and Daniel Brown?" The captain asked; almost smiling.

The Lieutenant nodded; "That's the pair we have sitting in our cells; Mr. Tibbs has a warrant for them. It appears the dumb bastards have tried their hand at forgery. He needs to speak to them before we hang them for treason." The Lieutenant shifted in his seat; "The Lord Advocate has authorized their pardon, if they co-operate with Mr. Tibbs. The finding of the forger and the document is paramount apparently. Its recovery is critically important for the future of English rule in Scotland."

The captain grinned broadly and clasped his hands like a child at Christmas: "Well, the Lord Advocate will be impressed with the Garrison Commander of Scone Castle because the very same pair are sitting in his dungeon." Lt. Dunbar stood and placed his hat on; "I'll inform our guests that their prey waits in our dungeon."

He bowed a little and made for the South corridor, where the 'guests' had been given rooms.

Wilson and Owen held aloft two lamps as the small group - with Lt. Dunbar - passed down the old stone steps towards the dungeons. Alex actually covered her face with a scented hankie; "What is that bloody awful smell?" She asked Owen, who smiled and waved a hand across his face; "Welcome to eighteenth century prison care. There are no showers, baths or toilets down here, just a big bucket." Alex groaned and held the hankie close. She caught Lt. Dunbar smiling at her - yet again – she just sighed.

"He's real keen Alex and his father is loaded; a mill owner near Manchester I believe, the sergeant told me." Owen whispered and grinned at her breasts protruding from that tight bodice; "He's seen some of the goods on offer and wants the rest I expect." Alex didn't answer; they had arrived at the cell containing McKenzie and Brown.

The old jailer rose from his rough wooden stall and tipped his hat to Alex and the Lieutenant; "Quiet pair these two, they hardly talk. They just sit there staring at nothing." He scratched his chest under a ragged shirt and then his crotch. "But they eat anything given to them." He added, with a toothless grin and then stared straight at Alex's breasts - licking his lips - he was quite repulsive, and Alex turned from him and peered into the cell.

William McKenzie and Daniel Brown sat upon some filthy straw, both chained to the wall with leg irons. They didn't look up as the cell door was pulled open. "On your feet you dogs!" The jailer shouted and kicked Brown, who was nearest to him, adding; "These are the Lord Advocates men and you'll be dancing a jig on the wooden lady sooner than later, if you disrespect them." Brown and McKenzie rose slowly, and both stared at Alex, who pulled her cloak about herself.

Brown smiled; "I don't give a fuck about the Lord Advocates men, but the Lord Advocates woman I would fuck." He and McKenzie chuckled and sat back down. The Lieutenant gestured towards them, and the jailer suddenly produced a wooden stick from somewhere and struck Brown full across the face. He lay in silence upon the floor, a little blood around his mouth and chin. "You will show both, the Lord Advocates men and women respect." Lt. Dunbar said quietly, as the jailer lifted the stick again. Jericho stepped in, smiling. "Thank you, Lieutenant, we'll take it from here, if you could just post a guard outside while Mister Brown and McKenzie have some words with us." Lt. Dunbar was most reluctant to leave Alex in the room, but she persuaded him with a big smile and some quiet words. There was silence until the Lieutenant and the jailer left; slamming the heavy cell door behind them.

Jericho knelt a few feet from the pair and held up a lamp; "Well gentleman, you seem to have got yourself into some trouble here. If you co-operate with me, I can guarantee that your necks won't be stretched and all I ask is for one name; just one little name and you will walk away from here and not carried out in canvas to a dark hole and a nameless grave." Brown and McKenzie exchanged a glance but said nothing. Brown wiped his bloody face and coughed.

Alex produced a small flask of brandy from her skirts and threw it to Brown; "That will ease the pain a little." Brown took the bottle and pulled the stopper out; he spat a loose tooth from his mouth and took a swig, passing it to McKenzie. "Thank you, Ma'am." He said quietly and spat more blood out.

"We know who the Mastermind behind the forged Scottish Accession document was and he has already been dealt with. All we ask is the name of the forger or failing that, where the document is now. Either one given to us will ensure you walk from here free men." Jericho gestured around the room; "Unless you find the King's hospitality too good to forsake?"

McKenzie stared at Wilson and spat upon the floor; "How can a Blackman supports this bastard King; your people are slaves and all we want is the same freedom your people cry for?" Wilson shrugged his shoulders; "I'm a freeman here in Scotland, at the King's kindness and mercy. But in the land of the so called free, those rebellious bastards that now call themselves 'Americans' would have me in chains. It was a very easy choice for me, my friend and now you have a similar choice." Alex had to smile at the supposed sincerity in Wilson's voice; he had always been a diehard American patriot whilst still breathing and she believed that hadn't changed since he died!

McKenzie just shook his head and said nothing more. Brown threw the empty flask back to Alex with a crooked grin; "Thanks Ma'am, now if those English bastards are going to hang me, I would like to ask one last thing." Alex folded her arms and said quietly; "And what would that be?" Brown chuckled, then groaned and held his chin; "Just lift those skirts of yours and show me your cunt and I'll swing a happy man or better still, let me kiss heaven's slit!"

McKenzie laughed at his friends words and then turned angry; snarling, he shouted; "Fuck off! You'll get nothing from us; you fucking stinking little lap dogs!" Both men slumped against the stone wall and stared up at the ceiling. Jericho sighed; "When you're ready to talk, let us know; the offer still stands." He then rose and banged upon the cell door and the Jailer opened it slowly and the group left in silence.

The jailer stood in the doorway and chuckled; "I have news for you two fools, that fancy lawyer from Edinburgh has been sent away with his tail between his legs and the Garrison Commander has signed your death warrants for high treason. You'll swing in the morning, so sleep well tonight." He slammed and locked the door; laughing loudly.

Both men sat in the dark, damp cell and contemplated what the morning would bring. Softly at first, they sang and then standing, sung as loud as their voices would allow. The old jailer, perched upon his rough stool, sighed to himself and slowly drank from his tankard. "Stupid brave bastards." was all he muttered.

8. SCOTLAND THE BRAVE.

The dining room had been laid out for the Garrison Commander and his guests; Lt. Dunbar was joined by Lt. Fairfax, a quiet, chubby young man who seemed uninterested in Alex, but enjoyed Owens's company and conversation at the table. Wilson watched the lieutenant with a growing smile; he certainly did like Owens's company - a lot.

Lt. Dunbar appeared totally engrossed with Alex who sat opposite him and paid little attention to anyone else - mush to the apparent annoyance of Captain Sackville - who couldn't get a word in with Alex: his 'seduction plan' wasn't going too well!

Jericho and Wilson exchanged amused looks, but the meal was excellent and enjoyed by all. The captain led the toasts to the King and the Ladies present; there was only one; Alex, who gracefully received them with apparent pleasure and modesty. The after-dinner conversation turned to Brown and McKenzie; they would be hung at nine o'clock the next morning - unless they decided to co-operate with the Lord Advocates men - Owen cleverly steered the conversation around to the dead men already hanging on the gibbet. Lt. Dunbar managed to pull away from Alex and joined the conversation about the pair.

It appears they were hung last week after a very short trial for treason. They gave their names as Mark Bolland and Clifford Richards; "A very odd pair actually and they died quite miserably, kicking and screaming, they had to be dragged to the scaffold by force. They died disgracefully, not like men at all. There was a good crowd and they ruined it for everyone." Lt. Dunbar sipped his brandy and gestured to the grand window, adding; "With all this snow coming down, Brown and McKenzie will be lucky if Father Stephen bothers to turn up."

"I think they will be happier if the hangman's doesn't show up, rather than Father Stephen." Alex muttered and emptied her brandy glass. Everyone at the table chuckled and Lt. Dunbar seemed quite amazed that a woman could make such a joke - he was impressed - very impressed. Later, he pulled Jericho to one side and asked about Alex; was she married? Promised? Who were her parents? He went on so much that Jericho actually held up his hand to cut the conversation and promised they would talk more tomorrow.

Owen discovered more about Mark Bolland and Cliff Richards from Lt. Fairfax; they had been discovered with various letters and documents from the former American Colonies that must have been treasonous in nature. They appeared to show future battle plans and they clearly planned to replace the good King George with some pretender to the throne; a woman called Victoria. They really couldn't believe they were to hang and screamed and shouted right up to their necks being snapped. "A real strange pair, I think they were from the rebel colonies, here to stir up support and trouble no doubt." Lt. Fairfax then wondered if Owen wished to see his drawings of Highland people and places that he kept in his bedroom; Owen politely declined.

The following morning, Jericho again attempted to convince Brown and McKenzie to talk; without success and thus a small group gathered below the gibbet just before nine o'clock; it was still snowing and bitterly cold. Wilson passed a flask of brandy amongst the team and Lt. Dunbar again, tried to persuade Alex not to watch the execution and like Owen before, she politely declined his request. But he walked away with a real smile on his face; 'what a fucking woman', he muttered to himself, as he finished organizing the hanging to his satisfaction.

McKenzie and Brown were marched out just before nine o'clock; hands tied behind them and still wearing their leg irons; neither had a coat or hat on in the bitter cold. The two-hangman half frog marched, and half dragged them to the gibbet, the nooses were slung causally about their necks and they were stood by the edge. McKenzie started to shout something, but Brown remained silent; his face had swollen up overnight following the blow from the jailer the previous evening.

Without further ceremony, the two hangmen simply pushed the pair from the floor of the gibbet, and they dangled in the air; kicking and choking. It took a couple of minutes for both men to die; the hangman had fucked up somewhat, but no-one was really bothered about that.

Alex discretely pointed to a small hill about half a mile away in the snow flurries; standing upon it was a lone piper. The team could just hear the sad lament being played through the wind and snow. Lt. Dunbar shouted for horses and he, with several men, mounted up to go after the lone piper.

Jericho explained; that by the playing the pipes at a traitor hanging; they were guilty of treason themselves. Alex watched Lt. Dunbar disappear through the grand gates with his mounted infantry following. They all stared at the small hill; the piper was gone. They turned back to the hung men and saw the strange figure in a nice black suit standing in the snow, just below the dangling pair.

Only Jericho and his team could see the collector standing by the gibbet, soul ledger in hand, he was soon joined by Brown and McKenzie and without a word said; the three walked to the bright light and disappeared. A soldier swung each body back onto the platform and fixed a little wooden sign about their necks; 'Traitor' it sated in chalk. He let them swing back out and there, they hung for several days, until replaced by two fresh 'traitors' the following Monday.

The team assembled in the castle's drawing room and sipped warming brandies in relative silence. A young soldier appeared carrying a bucket of coal and built the fire up until it roared and crackled. Alex slumped in a comfortable chair by the fire and was joined by Wilson; "Well, that's made the mission come to an abrupt end." He said quietly and sipped his brandy. "How so?" A puzzled Alex asked; the document had not been found and they still didn't know who the forger was.

Wilson chuckled; "That dumb pair were hung the week before they originally delivered the pouch to that damn solicitor. They actually knew nothing about what Jericho was talking about because they had not met with our not so friendly demon; Monsignor Francis de Ville, which means it never happened; none of it!" He slumped back into his chair and continued; "Don't need to find the forger now or recover the document; the current Human Time-Line has been restored."

A frustrated Lt. Dunbar returned from his fruitless hunt for the lone piper, cursing his bad luck and the worsening snowstorm; but he cheered up whilst sitting and chatting with Alex.

Alex admitted to her friends that young Lt. Dunbar had spoken about marriage and she really needed to exit this mission! After consulting his mirror, that very afternoon, Jericho called the team together in his rooms and they jumped back to the lighthouse together.

John Cordless walked slowly through the snow towards his little office, pulling his heavy coat around and adjusting his scarf and hat. He had money on his mind; if only he could get enough to marry Mary and maybe hire another clerk, his fortunes could rise. He kicked snow from his boots and hung his coat, scarf and hat upon the back of the door, then threw some coal upon the small fire and read the paper with little interest.

Yet another two old Highland warriors had been hung for being traitors; he didn't recognize either of their names and so he turned the page and then an advertisement in the 'Personal' column caught his eye. A Scottish clan leader in the Highlands required a Lawyer for his estates and they could be newly qualified and in-experienced. The pay looked good and a modest house would be provided with two servants included.

John Cordless opened the desk drawer and pulled some sheets of paper from it and dipped his quill pen into the ink pot; working for an ignorant, smelly Scottish Chieftain would be better than going bankrupt and ending up in the street.

THE END

EPILOGUE:

"A very difficult case for Team 74; especially for Alexandra, who was sexually assaulted at one point But the Team succeeded in getting the forged 'Scottish Accession Document' removed from history and the original human time line restored. That total enigma - as Jericho calls him - McIves, had basically saved them and the mission at one point. Just WHO he actually is, remains a mystery."
SJW

CHARACTERS:

There would be no 'Cordless, Cordless & Fraser (Solicitors) in the old quarter of Edinburgh City; John Cordless would die of influenza the following winter; in a damp cold cottage of his master who paid little and expected much. The Highlands proved no place for the delicate young man. John never did marry Mary. His soul was collected and processed.

Sir David Fraser obviously never became a Partner in the famous old firm of Solicitors, but had his own practice in Edinburgh during the 1980's. With the timeline restored to its original path; he never encountered Alex. He was married three times and had two children. He was tragedy killed in spring 1991, when his New Mercedes was hit by a speeding lorry on the M9. His soul was collected and processed.

Lt. Dunbar searched Edinburgh and the surrounding towns and villages for Alex. Even obtaining an interview with the Lord Advocate and was bitterly disappointed that a certain Mr. Tibbs and Mistress Alexandra didn't work for him; nevertheless, he continued to search for her in the coming years and died in 1786 when his horse threw him during a fox hunt. His soul was collected and processed.

Young Peter Davidson obviously never worked for Cordless,

Cordless & Fraser (Solicitors) and joined the British Army in 1980. He was killed on active service in Bosnia, when his lorry left a broken road and collided with a stone wall in 1994; he left a widow and three children. His soul was collected and processed.

Carl McDonnell [Peter's assistant] also was never employed by the solicitors; he worked for several fast-food outlets around Edinburgh in the 1980's and became, sadly, involved in the drug culture of the time. He died in 1987 after consuming a 'cocktail' of drugs whilst drunk. He never married nor had children. His soul was collected and processed.

Hamish Brown [junior clerk at the Solicitors] was found floating in the Forth River in the winter of 1981. He had been brutally murdered. It was understood that he had connections with a certain Glasgow Gang that didn't like him selling drugs on their 'patch'. No-one was ever arrested or brought to trial for the murder, and it remains unsolved to this day. His soul was collected and processed.

Alexander McIves - 'Black Sword - was reported many times in different times and places, always with his legendary sword at his side. He remains an elusive fugitive from the Temporal Detective Department to this day. His soul remains missing.

Colin Coves - 'Colin from Aberdeen' - was killed in a car accident in the Highlands in 1984. He was four times the legal limit for driving, both his two passengers were also killed: two young sisters from a local village. His soul was collected and processed.

Rosemary Alice Cairns [Rosie the medic] worked in a factory during the 1980's and married in 1984. She had three children and seven grandchildren. She died in 2031 and her soul was collected and processed.

Captain Edward Sackville retired from the British Army in 1783 – he never advanced beyond the rank of Captain - and returned to his uncle's farm in Kent. The pair quickly fell out and on Christmas Eve 1785, his enraged and drunk Uncle took a hunting gun to Edward. His soul was collected and processed. His Uncle was found 'not guilty' of murder at Maidstone Assizes that year.

John Dawson Butcher [the 'Redcoat' sergeant] retired from the British Army in 1786 and returned to his native Yorkshire and ran a tavern in the city of York. He lived to be over ninety years old - a staggering good age for the times - and died in 1827. His soul was collected and processed.

Mark Bolland and Cliff Richards [the first pair hung at Scone Castle] were, in fact; Simon John Parks and Phillip Wallington from Liverpool in 2026. The Temporal Detectives encountered them previously at Gettysburg in 1863. The two time travelers had failed to alter the outcome of the battle and had turned up in 1780 in Scotland. That was their fatal mistake; they were mistaken for 'Traitors' and hung. The pair was both humans out of their ordained time period and thus, their souls were lost: they remain missing to this day.

William McKenzie and Daniel Brown have no song or plaque in their names: for their stand against the British. They are totally forgotten to history. Their souls were collected and processed.

Lt. John Fairfax served for some nine years in the wilds of Scotland and returned to his home city of Manchester in 1789. He was embroiled in an early 'Rent Boy' scandal and fled to the new United States of America. There he opened a small bookshop and died, aged 73. He had never married nor had children. His soul was collected and processed.

The demon Kiri - defeated by James - returned to his master a failure, but the 'Dark Prince' wasn't too disappointed and treated Kiri well. The demon has vowed vengeance on both Jericho Tibbs and 'Black Sword'.

The very talented 'Forger' remains unknown, and the forged Scottish Accession Document has never resurfaced. After three Referendums regarding 'Scottish Independence and Scottish Devolution'; Scotland remains part of the United Kingdom: for now.

EPISODE 9: "PHARAOH AMENHOTEP V AND THE MIRROR OF TIME."

MISSION SUMMARY:
"Pharaoh Amenhotep V's magician has been ordered to investigate a strange mirror that appears to show alternative versions of the future - apparently, the mirror was robbed from an ancient tomb which belonged to the legendary magician; Tha, who is said to have received it from the God Thoth himself. But the King is known as the 'Dark Pharaoh' and plans to use the device for his own benefit and alter the destiny of his ancient Empire. Mr. Tibbs is dispatched to protect the current Time-Line from change."

NOTES: contains strong sexual references and a description of a sexual assault.

 ALCOHOL, VIOLENCE, STRONG SEXUAL REFERENCES [including sexual assault] STRONG LANGUAGE & MILD HORROR.

15+ AGE 15+ ONLY.   **45 Minutes reading time.**

1. ROYAL COURT OF PHARAOH at THEBES [LUXOR] during Peret [Growing Season] around 1320BC.

Simhenta-Kara carefully placed the brightly painted chest upon the stone floor and looked about the room that he and his master; Sentus-Kasim had been provided by the Royal Chamberlain. He walked to the large open window, covered by two embroidered curtains and stared out. The city was sprawled out below the window; "Typical, we're at the back of the palace with no view of the river." He sighed and watched, as his master's two household slaves, started to unpack the personal luggage and set the room up.

The Royal magician; Sentus-Kasim would only allow his young assistant to move or handle the magic props. Lulha wandered in and also stared out of the window which dominates the room. "No bloody view of the river; great!" She muttered with some sarcasm in her voice. Simhenta watched her with envious eyes; the pretty young girl was the old Magicians slave of the bed chamber. Simhenta found it hard to stomach, that the old man bedded such a lovely young girl, just because he had paid gold for her.

He quickly averted his eyes, when Sentus appeared and slumped in a newly placed chair and pulled the thick plaid wig from his head and cursed. He waved at Simhenta and groaned; "Some bloody emissaries have arrived from the Kadesh King and will receive audience with Pharaoh tonight, which means my performance will now be tomorrow night." Ghusan, the old magician's personal body slave, took the wig and placed it upon its stand and checked for new lice.

Lulha handed her master a cup of wine and said nothing. The old man ran his free hand up her thigh until it rested against her taught belly. "Still, it gives me more time to enjoy my new young bed slave." The old man grinned and sipped his wine, running a hand over the girls bum and between her legs; she didn't smile or react.

His unwelcome gropes were ended by the arrival of the Pharaoh's personal secretary, who informed Sentus that the Pharaoh demanded his presence now. "It is not for performance, but council." The secretary reassured the near panicked magician.

Thus, Sentus and Simhenta, suitably dressed to greet Pharaoh, made their way to the King's personal apartments; both were impressed by the King's bodyguard - Nubian soldiers dressed in silver and gold tunic's with vicious looking curved swords - they were known to be totally loyal to the King. They knew something was up, when they were shown into the King's inner sanctuary and were greeted by two naked young girls, bearing cups of wine. Simhenta smiled broadly at the pair and received quite a smile back; they were wearing nothing, but thick decorated collars and lotus flowers entwined in their long dark hair. "The King will be here in minutes." Dushan, the King's secretary announced and took a cup from the girls, then shooed them away; with a wave of his hand.

Dushan looked about and pulled the pair close to him; "What the King is about to impart could get you both killed, if you unwisely speak of it, to the wrong person." He then bowed quite low, as a dark curtain was pulled aside by a particularly fierce looking Nubian. Simhenta whispered to his master; "That's Talin, the Pharaoh's personal bodyguard, he never leaves the King's side, he never speaks; except with his sword."

Old Sentus-Kasim gulped and nervously smiled as Pharaoh Amenhotep stood before them; everyone bowed quite low. Simhentra immediately noticed the physical difference between the new King and his late predecessor; Pharaoh Tutankhamen who had lain in his tomb, these past three years. Amenhotep was a powerfully build man with cold, cruel eyes of black. He was not known for his mercy. He had taken the throne of Egypt by marriage to the young king's widow, and none defied him; he had commanded the Egyptian Army [at the time] and was a great warrior. He was also pious to the old Gods and had overthrown Tutankhamen's father's change, to a single God; the Aten, reverting the Kingdom to the religion of the ancient Gods.

The 'heretic' Pharaoh Akhenaten's name and very existence in Egyptian History had been obliterated from monuments and court records. Even his new capital had been deserted and was turning to ruins in the Armana desert.

Simhentra knew one fact, well known to every Egyptian; you didn't fuck with this Pharaoh. The Pharaoh pointed directly at Simhentra and spoke to Sentus; "Can this young man be trusted with Pharaoh's secrets?" The old Magician bowed even lower, well as much as his age and back allowed him; "Yes my Lord, Simhentra is my trusted assistant and apprentice. He only speaks of matters that I allow him. I would trust him with my life."

The Pharaoh smiled and grunted; "If you're wrong in your trust Setus, then it will be your life." Simhentra saw the look of sheer fear upon his old master's face but said nothing. The King folded his arms adding; "And your life as well." He indicated to Simhentra with another evil smile.

A young naked girl brought a tray with cups of wine and Simhentra noticed that the King's goblet was solid gold, encrusted with jewels, while they received plain silver cups. The Pharaoh gripped old Sentus's shoulder and spoke quietly; "My Captain, who guards the old tombs upon the Giza, discovered that a local family had indulged in some grave robbing. He had them all thrown to the God Hapi and the good God's servants [Nile crocodiles] devoured them. No afterlife for such villains." He grinned broadly and clapped his hands. The young girl disappeared with some haste; like her very life depended upon it. "If anyone here speaks, writes or even whispers about what they see; the God Hapi will have more tasty morsels for his children." Pharaoh nodded to Talin, who walked to the dark curtain and pulled it aside.

Two large Nubian servants carried in a heavy chest and placed it before Pharaoh, standing to one side, when indicated to do so, by Talin. Pharaoh patted the box gently and Talin carefully unlocked the chest, which was entirely painted black with no writing or symbols. "A funeral chest." Sentus muttered and wiped his face with a very nervous hand.

The big Nubian slowly opened the chest which contained bundles of black cloth and Pharaoh pushed his hands inside and slowly lifted a small, square shaped object that easily fitted into one hand. It glinted and sparkled in the light of the rooms lamps; Setus and Simhentra gasped as they could clearly see their reflections upon its strange surface, which also contained hieroglyphs they did not recognise or understand.

"This was robbed from the tomb of a long dead Magician, who served a great Pharaoh some thousand years before." He turned the object in his hands slowly, almost with reverence. He smiled a little, adding; "I've had several of my best and most educated servants and priests examine it. Four are dead and two simply vanished – gone - no trace of them found. Now I want you to discover how the thing works and what purpose it serves."

He placed the object into Setus's trembling hands and patted the old man; "It's our little secret my new friend, after all, no Pharaoh wants to be accused of receiving goods that were robbed from a tomb; now does he?"

Sentus nodded and whispered; "Of course not my Lord." He carefully wrapped the strange, and apparently deadly, object up in the cloth. Pharaoh pointed to the exit; "Go now and see what you discover. But remember, you cannot leave the palace without my express permission - on pain of death. Everything you require will be provided by my secretary Dushan; food, wine, gold and silver, girls, just ask and it will be done."

Sentus and Simhentra bowed and backed slowly towards the door, they were almost outside the chamber when Pharaoh called after them; "Oh, and please don't fail me, as that could have quite unpleasant consequences; for you." The King smiled broadly and walked away with Talin just steps behind him.

They both knew what Pharaoh meant by that - death; thrown to the crocodiles - if they were lucky and if Pharaoh was merciful that day! And that's if the strange device didn't kill them first.

2. THOTH'S MAGIC MIRROR OF TIME?

The pair sat in the gathering gloom of night and stared at the object, now placed upon a small table before them. They both sipped wine and for several minutes nothing passed between them, until the old magician sighed loudly and allowed a few tears to fall; "I know what it is." He said simply and gulped down his wine, allowing Simhentra to replenish his cup.

Simhentra could see fear - real fear - in the old man's face and hear it, in his trembling words. "You didn't tell Pharaoh what you knew because he would have killed us. Once we're of no use anymore, that will happen, and it will keep his dirty secret of receiving robbed tomb goods. I strongly suspect he kept all the gold and other precious items from those ransacked tombs, for himself." He whispered to the old man who nodded. Sentus pointed a shaking finger towards the object and spoke very quietly; "It was robbed from the tomb of the great and legendary magician; Tha. He died over a thousand years ago and his name and exploits are still known to this day. Whilst the many Pharaohs that have passed since then are mostly forgotten, with their temples gone and no one recalls their names. They have left history, but Tha lives on, in people's memories and hearts. He was a good man, kind and generous to the poor and a magician who almost equalled Thoth in talent. It was said that he was able to part the Nile waters with simple words of power and Hapi didn't mind. He could cure blindness and leprosy with potions and magic. There is a story that he could even raise the newly dead - before the fucking undertakers and priests pulled everything from their bodies and mummified the poor bastards." The old man sipped more wine and ran a hand over his face.

"Promise me Simhentra; that you will not allow them to disgrace my body in such as manner but bury me according to the instructions I have left for you. I have no family to object or prevent such a burial. You will inherit what little I have - as the son I never had - Do you promise me this?" The old man gripped Simhentra's arm with hidden strength.

The young man nodded his agreement; "Everything will be done as you say Master." That made the magician smile and he rose and walked slowly to his bedroom and rather strangely - to Simhentra's mind - he turned and said quietly; "May your God's bless you and let happiness into your life and love into your heart." The old magician retired for the night, leaving his apprentice to ponder his words.

Simhentra knew his master practised a strange religion which declared just one God and grand stone tombs, mummification and offerings were not needed to enter paradise or gain its favour. He had also been an admirer of the heretic Pharaoh Akhenaten and often spoke about the religion that the Jewish slaves adhered to.

"A very complex old man, but he has always treated me well." Simhentra whispered to himself and knew that the real legacy, the old man had bequeathed to him, was the much-acclaimed art of magic. He was the royal magician, because in a land full of magicians; he was simply the best. His only rival in talent and fame was probably the young Menes; the great magician from the North.

The old man's words about Tha made him recall what every magician knew that part of the story kept from the adoring masses; that Tha had been visited by Thoth himself and given a mirror from the God's, which showed both the past and the present. The mirror also had the ability to carry its owner to the 'hereafter' or back to the distant past. Simhentra actually shuddered, despite the heat of the night. He had just imagined what Pharaoh would do with such a device.

Simhentra recalled the old man's story, spoken in whispers; "As a young magician, I heard some of the stories about Tha. It is said that he travelled to strange lands and encountered unbelievable beasts, people whose skins were of many colours and even birds made of metal that roared and swept through the sky, where only God's should go. Tha served three Kings, but was murdered by a black hearted Pharaoh, who heard his story about the fall of the Egyptian Empire and how the God's were replaced by a single entity, who demanded nothing from his people but love."

The old man had slumped in his chair, muttering curses upon the device that lay before him. "We should smash it and flee for our lives." He had whispered and stumbled towards his bed, calling for Ghusan to attend him. "Hide it well Simhentra, let no other person be infected by its presence." Simhentra did as his was told and wrapped the device up and carried it to his bed, where he lay sleepless for many hours, until he finally slept and suffered a horrendous nightmare.

But it was Lulha shouting that awoke him just before dawn. He scrambled from his bed and ran to his master's chamber to find Ghusan kneeling and weeping by the old magician's bed. Luitha gripped Simhentra by the arm and whispered; "He's dead.... but look at his face....demons from the afterlife must have visited him!"

Simhentra approached the bed slowly and held a hand over his mouth; the old man lay face up and that face was contorted in pain and fear; the eyes and mouth wide open. "Fetch the physician." he spoke quietly to Ghusan and held Lutha tightly in his arms; it felt good.

The royal physician examined Sentus and pronounced that he had expired due to his heart suddenly stopping; "That would explain his contorted face and outstretched hands." The physician concluded and bowed to the Kings personal secretary, who nodded his agreement and acceptance of the good doctor's diagnosis. Dushan stood by the bed and shook his head: "The Pharaoh will not be pleased by this turn of events." He sighed and told a servant to inform the king of the magician's untimely death. Dushan pulled Simhentra to one side and spoke quietly; "You will need to convince the Pharaoh, that you can finish the task assigned by him - despite the death of your master - and produce the results he wants. Do you understand me?"

Simhentra nodded; he understood all too well; what the King's Secretary meant.

"I understand that the old magician had no living family, so I will instruct the Priests at his local temple to find in your favour; you had served him for many years and was born a free man?" Simhentra nodded again. Thus, Dushan would arrange for the Chief Priest, at the old man's temple, to declare Simhentra as sole beneficiary to Sentus-Kasim. This would mean, the young man now owned slaves [including Gushan and Lulha] a house in Thebes and a small country estate in Edfu. - And of course; the magic act - if he stayed alive long enough to enjoy his new fortune!

The Pharaoh; was certainly not pleased at the death of the magician but was impressed enough with Simhentra to allow him to continue working on the strange mirror. As he walked from the King's private audience chamber, distant screams punctuated by wailing and crying, floated within his hearing. He stopped and stared towards the city wall that fronted the Nile.

He heard several splashes and more screaming, which continued for some minutes before silence. Well, not complete silence; the wailing of mourning women now replaced the screams of dying men; the children of Hapi had been fed again.

He slumped upon a chair in his rooms and stared out the window. There were now two Nubian guards posted to his quarters and they had orders never to leave the young magician alone. The King called them 'bodyguards' but Simhentra knew they were Wardens; looking after the prisoner before his execution.

He had arranged for Gushan and Lulha to be taken to the country estate, away from the King; out of sight - out of mind - well, that's what he hoped. Simhentra poured some wine and picked at the figs left out for him. Now he needed to apply his mind to the unusual funeral of his old master.

3. A COSTUME DRAMA.

Alex, at first, steadfastly refused to wear the outfit. She dug her heels in and said NO. But Jericho patiently pointed out that the clothes were totally appropriate, for a woman of high birth in ancient Egypt, particularly at the royal court of Pharaoh. They were very necessary to the mission and Jericho knew that Alex understood that and so pushed the point home. Finally, after some heated discussions, Alex reluctantly agreed. But still under protest!

She appeared in the study wearing a long dark trench coat, wrapped closely about herself, which drew some odd looks from the others. Jericho grinned and shook his head; "Come on Alex, we're in our costumes and I look a right twat in this skirt thing. You can't wear a trench coat in Ancient Egypt; besides you'll sweat to death!" He held up his hands, adding; "Best get it over with and you'll quickly get use to wearing next to nothing. It may be very liberating; we are all good friends and professionals here, you know."

Alex slowly unwrapped and dropped the coat to the floor; Young Ruth gathered it up and tried not to stare. She had never seen an outfit that high born women of Ancient Egypt wore - well, almost wore - it was very revealing and would cause a sensation, even in the 21st Century.

"I didn't know, that by becoming a Temporal Detective, a condition of service was that I had to show my fanny and bum to anyone who cared to look." Alex said, with her arms folded and then dropped them to her sides. "Well have a bloody good look and get it out of your system." She spoke softly and didn't smile. Jericho and Wilson chuckled and said, "Well done Alex." but Owen said nothing, He simply could not take his eyes off Alex.

Wilson slapped Owen on the back and laughed; "Take a good look boy; that is a real woman in all her glory. Most men would happily murder their granny to possess such a beauty." Even the normally reticent Jericho had to agree with that statement. Alex was simply stunning in her costume.

Alex was dressed as high-born women of the Royal Egyptian

Court: with a full plaid black wig festooned with jewels, a long thin dress of the finest cotton which was almost transparent, and gold covered sandals. Her arms had amulets of gold and silver; she was completely naked beneath [as was the custom for such high-born women]. She placed both arms upon her slender hips and stared at Owen; "Would you like me to do a twirl, so that you can see everything?"

Owens's eyes fixed upon her magnificent breasts and dropped slowly to her thighs. He took a very deep breath and felt giddy; his life in the monastery hadn't equipped him to deal with such a sight. He actually couldn't say anything, and he simply couldn't look away; no matter how hard he tried to force himself.

She lifted her arms and turned around slowly. Poor Owen was already the colour of a tomato and he simply blurted out; "Sweet Jesus Alex! Your arse could drive demons mad!" But when he saw the look Alex gave him, he gulped and tried to apologise, but Alex actually smiled; "I'm joking Owen, I'm sure you didn't have many dealings with women in the Monastery, that your father dumped you in. I do know that you don't mean any offence by staring. Fill your boots!" She did another little twirl and patted his shoulder, then walked to the table, picking up a glass of brandy - she really needed it - and no-one looked anywhere else but at her bum, moving from side to side with her little strides and Owen actually groaned quite loudly!

"Now you don't get an offer like that every day." Wilson chuckled and gripped Owen by the arm, adding; "Best put your eyeballs back in their sockets before they roll about the floor. But, by Christ, your right about our girls arse; it could easily drive dead men into a sexual frenzy." Wilson turned to Alex, smiling; "Just one question baby girl, where the hell did you hide your mirror?" Alex grinned back and said softly; "Wouldn't you like to know!" she had recovered her humour, much to the relief of her colleagues. Owen kept looking at Alex and sipped his brandy with a strange look upon his young face. Wilson noticed it and whispered to Jericho; "I think our young apprentice detective has discovered what he missed, whilst he still breathed."

Jericho - still smiling broadly - clapped his hands and pointed to the door; "Let's go people and I hope you really like camels." The little group headed for the light room and jumped to Ancient Thebes in the year 1320BC.

They camped some kilometres from the city and sat about the fire, drinking brandy from silver cups and eating roast chicken and bowls of milky lentil's, garnished with herbs and a little spice. Angel Margret had provided servants and Nubian guards from the period, whilst Temporal Inspector Fabien Bisset had arranged for them to meet his human agent for this period.

Jericho recounted the brief he had received about the mission, they were now undertaking; "It was young Herbie the collector that reported what the old man had told him, to his boss. Who passed it onto Angel Margret and now we must investigate and recover the damn thing."

Alex - happily wrapped in a thin cloak - nodded; she had heard the rumours about the missing mirror. Apparently, it had gone missing from a member of Inspector Fabien's team, some thousand human years before this time. He had been investigating a breech in the Timeline [someone from 1935 had arrived in 2350BC] when it disappeared. According to regulations, Inspector Fabien would not be allowed to investigate an incident concerning a member of his team and so tracing the missing mirror had been passed to Jericho and his team.

Owen added to the discussion with his research on the incident: *"It appears that whoever arrived from 1935 managed to steal the mirror and disappear. The suspect was an American called Russel Hudson who discovered a natural tear in the timeline and travelled back to 2350BC, where he attended the Pharaoh's court, using a magic act to fund his life here. He became a legend; still spoken about today [1320BC]. Unfortunately, he hadn't done much preparation about the period and upset a few powerful men by sleeping with their wives and daughters. He was murdered by a close friend of the third Pharaoh that he served, who covered up his friends crime. But his reputation forced the authorities to bury the magician with full honours. Inspector Fabien did search his tomb; but nothing was found."*

"It was probably taken by thieves before the tomb was even sealed up - grave robbing was a full-time business - for some families around here." Alex spoke quietly and finished her brandy.

Jericho nodded at that and said softly; "Our mirrors have a defence mechanism which does not allow living humans to operate them. Should one try, the mirror will freeze them and their time period. Then send a warning message back to the Control Centre, who would arrange for temporal detectives to attend. Since that did not happen, we can only deduce that the mirror is damaged; it has become a very dangerous object to leave around."

Wilson coughed and sipped his drink; "Herbie the collector was told by the old man - who was a magician himself at Pharaoh's court - about 'Thoth's Mirror' and realised it could be the missing mirror - It had resurfaced after nearly a thousand years. As Jericho said, the thing could be damaged, four people from here died trying to operate the damn mirror and worse; no souls were collected, and the mirror sent no SOS; very odd. Two managed to open the travel app and they ended up in Brazil in the year 875AD - local natives killed and ate them - The pair had stupidly or in ignorance, left the bloody mirror behind. They couldn't get back and being out of their own time; no souls were collected. The Collector's called the finding of all these soulless bodies in. All the men were traced back to this period of history, but it was assumed that the group was playing around with yet another time portal, they had discovered locally. Only when Herbie the collector called the old man's story in, was it realised that the missing mirror could be the key to their soulless deaths." Wilson downed his drink and smiled a little.

"The old magician was murdered in his bed, by the slave girl that he raped on a regular basis; she suffocated him whilst he slept. It's a pretty good bet that the old man's apprentice knows where it is." Wilson added, refilling his cup.

"He's, our target." Jericho said simply and allowed Wilson to refill his cup.

One of their guards shouted that a rider approached on a camel. "Our human agent, I do believe." Jericho smiled and they stood and awaited the arrival of Inspector Fabien's contact for this period and place.

The following morning, a very grand camel train entered the ancient city of Thebes. Crowds of people watched the convoy passing through the great North Gate and whispered amongst themselves that the train contained Northern Egypt's Governor's daughter; the Lady Isis, who was rumoured to be the most beautiful woman in the Kingdom and a devotee of the Goddess, whose name she bore and whose powers she could enact at will. No man dared to try and possess such a woman [without her consent] because of the protection the Goddess bestowed upon her Priestess; few pious Egyptians would risk the wrath of the Goddess Isis.

Most agreed that it was appropriate, that she was accompanied by the North's greatest magician: Menes. The caravan reached the royal palace of Pharaoh Amenhotep V by mid morning and were greeted by the King's personal Secretary; Dushan.

4. MENES THE MAGICIAN.

Jericho bowed low and introduced his personal servant and travelling steward to Dushan; young Ossan. "Don't be fooled by his youth my lord, his mind is sharp and quick......" But the King's secretary stared beyond them both, at the large, imposing Nubian bodyguard who towered above everyone. "I take it that this man - if indeed he is a man - is the Priestess Isis's guard?" Jericho smiled and clapped his hands for the six litter bearers to lower their burden to the sand. "My lord, may I present the flower of the North, Goddess Isis's own Priestess who bears her name and enjoys the Goddess's blessings; the Lady Isis!"

Two slaves pulled the curtains of the litter apart and the Priestess stepped from it into the warm sunshine. There were loud gasps from the crowds, and many knelt down, Jericho heard several shout; "It must be herself!" Alex walked slowly towards the King's Secretary, who simply stood with his mouth half open; the old man was transfixed. "By the God's Menes, she IS the Goddess in living form. No woman walking this earth could compare with her!" He actually bowed low himself and managed to mumble out an official greeting.

The crowds were cheering wildly; they knew that the priestess's visit would bring much luck to their city - and them. Alex thanked Dushan for his words and gave a small wave to the adoring crowds, some men in the throng were actually fighting to get a better look and city guards had to separate them, using their sticks.

Dushan escorted Lady Isis and the magician Menes into the state rooms of Pharaoh's palace where food and drink awaited them.

Dushan whispered to a trusted servant to fetch the King; he knew that the King would wish to greet Lady Isis himself. Walking behind Alex, dressed a little more modestly, but still naked beneath her thin dress, was Thy, the Priestess's maid and the local human agent for this time. The difference in height between the two women was noted by all; Alex would be much taller than most grown females of this time because of human evolution - women had gained a little more height - over the centuries and the difference was now pronounced.

But it added to Alex's mystic; the God's were much bigger than mortal humans and so that just confirmed her position, in the Goddess's blessings, to most citizens and palace staff. Owen and Wilson noted that the ladies of Pharaoh's court were dressed similar to Alex and there were some beautiful women amongst them. But none compared to Alex [they both agreed on that]. Owen smiled and whispered; "Best fill our boots as Alex says." Wilson chuckled and definitely enjoyed the views on offer.

Owen recognised that Thy was an attractive young woman in her own right and watched her swinging backside as she walked in front of him. Thy was the youngest daughter of the local magistrate and had received a good education for a woman of this period. Her father had signed a marriage contract with a certain captain in Pharaoh's army of occupation in Kush; the pair would formally marry upon his return in a year or so.

Alex was not surprised that Thy considered Wilson a very handsome man; her future husband was of Nubian descent himself and no one really cared about 'mixed marriages' around here. Thy was pale skinned with green eyes and that didn't matter to him either. "He's a good man and he calls me his 'Isis'." She had confided to Alex. Apparently, Inspector Fabian also admired the big man; he was Fabien's man in Kush!

Both Alex and Wilson admitted they would really like to meet this army captain, who had quite modern ideas about his forthcoming marriage. They were now in the centre of the magnificent State rooms and could see it was filled with dignitaries of Pharaoh's court.

The High Priest of the temple of Amen-Ra [the father of the Gods and Egypt's Principal Deity] stood watching with his own secretary. Kumanine was also the pharaoh's Chief Minister and the second most powerful man in the Kingdom. He drew a heavy breath and turned to his man with a worried look upon his face. "In forty years walking this earth, I have never seen such beauty bestowed upon a mortal woman. There will be trouble in the King's harem when he casts eyes upon her. We both know his appetite for women - beautiful women." He sighed loudly and added; "Then we have the most urgent question of the succession, so this lady may be the answer to all the king's problems."

Then Kumanine hesitated and groaned a little; "Or be the cause of all the King's problems, if she refuses."

The young secretary nodded; Pharaoh's Queen was a sickly young girl, who by marriage had bestowed the throne upon Amenhotep - she had no choice in the matter - her husband was dead and she had produced no male heirs and still hadn't done so. The King's two chief Concubines had also failed to produce a boy, giving him three daughters. Two of them already in their tombs; Infant mortality in the ancient world was common and affected rich and poor alike.

The King did have some twenty-one children by women in his harem - he had over a hundred women and girls - but none had the rank to be Queen or even produce a son that the Empire would accept as Pharaoh. The secretary stared at the Priestess and one thought passed through his mind: A real Queen - acceptable to all. - But more importantly, able to have a son with a full claim to his father's throne.

The High Priest and his man exchanged glances, both knowing what the other was thinking; this woman had the sheer beauty to be Queen and her position as Priestess of Isis certainly gave her the rank to be Queen - there would be no argument about any son sitting upon the Gold Throne - none whatsoever. But her position also created a real problem for the King, if she refused his offer of marriage and the throne. He could not just take her; that would be sacrilege and blaspheming in Egyptian law and could easily cause civil war amongst his nobility and Priests.

The High Priest wiped his face, terrified at his own thoughts. Such action would certainly incur the wrath of the Goddess and the people would not stand for that. The kingdom could be in bloody chaos and fighting in just weeks, in the event of a disastrous decision by the King. Few Egyptians had forgotten the turmoil and trouble caused by the heretic Akhenaten, just a few years ago. Egypt could not afford another religious civil war. "If our prince so desires her, then she must be persuaded to submit for Egypt's sake." He whispered and turned to the grand entrance; Pharaoh was here.

The King desired to see the magician Menes about a certain little matter and thus came straight away. But all thoughts about the mirror simply faded when he was introduced to the Lady Isis. He eased himself onto a gilded chair and just sat staring at her; saying nothing.

The Lord Chamberlain gave a nervous cough which broke the silence in the packed chamber; "Your majesty, maybe the great Northern magician will be allowed to entertain us?" The old man had to repeat his request twice before Pharaoh pulled his eyes away from Alex and mumbled a 'yes'.

Everyone in the chamber exchanged glances - but said nothing - they all knew their King was utterly captivated by the Priestess and each wondered if they were looking at their new Queen.

Menes stepped forward and bowed; "You Majesty, may I present a very humble performance called the 'empty chair?" The Pharaoh nodded and smiled broadly at Alex, who sipped wine with some grace from a golden cup. The King's eyes followed her body from its toes to her face [again] and felt his mouth dry. He actually muttered which only Kumanine and the Lord Chamberlain heard, and both winced at his words - especially one of them - 'Queen'.

 A simple plain wooden chair was placed before Pharaoh and the audience shuffled a little forward to catch a better view. Menes unfurled a bright red sheet and showed it to everyone and then asked the Priestess to sit upon the chair, which she agreed and sat down. The magician carefully placed the sheet over the Lady Isis, covering her completely. She made the chamber laugh by complaining that the lamps had gone out. Pharaoh gulped down wine and leaned forward; "I trust the lady will come to no harm magician, for if she does, you may find yourself swimming in the Nile with some new friends." The King didn't smile.

Menes smiled and clapped his hands; the bright red sheet

fluttered to the ground; the chair was empty.

There was silence for a few seconds, then huge applause and shouts of praise rang around the chamber. Pharaoh rose and walked to the chair lifting it slightly; like everyone else, he was totally amazed; the great lady had simply vanished. Disappearing in a packed chamber with no hidden traps or mirrors, that could have been prepared in advance.

Simhentra could not believe what he had just seen [like everyone else - well, except Wilson and Owen - who smiled to themselves] the magician had performed an incredible disappearing act with just a chair and a sheet, whilst surrounded by a packed audience. "It's totally impossible!" he whispered and couldn't even begin to see how it was achieved.

The King slumped back in his chair; he had seen many magic performances in his time, but this simple little act was the most incredible thing he had ever witnessed. He stared at Menes, who was taking bows from the crowd, and knew this was the man to prise open the secrets of 'Thoth's Mirror'.

Menes placed the sheet carefully back over the chair and called upon Thoth to return the Priestess, then slowly lifted the sheet high above his head; revealing the chair was no longer empty; the Lady Isis sat drinking her wine and smiled at the crowd; "Have I missed anything exciting?" She said and laughed, to the delight of the audience and particularly Pharaoh, who had already made up his mind about both the magician and his new Queen.

Simhentra eased his way through the excited crowd and introduced himself to Menes, who appeared quite pleased to meet the young magician. But the chamber fell silent as Pharaoh arose and gripped Lady Isis by the hand and ran a soft finger across her lips, "My Lady you are truly beautiful, intelligent, pious, funny and graceful. You are already judged a Queen, just by those gifts that the God's have bestowed upon you. Now you WILL be Queen in truth."

Alex was caught totally unprepared, as he simply gripped her and placed a kiss upon her lips. The King was most reluctant to release her, and Alex pulled away from him with some effort and stood back from the King. "I am no tavern whore to be handled and taken at will. I will retire for the night and hope your majesty will be in better condition come the morrow."

But the King grabbed her back with some force, causing her to yelp; "Yes, you retire for the night sweet lady and sleep well, for tomorrow you WILL become my Queen." He released the shaking woman, who was immediately attended by her maid; Thy. "No, I will not sir." Alex said with real defiance in her voice. The chamber was in absolute silence, and many stood quite shocked by what had just happened. The stand-off between the Priestess and the King continued for a few painful seconds and then Kumanine, Dushan and the Lord Chamberlain diplomatically intervened.

"This great matter must be discussed with your council your majesty, a Pharaoh cannot be seen to defy the laws of his brother and sister Gods. She IS the Priestess of Isis herself - she cannot be compelled to marry by threat or force - it will tear your kingdom apart. Remember the heretic Akenaten and those troubled times my lord." Kumanine spoke in a whisper and the Lord Chamberlain agreed with him, adding; "Let us persuade the lady with reason and argument - she is a very intelligent woman my lord - she will see sense."

Pharaoh grunted his agreement with their words; "Make sure you succeed, for she will become my Queen - regardless of what happens - I will have her." He turned to Talin and ordered; "Escort the lady to her chambers and see that she has anything she wants." The King's personal bodyguard obeyed; Alex and Thy said nothing but followed the soldiers. Alex glanced back at Jericho with a real expression of concern upon her face. Jericho nodded to her and found Wilson and Owen. "I think we may have over-egged the pudding this time. But I've made contact with the old magicians apprentice, and he does possess the mirror."

"To quote a very wise man Jericho, I think we should grab Alex and Thy, then the mirror and get the fuck outta of Dodge City!" Wilson shrugged his shoulders and smiled, but he - like Owen and Jericho - was now concerned for Alex's and Thy's safety. They had seen that; the 'Dark Pharaoh' was quite capable of anything.

5. RUNNING TO STAND STILL.

Alex and Thy sat quietly in their rooms, which were spacious and comfortable, drinking wine and nibbling at figs and dates provided by members of Pharaoh's harem. "I'd bloody murder for a coffee." Alex muttered, sipping her wine and stared about the rooms; for the period, they were the ultimate in luxury with tapestries and pieces of 'artwork; - nearly all connected with some God.

Thy rolled her silver wine cup around in her hand and whispered; "I've tried coffee. It was really good, even if it was heated." Alex shook her head; "You can't have done Thy; it won't be around for another couple thousand years."

Thy leaned forward and grinned; "Mr. Fabien brought me some in a strange vase he called 'a flask' and let me try it." Alex did smile; "You like Mr. Fabien then Thy?" The young girl nodded and really did smile broadly. The pair were interrupted by the arrival of Menes the magician with Ossan and Lady Isis's guard close behind [that mean's Jericho, Owen and Wilson turned up] and Alex was really pleased to see them.

She noticed immediately that Jericho was not a happy man and he explained that the old magicians young apprentice had fled into the night - taking the mirror with him - So Pharaoh was not a happy king; ordering Talin to take several men and go after Simhentra. He had decamped because he knew the Pharaoh would replace him with Menes; and that 'replacement' would mean death - for him.

Jericho informed Alex that several members of the King's council would soon arrive to 'persuade' her to marry Pharaoh; to save Egypt from further turmoil and possibly; civil war. Alex shrugged her shoulders; "I knew this bloody outfit would be trouble; you can't walk about in public, showing your bits without some sort of trouble." Everyone chuckled and Jericho rubbed his chin and asked Thy, if she had any idea where Simhentra could have run to.

Thy nodded; "The old magician left him a small estate in Edfu and I'm pretty sure that Pharaoh doesn't know about that - yet." Jericho sighed and pulled his mirror out; "Let's locate the estate of the late Sentus - Kasim in this time period." Alex noticed that young Owen was staring at her - again. She smiled; "I thought you would have seen enough Owen." with no censor in her voice and folded her arms. Thy just chuckled to herself.

Owen openly blushed and muttered several apologies and pretended to study a piece of 'artwork' on a pedestal near the windows. Wilson chuckled; "I think our boy has fallen in lust with you." Alex nodded and Thy even agreed; "He hasn't taken his eyes off you in that gown." She hesitated and added; "Mind you, neither have any of the males we have met so far." Both women laughed quietly.

Owen was now intently studying the little statuette and turned the piece around carefully in his hands. He pulled his mirror from the satchel he was carrying and for some minutes concentrated on both. Alex asked him what was so interesting about the little piece of stone; a small fat man sitting upon a chair.

Owen tapped the rear of the small statue and pointed out the few hieroglyphs scratched upon the back of the seat. "It says that this is an image of Tha - the magician. But according to human records on Ancient Egypt, this statue is on display in the Cairo Museum as being the only discovered representation of the Pharaoh Khufu; the King who is credited with building the great pyramid. That piece has no name marked upon it. Interesting that."

Alex accepted the piece and showed it to Thy, who nodded; "That's an image of the magician Tha - everyone knows that - well everyone living here now."

"Modern archaeologists must have the issue confused." Wilson muttered and wondered why his young friend - who was staring at Alex [yet again] - found it as interesting as he now found Alex!

Jericho called for everyone's attention and tapped his mirror. "We're off to Edfu and pay a visit to young mister Simhentra. It would be a lot easier if he could just turn the damn thing on and we could trace him in a second." Thy pulled a beautiful dark cloak about Alex and she was more than happy with it. The little group disappeared and arrived in the metropolis of Edfu, which was dominated by its famous temple to the God Horus.

"He now has a large house in the street of the Baker's." Thy informed Jericho, as the group made its way through the quiet streets as night gathered in. "He's probably still travelling down

the river: that would be the quickest way from Thebes to here.
So, we'll wait at his house." Jericho spoke quietly and smiled
when Owen warned everyone to keep an eye on Lulha - she was
a murderer - after all. They found the house after about half
hour, a whitewashed villa with a roof garden. Thy pointed out its
name; 'House of illusions.'

Ghusan was a little surprised to see the famous magician Menes
[and rival to his old master] at the door and even greater
surprise at finding the Priestess of Isis standing there too.
Simhentra had not yet arrived and Ghusan felt compelled to
allow the Priestess to rest in his new master's humble abode.

Figs and wine were produced for the guests by Lulha, who bowed
really low to the Priestess and asked if she knew when, her new
master would return. Before Alex could answer, Owen stepped
back from the doorway and said quietly; "Pharaoh's soldiers are
in the street - heading this way - I think."

Jericho pointed to the back room - away from the servants - and
everyone quietly made their way there. "Well, our magical friend
won't be turning up here at any time in the near future. Not with
Pharaoh's troops swarming over the city. So back to the office for
now." Jericho spoke softly, as there was loud banging on the
door and shouting. He operated his mirror and suddenly the
room was empty. Lulha stood in the doorway and allowed the
tray of cups to fall slowly from her shocked fingers and smash
upon the floor.

The villa was suddenly full of soldiers, shouting and searching.
Talin gripped her arm and demanded where the bloody magician
was. Lulha couldn't speak for a few seconds and Talin could see
the look of horror upon her face. "They just disappeared - into
thin air - I saw them with my own eyes." She whispered and
came over faint. Talin heaved the girl up into his arms and
carried her to a nearby chair.

One of his soldiers shouted that the magician wasn't here; but
the magician Menes and the Priestess of Isis - with their servants
- had been here just minutes ago. "That's impossible; we have
the villa surrounded." He muttered and then looked at the Lulha,
who was drinking wine offered by Ghusan, and how she was
shaking from fear. He wiped his face - Pharaoh will not be happy
at this turn of events - especially now he has lost both the magic

mirror and the beautiful Priestess. But he would definitely be interested in the Northern magician's latest incredible trick.

Talin grunted and ordered his men out of the villa, after yet another search which yielded nothing, and headed back to their boat docked on the Nile. He would send a runner back to Pharaoh; especially informing him about the Northern magician Menes, making five full grown adults simply disappear in a room without windows and the only door had a serving girl standing in it!

That made him turn back to Lulha, who was sitting on the small chair; smiling at him - her legs open and arms at her sides - she was offering sex for protection. Talin rubbed his chin and reckoned that he would not hear from his master for some time. The big Nubian took hold of Lulha by the arm and marched her into the bedroom. The girl had only ever been with her old master and the 'big' Nubian came as quite a surprise; she screamed the whole time that he took her and when he left some one hour later; she lay half on the bed and half on the floor; wrapped in a blood stained sheet; sobbing.

Talin couldn't believe the girl was almost a virgin and smiled to himself, as he returned to the boat - her old master must have had a cock the size of a finger - he laughed out loud and was watched by Simhentra from a street corner - wrapped in a dark cloak and full of hatred for the Nubian because of what he had done to Lulha. He clutched the mirror to his chest and headed for his boyhood friends house in the street of the sailmakers.

6. SMOKE AND MIRRORS IN STONE.

Pharaoh sat slumped in a little gilded chair with a gold cup in his hand, whilst a naked serving girl filled it with wine. He had received several messengers that night; the one from the Northern Governor made him throw goblets, overturn furniture and kicking the Lord Chamberlain up the arse. He rubbed his face and stared at the floor, sipping his wine. The Northern Governor had informed Pharaoh that his daughter Isis was still at her Temple in Memphis and the great Northern magician: Menes was performing at the very same temple; they had been nowhere.

"All fucking imposter's. But the magician was no fake." The King yelled at Dushan, who stood in silence; he knew how to handle the King's anger. Finally, Pharaoh had calmed down enough to think clearly and make decisions; the Lord Chamberlain had no answers, when the King asked him; "Who the fuck were those people and where is the woman?" He had already decided that the woman [when found] would be a royal concubine, regardless of her current rank amongst women; he really didn't care; even if she turned out to be the fucking illegitimate daughter of a camel dung salesman!

The runner from Talin made the King pace the floor; "Where is the little bastard with my mirror?" He yelled at Kumanine who also said nothing. The King announced a large reward of gold for Simhentra's whereabouts and an even greater amount for the woman posing as the priestess of Isis. Just for good measure, he had all Simhentra's property and land seized, handing the battered and abused Lulha over to her new 'master' - Talin. He kept Ghusan [who actually was a very good servant] for his own household.

With no family or Simhentra to bury him, the old magician's body lay in the Temple mortuary at Edfu; until the smell forced the priests there to bury him without ceremony or mummification [which was expensive]. They felt little sympathy for the old man, as he was placed in a sand-pit grave and covered up - strangely enough - just as the old man had wanted!

Pharaoh knew that the lure of so much gold would produce results - he especially hoped - that it would in the case of the missing beauty; he really did ache for the woman. She had fooled them all with her believable performance. That thought actually made the King smile; a beautiful, intelligent, cunning and resourceful rogue! What a Queen she could have made - in his dark heart - he had already forgiven her.

The little group of camels passed quietly across the sand, heading for the city of Memphis, as the coolness of night approached. Jericho consulted his mirror and stared up at the darkening sky which was full of stars. His thoughts were disturbed by Owen, who rode next to him. "We can get a visit to the Great Pyramid, can't we?" Owen asked, desperate to see the structure as it was meant to be seen; before the outer casing was stripped away some three thousand years later and used to build a mosque. [This followed a large earthquake which loosened some of the outer stones which made removing them easy.] Jericho had to smile and he nodded. That made Owens's day and he volunteered to cook for the group, when they camped that night just outside the city. Everyone chatted and ate, sitting around the campfire and Jericho briefed his team between mouthfuls of curry and sips of wine.

"Thy tells me that a close friend of Simhentra has informed Talin that the young magician has fled to this city. He has managed to avoid capture for nearly a year despite the large reward offered in gold. The same informant also confirmed that he still has the mirror in his possession - and that's our priority; get the damn thing back - by any means."

Wilson chuckled and spoke directly to Alex; "You know that horny old Pharaoh has offered a massive reward if you give yourself up to him. I mean, Thy says its huge and all in gold. You would be the wealthiest woman in Egypt bar the Queen herself." Alex smiled and ate her curry slowly; "I think, I'll decline the dirty old sod's generous offer and stay with the team; thank you very much."

Owen coughed and held up the little statue of the fat man sitting on a chair, that he had 'borrowed' from Pharaoh's apartments; "I think I've worked out what the real story is about, despite the confusion that surrounds this." Jericho was now interested; he knew that Owen had a quite powerful deductive mind; that's why he picked the boy for his team.

Everyone sat in silence around the little fire and listened with real interest.

"Thy tells us that this little statue is actually of Tha - the legendary magician - and NOT Pharaoh Khufu who is credited with building the Great Pyramid. Why the confusion? Tha WAS King Khufu's magician and so is known to everyone at the time and even now, is still known. So, here's something to ponder; Pharaoh wants a tomb that will not be robbed, so he builds a fucking massive structure right where everyone can see it and, most importantly, knows that the King's incredible fortune in gold and other precious stuff are sealed up inside. That's just plain crazy; every tomb robber then and now will try to get in and steal the stuff. It's staring them in the face!" Owen sipped his wine and pushed the statue back into the bag he was carrying and smiled.

Alex pulled the cloak about her shoulders and nodded; "Your right Owen; it doesn't actually make any sense; Pharaoh Khufu MUST have known about the robbery of the other royal tombs - even the ones that were hidden - at the time. So why built a bleeding great tomb that everyone knows is full of treasure?"

Owen grinned broadly and said simply; "Tha."

Jericho started to chuckle and slapped Owen on the back; "Absolutely brilliant my young friend, fucking brilliant!" He looked quite amazed and shook his head in realisation of what young Owen had deduced. Alex actually clapped and stuck up a thumb; "That is just incredible; little wonder Tha is a legend."

Wilson looked quite puzzled, and Owen grabbed his arm; "What do magicians perform all the time, in nearly every trick big man?" Wilson shrugged his large shoulders; "Deception, distraction and illusion?" He ventured, then what Owen meant, struck home and he started to laugh.

"It's the greatest piece of deception ever performed - smoke and mirrors formed from stone; the whole world believed Pharaoh was buried, with all his treasure, in a fucking huge lump of stone that everyone knows about. But it was a bloody big deception thought up by Tha and it's simply brilliant. No-one would search for Khufu's tomb to rob because it was right there, staring them in the face. That's why it's never been found. Simply brilliant - no-one has ever looked for it - making it the safest tomb ever created for a Pharaoh." Owen Chuckled and sipped his wine.

"So the cunning old Pharaoh still lays undisturbed after three thousand years; simply protected by the fact; that no-one ever looked for him!" Alex gripped Owens's arm with real pride; "Brilliant." She repeated softly.

"Rider on a camel approaching." Wilson said and stood up; "Its Thy." He added and walked over to greet her. Alex was well pleased to meet up with her 'maid' again and handed Thy a cup of wine, as she joined the little group around the fire.

Thy sipped her wine and spoke softly; "I have really terrible news. Simhentra was betrayed by his childhood friend for the gold reward. Pharaoh tortured him but didn't find the mirror. They killed him just a few weeks ago."

Alex sighed; "A brave young man, I guess he knew what bloody Pharaoh would do if he regained the mirror and learnt how to operate it." Everyone nodded at that, and Owen asked; "I take it, they made him swim with crocodiles?" Thy shook her head and looked quite sad; "No, his death was worse than that."

Owen sipped his wine and asked; "What could be worse than eaten alive by really big reptiles?" Thy took a deep breath; "They buried him alive. Wrapped him up in bandages, placed him in an old sarcophagus and entombed in some hidden place. Probably at Saqqara, where there are lots of old empty tombs they could reseal and hide."

They sat in silence until Jericho spoke; "We really must recover the mirror before that bastard gets his hands back on it." Again, everyone agreed with that.

7. IS HE DEAD OR ALIVE?

Thy had arranged for the group to stay at her father's estate in Memphis for the time being. It was a beautiful two-story villa with a roof garden that backed onto the Nile.

Jericho sat in the roof garden, enjoying the smells of the plants and the cool breeze coming off the river. He was consulting his mirror and looked up and smiled when Alex joined him - dressed far more modestly - now that she wasn't playing a high-born woman. She watched as Jericho expression changed to one of puzzlement, then real concern.

"What is it?" She asked and sat next to him, gripping his arm. Jericho tapped his mirror, and his face was grim; "No soul was collected from Simhentra, no Collector was sent because Dispatches have no record of his death - yet - and the missing mirror logged an attempt to use the Travel App."

Alex was slightly confused; "But Thy is certain that Pharaoh put him to death in that bloody awful way." Jericho nodded and rubbed his chin; "There can be a couple of explanations. The first is Simhentra was out of his time [a time traveler] but why couldn't the collector find a body? The second is he's still alive - but he's been buried for almost four weeks now - that's simply impossible. It really doesn't make any sense with no soul and no body. There always has to be one or the other."

Alex leaned back and stared at the Nile; "So he's appears to be alive - yet we know he must be dead. - No one could be buried for four weeks without food or more importantly; water. So, what is he: dead or alive?" Jericho admitted he didn't know - it was one strange set of circumstances. Then he stared down at the message just received from a Senior Time-Controller; he re-read the message a couple of times.

"This gets stranger by the minute. Time control has reported that someone attempted to use the missing mirrors travel App and was successful - well almost - they logged to travel to Egypt in 1970 but didn't arrive. They never made it which is nearly impossible...." Jericho stopped speaking and drew a real full breath; "The poor stupid bugger; he's trapped between the two."

Alex asked Jericho, what he meant by trapped between two; two what?

Jericho folded his arms and said quietly; "He's trapped between the living and the dead - he's actually neither and there's no way we can help him. The bloody mirror is clearly defective, and his soul is still with his dead body, which cannot be located because Dispatch Records still show him as living!"

"Poor bloody sod." Muttered Alex and the pair were joined by Owen and Wilson - eating of course - they loved the local figs. Jericho bought them up to speed on the fate of Simhentra but added that Time Control had pinpointed where the mirror was operated from and that's where they were headed.

"It was activated at Saqqara, where Thy believes they disposed of Simhentra just four weeks ago. He must have tried to escape by using it and the bloody defective mirror threw his soul into limbo and Pharaoh must have come across his lifeless body." Jericho looked quite puzzled and rubbed his chin adding; "But if that's the case, why did Pharaoh bother to go through the whole *let's bury the fucker alive* routine?" Everyone shrugged their shoulders; this case was becoming stranger by the minute.

Owen folded his arms and sighed; "How could he operate the mirror and end up apparently lifeless, when Pharaoh finds him and takes possession of the body; but no mirror is found on him?" Wilson whistled and ran a hand over his face; "Owen Is right; Pharaoh should have found the mirror by the dead body -

but we know he didn't - how could that happen?"

Alex wrapped her cloak about herself; "Someone else was there and witnessed the mirror apparently kill young Simhentra and cleared off with it, just before Pharaoh turned up. But who could Simhentra trust? Who could have been his accomplice?"

Jericho pushed his mirror back into his tunic and took a deep breath; "I asked Control to give me some details on what the defective mirror could have done to Simhentra and one possibility, may be the answer why Pharaoh still buried him alive - apparently. With his soul stuck between the living and dead, his body would appear just like a man in a coma. The Pharaoh probably tried a little torture to wake him, but with no success and so buried him 'alive'."

"The bloody mirror is still out there. Let's go people." Jericho added and pulled his mirror out again and tapped details into the Travel App and the team was gone.

"The city of the Dead." Alex said quietly, as they walked through some low stone walls and stared at the Step-Pyramid silhouetted by the moon, which was rising in the darkening night sky. "I thought that was Hamunaptra." Owen whispered and smiled. Wilson murmured; "You watch too many movies." and pointed towards a small stone compound which had lights showing.

Jericho checked his mirror and nodded towards the building; "That's where our mirror may be." Keeping low, they made for the compound and found some statues of a dog headed God to hide behind. Owen gripped Jericho's arm and pointed near the wall of the compound; "Jericho; there's a dead soldier on the ground and it's so fresh, there's the bloody collector!"

Jericho waved Ali the Collector over - with the soul of the bewildered dead soldier in tow - They greeted Ali warmly and he bowed a little to Jericho, he gestured to the dead soldier's soul; "He said that tomb robbers are searching near the old temple wall, for some nobleman's burial. He was looking after the office, whilst his colleagues - six of them - have gone to the site, which is located on the other side of the complex. Then someone came up behind him and drove a dagger through his throat. He couldn't even scream, but he saw who killed him and he knew the man." Jericho nodded and spoke to the soldier directly; "You say you know the man who killed you?" The soldier spoke softly; "Yes Sir, all soldiers know Pharaoh's personal bodyguard: Talin."

Wilson drew a breath; "Do you think the so-called Tomb robbers are also Talin's men and; thus, Pharaoh's men?" Alex folded her arms; "They think they know where the mirror is." She said simply.

"This soldier's death will be blamed on grave robbers and their supposed appearance here will also cover Pharaoh's activities in the cemetery, quite clever really." Jericho grunted and stared at the small building; how could Simhentra hide the mirror in a building constantly used by Pharaoh's troops?

No, the young magician would hide the damn thing somewhere else - in plain sight. Jericho smiled at that thought.

Owen pointed to the small, whitewashed building; "Someone is still inside; it must be Talin." Jericho told Ali to take the man's soul and depart, which he did. Jericho spoke quietly to his team; "If you were a magician and needed to hide something really well; where would you hide it?"

"Smoke and mirrors." Muttered Owen and Alex wrapped her cloak around tighter against the chill of night. "In plain sight." She volunteered and then Thy chuckled quietly; "In Pharaoh's palace?" Jericho really did smile at that remark; "No, the mirror was activated around here; somewhere."

Alex held up a hand; "But what about poor Simhentra, shouldn't we try and find him and his soul?" Owen grunted; "No can do, I checked my mirror and he is not shown amongst the living anymore and worse; he's not shown amongst the dead either. We will not be able to locate his body or soul." Wilson waved a hand and said, "He's buried around here somewhere, and no-one will come digging for antiques and mummies for another four thousand years. The poor bastard."

8. HIDDEN IN PLAIN SIGHT.

Owen crept back from the compound's little office and re-joined the team by the low stone wall. "Talin is practically pulling the place to bits; he's even knocking holes in the bloody walls!"

Jericho wiped his face and stared about the extensive cemetery of Saqqara; "Where would a magician hide the bloody mirror?" Alex and Thy were chatting quietly and Wilson was consulting his mirror.

Owen suddenly snapped his fingers and drew everyone's attention; "I know this sounds crazy, but what if Simhentra decided to be inspired by his hero; Tha. And like the Great Pyramid, come up with a wonderful distraction and hide the bloody thing in plain sight? Or rather instruct his accomplice on where to hide the damn thing after he was dead?"

Wilson nodded; he liked that idea; "But where?" He asked. Owen grinned and jerked a thumb towards the North wall; "What about Tha's tomb, where it was originally stolen from?" Alex chuckled; "Now that would be really ironic if Pharaoh and his merry men are ripping the place apart and it's hidden in the last place they would even think of!" Thy folded her arm and smiled; "It's not such a crazy idea; remember they captured him in this place."

Jericho decided that since they had nothing else to run with, they would check out the old tomb of Tha the magician. The little group made their way quietly across the sand and stones of Saqqara. Some distance behind them they could see flaming torches; "Pharaoh and his men searching." Thy whispered, adding; "They can't be seen during daylight now they have Simhentra, they would have to explain why they're in the cemetery and what for. Pharaoh doesn't want anyone to know about the mirror, which was looted from a tomb."

Owen guided them to a quiet spot near a small ravine and the broken and derelict entrances to looted and abandoned tombs from the glorious 'Old Kingdom' of Egypt. "That's the one." He spoke quietly and the group disappeared into the dark recess, leaving Thy hiding in the entrance as lookout.

They followed the roughly cut tunnel, bent low because of the ceiling, into a three chambered burial area. It appeared empty apart from broken stones, pieces of dried wood and rags. Wilson was admiring the engravings upon the walls, now faded with age and smashed in many parts. "I take it that this magnificent looking fellow was Tha. They certainly used a lot of artistic license in their rendering of the tomb owner. But then he was paying their wages!"

Owen chuckled; "He was small and plump in real life." He shone his mirror about; "Look for anything that appears newly disturbed." Alex and Jericho took one wall and started to search away from it - Owen and Wilson started from the opposite. They searched for several minutes without success until they met in the middle of the abandoned tomb. Jericho sighed; "Nothing."

Everyone stood in silence and stared about the room, then Owen grinned and shone his mirror against the wall opposite; "That figure of Tha is holding something. It looks like a square box." Everyone headed for the wall and Alex ran her soft hands over the engraving. "There's something under the paintwork." She said softly and Wilson produced his 'Swiss Army knife' and started to scrape about the paint and plaster.

They stood back; "Well, he certainly lived up to his reputation as a bloody good magician, I have to admit that." Wilson eased the much sought-after mirror from the recess in the wall and handed it to Jericho. "I wonder who the hell Simhentrra's loyal accomplice in all this was. I mean, they could have handed it over to Pharaoh and received a mass of gold; but they didn't. They probably carried out Simhentra's wishes even after he was apparently dead. That's a real loyal friend."

Everyone smiled with relief at finally finding the mirror and then they heard Thy calling softly from the entrance. They made to the tomb opening and joined her, crouching low amongst the scattered stone blocks and mounds of sand.

"Tomb robbers." Thy whispered and they could see a group of men against the ravine wall opposite, emerging from a dark and shadowed clef in the ridge. They were carrying bags and boxes and worked in total silence, one old man carrying a wooden staff, appeared to be using hand signals to guide his fellow robbers. They disappeared into the darkness of the night without making a single sound. Thy leaned against the large stone and breathed deep a couple of times; Alex asked her what was wrong and Thy ran a hand across her face; "I know that old man and what I just saw could get me killed."

Jericho nodded and operated his mirror and the group found themselves back at Thy's fathers villa, where servants bought them wine and bread. Alex and Thy spoke together for some time before Jericho called everyone to order; it was time to return to the lighthouse and hand over the retrieved mirror to Angel Margret.

Everyone took their leave of young Thy and thanked her for all her assistance, especially Alex and the pair embraced like old friends. Then Thy was left alone in the house to contemplate what she had seen and the terrible consequences it could bring, if she ever revealed the identity of the old man who commanded the team of grave robbers.

Thy slumped upon her bed and sipped some wine, staring at the flickering lamps which illuminated her small bedroom. The scene she had witnessed earlier passed through her mind - yet again. She would have troubled sleep tonight and placed her wine goblet down and closed her tired eyes. Thy slept badly, turning frequently, wrapped in a single sheet.

Something made her wake suddenly and she sat up. Talin and three soldiers were standing at the base of her bed. She stifled a scream with a hand across her mouth and pulled the sheet around herself. Talin grinned broadly; "Well my little maid to a fake Priestess, the King would really like to speak to you."
He gestured to his soldiers, and they grabbed Thy, binding her arms and hands. She said nothing but breathed deeply as they dragged her from her father's house into the dark night.

9. SAME PLACE - NEW PROBLEM?

Jericho placed the file down upon the desk and rubbed his face with both hands. He looked up as Owen stuck his head around the door: "Alex and Wilson will be back from Human Records in a few minutes." He informed Jericho and sat in a chair opposite with hands upon his knees. The message 'little Ivan' had delivered was not good news.

Thy, their human agent had been taken by the 'Dark Pharaoh' who wanted to find out where Alex had disappeared to. Luckily, he did not connect her to Simhentra's theft of 'his mirror' and it only concerned his desires for the woman [Alex] who had played the Priestess of Isis. Owen shook his head; "He's a persistent old pervert, I'll give him that."

Jericho nodded and tapped the file; "This would never have happened to Thy in the original Time-Line. But because she assisted us and fell afoul of Pharaoh, the Timeline could now change and Margret wants it sorted out."

"We just heard about Thy; what's the plan Jericho?" Wilson sauntered through the door and dropped into a nearby chair and after a few moments Alex swept in and eased herself into her favourite armchair. "I really don't fancy meeting that dirty old Pharaoh again, but we do need to rescue Thy from his clutches; thank heaven he doesn't associate her with that bloody mirror." Alex accepted a brandy from Mr. Harris and sipped it slowly, adding: "But how can we do that? - Everyone in that time and place -would recognise us."

"They would certainly remember you and that dress." Wilson chuckled and accepted the file from Jericho. "Alex has a really good point there Jericho; how can we return without being recognised?" Owen accepted a glass from Mr. Harris and sat back in his chair, looking quite concerned. Jericho sighed; "Well, we certainly have to do something, we've all seen what the 'Dark Pharaoh' is capable of and there's no way we're leaving Thy at his mercy." Everyone nodded their agreement at that.

Owen placed both hands upon his head and stared at the ceiling. He then sat up; "Simhentra never blabbed about our involvement in retrieving the mirror, we know that because Pharaoh didn't link Thy with the disappearance of his precious mirror, just with our little deception. He certainly admired you as a magician and that could be useful."

Wilson sighed; "You seem to forget that Pharaoh's soldiers came to Simhentra's villa while we were there; the servants are bound to have informed Talin about that and then it's no small leap to link us with him [Simhentra]. But I am puzzled why Pharaoh hasn't linked Thy to the mirror - she was Alex's maid after all, and he would know that Alex was at the villa with her."

Owen had to agree with Wilson's deduction and sat back in silence. Everyone turned to the door as Mr. Harris appeared and whispered into Jericho ear, which made him smile. "It appears that Inspector Fabian has arrived to thank us for recovering his team members mirror and update us on young Thy. He's just returned from there."

Mr. Harris showed the Temporal Inspector in and Jericho

introduced Fabian Bissit to his team. He was a short plump man wearing a fine three-piece suit with shirt and tie - but everyone noticed the bright red training shoes that he wore. Fabian sported a black 'goatee' beard and a red beret. He was regarded as a 'little eccentric' or slightly crazy, according to Owen. He was delighted to be invited to dinner and the team made for the dining room, quietly chatting amongst themselves.

Wilson, with a little grin on his face, just had to ask Alex; "When Jericho did the trick with the empty chair that amazed everyone back there, Owen and I knew that you would simply operate your mirror and disappear; then return." Alex nodded; "Yes, quite simple really, so what bothers you about that?"

Wilson sighed; "Where the hell did you hide the mirror in that bloody skimpy outfit?"

Alex chuckled and pointed to her hair. Owen grinned; "Of course, you could get a dining table in that bloody wig, never mind a little mirror!" Alex rolled her eyes; "Some bloody detectives you two are!" They laughed quietly amongst themselves until dinner was started.

Fabian sat smiling, as he anticipated the famed cooking of Mrs. Harris and the conversation turned to young Thy - he certainly had some good news on that score. He slurped his soup and between spoonful's explained that Thy's fiancé - the big Nubian Captain - had returned to claim his young bride and wasn't happy about Pharaoh keeping her prisoner, until she told him about the whereabouts of 'Lady Isis'.

So the brave young man broke into the palace one dark night and the pair escaped - after he killed a couple of guards. They fled to Kadesh, where the King there, granted them sanctuary and the captain became a Commander in the King's army. They are now married - quite happily - it would appear.

Alex actually clapped at that statement and lifted her glass to the pair; Fabian and her teammates joined her for that toast. The relief amongst the Temporal Detectives was palatable and the atmosphere at the dinner table had changed completely. Fabian went on to explain, as the chicken in white wine was served, that Pharaoh's sickly young Queen had died, and he still had no son's by his two royal concubines. He was not a happy man by all accounts; prowling the palace at night and drinking.

Alex asked if he had any news about poor Simhentra and Fabian sadly shook his head - nothing had been uncovered about the young magician's whereabouts, but he had some news about the slave girl Lulha. Apparently, she had run away from her master - which carried the death penalty - and was in hiding, in Kadesh. He didn't drop the bombshell about her until the pudding course arrived.

"The poor girl gave birth in that country and unfortunately died from complications of the birth. There would have been no one to care for the infant, since Lulha had no family living there. The child was, of course, Pharaoh's man Talin's baby. The little boy was clearly of Nubian ancestry and was taken in by a kind young couple, who raised him as one of their son's.

Fabian grinned and lifted his glass; "The little boy fitted in quite nicely with his new family despite being of mixed blood because the couple was Thy and her Nubian husband!" Alex nodded with real delight at that turn of events, then came the bombshell as the biscuits and cheese was served.

"She may have bumped off her old master - I think she had pretty good cause to do so - but she must have felt something for her new master Simentra because after fleeing from Talin, the pair were on the run together for some time. She shared his poverty and fear, constantly on the move and hiding. She stayed loyal to him until death." Fabien helped himself to some blue Stilton Cheese and a couple of crackers, adding: "I take it you worked out that Lulha was the one, who hid the mirror in the old tomb; on Simhentra's instructions before fleeing to Kadesh. You have to give her credit for that sort of loyalty."

Owen grinned and whispered to Alex; "How the hell did we miss that one?" But the Inspector had one more little 'bombshell' to drop. The dinner party broke up and Fabian took his leave, but not before informing Alex that she was almost a legend in the Temporal Detectives Department. She was quite puzzled by that and asked why.

He grinned; "That incredible dress that you almost wore; someone lifted a picture of you from the life tape of that time and copies are appearing everywhere. I even have one!" He bowed, kissed her hand and left the slightly shocked Alex standing in the study.

Owen and Wilson said a hastily good night to her and tried to head for their rooms - but she stood in the doorway; unsmiling and held out her hand: "Thank you boys, I will take them now."

Both sighed and very reluctantly handed the pictures over quite slowly, then sheepishly departed for their rooms in silence. Jericho sat by the study fire and allowed himself a small laugh. Alex bid him good night and ripped up the pictures; throwing them into the blazing fire and went to bed a little happier.

Jericho sipped his brandy and smiled, he reached into his jacket pocket and pulled the picture out and studied it; "Very nice, but nothing on seeing the real thing." He whispered and laughed quietly - again. He sighed deeply and tossed the photo upon the fire, finished his drink and headed for bed.

He passed a happy Mr. Parker chasing a tennis ball down the stairs and stopped to pat the cat. "Alexandra and Elizabeth are much alike." He whispered and watched the cat disappear down the hall with his ball.

THE END

EPILOGUE:

"This mission twisted and turned, but was considered a success by Angel Margret; the missing Temporal Mirror had been recovered. Poor Simhentra-Kara would remain trapped between the world of the living and dead for nearly five thousand human years. He remains in the world of the living to this day; but is dead! That is definitely another story!
SJW.

CHARACTERS:

Simhenta-Kara [the old Magician's assistant and apprentice] fate remains a mystery; Human Records still have him listed as 'alive', whilst Dispatches show him 'dead'. No soul has been collected and the matter has been drawn to the attention of Archangel peter himself. It appears that the young man is trapped between the world of the living and the world of the dead. The matter came to a head, when his body was found by Archaeologist Sir George Hadden in 1888 and his soul was still with it! But that's another story.... [See the book series: **'Miss Dorothy Hadden'** by the same author.]

Sentus-Kasim [the old Magician] who was murdered by the young woman [Luiha] he raped on several occasions, was the catalyst for Team 74's mission to ancient Egypt. His soul was collected and processed.

Lulha [the old Magician's sex slave] died from complications following the birth of her son and her soul was collected. She escaped any quarantine and re-joined the human life cycle immediately. It is understood that Jericho spoke up for her to Angel Margret, which may have swayed the Angel's decision.

Ghusan [the old Magician's servant] served his new master [the Pharaoh] for some years and was freed from slavery upon the death of that Pharaoh. He lived out the remainder of his life in Thebes, as a Temple servant of the Goddess Isis. He died aged 34 and his soul was collected and processed.

Dushan [the King's Scribe or Secretary] continued to serve the Pharoah until Amenhotep death. The new King had his own scribe and Dushan found himself poor and unemployed. He went into the grave robbing business with his grandfather [at first] and became very wealthy and powerful. He died aged 63 [a staggering good age for the time] and his soul was collected and processed.

Pharaoh Amenhotep V [the Dark Pharaoh] was not a happy man. despite all the power and wealth, he commanded. None of his numerous harem could make him really happy. He was to marry three more times and not a single wife produced a son, just daughters. Upon his death at the age of 44, the throne [through marriage to his eldest daughter] passed to Ramses I. No soul was collected upon Amenhotep death and Inspector Fabien Bisset is currently investigating; with no resolution so far.

Talin [the Pharaoh's personal bodyguard] continued to serve his master for some years, gaining a reputation for violent deeds, indiscrete murder and further rapes. He was savagely killed by several men in the Royal Palace within days of Pharaoh's death. His soul was collected and placed in quarantine until the year 67.

Tha [the legendary magician] aka Russel Hudson? Produced no soul to collect; it appears he was a human out of their own time and his true identity remains undiscovered. Inspector Bisset has been tasked to discover who he was and from which time period he came; the case remains unresolved to this day.

Temporal Detective Inspector Fabien Bisset received a caution for his team member losing the mirror. He continues to police the 'Stone-age' for Angel Margret. This eccentric character is quite an expert on the period. Thy and Seti's grandson also became a human agent for him. Fabien continues to head team 42 to this day.

Thy [the Priestess's - Alex's - maid] had to flee with her husband [Seti] to Kadesh. She produced five living children during her marriage to Seti and her dependents are today scattered all across Africa and the Middle East. She was known for her kindness to the poor and sick. Thy died aged 31 and her soul was collected. She has not re-joined the human life cycle and firstly worked as a Collector for some centuries, before joining Team 17 as a Trainee Temporal Detective. Thy already is showing talent and commitment to her new role; she will go far in the Department. Her and Alex are very good friends.

Kumanine [Pharaoh's Chief Minister and High Priest of the God Amen-Re] was dismissed by Pharaoh shortly after the visit of Team 74 and retired to his huge estate in Memphis. He frequently plotted against his old master but escaped being brought to justice. He died in the final year of Amenhotep's reign. Little wonder Thy was so scared at seeing who was leading the tomb robbers; it was Kumanine! He wasn't a very pious Egyptian despite his position. His soul was collected and processed.

Ramses [the King's Chamberlain] was accidently killed in a hunting accident in the desert. He was hunting lions with the King when his chariot overturned, and he broke his neck. No soul was collected and that is being investigated by Inspector Fabian and Team 42. There is no resolution yet.

Ankhesenamun was queen who lived during the 18th Dynasty of Egypt as the pharaoh Akhenaton's daughter and subsequently became the Great Royal Wife of pharaoh Tutankhamen. She died in 1323BC. Her soul was collected and processed.

Seti [the Nubian Captain and Thy's husband] enjoyed a privileged life under the King of Kadesh. He led the King's army in several successful campaigns, including two against Egyptian forces. Seti was always merciful to prisoners he captured and wouldn't allow the looting of poor villages or towns. He died in his bed at 57 [a good age for the time] and his soul was collected and processed. But his career didn't stop with his death! Some four centuries after that, Seti was made a Knight of God. He still says to this day, that Thy would have been so proud of him - it appears that after nearly four thousand years - he still loved his wife.

EPISODE 10: "THE DEVIL'S CIRCUS."

MISSION SUMMARY:
"Damian Coffin is the Ringmaster of 'Circus Diablo' who tour late Victorian Britain, but this is no entertainment for families as they perform only for the ultra wealthy and the powerful. Only the morally corrupt and sexually deviant are their Patrons - and some of them are prepared to pay their Soul for a very special performance; 'The Dance of the Black Queen'. Mr. Tibbs is back in 1889, in the East End of London; because the Devil's Circus has come to town!"

NOTES: This episode was the 'Seasonal Special' for Series 1 [online at website] and was written with humour to the fore!

TRIGGER WARNING ALCOHOL, COMICAL VIOLENCE, SEXUAL REFERENCES, STRONG LANGUAGE & MILD HORROR.

 **AGE 12+ ONLY.**  **30 Minutes reading time.**

1. THE DEVIL'S CIRCUS COMES TO TOWN.

Several Constables had been required to clear the throng of on-lookers from around the body and allow Detective Inspector Maurice Mountjoy access to the corpse. He was accompanied [as usual] by Sergeant Thomas Bass, who blew his nose several times into a gaudy bright red handkerchief and cussed loudly, "This bloody cold is really pissing me off!" The Inspector smiled and tapped his assistants shoulder; "Try some rum with hot water and lemon that normally works for me." The sergeant grunted and blew his nose again. "How the hell did I catch a stinking cold in the middle of summer?" Sergeant Bass wiped his nose again but smiled at the thought of hot rum and spices. They approached the street corner, now cordoned off with Constables and could see the figure lying covered with a dirty tarpaulin, hastily borrowed from the builders yard several doors down. Divisional Surgeon Clive Roberts was writing into his little red notebook and looked up; he smiled, adjusting his small round glasses and pointed to the body with his pencil.

"A real queer one this Inspector." He spoke softly and pushed the notebook into his coat pocket. "Been dead for about four to six hours and by the look on his face, he died in utter fear and horror." Inspector Mountjoy and the Sergeant exchanged glances and big Tom Bass reached down, lifting the canvas sheet slowly from the head of the body. In the warm early morning sunshine, they both stared at the contorted face of the dead man.

"Sweet fucking Jesus!" Tom muttered; the old Police Doctor wasn't kidding one little bit; the poor bastard looked like he had seen the Devil himself. "What's the cause of death?" He asked the Doctor, who was closing up his 'Gladstone' bag and lighting a little brown cigar.

"I would say heart failure; there are no obvious marks upon the body. I will know more after the autopsy. But according to your Constable Lofthouse he had nothing on him – perhaps he had been turned over by footpads and simply dropped dead. But that certainly wouldn't explain the face." The Doctor looked down at the body and all three men could see that the corpse's suit was on the very expensive side of good quality.

What was an obviously wealthy man doing in this grim part of the East end in the middle of the night? Mountjoy pulled his cigarette case out and popped one into his mouth – he offered Tom one, which was reluctantly refused – smoking really aggravated his bloody throat and made him cough now.

The Inspector called over Constable Lofthouse and asked him about the man's possessions – or rather lack of them.

"Not a thing Sir, nothing in his pockets and no rings on his fingers. The suit jacket is missing and maybe his overcoat and hat have gone too – if he was wearing them - when he died." Constable Lofthouse was a veteran of nearly ten years service and had seen lots of dead bodies, but the face on this one gave the old Policeman the shivers.

"Old Stan Cornish and his youngest boy found the body at six thirty this morning – he was here to deliver a couple of sacks of coal to the little toy factory in King Street and saw the body in the kerbside." The Constable pointed over to old man Cornish and his coal cart. The boy was feeding the horse with a couple of apples whilst Stan Cornish sat smoking his pipe; he lifted his dirty hat to the Inspector and sucked hard on his large cob pipe. Inspector Mountjoy didn't bother having the old coal merchant or his cart searched; he had known Stan Cornish since his boyhood and whatever Stan was, it wasn't a thief. Constable Lofthouse held up his Police notebook and added; "I have his statement written down and I've asked him to drop into Brick Lane nick to make a full one; Can I let him get on with his deliveries?"

Mountjoy nodded affirmative and smoked quite slowly, staring down at the body and wondered who the corpse was and what the hell he was doing here at his age; which the Doctor estimated to be the late fifties. Mountjoy watched the coal cart pull away and could see the Police Ambulance turning into the street from Queen's Square. It was the gaggle of reporters following that made him groan and motioned to them, telling Bass to keep the bastards away from the removal of the body.

"With bloody pleasure." Sergeant Bass muttered and told a couple of Constables to keep them away from the stiff. The Inspector peered down the entrance of the dark alley, which the body lay in front of, and threw down his cigarette. He wandered across and stared down the alley; a typical grim East end collection of dilapidated houses and boarded up shops. He looked up at the street sign: 'Hobbs Lane.'

He nodded to himself; the place had a dark reputation stretching back many years for death and violence. Most of the decent locals avoided the place at night because it was now filled with the dregs of Europe, as he called them. Refugees from Russia, Serbia, Poland and even the Ottoman Empire now called it home – it was a ghetto of crime and vice – but it had always been so, if he was honest with himself. He smiled at his thoughts; if the old man had been robbed and murdered, then he wouldn't have to look too far for suspects! He watched as two burly Constables lifted the body upon a rough wooden stretcher and placed it in the Police Ambulance. The Inspector walked slowly over to the group of reporters, and they gathered about him, shouting questions and waving notebooks in his face.

Amongst the slightly interested crowd was a tall young man in a cheap suit and boots; he certainly watched with real interest and took a deep breath. "He went too far last night, changing back to his true form in front of that poor old twat, but who the fuck has the balls to tell him that?" He spoke quietly to Peter who nodded his agreement - he certainly wouldn't tell the master how to behave; he was a fucking demon, and you didn't really argue too much with them.

The odd-looking pair walked away from the Inspectors impromptu press conference and headed for the Queen's Head, which was open and packed with Dockers leaving the night shift. Damien Coffin checked his pocket watch and Peter pushed open the pub door and Damien walked in, his thoughts centered on tomorrow night's performance - the big one, as Lord Arthur referred to turning this very important trick, who would be played like a fish and landed.

"Katrina had better keep off the fucking gin until this is done." He muttered and ordered beer and whisky for himself and Peter. The fat publican: Dave 'dogface' Sellers stood arms folded, bowler hat pushed back, behind his bar and smiled; "It's still on for tomorrow night then?" he asked quietly. Damien nodded and jerked a thumb towards the two young barmaids; "Only those two Dave, they know what they're doing around toff's. I can't have any fucking upsets; this is too fucking important for that. It has to be sweet, like a clock; tick-tock."

'Dogface' grinned; "Yeah, ten bob each for them and two quid for me. I know we agreed ten bob for the pair and a quid for me. Sorry, but I'll need a little more, because of all the police activity now. You know, with that toff turning up brown bread [dead] by Hobbs Lane. It's fucking risky." Damien sighed and nodded his agreement; "Just make sure the tarts are washed and looking good. Just aprons and stockings; nothing else." He tapped the bar and pushed three pounds across to Dave, who grabbed the money up. "Sure, I'll scrub the bitches myself!" he smiled and pushed the notes into his gaudy waistcoat pocket.

The barman wandered down his bar and spoke to the girls, who turned and smiled at Damien. "Fat grasping bastard." Muttered Peter and swallowed his beer down. Damien tapped his shoulder; "Steady mate, we need that fat bastard for the girls and the booze he's supplying; at cost price. He's laid his fat hands on some decent champagne, and we can't dish up anything fucking less. The bloody toff's will smell crap a mile away and the game will be up. Nah, we need the fat fucker - for now." He smiled at Peter, who nodded and picked up his whisky glass; "Then he's mine." He whispered.

Damien and Peter finished their drinks and headed for the doors. From a quiet corner, Sir Francis Drake had watched the pair and the fat barman interact, he rose slowly and followed them out. Well, it actually wasn't Sir Francis Drake himself - he's been dead for over three hundred years - it was some twat dressed like him. Outside the Queens Head, he rubbed his chin and wondered what old 'Dogface' was up to with this pair of shifty strangers. He could smell a few shillings in it for him.

Two old women in shabby shawls walked past and the tall one cackled; "What's up William? Lost your bloody stage?" They both gripped each other and laughed like hyena's watching a gazelle die. "It's fucking Sir Francis Drake you fucking old crones! He shouted after them, but they were gone. "Bloody Philistines." he said and headed for home.

2. MR. TIBBS IS ON THE CASE.

Jericho and Owen watched the Police Ambulance depart and turned back to Ali Mennza, the Collector who had asked for Temporal Detective assistance after finding no soul to collect. Little Ali smiled at Jericho and held open his Soul Ledger; "He's in here for this morning, but he was supposed to die on some wasteland at the rear of Victoria Park – not on this street corner, miles away!"

Ali tapped his book and continued; "I waited for a few minutes at the wasteland, and then did a body search which bought me here, but again; no soul present." He folded his arms and smiled again; "That's everything Mr. Tibbs."

Owen consulted his mirror and read about the deceased; "Lord Henry Snowfield, passed over at 2.10 AM, using local time and dates; on the 7th of June 1889 on wasteland at the rear of Victoria Park, London. Now classified as a 'lost soul' with the body appearing at the entrance to Hobbs Lane, there are no apparent changes to the current human Timeline. Oh, and his soul Marker is 3241202 – it was his first time in the 'Life-Cycle, so he's quite a fresh one." Owen shrugged his shoulders and added; "He died on time, so that helps – but what the fuck happened to his soul?"

Jericho tapped Ali on the shoulder; "Thanks Ali, we'll take it from here." The Collector smiled broadly and flicked open his Soul Ledger to see the soul's details had vanished; replaced by a simple reference number: '048124 – 2 – 2600 TIBBS'.

The matter was now allocated to Temporal Detectives and the Collectors involvement was at an end. "Thanks Mr. Tibbs, I'm staying local for the next pick-up; the mum of a stillborn in Nelson Road. The kid didn't even know she was expecting; but her dad certainly did." Ali waved and vanished, leaving the pair of Temporal Detectives watching the crowd dispersing in the morning sunshine.

"Good man that Ali, he gets lots of compliments from the newly dead about his manners." Owen spoke to Jericho whilst reading his mirror again. He looked up and added; "Cause of death was a massive heart attack...." He hesitated for a few seconds, then shook his head in disbelief; "According to the Dispatch Department, the poor bastard died of heart failure bought on by fear and shock." He glanced at Jericho who just nodded his head.

"Can someone really die of terror?" Owen asked and pushed the mirror back into his pocket. Jericho just smiled in reply and the pair then disappeared to the wasteland at the rear of Victoria Park. Jericho pulled a glass orb from his inner pocket; no bigger than a golf ball and held the strange object out in his open hand. The little clear ball immediately showed red streaks flowing about its circumference.

"A Minion of the 'Dark Prince' was here." Jericho stated and pushed the orb back into his pocket. "The trail is still very fresh, just a few hours old and its presence was a strong one; strong enough to steal a soul." He added and looked about the litter

strewn ground and wondered why there was so much rubbish
here? Jericho then noticed the small parade of shops opposite
and he motioned for Owen to follow.

The little bell attached to the Tobacconist's door tinkled as
Jericho wandered in and started looking at the jars of tobacco
and boxes of cigarettes. Owen followed and breathed deeply'
"That's a bloody gorgeous smell!" He exclaimed and then, the
young clerk appeared behind the counter and asked if he could
be of assistance. Jericho picked a handful of large cigars and
placed them on the counter; the young man carefully wrapped
his purchase which was a whopping nine shillings and smiled
broadly; this was a cracking start to his day.

Jericho started up a conversation with the Tobacconist about the
rubbish strewn wasteland opposite and why the local Council
hasn't cleaned it up yet. The young man informed Jericho that
some travelling show people had camped on the ground for the
last week, but when he opened the shop this morning, they had
cleared off.

"What sort of show people?" Jericho asked, pushing his purchase
into one of the many pockets of his overcoat. The young man
rolled his eyes and laughed; "They were supposed to be a Circus,
but they played no shows – well, not for anyone around here -
some kids rushed across there to see the Clowns and came back
frightened and crying. Apparently, the Clowns looked fierce and
miserable. One of the little girls said they were 'bloody evil
looking'. Some flipping Circus!"

"What was the name of the show?" Owen asked, sniffing a
circular carton of Turkish cigarettes. He grimaced and put the
carton down quickly, muttering; "Smell's like horse shit." The
young clerk laughed and thought for a few seconds; "Circus
Diablo....or something like that. A real strange, dark bunch of
characters I can tell you. Foreigners most of them, but the Ring
Master was quite pleasant and spoke good English – he liked
those very cigarettes you just picked up, so I guess he was a
refugee from Turkey."

The young man busied himself wiping down his counter and then
laughed; "They had a couple of young women travelling with
them and they certainly caught the attention of the men around
here – they were a couple of stunners – olive skinned with dark

eyes and figures they didn't mind showing off. I suppose modesty hadn't reached Turkey yet."

Owen and Jericho chuckled at the young clerk's words. The young man brushed down his apron and smiled broadly; "I did see the woman they all seemed to fall over, [the circus crew] the way they treated her, you'd think she was some kind of princess. Tall blond lady with a figure like a Greek statue and I mean a figure." He formed big breasts with his hands and smirked; "Probably had legs all the way up - a real gorgeous piece of skirt. You don't see many ladies of that quality around here." He seemed unhappy about that particular omission and groaned a little, when a woman's shrill voice called him from the rear.

"Just serving some gentlemen, my dearest. He shouted – unsmiling - then he sighed; "The little woman; bless her." and the look upon his face spoke volumes. Owen had to restrain a laugh and coughed, then said quietly to Jericho; "What would a circus want with such a woman?"

"Honey trap." Muttered Jericho and thanked the young man for his time and the cigars, then left the little shop and its 'happy' owner and stood outside in the sunshine. The street was now quite busy with passer-by's, tradesmen, and carriages. Owen stood, hands in pockets, watching the street filling with people and traffic; "Who would operate such a Circus?" He asked the thoughtful Jericho.

Jericho folded his arms and sighed; "The Devil."

3. TICKETS TO THE DEVIL'S CIRCUS DON'T COME CHEAP!

Tim's the Butler stared at the young man standing in the doorway. He wore a cheap three-piece suit with a cheap Homburg hat and Tim's noticed that he wore cheap machine-made boots. He sighed, what on earth would his lordship want with such a fellow? Especially one that smiled so much - for no apparent reason - But Tim's was a professional and he bowed and smiled.

Reluctantly, Tim's showed the young man into the Front reception room and made a mental note to check for any missing items after the strange young man had departed. "I will inform his lordship that you are here...Mister...."Tim's had already forgotten the name offered and adjusting his glasses, looked again at the yellowing business card the man had offered. "Mr. Coffin." He said simply and walked to his lordships study and knocked gently upon the door and entered.

Lord Arthur Horewood - 9th Earl of Rochford - sat behind his uncluttered desk and stared at the afternoon edition of the local paper. He reached into his desk drawer and pulled a thick brown envelope from it and placed it upon the table. He also stared into the drawer at the small, loaded pistol that also lay there. He sighed loudly and looked up as Tim's announced the arrival of a certain Mister Coffin. The Earl just nodded and gestured for Tim's to show the young man in. He looked back down at the envelope and snatched it up, placing it back into the drawer; "We'll see." he muttered.

Lord Arthur also checked that the pistol was loaded and left the drawer half open, then rose slowly as Mr. Coffin was shown in - his cheap Homburg clutched in both hands. Nothing was said until Tim's left the pair. Lord Arthur pointed to a chair in front of the desk and sat back down. Mister Coffin eased himself onto the chair and fumbled in his jacket with one hand whilst the other gripped his hat tightly. He held up a small gold and silver bracelet; a snake and a circle.

 "Verax enim Pater Salutat." He spoke softly and smiled, then pushed the bracelet back into his jacket pocket. Lord Arthur nodded; "Omnes laudes fater tenebris." he replied and held up a matching bracelet, which he quickly pushed back into his waistcoat.

"I take it you've seen the afternoon edition of the local paper for the bloody East End?" Lord Arthur clasped his hands together and sat back in the chair; "What the fuck happened to the old man?" Damien Coffin squirmed a little in his seat; the smile was gone. "He just fucking dropped dead, honestly governor. One minute he was full of life, enjoying the show and the next, he was stone fucking dead. Little Ivor reckons he had a massive heart attack. What the fuck could we do but dump the bloody body and get the fuck out of the place. We can't have coppers near the show; you know that."

Damien hesitated then thought; fuck it. He ran a hand over his face; "It didn't help the situation that the master changed in front of the poor old sod and I suspect that killed him; stone fucking dead." Damien felt a little better getting that off his mind.

Lord Arthur sighed and stared up at the ceiling for a couple of minutes in silence and then turned back to the obviously nervous young man in the cheap suit. "Are you sure no-one can trace his visit back to the circus?" He asked and leaned forward; one hand hovering just above the open drawer. Damien grinned and relaxed; "Yep, no fucker even knows he was with us last night – nobody - The fucking coppers haven't even identified him yet. I thought of that, and we stripped the old bugger of anything that could identify him. I came up with that governor; good, eh?" Damien tapped the side of his head and grinned broadly.

The Earl ran a hand across his face and stared hard at the young man sitting in front of him; "You had better be right in that Damien, our master is not generous to failures and the circus is his special little project and he will protect it. You understand that?" Damien nodded vigorously; "Yeah, no sweat governor. It's all sweet. No fucker saw anything I can guarantee that."

"It had better be 'all sweet' as you say, the master has too much time and resources ploughed into this; to allow fuck ups. The big job is now underway, and you had better come through it smelling of bloody roses or we're both in fucking serious trouble - do you understand that?" The Earl reached into the drawer and pulled the envelope out and slapped it upon the desk. Damien swallowed hard and managed a smile; "Yes Governor, everything will go like a clock - good and sweet - tick tock, tick tock."

The Earl snorted and sat back in his chair; he indicated to the envelope and Damien slowly lifted it from the desk and stuffed it into his jacket pocket. "There's a hundred pounds there Damien, make sure it's spent well and keep her off the fucking gin until the jobs done." Lord Arthur wagged a finger and relaxed a little.

"Everything is in place for tomorrow night, she's going to give the fucker some show to remember, and you'll have him governor; all sweet like."Damian said and smiled - again - to the earl's slight annoyance. Lord Arthur half smiled; "Who are using for back-up? Who's behind the mirror?"

Damien grinned yet again; "I've got 'Black Bart' from Brighton for that. You know he's sound governor and he's the best. But he wants ten quid for the work."

"Yes, that's fine; Bart knows what he's doing and always keeps his mouth shut. A good man to have on standby. That's a good choice and he's certainly worth ten pounds. Yes, that's good." Lord Arthur rose from his chair; indicating that the meeting was over. Damien stood up and held out his hand; "You and the master will be sweet with what's done. Like clockwork; tick tock, tick tock."

The Earl just stared at the hand offered and walked to the door; "Just make sure there are no more fuck ups Coffin; for both our sakes." Damien dropped his hand and disappeared through the door and placed his hat on. Tim's showed him the front door and shook his head. He had already checked the front reception room and found nothing out of place. The Earl told Tim's to fetch some whisky and glanced at the large clock in the hallway; he would be here soon.

Lord Arthur returned to his study and picked up the paper; he felt little sympathy for old Lord Snowhlll; the old fool should never have insisted that he see the show, despite Lord Arthur's warnings; he had bought a ticket. "Fucking expensive show Henry. It cost you your miserable life and probably; your fucking soul." He slumped into the chair and stared through the window into the gardens. The slim figure of his teenage daughter could be seen walking with her maid; "Reading another bloody book are we Dorothy?" He muttered, but just had to smile.

Tim's appeared with a tray of whiskies and placed them down; "Mrs. Cole asks if you will be wanting dinner tonight my lord?" Lord Arthur shook his head; "Myself and Lord Lewisham will be dinning at the club; thank you Tim's." He checked his pocket watch against the grand clock in the hallway; 6.45PM. He would be here soon, and Lord Arthur was already sweating. He glanced down at the open paper upon his desk and wiped his face with a hankie; that won't go down to fucking well with him, but bloody Coffin seems to have put a lid on it, he thought.

Lord Arthur actually chuckled; "Coffin...put a lid on it." Then heard the front doorbell ring. "He's here." He spoke softly to himself and straightened his tie and jacket and swallowed hard. This could be a bit unpleasant.

4. JUST THE FACTS - PLEASE!

The little group wasn't really noticed on the crowded street; the Temporal Detectives had gone to some trouble not to draw attention to themselves. But, of course, most of the men [and some of the women] noticed Alex in her costume. Even dressed as an East End 'street girl' or 'prossie' she drew attention. "I told you that those damn hooters wouldn't go un-noticed around here." Wilson chided her - but with a grin.

Alex just smiled but did try and restrain her magnificent bosom from escaping her bodice - again. Owen chuckled and turned to Jericho; "Christ, our Alex could earn a fortune around here. How many 'gentlemen' have tried to hire her now?" Jericho checked his fob watch and sighed; "Several, as you know Owen." He pointed to the entrance of a closed down theatre; "There it is." He said and gestured towards it. Wilson nodded and smiled at Alex; "He certainly seems to know his way around here." Alex managed to refrain from grinning at Wilson's comment and continued to struggle with her breasts, in an effort to stop them from escaping again.

"He's human agent for these parts, has some information on that bloody grim circus that seems to be connected with the lost soul." Alex spoke quietly, as yet another well dressed young 'gentleman' lifted his hat to her and was about to speak. But he said nothing and hurried away - really quickly - when Wilson simply opened his coat and displayed the long, shiny knife that was strapped beneath his arm. "Remind me to invest in one of those." She murmured to Wilson and a man like Wilson to carry it, she thought.

"Why the hell did I have to dress up as a bleeding tart?" She moaned to Jericho, who stopped and waved his hands about; "We're in the slums of Victorian London, do you really think a lady of real quality would be seen dead around here? Believe me, if you had dressed up as one of them and came strolling around these streets, your dress would be up around your waist, with some dirty fucker enjoying himself, whilst his friends slit our throats. Do you get that?" He said in rebuke; but did smile. She nodded and pulled her coat about herself. "I always have to play the bloody tart." She muttered under her breath.

They stood outside the derelict theatre and Jericho knocked hard upon the shabby door. "He's name is Crispin St. Michael; an actor currently resting between jobs; apparently." Two old ladies in dirty shawls passed the group and the skinny one cackled loudly and gestured towards Alex. "I bet she gets tuppence from punters just to suck those puppies!" They laughed together and disappeared down the street. Owen stared up at the sign above the door; "Who the fuck are they trying to fool?" He said to no-one in particular. The sign read: 'The Magnificent Apollo Emporium'.

The door creaked open, and Jericho removed his hat and smiled; "Hello Nelly my girl; is he in?" The young girl was about thirteen or fourteen, dressed in a short colourful child's dress [her working clothes] that had clearly seen far better days. She was smoking a delicate little cob pipe which she removed from her mouth and blew a little smoke ring. "Good evening Mr. Tibbs, he is in. He's expecting you." She grinned and then stared at Alex; "Jesus fuck Mr. Tibbs! - That is a real pot of honey you've got there - I bet you get ten bob just for a five-finger tug job off her." [ten shillings - fifty pence nowadays - worth about twenty pounds in today's money].

The young girl stepped aside and allowed the group to enter, she clearly liked Wilson and pushed up close to him; "I do like really big exotic gentlemen; the blacker the better." She smiled broadly and suddenly pulled the front of her dress up, exposing her dirty thighs. "You can have the first one for free." She said softly and smiled again.

"No thank you." Wilson managed to sputter out - He was saved by a smiling Mr. Tibbs. "Where is he Nelly?" Jericho asked and the girl, somewhat disappointed, pushed her short dress down and turned, pointing to a shabby curtain covering a doorway. "In there Mr. Tibbs." She walked towards the curtain, gesturing for them to follow; scratching her bare arse as she walked.

Wilson, looking a little concerned, turned to Alex and said quietly; "I think you really should have motherly words with that girl." Wiping sweat from his face and adjusting his tie. Alex sighed; "Sadly, I think it's rather too late for that...and obviously way too late for her mother." They followed Nelly onto the rear of the stage and found 'Crispin St. Michael' sitting on a large up-turned bucket, reading a newspaper. For some reason – known only to himself; he was dressed as Sir Francis Drake; complete with feathered hat and fake sword. He leapt from the bucket, throwing the paper down and bowed quite low, waving his hat in a sweeping downwards motion. The large ostrich feather fluttered to the floor.

He grinned and retrieved the feather slowly; "Verily, a pox upon the hat maker for such neglect in his constructions!" He smiled at Jericho and adjusted his sword, which had become entangled with his brightly coloured hose. "And a pox upon the Cutler for this damn sword." He added, then saw Alex. He bowed again; carefully holding onto his hat feather. "My lady of Venus, you could easily eclipse the very...." he didn't finish as Jericho held out a couple of gold sovereigns and asked; "What have you got for me Reggie?"

Reginald Norman Sponge sheepishly replaced the feather onto his hat and slapped it upon his head. "Blimey Mr. Tibbs, you know I like to be called..." Jericho just sighed; "What have you got for me?" He repeated and waved the coins under Reggie's nose. Owen chuckled; "Reginald Sponge?" and folded his arms. Wilson appeared quite glad that Nelly had gone 'for another bleedin' piss' - as she put it - in her ladylike manner. Alex wondered why Reggie was dressed as William Shakespeare, when he was supposed to be 'resting' between jobs. She really did want to ask but didn't want to interrupt Jericho.

Reggie - sorry, Crispin St. Michael - threw a loose arm into the air and striking a dramatic pose, began his practised oration for Mr. Tibbs; "I came close to much danger my generous patron, for we are dealing with desperate men here. I do swear that nothing short of foul murder plays upon their twisted and deranged minds. At great risk to myself I...." Jericho held up a hand; "Just the facts -please." Reggie stopped in mid-sentence and smiled, he stared at the coins and said, "Alright governor, straight to the chase, as you like it."

They all heard the sound of water hitting metal from behind a shabby curtain at the rear of the stage, followed by Nelly softly groaning; "Gawd that's bleedin' better." They watched in silence as the girl emerged from the curtain, pulling down her dress and carrying a metal bucket. Nelly walked to a half open window and emptied the bucket through it. She turned and smiled at the silent group. "I'm pissing like a bloody horse these days." Nelly explained and shrugged her shoulders; she lifted the pail and grinned; "Anyone for a cup of tea? I'll fetch some fresh water."

Surprisingly enough, everyone declined her generous offer - quite politely - and she returned the bucket to behind the curtain. Owen whispered to Wilson; "Why is Reggie dressed as Robin Hood?" Wilson didn't smile; "You mean Ivanhoe. He's dressed as Ivanhoe - obviously." He replied with a deep sigh.

Jericho gently placed the coins into Reggie's hand and smiled - again. Reggie gripped the coins tightly and looking around - as if anyone else could hear in the deserted theatre, pulled close to Jericho and whispered for some minutes. Jericho nodded a couple of times and then walked back to his waiting team.

They huddled together and Jericho pulled his mirror out; "There's a certain Damien Coffin, who's the supposed Ring-Master of a black circus called Diablo, he has been hanging around some very wealthy local men - one of them was old Lord Snowfield - apparently the circus performs only for rich patrons. The tickets can be fifty guineas a piece. A hundred if you want to see a very special performance called the 'Dance of the Black Queen'. That is bloody serious money for these times; equivalent of thousands of pounds in, say, the 21st century. I've instructed Reggie to find out where their next performance is to be held." Jericho operated his mirror and the group returned to the lighthouse.

As they walked towards home, Alex just had to ask Jericho why Reggie was dressed like William Shakespeare in the deserted theatre. "I thought you said he had no work?" She questioned and Jericho nodded; "He's had no paid performances for months; he's a lousy actor but genuinely loves the theatre. I really don't know why he's dressed up as a bloody Musketeer." Everyone nodded but was none the wiser for Jericho's answer.

Alex still looked a little puzzled and asked Jericho; "Why did Reggie have to whisper his information just to you, when he clearly knew you would tell us what he said anyway?" Jericho stopped walking and shrugged his shoulders; "Maybe because he's a bloody idiot. I really don't know Alexandra."

The dinner conversation was quite lively that night.

5. THE 'BLACK QUEEN' IS PISSED – AGAIN.

Little Ivor sat at the rough little table and stared at his cards, then at the small pile of coins upon the table. He scratched his shaggy black beard and cussed a little in Russian. He looked at the other three sitting around the table and cussed some more. "Come on, fucking hell Ivor make a call; are you in or folding?" Peter the 'clown' was fast losing patience with the big Russian and it showed. Ivor actually bared his strong white teeth and growled like a Siberian bear with his wedding tackle caught in a hunter's trap. Peter got the message and fell silent. Finally, he smiled grimly at his big colleague; "When you're ready mate." He muttered.

The other 'clown' chuckled and lit yet another cigarette, coughing and wiping his mouth. "Did you tell MISTER Coffin that 'Black Bart' has arrived?" He directed his question to the little man sitting opposite, who was staring at his cards. Santo, the dwarf, screwed up his face in puzzlement; "This is the third hand where I have been dealt four aces of spades." He looked up at the others and placed the cards face up on the table.

Everyone stared at the cards in total silence. Peter threw down his cards in some anger and disbelief; "Fuck me!" He exclaimed; he had four aces of spades too.

The big Russian growled again and started to eat his cards with some frustration; he had four aces of spades too. The chain smoking man: a thin weedy fellow called 'Suet' because his surname was 'Pudding' also groaned - he had the same. After a few moments of silence, Peter slumped back in his chair; "We've been fucking playing with old 'Marvo's' fucking magic cards; again!"

The poker game broke up with the table being kicked over and the cards and coins scattered over the dirty floor. Santo then cussed loudly; "To answer your fucking question; no, I fucking haven't!" He yelled at 'Suet' the smoker, who had asked him about MISTER Coffin. "I'll do it fucking now." He muttered and headed out the small tent towards Coffin's elaborate wooden, horse drawn caravan. He couldn't believe it; they had played three hands of poker with the same fucking single card, and no-one had noticed! MISTER Coffin was right; they truly were fucking retards. He banged loudly on the door and waited.

'Marvo' the pathetic magician, was also hurrying towards the caravan with some really bad news. He walked briskly, then stopped to grab at his shirt and a fat grey pigeon fluttered out and returned to its coop. "Fuck!" He muttered; he must remember to empty his shirts after each fucking performance. He saw Santo at the bosses' door and slowed to a stroll. He smiled a little; he's really bad news can wait until Santo had been shouted at.

Damien stood in the doorway, just in his underwear. Surprisingly he didn't shout at the little man, he just nodded and told Santo to show 'Black Bart' where to position his cameras. Santo passed the magician, while returning to the tent, and he grabbed Marvo by the trouser pockets - that's all he could reach and snarled; "Keep those fucking cards of yours in your fucking tent or I'll shove them up your fucking arse and you'll need some real magic to have a fucking crap then!" He shouted at the crotch in front of him; Marvo just grinned and nodded.

The little man disappeared into the tent - still cussing; they were the best hands of poker he ever had. Marvo grinned at Damien; then decided that looking grim would go down better with the news he had to impart. There was no other way to say it; "She's pissed out of her head - again." He said with an appropriately solemn face. Damien said nothing, but quietly sat upon the small bed and placed his head in both hands. Marvo said nothing more for a few minutes, then just had to smile; "Lucy is her stand in - ain't she? - she'll have to turn the trick."

Damien looked up and simply could not smile, or strangely enough; shout at Marvo; he simply sighed, long and slow. "Lucy couldn't stand in for a dog having a crap in Victoria Park. Not even if we printed the fucking instructions on the fucking toilet paper for her." He said between clenched teeth and was amazed at his self-control. He stood very slowly and scratched his crotch - that was another little matter he needed to speak to Lucy about - But that would have to wait. He groaned loudly; "We need a real fucking classy tart, a real East end princess for this fucking trick. For Christ sake, even I only fuck Lucy because it's free!"

Marvo nodded and scratched his own crotch; he needed to speak to Lucy about that, even if it was free. There was silence for a few minutes and then Marvo had a rare intelligent thought. He coughed and smiled; "I think I know where we can get one of them Boss."

Damien stared at the magician and was about to scream, but he calmly asked; "Where can we get what?" He said and half smiled. The magician smiled broadly; "That useless actor, Crispin St... Something, you know, the one who lives with Nelly could have the answer to this." Damien stared long and hard at the magician; he had decided to shoot him and wondered where he had put his little pearl handled pistol. But unable to find his gun, so he finally muttered; "Nelly is a good kid and gives value for money to her tricks, but if you hadn't fucking noticed - she ain't no East End princess. We need a classy, big tit tart with long legs and a fucking big, pretty smile for this trick; nothing else will fucking do."

Marvo grinned and told Damien what Nelly had told him about the classy tart she had met yesterday. Damien scratched his crotch again; he knew Nelly wasn't one for exaggeration or tall tales; she left that, to her useless brother Reggie. He listened with real interest, to what Marvo said and then rubbed his chin - which made a change from his crotch - and made his mind up; he didn't have much of a choice really.

"Get Peter and little Ivor over here, we're going to pay a visit to that twat actor and tell them to tool up - just in case." Marvo nodded and walked away - truly surprised that Damien hadn't shouted at him or pulled his fancy little pistol out and threatened to blow his balls off. He smiled to himself, then stopped and grabbed at his crotch, loosening his belt and out popped a large white rabbit.

"Sweet fucking Jesus!" He muttered; maybe he didn't have to speak to Lucy after all.

6. AN OFFER YOU CAN'T REALLY REFUSE.

Nelly, despite having no medical training whatsoever, had managed to extract the ostrich feather from where little Ivor had placed it - quite forcibly it must be said. "Do you know that fat Charlie, the hat maker, will pay a shilling for a feather like this?" She dropped it carefully onto the table and made a mental note to give it a quick scrub before selling it to 'fat Charlie'.

Reggie groaned with relief and reminded himself that it could have been a lot worse; little Ivor had wanted to shove something else up his poor back passage and the term 'little' didn't match what he was holding at the time - with a real grin upon his face. He tried to sit - but simply couldn't, so he stood by the window and sipped a cup of tea, just made by his little sister. "Did you use fresh water?" He asked Nelly, adding; "It has quite a tang to it."

Nelly just nodded; her thoughts were all about her 'Fiancé' as she called him; a strapping big sailor from HMS Colossus called Tom Bell - he had proposed after a particularly passionate session of love-making last night. Well, it was for him apparently, but Nelly wasn't too happy; she had dropped several stitches whilst repairing her best jacket.

She was in two minds about being his wife, the main stumbling block was her future married name; Mrs. Nelly Bell. It sounded like the fucking name you give a pet goat, she reasoned and thought about Tom's best mate, another sailor from the same ship - Fred Crapps - He had paid Nelly sixpence to watch, while he enjoyed a bottle of beer and had told her, when it was his turn, that he would also happily marry her. Then she groaned; Mrs. Nelly Crapps. What the fuck should a girl do? They were the only genuine offers on the table at the moment.

So for now, she remained Miss Nelly Victoria Sponge - strangely enough - she never used her middle name!

"She'll have to do it, Mister Tibbs will convince her." Reggie was wandering about the stage, muttering and gripping his poor abused backside. Nelly sighed; "How the fuck did mum [old Nelly as she was called] land me with this useless twat of a brother?" Reggie grinned at his sister and placed his cup down; "What's that you say?" Nelly shrugged and held up both hands in mock despair; "Shouldn't you at least get hold of Mr. Tibbs, I mean, they're want that classy tart for tonight and they'll pay fucking good money for her to perform for that bloody toff."

"Oh shit!" Reggie exclaimed and grabbed up his hat, then picked up the feather and carefully replaced it. He made for the door shouting for his sister to get his best suit [well, his only suit actually] out of the pawn shop. He couldn't keep wandering around London dressed as Sir Francis Drake; people were starting to ask embarrassing questions. Nelly nodded; "That's a whole fucking shilling walking out the door." She muttered and also remembered, she hadn't cleaned that damn bucket this morning: still, she couldn't be expected to remember everything in her delicate condition.

Nelly pulled on her jacket and placed the straw bonnet on her head, carefully folding her long dark hair underneath. She fetched ten bob from the jar in the small kitchen, at the rear of the disused theatre, and headed for Samuel Franks Pawn shop on the Whitechapel Road. The money Mr. Tibbs had given Reggie, had provided a God send for the pair - especially Nelly - she could now buy some decent secondhand baby clothes and maybe, an old crib. She smiled, and maybe old Sam would like a little fun while she was there; he always paid a shilling but kept his hat on for some strange reason.

As she walked to the shop on the crowed pavements, she remembered the conversation with her brother about old man Samuel and his bleeding hat. Reggie had thought long and hard about his sister's question, then broke into a huge smile; "It's because he's Jewish; old Samuel practices the religion of old Israel!" Then added, with a dramatic change in voice and crossing himself; "They killed the Christ you know." That confused Nelly somewhat; old Sam had the same strange religion as old Israel Stoneman?

Old Israel Stoneman ran the chemist shop in Queen Street - but old Israel never kept his bloody hat on; while doing it – besides; everyone knew it was the fucking Romans that killed Jesus. She decided that asking Reggie anything really important was a total waste of bloody time.

That afternoon, Jericho and Owen sat in the lounge bar of the 'Royal Oak' tavern and sipped their beer quietly and slowly. It was quite crowded, and Owen asked Jericho if anyone actually worked around this place - the East End. Jericho just chuckled and gave Owen a quick history lesson about London Docks and that, the workers did shifts. So, the pubs were open nearly all the time - there were no real 'Licensing Laws' - yet. They would come during the First World War, to stop vital war workers from turning up pissed.

Owen hoped that the bloody actor would turn up suitably dressed and so draw no attention to them. He was greatly relieved to see 'Crispin St. Michael' arrive in a shabby three-piece suit; fresh from the pawn shop. Owen collected more beer from the bar and

Reggie poured an entire pint down his throat without stopping to say anything. Suitably refreshed, the whole dreadful story of Damien Coffin's visit was played out, complete with theatrical gestures and the placing of that awful feather.

A big drunk dicker, watching from the bar, then staggered over and gripped Reggie by the shoulders; he was actually crying. "For fuck sake my poor friend, the same bloody thing happened to my horse; Hercules." The big man sobbed openly; "The fucker called himself a Vet, but Hercules was never the same again." The big man slammed several loose coins upon the table and cuddled Reggie tightly, finally releasing him, when Reggie started to turn a mild shade of blue. "You poor bastard; they did that to your fucking ostrich. Have a drink on me." He staggered away and fell through the pub's door. Several people stepped over him, but a couple did help themselves to the contents of his pockets.

Gasping a little, Reggie managed to finish his story and plead with Jericho to convince Alexandra to perform for the sake of his poor arse - and dignity, of course. With the promise of assistance, Jericho finally managed to solicit the location of Damien Coffin and his Dark circus from Reggie - after several pints – and some silver coins.

They managed to get Reggie onto a bus. Jericho had to pay his fare - of course. Their 'good' deed didn't end well. They had put Reggie on the wrong bus, and he ended up in Bermondsey. Still a little worse for drink, he tried to explain his sad predicament to some passing gentlemen, repeating his performance from the 'Royal Oak'. He was a little unfortunate; both were foreign gentlemen visiting London from some far-flung foreign climes. He actually had to run for it when they started to pull down their trousers and press coins into his hands.

He made it - only just - and found refuge in a local graveyard, where he slept it off, sprawled upon an old grave. It had started to rain, and the night was drawing in. A couple of stray dogs pissed on him and chewed his boots. It wasn't going well for the Thespian.

Jericho and Owen found a quiet alley to operate their mirrors and returned to the lighthouse. For some reason, Jericho kept chuckling to himself, as they walked to their home, looming above them. Owen heard him mutter; "She'll go bloody nuts when I tell her. I hope for the sake of Reggie's backside, that he's got rid of that frigging feather." Owen just grinned but was a little angry with himself; he had forgotten, in all the excitement, to ask Reggie why he had dressed up as Robin Hood, when he wasn't even in a play; any play.

He had a bet running with Wilson over the costume and he desperately wanted to get something over the big man, for a change. But Wilson and Owen both couldn't hide their laughter when Jericho informed Alex of her dramatic new assignment. But they knew she would eventually give in - for the sake of the mission and to help out poor young Nelly - who would struggle without her brother, so Jericho explained to her; fingers crossed behind his back.

It worked. "Yet another bleeding tart." Alex groaned; a little disappointed. Then she sighed, it seemed to be her lot in life [sorry - death] to be a tart. Even when she played a grand Egyptian princess, she was dressed like a frigging tart!

The Supplies Department came up with a cracking costume for Alex and the two dressmakers told Jericho, that the outfit would rekindle the passions of a dead eunuch - never mind some perverted Victorian toff. Owen stared at one of the seamstresses; he would have sworn, he had seen her before - but where?

Wilson watched the two ladies depart. He scratched his chin, deep in thought. He was sure that the tall skinny one was Elizabeth; a medieval witch the team had dealt with some mission's back. She turned out to be a real witch with real powers. What the fuck was she doing working for Supplies? He shrugged his shoulders; I suppose that jobs for witches were hard to come by in the afterlife and so she had probably diversified. Multitasking was the new catchphrase he thought.

Alex, to the bitter disappointment of Wilson and Owen, would only allow Jericho to see the finished item, while she modeled it. He came down from her rooms and grabbed up a full glass of brandy and swallowed it down. "I'll kill that bloody witch!" Jericho muttered. There was silence for some time as he carefully refilled his glass. Finally, Owen just had to ask; "What the hell does she look like?"

Jericho's mouth moved, but nothing came out. He grinned at the desperate pair and swallowed down his brandy, finally muttering; "If I wasn't already dead, I could now die happy." He said nothing more but slumped into his favourite armchair and stared at the fireplace. Wilson and Owen sat down slowly on the sofa and cradled their drinks. They exchanged sad glances and also said nothing further. Ruth peered through the doorway and was quite bewildered. She returned to the kitchen and asked Mrs. Harris about the boys.

Mrs. Harris simply smiled; she had just served Alex a couple of brandies in her rooms and seen her latest outfit. Finally, she said to Ruth; "Sometimes it's far better not to see what you really, desperately want. It would ruin everything else." Ruth was now definitely none the wiser. She had helped Alex dress and thought her outfit was a little sparse; but nicely made. She went about her duties and didn't think anymore on the incident.

The team gathered together for their return to Victorian London. Alex was wearing a tightly buttoned ankle length black coat that revealed nothing. The only clue to what she may be wearing, [or not wearing, as the case may be] was the silver & diamond tiara in her hair and piano black high heels. They jumped back in silence - apart from some heavy breathing from Owen - for which he received a slap from Wilson.

7. NEGOTIATIONS, COMPROMISES AND REVELATIONS.

The little group walked slowly through the light drizzle, Jericho holding his big umbrella over Alex, so her hair didn't get ruined. Wilson and Owen trailed behind, still quietly arguing over Reggie's bloody costume.

"The common is located at the bottom of the next street. Reggie said that Damien has a beautiful, wooden horse drawn caravan. He must have 'Romany' blood somewhere in the family." Jericho told his team as they walked slowly - for them - through the rain. Owen kept staring at Alex's bottom - shaped by her tight coat - as it swung in rhythm with her strides. The spring in her dainty little walk was helped by her high heels. He actually groaned a couple of times which made Wilson smile and despair a little. "Behave yourself baby brother." He muttered and slapped Owen on the back.

Young Constable George Jones [collar No. H211] watched the

little group approaching with some interest, standing in the doorway of Wilson's the Bakers, out of the rain. He gripped his lamp tightly and felt in his pocket for his notebook. He pulled it from his jacket, adjusting his black cape. George opened the book and read about questioning strangers in the area; especially if they didn't appear to look like locals! The woman particularly caught his eye. What was a beauty like that doing with a dumb looking boy, a big black fella and some toff?

Then of course, there was 'Jack the Ripper' - the evil bastard had killed five women last year - with real brutally and butchery; and was still at large, probably hanging around these very streets. That sent a shiver up the young constable's spine, and he pressed against the firm door. The bastard won't get through a door, he reasoned. Then slowly swallowed hard; A fucking door can be opened! He slowly turned and jumped with sheer fear; then realised it was his own reflection in the glass.

Sighing from relief, he started to breathe again. Then Mr. Wilson opened the door and asked; "Can I help you, George?" George jumped so high that his helmet actually hit the door lintel. He calmed down a little and said between chattering teeth; "No you bleeding can't; piss off!" Wilson shrugged his shoulders and returned to the backroom of his shop and removed his dressing gown; he was stark naked.

The two naked young girls sprawled over cushions, sipped their wine and Stella [the older one] asked; "Who was it Uncle John?" Wilson sighed; "That bloody idiot young George Jones. He couldn't police sheep - not even if they were locked in their bloody pen - Where's your mum with those mince pies; I'm bleeding starving?" Mrs. Trundle appeared - quite naked - with a tray of said mince pies. "Pie anyone?" she asked; smiling. They returned to their game of 'strip' Happy Families.

Now composed, George snapped the book shut and leaped into action; he would find out who they are and what the fuck are they doing on his patch. He stepped from the shop doorway and raised his lamp; "Excuse me, can I have word please." The little grouped halted - in silence. He walked over and held his lamp up and stared at Alex; "Are any of these gentlemen family members Miss?" Alex smiled; really smiled; "Yes, this is my brother Jericho and we're looking for a circus that has apparently set up around here, can you help please?"

Jericho was always impressed with Alex - especially how she could easily distract someone - usually young men - and deflect difficult questions. He just had to smile. The young copper smiled broadly and lowered his lamp slightly; "There's no circus around here Miss, just a group of gypsies camped on waste ground by the old brick works. They are quite a strange bunch, and I would advise you to stay well clear of them." Jericho coughed; "I think the officer is quite right Alexandra, you never know what people like that can get up to."

"Quite right Sir." The Constable said, but never took his eyes off the smiling Alex, who demurely lowered her eyes and quietly thanked the young officer. "Another bloody moth to the flame." Wilson muttered quietly and Owen chuckled softly at the big man's comments. Jericho told the group to wait for him, while he had private words with the officer. They walked on a little way and Jericho caught up with them; the smile on his face intrigued Alex; "What have you been up too?" She asked and handed back his umbrella.

"I always like to co-operate with the local Constabulary." He said and the little group came upon the 'Circus' at the next corner. They found Damien's caravan and Jericho knocked at the door. After a few seconds, Damien opened the door and immediately stared at Alex. "Hello Mister Coffin, A friend of ours - a certain actor - says you have a proposition for my lady." Damien nodded; "Just you and the tart, the other two can wait outside. There's not enough room for them; especially the big fella."

"Tart? Charming." Muttered Alex, then remembered what she was almost wearing beneath her coat and just had to nod her agreement - with that comment - and smile.

With Jericho and Alex inside, Damien closed the door and sat on the end of his small bed and lit a cigarette; "Its five pounds for a little work, no fucking questions answered, and the tart does as she's told. She'll be quite safe; my men will be ready to spring to her aid; if anything kicks off - agreed?" There was another knock at the door and Damien yelled for them to enter. It was Santo, carrying a rusty money box; he looked Alex up and down and then smiled. He stood by the bed and handed the box to Damien.

Jericho smiled broadly; "Well, that sounds fine - except its twenty pounds for the performance Mister Coffin." Both Damien and

Santo laughed loudly and Damien just shook his head; "For Christ sake Mister...whatever your name is, I wouldn't pay that kind of money to see Miss Lottie Collins fuck a donkey on stage!" Santo laughed out loud and shook his head too; "What the fuck makes this tart worth that kind of money?"

Jericho just smiled; "Alexandra, would you please settle this."

Both men were still chuckling, and Alex simply stepped forward and slowly unbuttoned her coat. "What, you've got fucking pigeons in your drawers!" Damien chuckled at his own supposed wit. Alex pulled the coat open and stood quite still, then turned a little, showing her backside to the pair.

Damien and Santo had fallen silent. Santo simply groaned and fell upon his back and lay still on the floor by the bed. Damien could say nothing, and the cigarette fell from his lips onto his lap. It actually burnt a hole in his trousers before he yelped and slapped his leg. "Santo, give the gentlemen fucking twenty pounds." He managed to say softly and lit another cigarette with shaking hands.

Alex closed her coat and smiled; "You can blink now."

Damien did blink, then kicked Santo and opened the money tin himself, pushing four white, five-pound notes into Jericho's outstretched hand. He stared down at the dwarf; he was groaning loudly and clutching his erection with both hands. Damien had covered his own with the small cash tin - it was certainly adequate for the task - finally, he said quietly; "Peter will show you and the lady, her dressing room. The show starts when all the marks are sitting." He actually groaned a little, then added; "You best keep her covered up till then Mister...." He looked up at Jericho, who folded the money and pushed it into his coat pocket.

"It's Tibbs - MISTER Tibbs." He said simply.

They left the little caravan and re-joined Wilson and Owen outside; Peter and little Ivor stared at Alex for some time, then Peter finally managed to say; "This way please Miss." They sat in the tent and passed a hipflask amongst themselves. Jericho and Owen had gone to check the 'ring' for the performance, whilst Wilson stayed to look after Alex, who sipped her flask and spoke about Reggie and poor Nelly.

Jericho and Owen returned and they huddled together, Jericho not talking above a whisper. They had found a certain gentleman called 'Black Bart' sitting by a couple of cameras; cleverly concealed behind a magnificent two-way mirror. "There's a little private 'ring' and the camera's are set up there, I assume to capture whoever the most important victim is, and I expect dirty blackmail follows. But this does not explain old Lord Henry's missing soul and take a look at this." Jericho pulled a little glass orb from his pocket - there were small red streaks around its circumference - traces of a demon; powerful enough to take souls. "I've already put a call in for a Guardian." He added and accepted the hipflask from Alex.

"If they going to all this trouble; they must be after someone important. I mean for these times." Owen accepted the flask from Jericho who nodded; "I think I know who." They all looked up as Peter stuck his head around the tent flap; "MISTER Coffin says the marks are in the reception tent and keep the girl covered up. She only performs for the mark in the private ring. The girls will take care of the others." He held up a thumb and smiled. Jericho replied with thumbs up and a big smile.

Jericho rose and headed for the flap with Owen in tow; "Let's see whose paid a small fortune to be entertained tonight." Alone with Alex, Wilson just had to ask what happened in the caravan; he and Owen had seen the dwarf carried out by little Ivor. Alex smiled; "He was a little overcome by something he had wanted and dreamt of all his life - and can never have." Wilson was none the wiser with that answer but didn't push the point - for now.

Owen appeared at the tent flap and indicated for the pair to follow him, and they quietly assembled by the rear of the main tent. Jericho was standing by a slightly open flap and he gestured for silence and they all peered through. Sure enough, there were half a dozen very well-dressed gentlemen beginning to take their seats. Damien looked resplendent in his Ring-masters outfit and was paying close attention to one of the gentlemen - very close attention indeed - and bowing often.

Owen tapped Alex on the shoulder and whispered; "That's the main mark, that's your man." Alex stared at the young man quite hard and turned to Jericho; "He was well known for big collars and cuffs. In fact, the Bloody Prime Minister, sarcastically, use to refer to him as 'Collar & cuffs'. Jesus Jericho, what's going on?" Wilson stared in and said, "Who the fuck is he?" Owen chuckled; "British Royalty not your strong point, big man?"

Jericho indicated they should return to their tent; his mirror had informed him that the Guardian had arrived and was waiting for them. "Well, who the hell is he?" Repeated Wilson. Owen sighed; "That's Prince Eddy, Queen Victoria's grandson and heir to the British throne after his father, Edward the Prince of Wales, who would become King Edward VII in 1901. A very important historical figure for this current time and place."

"So he becomes King some day; big deal." Muttered Wilson who was not impressed. Owen chuckled; "Wrong big man, he's really important because he never became King!" Jericho stopped the pair and spoke softly to them all - including Alex. "We know there's a demon hanging around the place and how does this little scenario sound; he gets compromising pictures of the prince and that means he can control the young man - a human vassal of the 'Dark Prince' - in a very important position."

Owen coughed; "But it won't matter, Prince Eddy dies long before he could even inherit the throne and so why all this?" Jericho grinned; "Well, it means the 'Dark Prince' has his foot in the door, for when the young man does die and what if, he re-animates the body with a carefully chosen minion and so everyone believes the young man has survived the illness that should have killed him. Britain has a demon on the throne when the world is about to go to War in 1914. The world war that changed history completely. The 'Dark Prince' is playing a very clever long-term game and if he succeeds, well, God knows what will happen to the current human time-lime."

"So the bloody demon could be here as an 'understudy' to the prince?" Alex said and Jericho had to agree with her. "Learning his ways and duplicating them, ready to take over, when the time comes." She added, now really concerned and with that revelation, they made their way back to the tent and greeted Emika Sato, the Guardian assigned to the case.

8. AROUND AND AROUND THE MULLBERRY BUSH.

They all greeted Emika with some affection - especially Alex -

and the pair hugged; "It's been too long since we worked together Alex." Emika said and smiled broadly at the group. She was a petite Japanese woman but was wearing a modern 'business suit' with trousers and bright pink 'trainers'. She gripped her 'Staff of Moses' firmly and consulted her mirror. "All the signs point to Hari, and we all know that he's a clever bastard. One of the Dark Prince's better new minions. I'll stay cloaked until needed."

Jericho was well pleased with the Guardian that the Demon Ingress Department had assigned; Emika was well experienced and could be totally relied upon - even if she was a bit 'quirky' - according to some who had worked with her.

Peter stuck his head in and coughed; "She's on." was all he said and was gone.

Jericho grinned and rubbed his hands together; "I've waited a lifetime to say this; IT'S SHOWTIME!" Everyone just stared at him, and Alex sighed; "Come on, let's get this done." They trooped from the tent in silence until Owen patted Jericho on the shoulder; "I got what you meant Boss." Wilson sighed loudly; "Bum licker." That made Alex and Emika giggle a little.

Wilson and Owen remained outside the tent with strict instructions not to enter or even look until called; Jericho really rammed that instruction home and they both agreed – reluctantly and waited for things to happen.

Jericho and Alex peered into the private 'Ring' through the two-way mirror and saw the young man sitting in his well upholstered chair; smoking a large cigar with a glass of champagne in the other. 'Black Bart' finished fiddling with the camera nearest to him and jerked a thumb towards the young man on the other side of the mirror; "I'll want another ten pounds off that queer little fucker, he didn't say it was him. I don't want fucking Scotland Yard crawling up my fucking arse over this." He didn't seem happy.

Jericho whispered to Alex; "No wonder he didn't end up on the floor like the little man - Our friend Damien plays for both sides, he was affected, but not like Santo." Alex nodded and started to unbutton her coat, 'Black Bart' grunted; "Keep your bloody tits and arse out of his face, that's really important; ok?" Alex turned and pulled her coat off; "I'm sure you'll enjoy the show." Her coat dropped to the floor, and she stepped towards the tent flap that Jericho pulled slightly open.

'Black Bart' simply stared, and his mouth moved a couple of times, but nothing came out. He hit the floor and groaned a little; still clutching a photographic plate and a camera cable; the camera went off with a small puff and so did 'Black Bart'. He groaned loudly and clutched his crotch. "Oh dear, the camera went off prematurely." Alex muttered and Jericho sighed; "So did 'Black Bart' apparently."

Alex stepped into the ring and curtsied before young Prince Eddy; "I do hope your Highness will enjoy the...."Alex never finished her introduction because the young prince looked up from his cigar and sat motionless. The big cigar fell from his fingers and rolled down his jacket, across his trousers and fell to the floor - the champagne glass followed - smashing on the floor.

He managed a little groan and quite slowly slid down the chair until gravity worked its magic and he slumped upon the floor - on his knees. This was followed by words that Alex and Jericho couldn't make out and the young prince fell upon his face, and he clutched his crotch and grinned broadly. Apparently, it took a couple of days for Prince Eddy to lose the smile.

Alex stood arms on hips and sighed; "Charming. I never even got to do my little dance...." She was interrupted again - by Emika - who shouted something about the demon Hari and burst into the tent. She stared at Alex and fell face down on the dirt, groaning and cussing. Jericho placed both hands upon his head; "For Christ sake Alex! Get your bloody coat on!"

Alex sprinted into the other tent and grabbed up her coat and pulled it on. She shouted for Owen and Wilson. Jericho pushed through the tent flap and groaned, then sort of smiled; "Well, that puts an end to some of the rumours about young Emika, I think. But now, what the fuck do we do about the bloody demon?"

Alex folded her arms; "I wondered why she kept following me into the toilet, whenever she could. Bloody hell, you really don't know people do you?" She asked Jericho, who didn't answer, he was staring at the tent flap and the strapping young man standing there. Hari was dressed in a quality Tuxedo, with a white rose in his lapel. He waved a hand behind him; "Sorry about them two Jericho, I just couldn't resist." Both Jericho and Alex stared out the tent flap and saw two goats wandering about. "Oh, you didn't; did you?" She asked Hari, who nodded and grinned mischievously; "Afraid so Alex."

"Oh bollocks!" Said Jericho and slumped onto the little folding chair that 'Black Bart' had been fond of [he was still laid in the dirt - grinning] and pushed his fingers through his dark hair. Alex recalled that Hari had actually been a handsome young man as a human - he didn't really need to manifest such a disguise - as most of the other male demons did, when in the realm of living humans.

"There's another two like that at the back of that small ring; a big man and a tall skinny one." Hari gestured to 'Black Bart' and added; "What on earth have you been up too Jericho?" Alex guessed that was little Ivor and Peter; they just couldn't resist taking a peek, she reasoned, then smiled.

"I suppose it was my really sexy outfit Sir." She spoke to Hari softly and started to unbutton her coat. He just chuckled; "You are a stunningly beautiful woman Alexandra, I'll give you that, but nothing you possess I haven't seen and enjoyed before." He lifted both hands; "Now you can join that pair out there, munching on the grass."

Alex dropped her coat and Jericho covered his eyes with both hands; just in case the immunity was wearing off. She placed both hands upon her hips and did a little twirl. Hari laughed; "I'm immune to your stunning, sexual charms..." and fell flat on his face, groaning and clutching his crotch, he managed to mutter; "The master will understand, he'll...." Then groaned even louder.

Alex grabbed up her coat and covered her charms. Jericho rose from the chair and surveyed the scene before him; "Now what the fuck do we do?" He sighed.

"I really would like to know; what the fuck is going on here Mr. Tibbs?" Inspector Mountjoy stared at the two moaning on the floor - but quite happy - strangely enough. Jericho shrugged his shoulders; "If you take a look in there, you may begin to understand Sir." Mountjoy turned to Sergeant Bass who pushed into the tent, cussing loudly and rubbing his backside. "Check the other tent, Tom; when you're ready." The sergeant nodded; "One of those fucking goats just bit me, all I did was pat the bloody thing." he wandered into the adjoining tent and after a few seconds shouted for Mountjoy.

"That'll be Wilson; that bit him." Alex whispered to Jericho. "How do you know that?" Jericho asked, smiling at Mountjoy. "Easy, Owen is way too timid to do such a thing. Simple." Jericho just sighed at that 'brilliant' deduction; "They're now bloody goats Alex and will behave like goats. Too timid my ar..."

Alex suddenly grabbed Jericho by the arm; "Emika is in there!" Jericho just smiled; "She's still cloaked for living humans; we'll collect her later." Mountjoy returned and shouted for more constables. He turned to Jericho and wiped his face; "I think you and your lady had better accompany me down to Brick Lane Station and make a statement about all this; don't you think?"

Jericho nodded and straightened his jacket; "But first we need to recapture our goats Sir. They're family pets and Alexandra here will be most upset if we lose them." Mountjoy just stared at Jericho, he couldn't speak for a few seconds; "You want us to round up goats when the fucking Heir to the throne is laid upon a dirty floor, clutching his...well, never mind what he's holding, that's his royal business. The bloody goats can wait." Jericho nodded at Alex; "Well, you can tell them I tried." and smiled - broadly.

The old Queen stared down at them from over the small fireplace in Inspector Mountjoys equally grim office. They both sat in uncomfortable chairs and said nothing. Constable George Jones stood by the door and kept smiling at Alex. Finally, he broke the cold silence; "Would you like a nice cup of hot tea Miss?" Alex turned on her chair and smiled; "That would be lovely, thank you Constable. Could my brother have one too?" She asked and adjusted her hair.

The young constable grinned; "Of course Miss, I'll see if they can conjure up some biscuits as well. My old gran always says that tea is too wet without them." He opened the door and shouted down the corridor. "Old Norman will fetch them." he said and straightened his uniform jacket. "You look very smart in that uniform and very professional Constable." Alex smiled; again,

and crossed her legs in a very dainty and ladylike fashion. "You
can call me George. If you like Miss." He replied and opened the
door for 'old Norman' with the tea tray.

Jericho slapped a hand over his face and quietly moaned;
"Another bloody moth to the flames."

9. ASSISTING THE POLICE WITH THEIR ENQUIRIES.

They were finishing their tea when Inspector Mountjoy returned
and dropped into the threadbare chair behind his desk. He had a
large wad of papers clutched in his hand and rather bizarrely, a
large black wooden dildo in the other. He slapped both down in
front of them. Alex had struggled to prevent the giggles from
escaping - but failed - She composed herself and shifted in her
chair.

"This is no laughing matter young lady, the life of the young Heir
to the throne could have been in jeopardy. The Prime Minister
himself has been informed of this matter by the Home Secretary.
The Commissioner had to call him from a very important state
dinner - he was not amused and both the officers who were
assigned to guard the prince have been fired." The Inspector
stared at the tea tray; "Jones get more tea here, I really could do
with a cup." The constable disappeared to fetch more.

Mountjoy carefully flicked through the papers, now placed on the
desk - he was using the dildo as a paperweight - and poor Alex
just had to chuckle. The Inspector peered over his glasses at her;
"Anymore of that and I'll have you thrown into a cell; do you
understand?" Alex nodded and whispered that she was sorry, and
it was her nerves; she admitted to the Inspector that she was a
little afraid and clutched her 'brothers' arm. "Oh, I see Miss - yes,
I have a young daughter - and I would not want her in a Police
Station at this time of night." He actually smiled, then returned
to the papers.

He picked up the dildo and moved it to one side and caught the
look upon their faces; "I found this strange object by the prince;
I can't believe it fell from his pocket." Jericho coughed' "it was
probably placed there by Coffin; to discredit his Highness." Alex
shifted on her chair and muttered under her breath; "Like hell it
was." Jericho gently kicked her under the table and received a
'death' stare in return. Mountjoy stared at the pair and Alex

smiled and clutched her 'brothers' arm; "You were saying sir?"
She said and fluttered her eyes; demurely.

Mountjoy nodded his agreement with what Jericho had said and
sat back in his chair with both hands on the desk; "So as I
understand it, this Damien Coffin fellow was using his so called
'Circus' as a cover to blackmail wealthy gentleman by getting..."
He shuffled the papers, lifting the dildo up and down, then
continued' "Getting a certain disreputable photographer, a Mister
Bartholomew Blackberry from Brighton to photograph them with
ladies of the night from behind a special mirror; is that correct?"

Alex breathed deeply as he lifted the dildo up and down again.
They both nodded. The inspector grunted; "Excellent. I will
charge Mr. Coffin with blackmail and attempted blackmail and the
rest of his merry band as accomplices'. The prince's name will not
appear in any police reports, and you will not mention him in
your statements. I'm sure your staunch patriots and love the
Queen. But I must know what you were doing there...Miss
Alexandra Tibbs?"

Jericho suddenly leaned forward and said softly; "Inspector, I'm
sure you will understand that this is a most torturous and difficult
confession, but I fell to Coffin's evil scheme and he insisted that I
allow my sister to perform....dance for the prince or expose my
own sad shortcomings to the sordid world of the tabloids. He had
to procure a very pretty young girl to entice the prince and I was
forced to agree; to my shame."

Alex dabbed her eyes with a little lace hankie; "I had to agree
otherwise my dear brother would have been ruined for one stupid
mistake which he clearly bitterly regrets." The Inspector nodded;
"So that's why you tipped off Constable Jones Mr. Tibbs; to
protect your sister and see an end to these dreadful
happenings?" Jericho nodded and placed his arm around
Alexandra; "I did Sir."

Constable Jones returned with more tea - and biscuits - and
placed them down, standing next to the Inspector, smiling at
Alex. "With your permission sir, I need to inform Miss Tibbs of
something that is clearly very important to her - may I?" The
Inspector nodded. George folded his arms and smiled - again;
"Don't worry about your precious family pets Miss; I had some of
the lads round them up and they are tied up in yard; safe and

sound." Mounjoy just snorted; "Don't mention those beasts to poor Tom; the Divisional Surgeon had to plaster his ar... backside with iodine."

Mountjoy grunted; "So you were only to dance for the prince Miss?" Alex nodded vigorously; "Yes sir, my brother made that completely clear to that blackmailing wretch Coffin." The Inspector tapped his chin; "I see, well it must have been one hell of a dance or outfit to keep a young prince of the realm in such an establishment. You've clearly had no time to change, so please, let us see this magical costume."

Alex shook her head; "I'd really rather not Sir." The Inspector shrugged his shoulders; "Well, if you cannot corroborate your brother's story, then we must look closer at his participation in all this. If what his says is true and you were there only to dance for the prince, then you both can go free. If not, then I'm forced to keep you here for some time and the press will be all over the story - it's out of my hands - sorry."

Alex quietly stood and started to unbutton her coat, Jericho stared at the floor; "Here we go." he muttered. She opened her coat and managed to smile. Mountjoy nodded and adjusted his spectacles, then pulled them from his nose and cleaned them; replacing them in an instant; "Yes, I can see that could keep a young hot-blooded man in such a place. But I would caution you young lady that such an outfit would only be suitable for viewing by your husband - and behind locked doors - You understand that? "An amazed Alex could only nod her agreement.

The Inspector turned to young Constable Jones; "Show them out and reunite the young lady with her bleeding goats." Jones nodded; "I will sir." He smiled at Alex and whispered; "I would be most grateful and proud if you would allow me to be that husband - please." He fell forwards and lay quite motionless on the floor, apart from a very happy little groan. The Inspector jumped from his seat in surprise; "For heaven's sake Jones - get a grip man; haven't you ever seen a..." Then collapsed over the desk, groaning loudly and slivered to the floor - smiling. "I've haven't had one in years...." He moaned, clutching his crotch.

Jericho grabbed Alex by the hand and headed for the door; "That's some delayed reaction!" Alex managed to button up her coat by the time they reached the police station's yard and collect the unhappy goats waiting there.

Alexandra was grinning; "That lovely young man actually proposed, you heard him, didn't you?" Jericho just groaned; "Alexandra, in that outfit, the bloody Pope himself would have proposed to you." They dragged the goats behind them and reached where the circus was. Jericho explained to the constables on duty there, that he needed to retrieve his coat from the tent.

Unsurprisingly, they folded their arms and said NO. The older constable wiped his nose and shook his head; "Sorry, can't let you Sir. This is now a cream scene; the CID officer told us so. No-one is allowed in there. Sorry." The younger constable chuckled; "Wally, you mean crime scheme! That's what Tom said, not flipping 'cream scene'." The older constable just nodded and wiped his nose again. Jericho realised these two were the not the brightest lights in the famous Metropolitan Police and smiled; "Gentlemen, I really need to retrieve my coat and it's so important, that I will make a very generous donation - via you two honest officers - to the Police Widow and Orphans fund." He produced the wad of white fivers that Damien had paid him earlier.

Both officers stared at each other and then smiled. The younger one adjusted his helmet and said quietly; "Bribing a police officer is a serious offence and bribing two of them is even seriouser. Get him!" They both leaped forward and grabbed an arm each, pushing Jericho to the ground; "Get the bleeding cuffs on him Wally!" the younger one was now actually sitting on Jericho and the older man struggled under his cape for handcuffs.

Alex sighed really loudly and unbuttoned her coat; "Gentlemen, would you like some of this?" She pulled open her coat and stood smiling. The old Constable stood slowly and wiped his nose; "Sweet fucking Jesus, I haven't seen anything like that since they closed down St. Mary's convent....Oh Fuck!...I don't.." He fell forward and lay in the mud - crying with happiness - clutching his crotch.

The young copper climbed off Jericho and stared at Alex; she turned and pulled the coat right up her backside. "Or would you prefer some of this?" She smiled and patted her bum cheek. The young constable said nothing and just stood there - and stood there - and stood there. Jericho pulled himself up and brushed mud from his jacket and trousers. He walked round and stood in front of the young policeman. "Cover yourself up Alexandra." He said and very slowly, pushed the young constable's shoulder with a single finger. It was like a mighty oak felled by a lumberjack; the young constable crashed to earth and lay motionless.

"Now that's different." Alex murmured and patted the goats.

Jericho knelt down and pushed the money into the young policeman's jacket and patted his arm; "Thanks, that'll pay for dry cleaning your coats." he stood and gestured towards the tents; "Come on Alexandra....and bring the bleeding goats." Alex wrapped her coat around herself and followed Jericho into the tents with the goats in tow; she was puzzled.

"What on earth did that old copper mean about St. Mary's bloody convent? I'm wearing nothing that remotely looks like a Nun's habit." She asked Jericho, who just shrugged his shoulders; "My old Uncle Septum always said the police were a queer bunch, but then, they harassed him over his hobby constantly." Alex stopped; "Since when was having a hobby a criminal offence?" She asked; a little intrigued.

Jericho stopped and rubbed his chin; "I don't know; he studied reindeer." The pair walked on and Alex stopped again; "Since when did studying reindeer become a crime?" Jericho shrugged his shoulders; "He use to photograph young girls dressed up as reindeer's, red noses, antlers, bells, the works." Alex shrugged; "That doesn't sound criminal. Probably quite cute, you know for Christmas cards and that, but a bit strange I grant you." Jericho nodded his agreement with that, then stopped again; "I think what the police really objected to was the fact that all the girls were stark naked."

"Oh...that' will do it every time." muttered Alex. They reached the small ring; "Fancy not having your bloody mirror on you." He scolded Alex and managed to find his coat - where he left it - and with some relief found his mirror in the pockets. "You can talk; you should have kept your bloody coat on." She said and they both helped Emika to her feet. She grinned at Alex; "Would you wear that for me?" Emika murmured to Alex.

"No." Came the reply and they grabbed the goats and Jericho

operated his mirror. Back at the lighthouse, they had to call upon James - a Knight of God - to return Wilson and Owen back to their proper form. Ruth wasn't happy; she wanted to keep the goats; she thought they were 'cute'. Alex was more than happy to change out of her outfit and into some proper clothes. She settled into her favourite armchair by the fire and enjoyed several brandies before dinner. Wilson and Owen sulked a little over not seeing Alex in her costume but were glad not to be goats anymore.

Jericho tried to settle the mystery of Reggie's costume; it was Sir Francis Drake, he announced. Everyone stared at each other; "Bloody never!" was all Owen said and Wilson still insisted it was Ivanhoe. Alex simply refused that answer; "No, he was playing William bloody Shakespeare, it's so bloody obvious, really...."

Jericho stared up at the ceiling and sighed - he said nothing further on the subject - ever. The only strange mystery remaining was the big bruise on Wilson's arse. He had no explanation for it. The dinner conversation was definitely, quite lively that night.

THE END

EPILOGUE:

"This 'Special' episode was written with some humour in mind. The demon Hari's little project was broken up and his plans thwarted by Team 74. It wouldn't be the last time that prince 'Eddy' would be involved in a temporal detective's mission before his untimely death in 1892. Alexandra's outfit remains a legend in the department to this day. When asked about what he saw her wearing, Jericho would only groan, shake his head and say nothing!"
SJW.

CHARACTERS:

Lord Arthur - 9th Earl of Rochford - was implicated by Damien Coffin in his statements to Inspector Mountjoy as supplying money and assistance to the blackmailers. But no criminal charges were ever laid against the Earl. He died in 1904 - not surprisingly - there was no soul to collect.

Lord Lewisham [aka the demon Hari] had disappeared without trace from that time period and it's reported, despite his failure, that he remains a favourite of the Dark Prince and this demon and Jericho Tibbs were to encounter each other again.

Damien Coffin was sentenced at the old Bailey to eleven years hard labour. He was in-castrated at Brixton Prison, where he was very popular with inmates of a certain persuasion, who called him MISTRESS Coffin or 'Tick-Tock'. He was released in June 1900 and joined the Royal Navy - he was accidentally killed in a freak accident aboard HMS Colossus, cannon accidently went off and blew him apart while at sea. No soul was collected. Two sailors were cleared of any blame for the accident. Able Seamen Bell and Crapps continued to serve on the ship until they both retired from the navy in 1902. They remained good friends for the rest of their lives and died in 1927 and 1933 respectively. Both souls were collected and processed.

Reggie Sponge [aka Crispin St. Michael) continued to try and find acting jobs - with little success but did assist Jericho on a couple of more missions in late Victorian England. Finally, the penny dropped, and he gave up acting, becoming a shoe salesman for 'Stead & Simpson' and ended his days as a Regional Manager for that company. He never married and died in 1936 - his soul was collected and processed - Jericho and Alex attended the funeral.

Nelly Victoria Franks [nee Sponge] married Mr. Samuel Franks in 1889 and the old man was delighted with their son, little Samuel - despite the boy being a touch on the dark side. They had no other children and Nelly was widowed in 1908. She was now quite a wealthy woman and remarried in 1912 to a Silversmith called Dean. [Nelly Dean!] - They had five children together and Mr. Dean never wore a hat in bed. She was widowed again in 1929. She didn't marry again and died in 1940, surrounded by her large family of six children, nineteen grandchildren and six great grandchildren. Her soul was collected, and Nelly became a very popular 'Collector' - she still works as one to this day - She counts Alex as a good friend.

Detective Inspector Maurice Mountjoy remained at Brick Lane Police Station until his retirement in 1899; his position was filled by a very promising young Detective; Harry Hadden who became [with his sister Dorothy] a human agent for Jericho Tibbs. Maurice didn't enjoy his retirement for long and died of cancer in

1903. His soul was collected properly.

Sergeant Tom Bass didn't look after his 'summer cold' too well and it progressed into influenza. He died in 1890. Temporal Detective Inspector 'Doc' Underhill dealt with his case - no soul was collected - the case currently remains unsolved.

Lord Henry Snowfield's soul remains missing; his case is marked 'LTDA' [Lost to Demonic activity] and is currently closed.

'Little Ivor' – the big Russian, served five years hard labour in Wandsworth Prison and upon his release in 1894 became a professional wrestler with the stage name: 'The Bear'. He was very popular and died in 1922 – quite a wealthy man - His soul was collected and processed.

Santo only served a year in prison; the Judge at his trial had many fond memories of circus clowns and dwarfs from his happy childhood days – he was lenient towards the little man. Santo gained a job with 'Walpole Salad's Travelling Show' in America, where dressed as a cowboy, he rode a large pig called 'Edith' and fired off pistols. It wasn't much, but it was a living. 'Edith' the pig died in 1907 and Santo simply walked to some wasteland behind the showground and blew his brains out with one of the pistols. His soul was collected and processed.

Peter Zackiskovy received eight years hard labour and never completed his sentence. Another inmate at Pentonville prison cut his throat over unpaid gambling debts and with no relatives to claim his body, was buried in a 'Paupers grave' at Whitechapel Cemetery – in an unmarked grave. His soul was collected and processed.

"Marvo the Magician';real name: Alistair McArden continued his magic act in Vaudeville – badly. He had escaped prison due to possible insanity; he had turned up for his trial with several rabbits in his trousers that escaped during his appearance at court. He actually did have no idea they were still there. Finally, he gave up show business and worked as a porter in a London Hotel. He had a fatal accident in 1910; he fell down a staircase – pissed – and broke his neck. His soul was collected and processed.

Katrina Boggavich – aka 'The Black Queen' - escaped any

prosecution because of lack of evidence and the sneaking possibility that she was stark raving mad. Police had searched her humble caravan on that fateful night and found her face down on the floor; drunk. The fact that she was dressed as a Durham Miner, complete with helmet, boots and coal dust aided her defence. Wisely, she fled Britain and became a 'mystic' in New York, reading palms and her crystal ball. Katrina became known for her prophecies until 1901, when, unfortunately, a milkman's horse kicked her in the head, and she died of her injuries. She hadn't seen that coming. Her soul was collected and processed.

Lucy Kassine and her twin sister Fatima also escaped prison. They became the mistresses of the judge who heard their case. Both had been born together and both died together of tuberculosis on Christmas Day 1896. Both their souls were collected and processed.

Emika Sato remains a Guardian - despite her failure to deal with the demon - and remains 'friendly' with Alex. Though she did stalk Alex for some time, sent her flowers repeatedly, turned up on missions when no guardian was called for and still followed her into toilets whenever possible. It's only been a couple of centuries and so Alex thinks she will get over it....

Constable George Jones [H211] remained in the police until he retired in 1917. He never married and died in 1931. His sister Lillian cleared out his small cottage in Kent to sell it [she was his only surviving relative and heir] amongst his possessions she found a sketch book [apparently, he kept his superb drawing skills to himself and sketched in secret] the old scrap book was full of drawings of a stunning young woman called Miss Alex Tibbs. He had never spoken to his sister about this girl; ever. His soul was collected properly. The scrap book was kept by his sister until her death in 1952. It was found in an antique shop in 1974 and purchased by a young woman for three pounds. Its whereabouts are now unknown.

Bartholomew Blackberry [aka 'Black Bart'] served three years at her majesty's pleasure and was released in 1892. He disappeared for a while but resurfaced in Hull. Still skilful with the camera, he actually became a noted 'Scene of crime' photographer for the police and also sold pictures to various newspapers. He married an exotic young lady of Welsh and Eskimo decent and died a happy man in 1913. His soul was collected.

Police Constable John Lofthouse {H241] dealt with many dead bodies and strange incidents during his twenty-seven years in the Metropolitan Police. He retired in 1916 and became a Post Sub master in a small Essex village. Both his two sons were killed in the Great War [WW1] and he never really recovered from such a loss. John hung himself in his bedroom in November 1920. His soul was collected and processed.

Roger 'Suet' Pudding received three years hard labour and was released in 1892 - sadly, he was a habitual criminal - and a lousy one - he was released in 1897, again in 1902, 1910 and 1922. Finally, the penny dropped, and he gained 'honest employment' in 1923 as a Road Sweeper. It didn't last long; he was killed by a car on his first day of work. He had spent so much time in prison that he really didn't understand; that you didn't carrying on sweeping when a motor car approached; at speed. His soul was collected and processed.

Stanley Edwin Cornish continued to run his coal delivery business until 1897, when his horse 'Neptune' suddenly dropped dead in Eastham High Street. He truly loved his old faithful companion and workmate and couldn't bring himself to replace the old horse. He survived a few years by delivering coal with a hand barrow but had turned to drink. He was found dead in the street one night and his family couldn't afford his funeral; he was buried in a 'pauper's grave' with no headstone. His soul was collected and possessed.

Percival Tim, Lord Arthur's snobbish Butler found himself unemployed after the death of his master in 1904. He was forced to seek employment on the stage, appearing in a 'drag' act called 'East & West'. His fellow artiste was a young Chinese man called 'Gan Ho' and the pair was quite successful until they were found in bed together - dead from an opium over-dose - in 1909. Both souls were collected and processed.

Dave 'Dogface' Sellers wasn't implicated in any crime by his two loyal barmaids and continued to run the 'Queen's Head' pub. The pub became a haven for crime and prostitution throughout the last years of Queen Victoria's reign and old 'dogface' died in 1904 in mysterious circumstances; well, they weren't that mysterious considering the type of people he dealt with. He was found hanging in his cellar - stark naked - with barbed wire wrapped around his penis and a dead rat shoved in his mouth. Strangely enough, the inept Coroner decided it was 'Death by Misadventure' and no one was ever prosecuted for his strange death. No soul was collected, and the case remains 'unsolved' by the Temporal Detectives assigned to the case; Inspector Gwyn Francine and Team 28.

SPECIAL APPEARANCE BY:

Prince Albert Victor, Duke of Clarence and Avondale (Albert Victor Christian Edward; 8 January 1864 – 14 January 1892) as himself. The prince was never mentioned at the trial of Damien Coffin or any of his merry men. No scandal was attached to 'Prince Eddy' [as he was known to friends and family] over the 'Devil's Circus' incident. But there were other episodes that linked his name to scandal.

He died in 1892 and when his father; King Edward VII died in 1910, his younger brother George, became King George V. Such was the prince's 'dark' reputation that some modern scholars have linked him with the 'Jack the Ripper' killings in London's East End. There is no evidence available to really add credence to such stories.

He had been engaged, at the time of his untimely death, to princess Mary of Teck. His brother George eventually married the princess who became Queen Mary.

Prince Eddy's soul was collected and processed.

He is sometimes referred to - in popular literature - as 'the King we never had'.

IMPORTANT NOTICE:
"Jericho wishes to point out that no animals were harmed in this episode – well, except a certain goat that was kicked up the arse by a certain irate policeman.
Thank you."

EPISODE 11: "GHOSTS IN THE DEVIL'S GARDEN OF THE DAMNED."

MISSION SUMMARY:
"There has been an error in the 'Dispatch Department' [They keep the records of deaths] and Mr. Jericho Tibbs must find and bring back Patrick 'Bends' McGill from the dead of the Underworld, despite being a man of evil disposition, he must be returned to the Dimension of the living. This will involve a dangerous trip to a part of Hell colloquially known as the 'Devil's Garden' - where the Dark Prince rules!"

 ALCOHOL, VIOLENCE, SOME SEXUAL REFERENCES, STRONG LANGUAGE & MILD HORROR.

 **AGE 12+ ONLY.**   **30 Minutes reading time.**

1. A KNIGHT PAYS A VISIT.

Alex sat reading in Jericho's study; she had finished 'Treasure Island' and now started to read 'Don Quixote' with growing pleasure and interest; "I wonder if Jericho has read this." She smiled and turned the pages quietly, adding; "Well I certainly know how the old Knight feels." The study door opened, and young Owen bounced in with a big grin and holding a brown paper file.

He dropped onto the sofa and held the file aloft; "You'll never guess where we are heading for Alex?" She marked her page and closed the book, placing it upon the small table beside her chair; "Go on Owen, you appear to be bursting to tell someone." The young man almost giggled with growing excitement; "Bloody Hell." He said and grinned.

Alex rolled her eyes and pulled the file from his fingers and read the summary of their latest Mission; Indeed, they were scheduled a trip to Hell, well, the place colloquially known as the 'Devil's Garden'. It wasn't quite 'Hell', but similar, in the old days and according to certain religions, it was known as 'Purgatory'. It was the 'Quarantine' area used by 'Collections' to house souls waiting final judgment. If a soul was sent to 'quarantine'; this is where they ended up.

All souls that failed the initial inspection by the Duty Death Angel [currently Angel Margret] were placed there; to await their final judgment; return to the human life cycle or dispatched to 'Hell' proper. The 'Dark Angel' currently in charge was Simon. He and Angel Margret knew each other well.

Alex peered over the top of the file at young Owen and asked; "Has Jericho seen it?" Owen shook his head; "I just received it from little Ivan, the Messenger, he's just left. Mr. Tibbs is apparently playing Chess with Wilson, or rather trying to teach him to play the damn game, without throwing the pieces about."

Alex nodded and handed the file back; "Best you disturb their game, Mr. Tibbs will need to see it as soon as possible." She watched young Owen jump from the sofa and disappear through the door, standing aside as Mr. Harris appeared with a large tray of drinks and he laid them upon the study table; "For the journey I believe, my Lady." Alex pulled from her over- comfortable chair and lifted a brandy glass; "Yes, I think we're going to need a good start for this particular show; thank you Mr. Harris."

The details of the Mission floated through her mind, and she slowly sipped the brandy; there had been an error in the Dispatch Department and a 'Patrick Bends McGill' had been collected three hours earlier than scheduled by the Human Timeline. Mr. McGill was a very unpleasant individual; a paid hitman for the 'Five Points Mob' and had several murders to his credit. He should have been killed at 6.15pm by another gangster outside his boarding house in New York City, but had been collected some three hours before that event and with his record of killings, was sent to 'The Devil's Garden' to await his final fate.

How he slipped through the system would be investigated thoroughly, but it appears that a slightly overzealous new collector might be the answer!

Alex could hear voices coming from the Hall and realised that Mr. Harris was escorting James - a Knight of God - into the Reception Room; she placed her drink down and headed there at once. She found Jericho and Wilson emerging from the small Games Room, both sharing the file between them with Owen trailing behind; still smiling.

James was a stunning young man, who when last alive, had fought for the Tsars of Russia, on horseback with sword and spear. His piety and devotion to God was well documented and known - as was his chivalrous nature. His enemies both feared and respected the young cavalier. He was killed at the age of 28, defending a church packed with women and children who were refugees from Cossack raiders. The legend states that he killed over twenty of the fierce warriors with sword and dagger, before being killed by a volley of arrows fired by hidden archers.

His dying words to his enemy were to leave the church in peace. The Cossacks did; out of respect for a fellow warrior and the legend of James of Kiev was written into the annuals of Russian History; pre-revolution of course.

It didn't survive the Revolution and now, few remembered the brave young man in his old homeland or his incredible sacrifice; there were no memorials or plaques to recall James or his feats of courage and devotion - but the BOSS [God] had remembered and within a century or two - the young man found himself made a Knight of God.

An elite company of the finest men and women that Humanity had produced, and they were nicknamed; 'The little angels', since they were considered just a step away from being an angel and with a very important difference: they could still pass into the Realm of mortals!

Young Ruth watched from the kitchen door with mouth open in

sheer awe of the handsome young man, until Mrs. Harris called her away. Ruth grinned broadly and said that Owen could easily end up as a Knight of God; Cleo Harris sighed and rolled her eyes; "Ruth, you certainly have a strong imagination!" The two walked back to the kitchen, passing Mr. Parker carrying a rubber chicken that Alex had given him to play with. Ruth reached down and stroked the big cat that disappeared into the Dining Room.

John, the reclusive friend of Jericho's, was waiting in the kitchen doorway to hand back an empty plate and cup. He thanked Cleo for the sandwiches and tea, the asked who the visitor was. Cleo explained about James, the 'Knight of God' and John almost smiled; "Yes, I do know James. A good man; a very good man." Cleo suggested that he join Jericho and James in the Dining room, but John shook his head and shuffled through the yard door and headed for his cottage.

Cleo sighed and placed the cup and plate in the sink; "Such a waste. If only he pulled himself together, he could achieve so much good." A puzzled Ruth asked Cleo what she meant, but Cleo just smiled and asked her to get on with warming the dinner plates and said nothing more about the hermit of Heaven's Edge Bay.

"Mr. Tibbs, I've placed himself in the Reception Room and will fetch more drinks." Mr. Harris disappeared into the Butler's Parlour with a determined step – having a Knight to entertain was the equivalent of serving Royalty - in his mind. Everyone gathered in the Reception Room and James was made comfortable and accepted large Vodka from the delighted Mr. Harris, who had changed into his best black jacket and trousers but was sporting a multi-coloured waistcoat beneath!

James glanced at the gaudy garment and had some difficulty not smiling. Owen stood respectfully to one side with the grin gone and was listening quietly to the Knight outlying the details of the Mission. James explained that authority for the Mission had come from 'above' – from 'HIMSELF' – and despite Mr. McGill having an evil disposition; he was entitled to his fully allocated life-span – even if, it was just three hours more.

He also mentioned that it was the first error in almost a thousand Human years and that the 'BOSS' had informed the 'Dark One' of the mission and there should be no interference from the dark side, and that the 'Dark Prince' had arranged a Minion to assist; if necessary or required.

Owen looked totally puzzled and whispered to Alex; "Why would the Devil do that – I mean assist us?" She smiled; "They are brothers and they do talk you know." Owen shook his head in mock disbelief; "I still can't get my head around that, and the fact they have a sister." He said quietly and accepted a glass of whisky from Mr. Harris which returned a smile to his young face.

The Knight gave his instructions with a smile, especially when he saw the look on Jericho's face, as he informed him that the Pilot of the 'Necrosub' was McAlister Semple. Alex grinned and tapped Jericho's shoulder; "You two will get on fine; this time." For the Journey to the 'Devil's Garden' a specialist craft was required; a 'Necrosub' which was created to cross between the dimensions of light and dark/Life and Death. McAlister made many such runs each year; taking condemned Souls there and occasionally returning a very happy Soul whose sentence had been commuted or pardoned.

With all his experience, he was clearly, the right choice for the Mission despite the falling out between him and Jericho, some years previously. McAlister was the Chief 'Necronaut' of the small unit of 'Necrosubs' that were operated by the 'Collections' Department – and the best Pilot by far; he had said so himself on many occasions!

James stood by the fire and downed his vodka in a single throw, he smiled at Alex; "Lady Alexandra may I say that when 'the BOSS' decided to bestow beauty, grace and intelligence upon the female, he gave you a full measure of each." and kissed her hand.

It was rare for Alex to colour at men's mere words of admiration, but on this occasion she did blush a little and murmured a quiet; "Thank you Sir." It was clear that the good Knight had fallen under her spell; like many had done so and would continue to do so! Wilson chuckled and said quietly to Owen; "Another bloody Moth to the flame."

The Knight turned to Jericho and raised his class, which Mr. Harris had rushed to refill; "To God and your safe return." He turned to Alex and whispered; particularly yours." Alex sipped her drink and said quietly; "To God and his good Knights."

2. McAlister SEMPLE.

Jericho just nodded his head at that remark and sipped his whisky without further comment. The Mission would commence that very night with the group heading for McAlister's office and home; an abandoned whaling station in South Alaska!

They arrived during a blizzard of snow and ice; "What bloody nutter actually chooses to live in this shit hole?" Wilson moaned, wrapping his coat tightly against the flying snow. "I bet he doesn't have many fucking visitors." He added, but Jericho smiled; "You would be surprised, never mind what I think of McAlister; apparently he's a very popular character. I have no idea why."

The group made their way through the numerous rusting and derelict buildings towards a couple of sharp lights, showing from what appears to be an old derelict Chapel. Alex was quite bemused by the stained-glass window at the front of the building - covered with rusting chicken wire - it appeared to be a large polar bear wearing a bright red three-piece suit and a black top hat. Jericho actually chuckled; "Rumour has it, that's based on McAlister's first wife."

Jericho banged hard upon the doors and awaited entry. The night was falling fast – as was the temperature - and Owen pointed out to his fellow travelers a pack of several large wolves, who were prowling around the perimeter of the ruined station. "They probably view us like we would a Pizza delivery." Owen quietly muttered; then grinned, wiping the snow from his face.

The big door jerked open and bright light streamed out; McAlister stood in the doorway and smiled. He pointed his rifle to the sky and fired – that actually made Alex jump, then laughed; "That's Tibbs and his pack, he's the really big fucker with the silver streaks in his fur. Mean and sneaky, but he's clearly a good pack leader." McAlister stared at Alex and lowered the rifle; "Jesus Jericho, you're a lucky bastard, what a fucking babe!"

Everyone watched as 'Tibbs' led the pack away from the buildings; stopping once to look back, then quickly disappeared into the night. "He's called a pack of wolves after Jericho?" Owen whispered to Wilson and smiled braodly.

McAlister was easily the size of Wilson and dressed like an 19th Century Snake-Oil salesman, complete with chequered trousers, bright red waistcoat and a small pistol tucked into his braces. On his head was a large black Russian style fur hat, sporting a 'skull and crossbones' badge. He pulled a half-smoked cigar from his pocket and grinned broadly; "Welcome to fucking Alaska!"

He stepped aside, and everyone quickly pushed into the Hallway and McAlister slammed the big door shut and placed a metal bar across it; "The local Eskimo's are a funny bunch: they'll steal the teeth from your gob; given half a chance." He hung the rife up and gestured towards a piano black door opposite.

"Tang! Tang! You lazy dog! Get off your arse; we have visitors, and one is a real babe!" The group trooped into the room and was quite surprised by what they found; it was a saloon bar! There was a fine, dark wood bar with gold railings and a large painting of a completely nude woman; holding a shotgun and standing upon a dead grizzly bear, which had a surprised look upon its face.

Alex looked about the place in amazement; it was exactly like one of those Wild West saloons you saw in Western films. She shook her head and smiled at Owen; "Our host certainly has a specific taste in clothes and furniture."

The door reopened, and a small Chinese man crept in and quickly ran past McAlister, who tried to boot the little fellow up the arse. "Get the drinks on the go; we got fucking visitors!" Tang slipped behind the bar and stuck two fingers up; "Fuck you! I get drink for people and beautiful lady." He grinned at Alex and bowed a little, jerking his thumb at the painting; "Your far more pretty than Stella – I wish to paint you – maybe getting out of bathtub!" He bowed again and started opening bottles of whisky and brandy.

"Tang painted the tart in the picture, some years back, he's a lousy barman and servant; but quite a good painter of nude women and walls and ceilings." McAlister laughed and coughed, pushing the cigar into his mouth.

McAlister lit his cigar and blew large smoke rings about the place and sat down on a gaudy red sofa, stretching out his legs and scratching his shaggy beard; "I got a message from Margret that I'm to do a run to Hell with you fellows and rather strangely; I'm to bring you back!" He laughed and coughed, drawing on his smelly cigar. Tang offered him a whisky and he took it slowly, eyeing Jericho closely; "So what's the plan Jericho, who's the fuckwit that has a second chance?"

Jericho accepted a large whisky from the grinning Chinese man and settled back in his surprisingly comfortable chair; he looked about the place and smiled slightly; "Just run us there, wait until we collect Mr. McGill and then return us here; we'll do the rest."

McAlister nodded his agreement and sipped his whisky; "I know you've been there, but what about these three – do they know the rules?" He waved his glass at Owen, adding; "He's a bit young to visit such a place; you could leave him with Tang, the old bastard will teach him Poker and how to cheat without getting his head blown off."

Jericho shook his head; "Owen wants to be a Temporal Detective and so he must learn the ropes, this mission will be good training." Owen smiled with some relief at that; he didn't want to miss out on the trip to Hell just because some crazy Necronaut thought he was too young. Wilson slapped him on the back and nodded. "Jericho's quite right; baby brother."

"The babe should definitely stay; Tang could paint her and I can show her my engravings when I return." McAlister smiled broadly at that suggestion and added; "A beauty like that shouldn't be risked in such a shit hole."

"Alexandra, my name is not babe, baby or anything else but: Alexandra." She spoke quietly and sipped her brandy; "I have been to 'The Devil's Garden' twice before and I know what I'm doing Mr. Semple."

"Never Semple, NEVER, always McAlister or Mac!" He groaned and lifted his class in salute; "Alexandra!" He said simply and swallowed the whisky down in one gulp. The door creaked open, and Omar stepped in, scratching his head and stubbly beard with some enthusiasm, declaring; "Mac, why have we got visitors at this time of night?" He made his way to the bar and Tang dished up a large dark rum, he took a couple of swigs and nodded at

Wilson: "Nothing beats a slug of rum for breakfast!" Everyone looked at McAlister who shrugged his shoulders and said quietly, "He likes to sleep late."

Omar Hussein [the subs co-pilot] was a tall, thin individual dressed like an 18th century Turkish brothel keeper and with the same cheerful disposition. Alex cringed as the young man took bites from a small red onion and picked at some bread Tang had handed him.

"He has Dark Rum, onions and dry bread for breakfast?" Owen didn't know if he was impressed or nauseous. Omar looked Alex up and down; then smiled. He pushed his hands through his long dark hair and spoke softly; "I never thought I could really fancy a bloody copper, but you are one hell of a piece of skirt and trousers don't suit you. Always wear a short dress that shows off your legs. They look long and lean and I bet they go right up to heaven. That's one ladder I'd climb any day!"

Alex said nothing initially but sipped her brandy, she believed a trouser suit was the most appropriate clothing for where they were headed and told him so. Omar disagreed – clearly - "Nay Alex, it's all wrong. I would have thought that you would know the Minions there are all in human form. They won't take a bite out of piece of skirt like you, showing those gorgeous legs and plenty of cleavage. If it all goes tits up, pardon the pun! That's your key to survival in that shithole."

McAlister nodded his agreement with Omar's comments and turned to Jericho; "You should either leave the babe here or tell her to dress up. Surely, when she made the other trips; the Necrosub crews pointed that out. Young Kate, the skipper of sub six, always wears skimpy shorts and an open blouse. She knows the score."

Alex didn't admit that both the crews on her two previous trips had made the same comment. Both the captains she travelled with, made the point of insisting, to her Inspectors, that she remains on board for her own safety. But she really didn't like being told what to wear; her husband Henri always ordered her about, when it came to dressing to please him and she hated that.

Jericho just smiled; "Alexandra can wear what she likes. If she's prepared to take a chance on those clothes, its fine by me. But, very reluctantly for once, I would have to agree with you, just to safeguard her." Alex sighed quite loudly and folded her arms in defiance. Then she saw the look of concern upon Jericho's face; had she badly cocked up on the costume front this time?

McAlister jerked a thumb towards a bright green door at the rear of the 'bar' and said, "Take a look around in there, there's lots of girl's stuff left by Omar's and my friends. You're bound to find something more suitable and safer than looking like a vulnerable young boy."

"You should wear something really revealing; a short skirt with stockings would be perfect and just a little black bodice, showing off those hooters; they are bloody stunning." Omar chuckled to himself and gulped down yet more rum. "We can wait." McAlister added and pointed to the door. Jericho shrugged his shoulders and said to Alex; "It's your call Alexandra."

Wilson, who had made several trips to the 'Devil's Garden' during his tenure as a Temporal Detective, said quietly; "For once they're right Alex. I suggest you slip into something that shows off your female charms. You'll have those bloody minions eating out of your hand - if needs be - so don't be a mule-head and get those legs showing!" He grinned and pointed to the green door.

Owen didn't offer an opinion, but what McAlister said about 'vulnerable young boys' gave him some thoughts to ponder; but he was still going.

Alex said nothing more but walked slowly to the green door and pushed it open. The team sat about drinking and chatting, with Jericho and Wilson giving last minute advice to young Owen. McAlister offered one piece of advice to him; "Don't bend over in the reception centre when we book in; the skinny minion; Simon, who's in charge there, really likes young boys!" He and Omar laughed for some time over that comment. Owen forced a grin and said nothing.

All the heads turned, as the green door creaked open, and Alex re-appeared. She was wearing a short black mini skirt with black boots that came to just below her knees and bright red leather, over bust corset, which certainly showed her magnificent breasts to their best advantage. Her long dark hair was tied back with a white ribbon and she wore a dark lace collar; she simply looked stunning. She did a little twirl and said loudly; "Will this do?"

There was a silence for a few seconds, then McAlister nodded; "Alex, you look fucking stunning. If I wasn't already dead - like everyone here - I would marry you tomorrow and live happily in lust for ever more and die a happy man, a very happy man." Omar grinned and said, "Ditto." The look on his face said all he was thinking.

They had one last drink before their trip to Hell and Alex sipped her brandy and turned to Jericho; "In another century, these two could easily pass for pirates!"

Jericho nodded his agreement with that statement and placed his glass upon the table; "Let's go people." McAlister sighed loudly and eased from his sofa with little enthusiasm; "Come on Omar, let's fire up the old girl and get this crap done."

3. "NOT A NICE PLACE TO VISIT AND YOU WOULDN'T WANT TO STAY...."

McAlister walked slowly down the steep staircase towards the basement with Omar just behind who was telling Owen what to expect when the 'Necrosub' drops. At the foot of the old stone staircase, McAlister opened a heavy metal door and pushed through; the rest of the group followed in silence.

"There she is; the Scallywag." McAlister announced with some pride in his voice. Alex chuckled; "My reference to pirates couldn't be more appropriate." Wilson nodded but looked puzzled. Owen sighed; "Scallywag is a pirate saying." Jericho and McAlister stood next to the 'Necrosub' and exchanged views about the mission. Owen stood staring at the craft; he had never seen anything like it. "It looks like a giant teardrop made out of plastic!" he exclaimed and walked round the small craft which was no bigger than an old London Double Decker bus, standing on it's head.

"How many souls can you transport in this thing?" He asked Omar directly - not impressed with the vessel - Omar shrugged his shoulders; "We normally carry about two thousand on a trip."

Now that did puzzle Owen; "Where the fuck do you put them?"

He muttered as the team started to board and could hear Alex and Wilson chuckling.

Omar chuckled and slapped Owen on the back with some humour; "You'll see my young friend." Omar dropped through the hatch first and eased into his pilot's seat, Owen followed and stood a little amazed; the inside was enormous. Wilson dropped down next and smiled at Owen; "Same as the lighthouse really; the inside is certainly not constrained by the outside." Owen just smiled and made himself comfortable in one of the six visitor's seats, behind the two pilots.

Everyone stared up at the hatch as Alex made her way day into the craft. "Now that's the sort of view that should be on an art gallery wall." Owen muttered and really did grin. Wilson gave him a gentle slap and shook his head in mock despair.

"Little white panties are an absolute favourite of mine." Omar interrupted the pair and smiled broadly. Alex simply stuck up a solitary finger at them and found a comfortable seat, then strapped in. Jericho and McAlister dropped through the hatch and then 'Mac' sealed it up behind him.

Jericho sat next to Alex and checked his mirror; "I take it we're not carrying any souls on this trip?" He asked McAlister who nodded. The soul chamber was empty. Owen scratched his head and asked Wilson; "If this craft can carry about two thousand souls, do they carry extra guards or something?" Wilson shook his head; "Don't need them; the souls are delivered in a couple of small, sealed crates which are only opened by the receptionists at the centre. The crew has no access to them, except to load the crates into what's called the 'Soul Chamber'. The Receptionists will unload the crates once the paperwork is processed; it's a really simple procedure."

Owen nodded; "Yeah, but why is it shaped like a teardrop; that's weird." Omar chuckled; "Well. If you're going to Hell, what better way to travel than in a tear drop?" Owen grimaced and settled in his seat.

Alex smiled and tapped Wilson's shoulder; "You haven't explained to our resident pervert about the ghosts in the devil's garden." She eased back in her seat and consulted her mirror. Owen stared at Alex, but spoke to Wilson; "Ghosts? What ghosts?" He asked with real curiosity in his voice. The big man sighed; "Sometimes there are errors - failures - in the system and the odd soul is lost on arrival. Sometimes, souls turn up there without warning and are lost in the 'Garden'. I understand that the 'Dark Prince' does allow his minions to carry out searches for them; but it's rare to find one in the vast space that is the devil's garden. Everyone there refers to them as 'Ghosts'."

Omar turned around and grinned at the pair; "Don't forget the poor bastards of crashed Necrosubs'. I know that over the centuries, two subs have crashed there and none of the crews were recovered. They're out there somewhere; now ghosts in the fucking garden." Wilson smiled at Alex; "Being a beautiful young woman, you'll have a far greater chance of survival than any of us blokes; most of the devil's minions there are male humans." He gestured to her outfit; "Hence the advice about your clothes." He chuckled and settled back in his seat. Jericho nodded to McAlister, and he fired up the 'Scallywag'.

"Next stop hell!" McAlister shouted and pulled down a vivid red lever just above his head. The ship dropped through nothing at incredible speed - Owen actually felt sick; his stomach was now apparently - just below his chin! He closed his eyes tightly as the craft appeared to drop further and faster. Then it stopped and his stomach was now – apparently - around his ankles. He felt awful and groaned loudly; he needed brandy urgently. Alex smiled and shoved her hipflask under his nose. "Well. We got here without turning into bloody ghosts." She muttered as Owen took a couple of sips from her flask.

"Are we really there?" He whispered and leaned back in his seat; his legs were no longer shaking, and his stomach had stopped moving about. Wilson grinned and released his safety straps; "We sure are baby brother, our day trip to Hell starts now!" Alex gripped Owens's shoulder and smiled; "Come on Owen, Simon and his staff are very good hosts to visitors like us, they almost view us as respected colleagues. You should enjoy - and learn - from our quick visit."

McAlister was up the ladder, unsealing the hatch as Jericho consulted his mirror; "OK people, let's get this done as quickly as possible. Mrs. Harris has Beef Wellington on the menu tonight." Owen felt sick at the thought of food [now that was a first!] and took another sip from the hipflask before handing it back to Alex.

Omar stood arms folded by the seats and grinned; "Mac and I will wait for you fellows at the Staff bar and restaurant; the food is very good there and the booze is completely free. The company can be difficult; not many have a real sense of humour down here."

"I'm last up the ladder; thank you gentlemen." Alex grinned and gestured towards the ladder. Omar and Owen both groaned; "Spoilsport." Jericho just chuckled and followed McAlister up the ladder, with Omar and Owen behind him. Wilson came next, then a happy Alex. They were in the reception area of the Devil's Garden.

Owen stood in amazement, staring at the huge stone interior of the reception area; it appears to have been built from Neolithic stones of enormous proportions. The reception desks look like they were carved from single pieces of gold and white marble. The place was packed with people, formed into orderly queues at the desks. He then noticed that there was two other 'Necrosubs' just behind where the 'Scallywag' had docked. That's when he saw they appeared to be standing on pools of dark water, he looked above each craft; there appeared to be similar puddles on the ceiling!

Wilson slapped him on the shoulder and pointed to a imposing desk in a quiet corner; the blue sign above said: 'Visitors Only'. "That's our one." He smiled at Owen, and they followed the others over to the desk. The Receptionist was a young man in a neat black suit, white shirt and black tie. He smiled broadly and opened the large, ornate book on the desk and offered an old fashioned 'fountain pen' to Jericho; "Would you please sign yourself and your team in Inspector."

Jericho nodded, and McAlister slapped him on the back; "We'll be in the bar when you're finished." He turned to Alex; "You'd be better off staying with us. The drinks are on me and Omar." He stared at her breasts and licked his lips; "You'll love the place; it's like an old-fashioned disco and strip bar. They play ABBA a lot here." Alex declined his generous offer; not very politely it must be said.

A little disappointed, McAlister shrugged his shoulders and with Omar in tow, headed for the bar. Owen had to chuckle; the place was called 'Dave's Inferno'. A bright red sign displayed above the two big red doors shouted that out. "I get it. The devil's real name is David; isn't it?" He spoke to Wilson, who just sighed; he guessed it was going to be a long stay, even if it only took a few hours in human time.

The receptionist - quite politely - asked the team to wait until their hosts appeared. He checked Jericho's time piece and wrote its number down in the ledger. Every temporal Detective Inspector and above, carried a custom-made fob watch. The time piece was their badge of office and authority to carry out their duties. Each Inspector received his watch from the 'BOSS' himself.

It was the first time, that both Owen and Alex had seen the fabled and almost legendary time piece. Jericho closed it with a snap and replaced it in his waistcoat pocket. Owen chuckled and said quietly to Alex; "Now I know why all Inspectors wear waistcoats; even the female ones!" Alex just smiled; she was watching the two people approaching the team from a door marked Staff only'.

The male - wearing the obligatory black suit - was a tall African male with strange horizontal scars on each cheek. He was quite handsome despite those markings. The female was in a matching black 'business' suit with a very short skirt. She had amazing burnt copper coloured hair, tied up with a black ribbon. Her skin was very white, almost like milk. She had real dark eyes and thick red lipstick. The young woman walked like a catwalk model and could easily be considered a 'real beauty'.

Jericho smiled and held out his hand; "Hello Peter. I hope this isn't too much of an inconvenience?" Peter returned the smile and shook Jericho's hand with some apparent affection; "You're always welcome Jericho." He had a deep voice; he could have made a fortune doing movie talk over's! He introduced his assistant; Tabitha to everyone. Apparently, Peter was her mentor; she was still learning the job. She and Alex stood chatting; Tabitha was pleased that Alex knew the ropes here and had dressed appropriately!

That's when Peter dropped the little bombshell; their BOSS [the Dark Prince] was here in person. He had arrived just a few minutes ago with his large retinue and had asked to meet the visiting detectives at some point, on their mission. The two minions never noticed how Jericho, Wilson and Owen all stared at Alex, when they were told the news. She just folded her arms and said nothing. Owen whispered to Alex; "Bit of a co-incidence that; he turns up when you're on a mission here?" Alex just ignored him; but she was actually quite concerned. He [the Dark Prince] had made it clear, at their last encounter, that he wanted her for his personal 'Harem'. She tugged at her short skirt and felt a little vulnerable. She really wished she had stayed in her business suit with its wonderful trousers.

Peter pointed to a pair of large glass doors - guarded by at least a dozen staff [easily recognizable; all staff wore the same uniform] - and said simply; "Shall we go?"

4. THE GARDEN.

They walked through the doors and the heat hit them; it was like stepping into an oven. Owen groaned; "Now I know how the Christmas turkey feels." Wilson chuckled; "I expect it's a little acclimatization for the real thing." Peter gestured to their transport; sitting a few yards away. "Captain Stabbings and her crew will take us out into the garden." Owen just stared and Alex joined him; their transport resembled a large cockroach on wheels!

As they drew closer, they realised just how big the vehicle was. It towered above them, black and shining in the bright sunshine. "It must be five stories high." Owen said to Alex, with real amazement in his voice. Alex nodded and then noticed; at the front was a moveable set of steps, like you see at airports, with two people waiting to greet them. Both women, in neat black uniforms with the mandatory short skirts and like Alex; wearing knee length boots. They smiled broadly and said together; "Welcome aboard the 'Lady Alexandra'."

Owen actually giggled at that, he turned to Wilson and said quietly; "Well, at least we can say, we have been in Alexandra!" But Alex had heard him and slapped his shoulder; hard. He just grinned and the team made their way up the steps and into the welcoming cool of the inside. The interior was like a hotel reception area. The two very pleasant ladies showed them the reception desk and departed. Wilson and Owen watched then walk away; their hips swinging gently in unison. "That's what I call a real pair of glorious ars...." Wilson never finished his sentence; he saw the look on Alex's face as did Owen, who could only chuckle softly. Wilson just smiled and shrugged his big shoulders.

The receptionist on board was another young woman in the same uniform that the greeters wore. She smiled at Peter; "I do understand that these guests are day visitors and do not require rooms, just access to the bar and restaurant Sir." Peter nodded and he asked the team to follow him. That's when they noticed the little clutch of staff around the door marked 'Staff only'. They were all chatting and gesturing towards Alex. Peter waved them away and smiled at her; "They're a bit excited. They have obviously never met the person - in the flesh - that a crawler has been named after. The 'BOSS' [the other one] named this himself; after you apparently Detective."

Alex didn't smile and that didn't go un-noticed by her colleagues. Finally, she said quietly; "I'm really flattered that he named a giant cockroach after me. Charming I don't bloody think." Even Peter had to chuckle at that. For a minion, he still had quite a sense of humour. They were shown to the bar; it was clearly marked 'VIP's ONLY'. It was stunning, all wood décor and furniture to match. It would not have been out of place in a five-star hotel.

Tabitha showed them to window seats and they were like large armchairs. Alex carefully eased herself into hers and stared out the window. There was nothing but desert - just endless miles of brownish red sand - she wondered about the strange humour of naming this place; the Devil's Garden'.

Everyone felt the gentle movement as 'Alexandra' got under way. The music playing - it was 'Lead Zeppelin' - stopped and a woman's voice was heard. She spoke with some authority in her words; "Welcome above the crawler Alexandra, the newest crawler in the fleet and Captain Stabbings and her crew are pleased and honoured to welcome aboard Assistant Director Peter and his staff. We are also pleased to welcome the visiting Temporal Detectives; especially Inspector Tibbs and detective Alexandra Cappanni, who this very craft is named in honour of. Thank you and have a pleasant voyage."

A very smart, good looking young waiter appeared and took orders for drinks. Alex asked for a brandy and some cold water.

He smiled and murmured; "You may have anything you wish Ma'am. Anything." Tabitha chuckled at that and ordered a large whisky and - again - some cold water. "The BOSS has instructed us, that you can order anything you like. Food, drink, hot bath, new clothes, anything. You are quite the VIP Alex." Tabitha smiled at her and pointed out the window adding; "Hopefully the Captain will take the Southern Pass to the 'Shadow lands' and you'll be able to see the mysterious ruins on the way."

Alex accepted her drinks from the young waiter who smiled broadly at her; he couldn't his eyes off her over-bust corset that was showing off her magnificent bosom. Tabitha took their drinks and waved him away, with a smile. "What are the 'Shadow lands?" Alex asked her, quite intrigued by the name. Tabitha nodded; "It's a remote district here; to get some idea of its size; it's about the size of North America; all of North America."

Alex looked impressed, then asked; "The ruins?" Tabitha lowered her voice and sipped her whisky; "No one really knows. They are very ancient. In human years they are reported to be millions of years old. No one has any idea who built them or what they were built for. You'll be impressed by them, if you like mysterious old buildings."

Alex sipped her water and said dourly; "That's more Owens's department." The young waiter was back, taking orders for lunch. Alex asked for the menu and the young man just smiled; "Sorry ma'am, there are no menu's. Just order what you wish, and it will be served." Tabitha leaned across Alex and whispered; "He really means anything, so order what you really fancy." Alex shrugged her shoulders and waved her brandy glass gently at him; "I would like Turbot with oysters, cabbage and bacon, with a decent bottle of plonk...sorry, white wine." He simply smiled and asked what Tabitha wanted.

Owen eased forward in his seat - opposite Alex and Tabitha - and said quietly; "Where the hell are they going to get bloody Turbot out here?" He sounded a little amazed. Tabitha ordered exactly the same and smiled at Alex; "The BOSS said you had exquisite taste Alex, and I must agree with him. You are a real pleasure to host." Owen grunted at the waiter; "Fillet steak - rare - and chips [French fries] with all the trimmings." He saw the look of sad disappointment on Alex's face. She sighed: "You could have ordered something with a little more imagination." Alex spoke with definite censor and disapproval in her voice. "I ordered all the trimmings." He replied, defensively. Alex just sighed and sipped her brandy. That's when she noticed that Jericho and Peter were deep in conversation. They clearly appeared to know each other very well; that puzzled her a little. But then she glanced out the window and saw the small group of people, standing by the roadside. They were in rags and wore no shoes. They looked like vagrants and beggars who had fallen on real hard times. They stood in silence as the 'Alexandra' passed. They didn't wave or make any gestures.

Alex turned to Tabitha, but Tabitha spoke first; "Settlers here. That's what we call the enforced residents of the Garden. They tend to gather in groups now and again, for company I suppose. Heaven knows what they have to talk about if they've been here for a while."

Alex just nodded. The 'Settlers' - as they were called - were condemned souls awaiting their final judgment. Alex also knew that they suffered all the human emotions and needs still. They hungered and knew thirst. They could feel the heat and the bitter cold of night. They still had sexual feelings and all their memories from their time amongst the living. But - and this was a big but - They could not physically eat or drink or copulate. That was all gone. They could dream and desire, but never realise any of them - ever.

The basic rule of the Garden - for visitors - was simple; you gave them nothing; clothes, shoes, trinkets or words of comfort. You must not help or assist them in any way. The penalty was simple too; you became one of them, if you broke the rules.

The waiter appeared and asked everyone to follow him to the dining room. Everyone rose and followed him. Alex took another look out the window at the disappearing group of 'settlers' and despite whatever evil crimes they had committed; she could still feel a little sorry for them. They had been fellow humans after all. Now they were just creatures of unfulfilled desires, and they could never change.

The meals were superb and Alex got exactly what she wanted; that did amaze Owen. After dinner, back in the bar, Jericho briefed his team about what lay ahead. They were going into the 'Shadow lands' and there meet an 'agent' who ran the place; he was a condemned soul that apparently could be trusted; like 'Trustee's' in normal prisons for the living. He would take the team to where Mr. McGill had been placed.

Through the windows, Owen and Wilson could see the passing settlements; made of brick, stone and canvas. Each one had little groups of ragged humans standing or wandering about. Not one condemned soul waved or gestured or even acknowledged the 'Alexandra' as she passed. But occasionally, they saw a much smaller version of the 'Crawler' they were aboard, parked near one of the ramshackle townships. Tabitha explained it was guards from the centre, sorting out various problems with the natives. Some of the guards did wave as the big crawler passed them.

Owen was a little puzzled and finally asked Tabitha outright. What was the difference been the condemned souls and their past actions [when they were alive] and the guards and staff, that ran and policed the place? Wilson thought that was a cracking question; and said so! Tabitha smiled - a little - and pointed out that the staff and guards had all been followers of the 'Dark Prince' when living and had 'sold' or given their souls to him. That way, when they died, they were never collected and thus, never faced the judgment of the Duty Death Angel.

It was a sort of 'get out of jail free' card. She summed it up, with an old expression, popular amongst the staff; "Better dark than judged."

"No bloody wonder the devil is so popular." muttered Owen and that did make Alex and Wilson smile.

5. THE SHADOW LANDS.

Night had started to fall as the 'Alexandra' passed a huge signpost, erected by the side of the road. It stated, 'DISTRICT 9. GUARDIANS ONLY'. Tabitha pointed out that the temporal Detectives Mission team had special permission to pass into the district. But the team would have to transfer to a 'Guardian' flyer at the Guard Station ahead. The 'Alexandra' would wait at the station for them to return with McGill. They would be escorted by Guards throughout their short stay; the place was especially dangerous at night. That remark really puzzled Owen; "How can it be dangerous? Everyone is bloody dead." Peter chuckled at that and pointed out that some of the 'residents' were carrying horrific injuries from fighting amongst themselves. Some had lost limbs, eyes, hands and even heads! Their existence was miserable enough without adding the burden of crippling disability to it. Plus, these people have absolutely nothing to lose; nothing. Owen nodded his understanding.

The 'Alexandra' pulled up outside the station and awaited entry through the large black gates. The place was constructed from huge, stone blocks and towered above the crawler. There was a tall metal watchtower at each corner, and they shone bright lights down upon the crawler. "It's like fucking Alcatraz' without the water." Muttered Wilson and stared about the huge complex.

Once inside the compound, the gates were closed and they were greeted by three Guards. They all saluted Peter [the Deputy Director of the Garden] as the team decamped from the bus. The Station Commander seemed extremely nervous that such a high ranking official from the Reception Centre would turn up at his station [No. 153] especially at nightfall. The two Senior Guards with him made no secret of their sudden and intense interest in Tabitha and Alex: especially Alex. They really did smile at her, which made her quite uncomfortable.

Wilson whispered to Alex; "See what we mean Alex? What we have been telling you? If you ever got stranded here; you wouldn't be short of some real protection. The buggers in the garden would tear you apart just for the fun of it. They have no use for women that way; even beautiful ones." Alex slowly nodded her agreement; the Guards and Staff retained all their human desires and many of the males would certainly protect and shelter her; for the sexual favours she could bestow upon them. It really didn't make her feel any safer.

The Station Commander showed the team to the flight deck of the station. He was a big man, clearly - originally - Japanese or Chinese in descent. He introduced them to the flyers who would take them out to where McGill had been dumped. The Pilot was a certain tall, athletic looking male who smiled broadly at Alex and Tabitha. He was called 'Mackenzie' [no one really used surnames on the 'Dark Side'] and admitted he was from Glasgow; when alive; "Not much difference between here and there on a Saturday night!" he chuckled and shook hands all-round.

Owen groaned; "Are all the bloody pilots we meet from Scotland?" Wilson slapped him on the back; "As long as the fucker can fly really well; I don't care if he's from bloody Nazi Germany!" Owen smiled at that. Wilson really fucking hated Nazi's - but then who didn't?

They all stared at his craft; called 'Jessabelle'. it resembled a large black mosquito and was about the size of a single Decker bus. Standing by the open hatchway was the Co-Pilot; a young woman of African descent and Mackenzie introduced her as 'Bugsy'. They gave each other a 'high five' and Mackenzie pointed to Alex and Tabitha, slapping a kiss on Bugsy's cheek; "You've a real couple of rivals here my girl."

Alex smiled; 'Bugsy' was actually quite a beauty. Bugsy pushed him away and smiled at the girls; "Never mind bloody Casanova; welcome aboard the 'Jessabelle'. We'll be flying for about two hours. Your man has been assigned to camp 477 - it's a mix of males and females - mostly newcomers. We're just waiting for young 'Tagger' to show up. He's the Trustee there."

Everyone climbed aboard and found a seat. Alex and Tabitha sat together; they were actually getting quite friendly, considering they were on totally opposing sides. Wilson sat next to Owen - who insisted on a window seat - whilst Peter and Jericho sat just behind the pilots. The last two rear seats were empty: for now. Everyone could feel the engines come to life and a small vibration could be felt through the seats and arm rests. There was very little sound from the engines. Everyone buckled up and Owen found a 'flight magazine' on the floor. He had to smile at the title: 'After death fun for travelers in the Garden'.

Peter stared at the hatchway as two figures squeezed through; one was a rough looking guard, with a big nasty scar running the length of his right cheek. The other was a young man - dressed in little more than rags - who said nothing and stared at the floor, as he made for his seat, but stood next to it.

"He knows where McGill is in the camp?" Peter asked the guard, who saluted and stood by the empty rear seats; "Yes sir, Tagger says he was put near the old towers." Peter nodded and gestured for the pair to seat. The hatchway closed softly, and Bugsy checked it before taking her seat next to Mackenzie. Everyone could feel the craft lifting vertically and increasing in speed. They were airborne in seconds. "We'll be flying for around two hours before we reach settlers camp 477. The weather is reported as clear. But don't hold your breath over that forecast. Storms can come up in minutes and can be really nasty for hours. If we shout to use the seat harnesses; then slap them on!" Bugsy's voice came over the intercom and everyone chuckled.

Owen stared through the window; Guard Station 153 - lit up like Blackpool Tower - was fast disappearing into the darkness. He settled back in his seat and said softly to Wilson; "I wonder what our young friend 'Tagger' did to get quarantined and for how long?" Wilson shrugged his shoulder; he certainly didn't know.

But Tabitha turned in her seat and said quietly; "Tagger was in the Russian army. His patrol entered Berlin in 1945 and was responsible for raping two German women - young girls really - he received quite a light quarantine, considering your Angel Margret heard his case. You know what she's like about such matters. But apparently, he didn't want to take the girls, but the rest of his patrol made him. He was killed - along with most of that patrol - by some Hitler youth just days later. He only received a human century in quarantine; all the others are here for some time more."

Alex stared at the young man - sitting head down - next to the burly guard who was picking his teeth with some determination. The boy was no older that Owen. She sighed and stared out of the window; there was nothing but darkness; no lights anywhere and then she realised there was no moon! She wondered where - exactly - was the 'Garden' located?

That's when Alex noted a small string of little white lights on the sand below. She turned to Tabitha; "Is that one of your patrols down there?" Tabitha didn't reply, but Peter shouted to the cockpit crew; "Lights on the sand. Call it in." Bugsy's face appeared by the hatchway door and nodded. "Yes sir." was all she said. Tabitha leaned back in her seat and didn't smile; "Illegal night movements by gangs of smugglers. We must have caught them out - this was an unscheduled flight - they were not expecting us up here, obviously."

Owen leaned forward and said to Tabitha; "What are they smuggling?" Tabitha smiled; "Trinkets, blankets, bits of furniture, clothes and stuff like that. Books especially, they're like gold down there. But anything that can make their miserable lives a little more comfortable, which is not allowed or tolerated."

Alex stared back at the ground; the lights had been extinguished -they must have seen the 'Jessabelle'. The rest of the flight was quite uneventful, apart from Wilson snoring loudly! Owen woke up the big man by shaking his arm. "We're here." He said and grinned; the 'Jessabelle' was starting her descent to the sand.

The craft landed softly - just a little bump - and the team spilled out onto the sand. Camp 477 looked like a third world village that had hit really bad times - really bad times. There was a small group of settlers watching from the crumbling brick entrance. They made no sound or gestures; they just stood and watched. Peter produced a simple looking black rod from his jacket and turned it in his hands. Both Tabitha and the unpleasant looking guard did the same. Peter turned to the temporal detectives; "I know I don't really have to tell you but keep your wits about you. This place is full of human rats, and this is THEIR nest." He smiled and gestured to Tagger; "After you boy." The guard shoved the boy hard, and tagger gestured for them to follow them.

The place was lit with little yellow lamps and the smell was appalling; Tabitha held a hankie to her face on a couple of occasions. Alex was clearly made of sterner stuff and that made the guard smile. He certainly would be having some pleasant or rather, unpleasant thoughts, about what he would like to do to her, after this shift had finished. Tagger led them through the silent streets, Alex stared at the hopeless people; men and women, huddled in doorways, wrapped in ragged blankets or scraps of heavy cloth, against the chill of the night.

Wilson pulled off his jacket and Alex - really gratefully - wrapped it around herself. The slow-witted guard smiled to himself and offered his jacket to Tabitha, who just stared at him and waved his gesture away. She may not like the smell, but she could suffer the cold, rather than accept 'charity' from a lowly guard. Now, if Wilson had offered his coat to her; well, that would be a different matter. She smiled at the big man and Wilson struggled to smile back. For some reason she sent a shiver up his spine!

Tagger stopped outside a small brick and canvas covered hut, below two ruined brick towers, whose purpose was totally unknown. He gestured inside and stood back. Peter tapped the broken wooden door mantle with his rod; "McGill. Patrick McGill, get your sorry arse out here." He shouted and stepped back. They could hear movement inside and the dirty door flap was pulled back. A young Asian woman, in utter rags and almost skeletal in appearance, appeared and pointed inside; then she folded her arms and stared down at the sand.

Peter and Jericho peered inside. A big white male was pulling himself from the dirt. He was dressed quite well compared to the others. "You McGill?" Jericho asked, pulling out his mirror, to confirm the man's identity. The man simply nodded. Satisfied that it was McGill, Jericho nodded and said quietly; "You're coming with us. You have been given a three-hour reprieve." The man just picked up his jacket; he had been using it as a pillow. He started to brush it down, when Peter slapped the rod across his chest; "Get a move on. No one is interested in what you look like."

It was obvious by his face and stance, that McGill wanted to shove that bloody rod somewhere very unpleasant. But he just pulled on his jacket and then touched the woman's face. Nothing was said. He followed Peter and Jericho outside. "What do you mean 'three hours?' What fucking good is a reprieve of three hours?" McGill's New York accent was quite pronounced. Owen chuckled and turned to Wilson; "He sounds like you. The pair of you should get on like a house on fire." Wilson grunted; "I don't fucking think so."

Peter turned and didn't smile; "Keep your mouth shut McGill. You're new here, so you can have that one for free, but next time you open it without permission; you'll pay for it. Do you understand?" McGill nodded; he certainly did.

6. Patrick 'Bends' McGill.

Tagger took the team back through the streets. Several of the settlers gestured to him but said nothing. Nearly all stared at McGill trailing behind with the guard. Peter instructed Tabitha, to ensure that the Station Commander gave Tagger a little something for his co-operation; extra blankets and some new clothes, stuff that he could trade or keep for himself.

Such gestures, normally strictly forbidden, could be authorised by someone of Peter's high rank.

Tabitha nodded; she would arrange it when they returned to Guard Station 153. They gathered around the hatchway of the 'Jezebels' and watched Tagger disappear back into the township. No one had thanked him and only Peter had actually spoken to him. Owen rubbed his chin; he would certainly speak to Jericho and the rest of the team - about the posters he had seen - pinned to crumbling walls and doors. They were asking for 'Volunteers' for a new and - hopefully - better life on the 'Outworlds' of the Dark Princes Empire. He wondered what the hell that was about!

McGill was placed in a rear seat with the not very talkative guard. Owen settled in his seat and stared at McGill with some curiosity, he spoke quietly to Wilson; "I pulled his file from Human Records. His has six murders to his credit. All other gangsters, apparently, he made a point of never taking out civilians. He appears to regard himself as some sort of soldier."

Wilson threw a glance at McGill; "He was a soldier - once. I also looked him up. He won the Silver Star in 1918 at the age of just nineteen. He took out a German machine gun post, whilst wounded, with just a spade and a pistol. The bastards had apparently killed all his friends in a patrol they were on. Took out seven of them single handed, probably would have got the Medal of Honour, if he hadn't punched the officer out, who sent them on the damn patrol, for no apparent reason."

"Brave, but evil bastard." He added and looked back out the window. Alex looked back at McGill, sitting up in his seat and staring ahead. If a rival gangster didn't kill him on that fateful day, then he almost certainly would have gone to the Electric Chair; eventually. He had a boxer's face with the usual broken nose and marks under both eyes. But those eyes were so green and bright. She wondered what had turned an apparently brave and loyal man into a paid killer.

Owen chuckled and said to Alex and Tabitha; "Do you know why he's gangster name is Bends?" Alex sighed but said no anyway. Owen grinned; "Well, before he killed people; sometimes, he would bend their fingers right back - until they snapped - hence 'Bends'." Alex just shook her head in a little despair; Owen almost admired the man. His years in that bloody Monastery had done him no good whatsoever.

Owen turned to Jericho; "Is it ok to talk to McGill?" Jericho looked at Peter, who just shrugged his shoulders; "Yes, there's no harm in that. He'll probably keep the memory of any decent conversations. He'll be back here quick enough." Tabitha chuckled at that, which gave Alex a strange, little uneasy feeling.

"What turned you into a paid killer McGill?" Owen asked the man outright - subtlety wasn't his strong point - and McGill just stared at him, then slowly smiled at the boy. Finally, he said quietly; "War and influenza." Wilson and Alex exchanged a glance but said nothing. Owen screwed up his face; "But that don't make sense?" He muttered, a little disappointed by the answer. He slumped back in his seat and Wilson gently tapped his arm and pulled him close.

"You didn't go very deep on your background research, did you?" Wilson said quietly. Owen said 'no' softly and looked back at McGill. Wilson sighed; "He fought in one of the worst wars humanity could come up with. Living in a filthy, rat-infested hole with the constant threat of death. Dead friends and colleagues littered around the place. Sometimes they couldn't bury them for weeks. Existing with little food or water and constant real fear, he then returned home to marry his childhood sweetheart and found that she had died of influenza in 1919. He had no family or friends left. He had been bought up in a Catholic boy's home - not known for the gentle way it raised its kids - in one of the toughest districts in New York. He came home a hero and was quickly forgotten; the Great Depression saw to that; they didn't need heroes anymore."

Wilson glanced at McGill and continued; "Firstly he made his living - if you can call it that - as a fair ground boxer. Knocked about four or five time a night; for bed and board and some drinking money; maybe. Joining a gang must have seemed like a holiday on Coney Island. Like the army, he was paid to kill other soldiers - gangsters - and I suppose that suited him just right. Ever heard the expression; 'there but for the grace of God'?"

Owen slowly nodded. Wilson almost smiled; "Secondly; he really enjoyed the work." He leaned back in his seat and closed his eyes, adding; "Wake us up, when we reach the station." Owen said nothing more and eased down in his seat.

Jericho smiled at Alex and they both knew that Wilson was going to make a cracking Inspector when the time came! Everyone turned to McGill as he chuckled loudly and gave a little clap. "So, it's true, you temporary defectives are really a bunch of fuckwits. Well, except the big black fella. He knows a really bad one, when he meets him, and that makes me think about another expression; 'it takes one to know one'. I wonder what the big fella is hiding." McGill grinned and eased back in his seat. He stared at Alex.

"That's about the best looking broad I've seen in years. A great fucking body and not ashamed to show it off, may dress like a fucking bar room tart, but I suspect there's real lady under the hooker's clothes. Give me a working cock again and I'll show her what a real fuck is." McGill grinned and stared up at the ceiling. The guard smiled and waited for the command from Peter.

He didn't wait long; Peter sighed and just nodded. The Guard touched McGill with his rod and the big man convulsed and dropped from the seat onto the floor, twitching and groaning. He had several fits and lay quiet. Alex rose from her seat, but Jericho waved her back down, saying nothing. Tabitha grinned and said to Alex; "He really had that coming. They keep a civil tongue in their heads, or we remove it."

Alex just stared at the grinning woman. Then realised why so many of the settlers said nothing; they couldn't. She actually felt a little nauseous and really needed a brandy. She turned, looking out the window at the darkness; away from the darkness sitting next to her.

After a few minutes, the guard hauled the groaning McGill up and threw him back into the seat. "You're lucky stupid; if you weren't going on a little trip; that would have cost you that foul tongue of yours." He grinned and tapped his rod with real pleasure. He was now a very happy guard.

There were no further incidents with McGill and the flyer landed back at Station 153. Bugsy pulled open the external hatch and smiled at everyone as they departed. Alex wondered what she had done to end up here. Then remembered what Tabitha had said about the guards and staff here; they had all been followers of the 'Dark Prince' before they died. She pulled Wilson's jacket tightly around herself and walked with him back into the Guard

Station. "I'll be glad to get home." She whispered to him.

Wilson smiled and said simply; "Ditto."

In the small visitors area of the Guard Station they were served Coffee and waited for the call to board the 'Alexandra' for the return journey to Devil's Garden Reception Centre. McGill was dumped in a small cell; he certainly wasn't given any coffee. He couldn't drink it anyway.

Wilson and Owen watched Peter talking into his 'Mirror'. They were very similar to the ones carried by Temporal Detectives, and he was clearly reporting that all was going well. They knew who he was talking to, Simon, the Dark Angel in charge of the garden. They knew this because he called the other one 'Sir', several times. Given Peter's position, the only person above him was, indeed, the Dark Angel himself. Peter walked over to them and gestured for Alex and Jericho to join them.

He spoke directly to Alex; "A suite has been put aside for you on the crawler Lady Alexandra, so that you and your companions can freshen up before we return to the Centre. There is going to be a little reception for the BOSS, and you are all invited. His has provided a couple of his ladies to assist you and hopes that you will be pleased with the dresses provided. Let's get going." They followed him back out into the cold night air and boarded the waiting 'Alexandra'.

Wilson smiled at Alex; "A really big bloody moth to the flame." Both Owen and Jericho chuckled at that, but Alex said nothing. Everyone looked up, as the big red flyer took off from the flight deck of the station - it had an incredible gold dragon insigne painted down the sides - the personal emblem of the Dark Prince himself. It had just delivered the Dark Prince's ladies and of course; gowns for Alex's selection. She was not happy. From her window seat in the bar, she watched McGill loaded into the back of the crawler, like spare luggage into a baggage compartment. The rear of the crawler – apparently – contained cells for the transportation of 'residents' when required.

7. DANCING WITH DARKNESS.

Everyone had noticed the extra security aboard the 'Alexandra'; there were three more garden guards in reception, chatting happily, with the Receptionist and the two greeters. But it was the guards in neat black uniforms with gold buttons and dragon insignia that caught the team's attention. They were the Dark Prince's personal bodyguards. But it was the tall, strikingly beautiful woman in a full-length black gown with all the accessories that really drew their looks. She was Bathsheba; a Dark Angel and she was heading their way.

Bathsheba was known to command the personal staff of the prince and for now, kept a close eye on his 'Harem'. That would fall, eventually, to the Queen, when the prince chooses one. That simple little act - or rather lack of - was the talk of the 'Family'. His brother - the BOSS upstairs - had wanted his younger brother to 'settle down' for some time now. But the right human female had escaped the young prince; currently. It spoke volumes that he had not 'promoted' one of his three Princesses to the role.

Jericho gestured for everyone to rise. She greeted Peter quite warmly and then turned to Jericho. He bowed a little and said nothing until spoken too. "Mr. Tibbs, your reputation does precede you. I guessed it would be you or old Doc Underhill that would have been sent. Has everything been satisfactory? Have my people been looking after you and your team?" Jericho bowed again; "Yes, you're Grace. The hospitality we have been offered has been superb and I thank you and your staff." The Dark Angel smiled; "You are most generous Mr. Tibbs. Now this must be Lady Alexandra Cappanni?" She turned to Alex, who actually managed quite a good curtsey, considering the outfit she was almost wearing.

The Angel just stood for a good few seconds, looking Alex up and down, then smiled. Wilson whispered to Owen 'like a snake viewing a rabbit.' Owen just nodded. "You really are quite a beautiful human female. Absolutely stunning, little wonder males fall at your feet." Alex didn't smile and said quietly; "Thank you, your Grace." She gestured for Alex to follow her; "David [the dark prince] has sent a couple of his girls with some gowns, for you to pick a suitable one for the reception. I know you will appreciate their quality and beauty." She chuckled; "The gowns, I mean. Not the ladies. Well, whatever you fancy my dear. Whatever."

Wilson turned to Jericho; "I take it we not on Earth at any time in its history, otherwise the shit would really hit the fan with dark

Angels everywhere." Jericho nodded; "The Garden is not on earth at any time in its history." He gestured out the window and sighed; "This is Mars; millions of years into its past when it still had a breathable atmosphere. We're millions of years into the past and on a completely different planet. That's why we need the Necrosubs to get here." Owen actually stood with his mouth open, staring at the reddish-brown dirt and no moon. "Bloody ancient Mars?" He whispered and slowly sat down; he needed a brandy.

The 'Alexandra' reached the Reception Complex and parked near the main doors. The moveable staircase appeared, and the two greeters stood at the bottom and thanked everyone for travelling on the 'Alexandra'. The reception area was totally void of all 'settlers' - just guards and staff - they were lined up in small rows, waiting. Peter stood by the Visitors Reception desk and also waited. Tabitha nervously smoothed down her skirt and jacket; then tidied up her hair. She turned to Owen and said quietly; "He's here with Mr. Simon." She joined Peter by the desk.

Owen knew that 'Mr. Simon' was the Dark Angel in charge of the garden and he certainly knew who the 'HE' was; the Dark Prince himself. A couple of guards helped drag McGill away; he certainly wouldn't be meeting the grand visitor. He was secured aboard the 'Scallywag' by McAlister and Omar; strangely enough, the pair weren't invited to the reception! They would wait on their craft until required.

Jericho noticed that the two huge piano black doors at one end of the reception area were slowly opening. It revealed the Arboretum; it looked like a ancient woodland with a circle of standing stones its centre piece. The team was impressed; very impressed. There were lamps hanging from trees and fairy lights decorated bushes. Just behind the doors was a large brick and stone 'Summer House' filled with tables and two bars apparently. Owen was actually speechless; that was a first!

Jericho turned to the pair; "If this is just his little playroom here; in this dismal place. Can you imagine his palace?" Wilson whistled through his teeth; "He certainly knows how to live." He then thought about the condemned wretches outside in the other 'Garden'. He was a little disgusted by the comparison.

The team noticed that the female staff actually curtsied to Alex, when she came into the reception area. That certainly wasn't normal protocol. Jericho and Wilson exchanged a worried glance; they could smell a rat - a large Princely one - behind that.

But when they saw Alex approaching them, she also left them impressed. She was wearing a stunning full length, white, backless gown of silk and gold. The bodice was cut quite low, and it certainly showed off her magnificent breasts. Her dark hair was piled up and held by an exquisite diamond tiara. Around her neck was a gold and silver necklace of stars. It looked priceless - a masterpiece of the jewelers art - She walked slowly in white heels, holding her dress with one hand, whilst the other held a clutch purse encrusted with diamonds and pearls.

The front split in the gown gave a glimpse of pure silk stockings with each step. Alex was dressed like a Queen, and you could actually hear little gasps as she passed. "I think, I'm in fucking love." Wilson muttered and wiped his face. Jericho stood by Alex and whispered; "Best behaviour please Alexandra; remember whose world we are now in." Alex nodded; she just wanted to go home, but she would play her part; diplomacy demanded it. The rooms were filling with guests; including Court ladies dressed similar to Alex; but as Owen pointed out; 'They couldn't hold a candle to our Alex.' Jericho sighed; "Yes, and that could be the problem here."

Waiters were serving glasses of champagne and Alex took a glass and asked about McAlister and Omar; she chuckled, when told they were sulking aboard their ship. "Sweet Jesus, they have a band." Owen said as music started coming from the Arboretum. Wilson just laughed; "It's probably a bloody orchestra." And the big man was right.

The place suddenly fell silent; their 'BOSS' was here. The Dark Prince strolled in with Dark Angels Simon and Bathsheba at his side. There was a small greeting line, with Peter at its head and the prince shook hands with everyone. Alex chuckled as she watched Tabitha trying to curtsey properly in her short skirt. Jericho spoke softly to Alex; "Keep your wits about you, I think our Dark Prince is up to something. He has made it clear that he wants you - anyway he can."

Alex nodded; she clearly remembered the encounter with the

Prince and having to ask him for a favour, in restoring Wilson and Jericho back to the team. [See: the episode; **'Lucy London's lost soul'**] She glanced at herself in the one of the grand mirrors; he had picked her clothing right down to the panties. Now that thought made her shiver a little and sipped her brandy.

That's when Alex realised that Bathsheba was gesturing to her. "Here we bloody well go." She muttered and handed Owen her drink [which he finished in one hit] and walked slowly across the room. Jericho and Wilson smiled; there was not a pair of eyes looking anywhere else; including the Dark Prince.

Alex curtsied and the Dark Prince took her hand and kissed it. Jericho, Wilson and Owen were all straining to hear, what the conversation was between the two; but they couldn't make it out. The prince placed her hand upon his arm and the pair walked into the Arboretum. Inside the circle of stones was a dance floor. He swept her into his arms and the pair danced - beautifully together - it must be said. The guests were all clapping and cheering, then one by the one other couples joined them on the dance floor; starting with Simon and Bathsheba.

Wilson and Jericho exchanged a concerned look and were joined by a very happy Peter. He stopped a passing waiter and handed everyone more champagne, then told the young women to fetch more. "You're in a good mood Peter; your BOSS happy with everything in the Garden?" Peter nodded and sipped his drink; "Most pleased. It's nice when one's efforts and commitments are appreciated." He gestured to the dancing pair; "The place is full of gossip and rumour about your young lady - which comes as no surprise - she's utterly stunning and knows how to behave at this level. That's really important Jericho, my old friend, really important. He's princess's [he has three of them and about another thirty girls in his harem] are real beauty's but have no real class. Not like young Alexandra."

Jericho and Wilson exchanged another concerned look and Jericho managed to smile; "Do tell? What delicious rumour and gossip is that?" Peter grinned; "That our Prince has finally found a real Queen." He raised his glass, adding: "To young Alexandra; Queen of Darkness – hopefully – and our Prince." The team raised their glasses slowly and stared at the dancing pair, who was clearly centre of attention at this party. Finally, Wilson whispered to Owen; "The really big shit has hit the fan full on."

Owen just nodded and downed another glass of champagne. Jericho just watched the pair dancing and realised his mirror was buzzing.

He walked away and found a quiet corner and answered, it was Angel Margret. Jericho watched as Peter and his partner Todd, took to the dance floor. The young man looked resplendent in his evening suit. They danced smiling at each other. Jericho finished his brief conversation with the Angel and walked back to Owen and Wilson. He didn't smile; "We've been recalled. The Angel wants us back with McGill, with or without Alex." Wilson ran a hand over his face and gripped Jericho's arm; "Who's going to get her? We are NOT leaving her here."

Jericho managed a weak smile; "Down to me I'm afraid, goes with the Inspectors job. You and Owen get aboard the 'Scallywag' and tell McAlister to fire up the engines." He stared at the dancing pair and added softly; "I've always wanted to piss on that bastard's strawberries. I just hope I don't end my days wandering around this fucking cesspit." Then made his way into the Arboretum; slowly.

Owen dropped through the hatch, followed by Wilson who shouted at McAlister to start the engines and be prepared to 'drop' as soon as Jericho and Alex came through the hatch and sealed it behind them. The pair was eating - what appeared to be - a takeaway curry. McAlister sighed loudly; "The fucking party sounds like it has ended with a bang." He grinned at Omar, who took their plates to the disposal hatch. McGill was sitting in his seat - saying nothing - the crew of the 'Scallywag' had handcuffed him to it. Wilson sat next to him and smiled; "Hope you've got a strong stomach." McGill just grunted.

McAlister stared at the monitor for the external cameras and chuckled. Jericho was running full tilt towards the 'Scallywag' with Alex in tow - holding her hand - whilst she ran with her skirt pulled right up and her heels gone. He shook his head; "I may not like him, but he's got balls of steel to go up against the fucking dark prince; especially over something the bastard really wants."

Everyone turned and stared at the hatch as Alex came down the ladder. Owen grinned, but sounded a little puzzled; "Nice white lace panties, but why do they have bloody pearls sewn onto them; who the hell is going to see them? - apart from Alex and whoever does her laundry?" McAlister and Wilson exchanged a despairing glance and both muttered; "Bloody monastery."

Alex jumped into her seat; quite breathless and straightened herself up. Jericho closed the hatch and sealed it, shouting; "Drop for fuck sake McAlister!" and leapt into his seat, snapping his harness shut. Omar stared at the external camera's monitor and ran a hand over his face; "Mac, I'd really fucking drop right now!" McAlister grunted loudly; then chuckled and pulled the big red lever above his head. He shouted; "Yippe-ki-yay you fucking motherfuckers!" The Scallywag dropped at some speed. Jericho sighed loudly; "Bloody Bruce Willis has a lot to answer for." Owen groaned; he really wished he hadn't drunk all that champagne and McGill shouted; "Yes! Fucking Yes!" He clearly loved it. Well; he was a murdering Psychopath after all and had always loved the big rollercoaster on Coney Island!

8. INTERVIEW WITH THE ANGEL.

The team sat on the clean marble seats outside the Angels office, somewhat bored. Jericho checked his mirror and then smiled at Wilson; the big man was slumped against the wall - arms folded - staring down the almost empty corridor. "Waiting for what seems an eternity, goes with the job. You'll get use to it. I must have spent the equivalent of a couple of lifetimes sitting here; waiting for the Angel to see me." Jericho said quietly to Wilson, who nodded, then sat up straight. Mr. Colgate, the Angel's personal Secretary, had appeared in the doorway of her private office. He gestured for them to enter.

Jericho threw a glance at Alex; looking very smart in her blue and white business suit and had to smile. That's one hell of a woman - just like Elizabeth was - little wonder the Dark Prince had *'thrown his dummy from the pram'* over her. It was now, clearly apparent that the prince wanted her, not just for his Harem, but as a Queen. The ramifications of that desire were enormous. His brother: The BOSS wanted his wayward younger brother settled down and taking a Queen - like Alexandra - would definitely be a step in the right direction. Except Alexandra was having none of it!

The team lined up before Angel Margret's desk. Unusually, she had several glass sheets laid upon it. All contained Confidential

Reports or forthcoming Mission summaries. She didn't look up as Mr. Colgate announced the arrival of Inspector Tibbs and Team 74. The door slid silently shut behind them and Mr. Colgate stood quietly behind the angel's back; his face expressionless.

Angel Margret sighed and sat back in her chair; hands clasped in her lap. She didn't smile. "Firstly, I must congratulate you and your team Inspector, upon the successful finding and return of the McGiff fellow." Jericho coughed; "McGill, Ma'am. It was McGill." He said quietly and refrained from smiling. The angel just stared at him and tapped a piece of glass upon her desk. "Secondly, there's the little matter of my Detective Constable Cappanni. Though, little doesn't really cover the storm that has closed in around her." She straightened up in her chair and picked up another piece of glass. To human's, it appeared blank.

"Detective Cappanni was the main topic of discussion at HIS Privy Council meeting." She explained, jerking a finger skywards, adding: "The unanimous verdict and their advice to HIM was simple; give her to the prince. That would solve a great many problems with the young prince and make HIMSELF very happy." She leaned over her desk and slapped both hands upon it. She looked straight at Alex, who stared at the floor in silence. "Except young Lady Cappanni was not very willing in this matter. No, willing is the wrong word; downright hostile is a better term, I think."

She addressed Alex directly; "Telling the young prince to shove his marriage proposal up his..." She picked up the glass sheet nearest her and peered over the top at Alex. "Sorry, told him to *'poke his proposal up his dark arse'* is not the language of a future Queen, or the diplomatic answer expected, no, required of one of my Detectives." Owen and Wilson couldn't hold it anymore; they giggled a little. The angel just stared at them; they both whispered; "Sorry Ma'am." and stared at the floor.

Alex slowly held up a hand and the angel nodded at her. "I don't want to be Queen of Hell, Ma'am." She said simply and looked back at the floor. The angel sighed and placed the glass sheet down. "With the situation between himself and those two sons of his, you would eventually be Queen of all this." She gestured around with both arms, adding; "Queen of all Existence. Do you realise that any woman in his harem, would probably murder their grandmother for that position?" Alex said nothing. The angel continued; "Any one of his three princesses would strangle their own children, for the title of Queen and you casually, tell him to poke it up his dark arse?"

That was the final straw, Jericho, Wilson, and Owen all chuckled. Alex just shrugged her shoulders; "Sorry Ma'am; he caught me unaware with that damn proposal and I just couldn't think of anything diplomatic to say....and well, it just came out. Sorry Ma'am." The angel actually groaned and placed a hand against her cheek, just staring at Alex, finally she said; "You would have been handed over to him; except Queen Mary just wouldn't have it. She pointed out that 'Free will' must be allowed to exist in humans. Fortunately for you, young lady; HE agreed with his Queen. Otherwise, you would be now resident in the Dragon Palace as Queen; willing or not."

She turned to Jericho and really didn't smile; "Then, there's my Inspector." She picked up another piece of glass, stared at it and replaced it on her desk; "*Let her go fuckwit'* is not the language I expect one of my senior Inspectors to use when addressing a high family member. I do have that right Inspector. You've not been misquoted there, have you?" Jericho shook his head and said nothing, but now Alex, Wilson and Owen all chuckled. Then they all muttered - very quickly - "Sorry Ma'am."

She turned back to Alex; "Apparently, you removed your heels and threw them at him and his two senior Dark Angels. Then pulled your skirt up, exposing your underwear to everyone, and ran for it - with your inspector - and made your getaway like thieves in the night? I do have that right?" Alex nodded. The angel folded her arms and sighed quite loudly; "At least you returned the necklace; it's a family piece - quite priceless - normally worn by high females of the family. It was yours girl, a little gift from that totally besotted young Prince, though heavens know why, with your behaviour to him."

The angel gathered the pieces of glass together on her desk and said quietly; "I think, I shall refer to you as 'Lady Cinderella' in future. Apparently, the prince keeps your shoes on his desk." Now that did make the team laugh outright. The angel just sat back in her chair and gestured towards the door. "There's a mission file being sent to the lighthouse, as we speak. Get it done without causing a major rift in the family or a diplomatic incident with the other side. Go on, just go."

As the team headed for the door, she called after Jericho; "You best keep a close eye on our girl in future. He will not take this laying down, Watch yourselves." Jericho nodded and the team spilled into the corridor; they couldn't keep the laughter in anymore. Mr. Colgate stood outside the door - unsmiling - he spoke directly to Jericho; "I think the common feeling amongst the angel's staff is that; *'she's covered your arse's - yet again.'* - Yes, I think that's what being said. Goodbye Inspector." He disappeared down the corridor and just for a second; they all thought, they heard the usually dour man laughing.

Jericho sat in his big armchair and sipped a well-earned brandy and stroked Mr. Parker, who lay sprawled across his lap. He picked up the brown paper file and re-read the next mission. It could wait until another day. He smiled to himself despite the fact that team 74 had been banned from any future trips to the 'Devil's Garden' - well, just for the immediate future. Anyway, the main success was that Alexandra was not now 'Queen of Hell' and lived to fight another day.

He glanced over to the card table and the three were arguing - again - about certain points of the mission. John was dealing the cards with an amused smile on his face; especially when Owen raised the question of Alex's panties; again. He couldn't understand why they were decorated with pearls, since only Alex [and whoever did her laundry – which was Ruth - would see them]. He argued; what was the point? Alex finally said, in some frustration; "They came with the damn dress; I suppose he wanted me to wear them." That puzzled Owen and then he seemed quite shocked; "You were going to show him your knickers! With yourself still in them? That's unbelievable."

Alex gave up and sat staring at her cards. John chuckled; "Knowing the Dark Prince's reputation, I really don't think he wanted to just look at them." He said quietly and laid down a full Royal flush; again. Alex slapped her cards down and folded her arms; "Can we please drop the subject of my damn panties for once." That remark creased young Owen up; "Drop the subject! Her bloody panties were the subject.... drops the subject!" He laughed and took a sip of his brandy and then realised no-one else was laughing; just staring at him.

Wilson dealt the cards out and remembered what he had said to himself, when he saw Alex in that dress, walking across the floor towards him. He sighed and could easily understand why the young Prince wanted her. He had always told himself that he wouldn't be 'another moth to the flame', but the damn flame was edging closer every day. He looked up from his cards and saw Alex smiling at him; "Your call." Was all she said. He nodded and tossed two custard cream biscuits onto the table. "I'll see you and raise you one." He smiled and could still see her, walking towards him in that dress, smiling.

THE END

EPILOGUE:

"Despite the 'diplomatic incident' with the Dark Prince, the mission was considered a success. Team 74 was successful in returning Patrick McGill to reclaim those extra three hours of life that he was accidently denied. Temporal Detective Alexandra Cappanni remains an object of fascination and desire for the Dark Prince and that will always be a danger to her and the Team." **SJW.**

CHARACTERS:

Patrick 'Bends' McGill was returned to the 'Devil's Garden after his three-hour reprieve. He had a quarantine of nearly three hundred human years to complete. But he was a clever man and volunteered for the Dark Prince's 'Outworld' project. His current whereabouts are unknown.

Alexei Andreyushkin - 'Tagger' - was sixteen, when he was killed in the fighting to take Berlin in 1945. His part in the rape of two young German girls cost him a century in quarantine. But the boy was clever and resourceful, becoming a Trustee at Camp 477. He was released, a little earlier, because of his 'good behaviour'. He re-entered the Human Life Cycle and is now an Amazon dirt farmer.

Despite the 'incident' between Team 74 and the Dark Prince; its business as usual for the Devil's Garden and its staff. McAlister Semple and Omar Kassam still make regular runs to the place in their Necrosub; the Scallywag. They often carry Temporal Detectives to the garden; to interview souls for missions they are currently on. But they do remember Team 74's trip with some affection and much amusement.

SPECIAL APPEARENCE BY Prince David, the Dark Prince, as himself.

EPISODE 12: "THE GALLOWS TREE HOTEL MYSTERY."

MISSION SUMMARY:
"In the early summer of 1999, Anne and Kent Murphy are excited - and dreading it a little - that work on the new restaurant extension for their hotel; 'The Gallows Tree' is underway. But contractors excavating in the old gardens have hit a problem; they have discovered the remains of ancient dungeons, complete with graveyard. Now work has halted while Archaeologists from Rutland University check out the uncovered ruins. Mr. Tibbs is on scene because two souls have gone missing from the current human timeline..."

NOTES: Contains language that is relevant for the time period but is now considered offensive.

 **ALCOHOL, VIOLENCE, SEXUAL REFERENCES, STRONG LANGUAGE & MILD HORROR.**

AGE 12+ ONLY.  **30 Minutes reading time.**

1. THE ARCHAEOLOGISTS.

Old professor Fielding Larbert walked slowly back to his caravan, hands in pockets, head down. His threadbare flat cap lay at an angle upon his hairless head. He stopped and looked back at the fenced off excavations; they were due to pack up the dig in a couple of weeks – the funding had basically dried up and the whole place would be closed up until – well, that was a mystery in itself. What the hell would happen to the Hotel now?

He sighed and removed the padlock on his caravan's door and stepped inside. He threw down his hat and well-worn jacket and slumped on the cushions beneath the big window with shabby curtains; closed to keep out the bright sunshine. He stretched out and remembered there were a couple of bottles of coke in the small fridge. He reached down and from a rucksack, discarded at his feet; he pulled a bottle of 'Johnny Walker' whisky – half empty – or half full, if you were the optimistic type. He wasn't.

A couple of loud knocks on his door made him hastily replace the bottle and shout; "Enter!" In stepped Ray Chapel, who grinned and gestured towards the rucksack with the whisky bottle half hanging out. "Just in time, am I?" He held up a full litre bottle of coke. Fielding had to chuckle and gestured for Ray to sit down – after he grabbed a couple of clean glasses from the small sink - which was crammed with dirty dishes and cutlery.

Ray stared at the sink and turned to the professor who was opening the bottle; "I thought you asked that student.... Emma, wasn't it? To clean up the caravan for you before they headed home for the weekend?" The professor grunted; "I did and received a lecture about female emancipation and the fact it was almost the twenty-first century and so on."

"Lazy feminist bitch; probably one of those ball breaking lesbians who think all men should be castrated." Ray murmured with real anger in his voice and joined the professor on the caravan's sofa. Fielding sighed; Ray was almost Victorian in his attitude to the opposite sex. He was a good assistant, but a lousy human. He poured the whisky and Ray topped up the glasses with a little coke. "So it's just two weeks then." Ray finally broke the silence as the pair sat sipping their whiskies. The professor nodded and sighed again; "We've no idea what's going to happen to the excavation, or for that matter, the bloody Hotel now." Ray nodded and then remembered the letter that had arrived this morning from the University, from the Dean's office.

He pulled it from his pocket and handed it to the professor; "Our eviction notice, I expect." He grunted and refilled the glasses. The professor placed small spectacles upon his nose and tore open the envelope; he read quietly for a few minutes and then slowly offered the letter to his sad assistant; with a strange smile on his face.

Ray read the two pages with an incredulous smile spreading across his face. "The old Dean must have finally lost the fucking plot!" He exclaimed and laughed, shaking his head in disbelief. He swallowed down his whisky and laughed again; "A fucking team of paranormal investigators!" He shouted and just stared at the letter, then dropped it upon the small table.

The professor shrugged his shoulders and refilled the glasses; "Well, it actually makes sense – in a crazy way – the police investigation discovered bugger all. Then of course, what about all those stories that started to appear around the ruins; ghosts, apparitions and noises. All that shit is bound to attract the nutters; even the so called professional nutters!"

Ray leaned back and raised his glass in mock salute; "Well, fucking good luck to...." He picked up the discarded letter and re-read part of it. "So, fucking good luck to Professor bloody Tibbs and his merry crew. May they find a bloody poltergeist climbing up their arses." He muttered and sipped his whisky; still smiling.

The pair sat in silence for a few minutes, then Ray's mood changed a little, his voice couldn't hide irritation with some of the letters content. "How the fuck, are they allowed to use the Hotel to doss in and we're stuck in this mobile flea-pit?" He asked, throwing the offending letter back on the table. The professor didn't answer that question but patted his aggrieved assistant's shoulder and smiled; "I thought the end paragraph would cheer you up a little; the local police liaison will be Detective Constable Sharon Smith. So, surely that will put a smile on your face and a spring in your step."

Ray had to smile at that and sipped his whisky slowly. He nodded and raised his glass; "To Detective Constable Smith." That's when the professor's mobile phone started to ring – the theme tune to 'The Dam Busters' filled the caravan - Fielding scrambled to the rucksack and pulled his phone out. He sat listening, grunting Ok several times, then switched it off and sipped his whisky.

"That was Maggie; the ghost hunters will turn up tomorrow morning." Fielding muttered and started to laugh softly, adding; "Apparently this Tibbs fellow has an envious reputation in the field of shifting through paranormal crap." They both laughed at that. "He must be quite a persuasive fellow; this Tibbs." Ray said and held up the fast-diminishing whisky bottle. Fielding chuckled; "I agree, if he managed to persuade 'old Dean, I can't make a decision' Cartwright to allow them on site, then the fucker should be a politician." They both laughed again. Fielding gestured to the small cupboard above his head; "There's a fresh one in there – I keep it for emergencies – like this."

The pair shared the new bottle for about an hour, then both stumbled to their respective beds and slept badly. But both were up early in the morning; neither looking the worse for their drinking session.

Ray sniffed at his bowl of cornflakes; "I think the bloody milk is on the turn. I'll get some more, where I pop into the village this morning." Regardless of the milk's condition, he scoffed down his breakfast and watched the professor eating yet more digestive biscuits; he must have eaten about a dozen this morning. There were packets of them scattered about the caravan. No wonder the bloody old boy was like a matchstick. Ray smiled to himself and poured more tea from the big metal tea pot and stared through the window.

He could see at the end of Gallows Lane [the small road that ran up to the Hotel] a white Transit van had just turned into the lane from Cooper's Road. He sighed; "I think the fucking ghost busters are here." The professor just grunted and rose from the table, finishing his tea.

"Let's go and welcome the spirit chasers to our little Shangri-La." Fielding, straightened his jacket and slapped his flat cap on, he peered out the window and wiped his face. "Jesus, that's a big black fella they have driving the bloody van, even the ghosts don't mess with him, I bet." He chuckled and watched the van park up. Ray eased himself up and adjusted his black jeans that had numerous pockets filled with bits and pieces. He picked up his dirty, off white 'safari' jacket and checked that he had some packets of soft mints.

The professor pushed through the small door and stepped into the early morning sunshine. Ray followed, slamming the door behind him. They both watched as the team of paranormal investigators decamped from their clean new van. "They are probably better funded than we are; there must be money in apparitions and ghosts." muttered Ray then caught sight of the tall, young woman in the tight blue jeans and white T-shirt that did not hide her impressive figure.

He smiled broadly and whispered to the professor; "I must be in the wrong fucking business." Fielding just nodded but slowly straightened his thin tie – she was a real beauty - no argument about that. The young man in the dark blue suit approached and held out his hand; "Hello, Jericho Tibbs; I believe the Dean has informed you of our coming?" He and the professor shook hands.

"Yeah, the Dean sent us a letter." The professor said softly and gestured towards the closed-up hotel; "Sorry, we don't have keys for the place, so we can't help you getting in." That made Ray smile until Jericho pulled a set of keys from his pocket and smiled; "No trouble; the police liaison officer gave us these."

"Oh good, she's a very efficient detective constable." The professor muttered but thought; she's also a hard-faced sarcastic bitch and he really couldn't see how his assistant could even fancy the damn woman - that was yet another bloody mystery around here - he restrained from smiling at his thoughts.

The little group headed for the hotel front doors and Ray stared at Alex's bum as she walked in front of him, then he caught Wilson smiling at him. He pretended to check his pockets and grin; "Mint anyone?" He asked, pulling a packet of soft mints from a pocket. No-one accepted his generous offer, and they reached the doors. The professor was a little impressed that Jericho found the correct key immediately, from the big bunch he held.

Jericho pushed the door open and smiled at the professor; "We'll settle in and meet up later. I'm sure you can give us some insight into the so-called mystery." The professor nodded and turned away, indicating for Ray to follow him. Ray smiled at Alex; "If there's anything we...I can help you with, just pop over to the caravan." He pointed to the scruffy little caravan at the far end of the car park. Alex just nodded and turned away.

Ray and the professor stood by the entrance to the excavations and watched the team disappear into the hotel. Ray rubbed his chin; "That's odd, they don't appear to have much equipment or even luggage." The professor just shrugged his shoulders; "It's probably in the van. They'll get it later I expect." Both men wandered into the dig area and made their way to the 'dungeons' which were covered with large dirty, canvas tarpaulins; held down with house bricks. Ray pulled one tarpaulin back a little and both men stared down into the circular pit. "I'm amazed that anyone survived down there for a few weeks, let alone years." He spoke quietly and thought, a place like this was bound to have ghosts - if they were real - He threw back the canvas sheet and stared up at the hotel. "I wonder what our amateur ghost busters will make of the mystery." Then smiled and joined the professor walking back to their caravan.

2. THE MYSTERY.

Jericho stood by the window and watched the pair disappear into the caravan. "I suspect that our neighbours are not happy that we're here, dossing in the hotel, while they sit it out in that little box." he said quietly; unsmiling. Wilson chuckled and lowered his mirror; "The younger man – Ray, is lucky to have anything. Apparently, he's not a good archaeologist or person. If his old mentor - the professor - hadn't taken him on; he would be probably selling white goods in a high street somewhere; badly."

"He certainly liked the look of your arse." Owen said to Alex, who just folded her arms and sighed. Jericho called the briefing to order; the mission was simple - solve the disappearance of two souls - still in their flesh suits, from the hotel. There were no witnesses and the police had drawn a huge blank, after investigating for almost two weeks. The team sat in the empty restaurant and checked their mirrors; the story was indeed strange.

The young couple who owned the 'Gallows Tree Hotel' had closed the hotel for the duration of the building works - an extension to the very restaurant the team were sitting in - so, the only people in the hotel were the owners and old Thomas O'Connell, the Night Porter who lived in a small backroom of the hotel. It was him that had raised the alarm about the couple's disappearance.

"According to the police report, O'Connell came on duty - as usual - at 10pm and simply couldn't find the couple; anywhere. He became suspicious because both their cars were still in the car park and found, in their private apartments, that dinner had been set out, but not eaten. They normally ate about seven o'clock in the evening when the hotel was closed. He searched for about half an hour, then went out to the caravan and woke up Larbert and Chapel who helped him search. Finally, they called the local police at 11.10pm. A police search turned up nothing; no signs of foul play or any disturbance - nothing out of the ordinary - They haven't been seen or heard of since." Owen concluded his report by asking Jericho if they could use the bar!

Jericho, sadly, said no. But told him and Wilson to fetch the two boxes from the van; they contained the emergency rations of brandy. They had already chosen their rooms, but Jericho believed they wouldn't need them. "We'll wrap this up and be back home in time for a delicious dinner." He pacified the trio, but Owen muttered to Wilson, on the way to the van; "When he says things like that, the bloody wheel normally falls off." Wilson had to agree with that; grinning broadly at his young colleague's cynicism.

Ray watched from the caravan as Wilson and Owen carried two large cardboard boxes into the hotel. Then he saw the old mini-car of the Night Porter - O'Connell - pull into the top of the car park. "He's early today. I wonder what the old fucker will make of his free-loading guests." He said to Fielding, who was studying photographs of the ruins, taken on their first day on site. He looked up and smiled; "Old Thomas must be dedicated; turning up for duty when there's no-one here to pay his bloody wages anymore." Ray just grunted and watched Thomas disappear into the hotel, behind Owen and Wilson.

"Maybe he has nowhere else to go." Ray muttered and sat down on the sofa and sighed loudly; "The police questioned him for nearly two days you know, and he never changed his story; not a word." The professor was staring hard at the photographs; "Where did we put the pictures that the builders took, when they first uncovered the ruins?" He asked Ray; who shrugged his shoulders; "I don't know, I thought you had them." The professor shook his head and said simply; "No." The missing photographs seemed to trouble the old professor and he searched the caravan - a couple of times - with no success.

The professor watched Ray from the corner of his eye as he looked in the kitchen cupboard; "I could never understand how such a small caravan could have so many bloody cupboards." He watched the agitation on Ray's face and his jerky body movements. Finally, Ray jumped up and smiled; "I think I'll pay the ghost busters a visit - see if they need anything – see what they're up to." The professor nodded, then in a quiet voice said; "Behave yourself around the young woman Raymond. Those people are total strangers who could take real exception to some of your comments and mannerisms."

Ray nodded, then grinned; "Yeah. Sure. I promise best behaviour; scouts honour." Then, wiping his face, made his way out the door. The professor sighed; "You were never a bloody scout Raymond. They certainly wouldn't have you." He went back to searching the caravan with some purpose. Ray wandered into the hotel foyer and found it empty. The two cardboard boxes were on the Reception Desk and Ray carefully peered inside; one contained six bottles of 'Johnny Walker' scotch and the other; four bottles of brandy, with a dozen mixed glasses. He actually laughed out loud and shook his head. The bastards certainly knew how to chase bloody spirits!

"Essential supplies." was all Jericho said. He was standing in the doorway with the Night Porter, who was smiling, which was unusual for him. Ray grinned; "You ghost busters certainly know to investigate spirits all right." Thomas walked behind the desk and started to write in the Guest Book and Jericho walked past Ray and stood in front of the desk. From his coat pocket, he pulled a thick brown envelope and started to count out twenty-pound notes. "That's for four rooms for two nights." He told Thomas who nodded.

Ray licked his lips; there must be at least a grand in that bloody envelope. He wondered where the cock teasing tart was and wandered off. Jericho watched him go and collected the receipt from Thomas, who placed the money in the safe beneath the counter. Jericho walked to a quiet corner of the closed bar and called Alex. The conversation was brief, and Jericho then called Wilson.

Owen appeared in the doorway and jerked a thumb behind him; "What's that sneaky fucker after?" As Ray walked slowly up the stairs; Jericho didn't smile; "Alex." He muttered and Owen turned to go after Ray. Jericho grabbed his arm and really did smile; "Wilson's on the case." Owen chuckled and stared back up the stairs; "Couldn't happen to a nicer scumbag." Jericho indicated to the front doors; "I think we should pay a visit to the old professor and have a little chat. Bring a bottle of scotch as a little peace maker." Owen nodded and the pair left the bar, heading for the caravan.

Thomas watched them go and sat slowly down. He rubbed his face and folded his arms. "If they are fucking ghost hunters, I'm the Pope's left testicle." he said softly to himself and pulled the shabby little red notebook from his jacket pocket. He carefully pulled off the fat elastic band that held the book together and flicked through the well scribbled pages. He stopped and read two pages with interest. "Oh fuck!" He said and looked about. The shit had hit the fan alright.

That's when he heard the altercation upstairs; he rose slowly from the chair and with a little smile creeping across his face, watched Ray hurriedly walk down the stairs and out the front door; not a happy man by any means. Thomas peered up the stairs; to see the big black man, arms folded and grinning; in his underwear!

Thomas chuckled to himself and headed for the kitchen - a fried egg sandwich was in his mind - He stopped and stared out the hall window, to see Ray jumping into the professors old jeep and head up Gallows Lane. Thomas smiled; maybe the bastard will learn that some women have very good - and powerful - friends.

The professor watched Ray go - apparently unconcerned - He had remembered that Ray was going into the village to get supplies, especially milk for his bloody cornflakes and more coke for their whisky. He turned back to Jericho and Owen; "We were called the very morning that the builders started to uncover the ruins. The Murphy's made no objections to us being on site or the fact that their work on the extension had to stop; completely. They were really good about it all. I think they actually were quite interested in the whole thing." He sat down and gestured to the papers and photographs, spread across the small table.

"It appears we have Anglo-Saxon period stone enclosures; probably pit-dungeons by their constructions." He tapped a photograph and continued; "Quite a rare find to be honest. We didn't find any forgotten prisoners in them - no bones, nothing really - except in one, we found a necklace that definitely wasn't Anglo-Saxon in origin; more like Edwardian or late Victorian." He accepted a cup of tea from Owen, who had made a brew in the old metal tea pot, "That's another real mystery Jericho, we dug out the structure; it looked like it hadn't been disturbed for centuries yet lying in the dirt at the bottom of the large pit was the bloody modern necklace." The professor shrugged his shoulders: he had no rational answer for that. "What about the stories that sprung up after the ruins were exposed?" Owen asked, sipping his tea.

The professor sighed at that; "Most are from old Thomas, he claims that he saw two figures by the large pit one night - just days after we arrived on site - the figures were all white and ghostly and appeared to jump into the bloody pit. Of course, when he finally managed to get up the courage and take a look; there was nothing in the pit." He tapped his cup with a nervous finger and stared at the ceiling. "Then I saw something one night, when I was sitting in the doorway there [he pointed to the caravans door] I would have sworn that I saw the figure of a young woman - dressed in a long white dress - running into the excavation. She had the most wonderful, full figure and was quite well built up here." He indicated large breasts and then half smiled; "I put that down to Mister Johnny Walker, I'm afraid."

Jericho and Owen chuckled at the professor's candour. Leaving the bottle as a present, the pair walked back to the hotel. "We'll start with the hotel, then the ruins." Jericho said but stared back at the excavations. He had a gut feeling about the place, and it wasn't good.

3. THE HOTEL.

The team gathered in the restaurant that afternoon and Owen fetched freshly brewed coffee from the kitchens that old Thomas had opened for them. Jericho informed his team that they would be staying the night - after all - and that Thomas had given Owen several 'takeaway' menu's for local fast-food places. But everyone settled on the menu from the 'Star of India'. It was also decided to invite the professor and his assistant - though nobody thought Ray would put in an appearance - after his confrontation with Wilson.

"Strange eh, we're in a country hotel noted for its location and cuisine. Yet we're ordering Indian takeaway." Owen chuckled and consulted his mirror once Thomas had left the room. He sighed; "Well, parts of the hotel itself go way back to the late medieval period - around 1460 - it was a manor house and belonged to the De Walt family, who owned it for about two hundred years. Then the house passed into the hands of the O'Connell family, they stayed for about a hundred and fifty years." He looked up and saw that he had everyone's attention.

"That's a co-incidence right there; the night porter in 1999 having the same surname as the family that owned the house from the 1680's?" Owen smiled, but Wilson just grunted; "O'Connell is a very common name."

Owen continued; "In 1810, the house was a 'coach stop' and ran by the Joiner family, who spent some real money on the place. They did all kinds of improvements, but the family apparently died out in 1882 and the house was sold to the Anderson family, who were textile and mill owners. It remained in their family until 1936, when the last surviving Anderson died. The house was almost derelict until 1950 when an American couple brought the place and opened it as small hotel. During the sixties and seventies, the place changed hands several times." Owen sipped his coffee and grabbed a couple of biscuits.

"Any paranormal activity reported over those years?" Alex asked and Owen shook his head; "Not a bloody sighting – nothing - Now I find that really strange for such an old house; don't you?" Alex had to agree with that and both Jericho and Wilson really did think that was odd. "So, all the paranormal stuff apparently started after the ruins were uncovered?" Jericho rubbed his chin as Owen nodded. "In 1989, a certain John Murphy bought the house and re-opened it as a country hotel - he appears to have made quite a success of it and when he died - his only son, also called John, took the place over and ran it with his wife. That's the couple who have apparently disappeared."

"Hold on, I thought the blokes name was Kent Murphy?" Wilson looked puzzled, but Owen smiled; "Kent was his middle name and he always used it to distinguish him from his father. I suppose he got so use to being called 'Kent' that he just let it continue, even after his father's death." Wilson grunted and finished his coffee, looking for a refill.

Alex topped the big man's cup up with a small smile.

Jericho held up his little glass orb; it was clear. "No demon activity detected in the hotel itself. Alexandra and I wandered around the place and found nothing to indicate the presence of a demon – well - not recently." Everyone sat in silence and enjoyed their coffee and biscuits. Wilson sighed; "Owen and I checked every bloody mirror in the place - and there were loads of the buggers - no Jerusalem Mirrors I'm afraid." Owen coughed; "No time portals either."

"So, the house is apparently clean for our purposes. Obviously, no souls have been collected here and so we are left with one conclusion - regarding the house - that the couple are no longer here, dead or alive. But where the hell are they? The pair are missing from the current human timeline, so we know that something 'un-natural' has befallen them; but what?" Jericho sipped his coffee; this was a real puzzle and very little made any sense; from a Temporal Detective's point of view unless they had encountered a rouge 'time portal'.

He rose from the table and stared out the window and saw the professor's jeep was back in the car park. That's when old Tom appeared in the doorway; he spoke directly to Alex; "Excuse me Miss, but Mr. Chapel would like a word." Everyone glanced at each other, and it was Jericho that answered, "Yeah, sure."

Ray stepped through the door with a sheepish grin on his face and was clutching a large bunch of colourful flowers with both hands. "I'm sorry about this morning Miss, I was wrong, and I would like to say sorry for my stupid behaviour." He held out the flowers and Alex accepted them with a quiet; "Thank you." Ray stood a little embarrassed for a few seconds, then nodded to Wilson and walked away. They watched him go in silence and everyone started to laugh; quietly.

"What the fuck just happened?" Asked the intrigued Owen, who sniffed the flowers and pulled a face, adding; "I can smell manure."

Wilson chuckled; "When Jericho gave me the heads up about him, I dived in Alex's room and she was waiting for me. So, she went to the bathroom and switched on the shower, whilst I found myself a big armchair and turned its back to the door." He couldn't stop himself chuckling again, then continued; "I pulled off my shirt and trousers and sat waiting. Sure, enough the pervert knocked softly at the door and came in, saying quietly 'Hello, anyone there? He spoke just above a whisper and went straight for the bathroom, knowing full well, that anyone under a shower wouldn't hear him. That's when I stood up and asked him what the fuck he was up to!"

Alex grinned; "I opened the door and stuck my head out saying; "Oh darling, do come and scrub my back." Everyone laughed at that. Wilson almost giggled; "He looked like he had shat his pants and mumbled something and then fled the bloody room."

Alex stopped laughing and held up the flowers; "The stems are covered in dirt and is that bloody shit?" She grimaced and dropped the flowers on the table. "Where did he steal them from, I wonder?" She muttered, wiping her hands on several table napkins.

Owen, still chuckling about the whole scene, waved a hand towards the doorway; "He probably nicked them from that derelict church we passed in Gallows Lane, the old churchyard is overgrown and full of flowers. Bit of a strange place, by all accounts." He sat down and poured himself another coffee - that's when he noticed everyone was looking at him. He shrugged his shoulders; "What now?" He asked and poured milk into his cup.

Jericho folded his arms and sighed quite loudly; "Why is the old church so strange?" Owen sipped his coffee and said quietly; "Oh, it has a history of ghosts, demons, apparitions and all sorts, including the disappearance of a young girl last century. When the church was closed up [in 1971] the locals gathered around and cast salt along its paths and around the church walls. Apparently, none of the villagers will go near the place. It's now owned by the Murphy's; well, until they disappeared. Don't know who would own it and the hotel now." He smiled broadly and picked up some more biscuits; "Do you think old Tom has any custard creams?"

Jericho held up his hands in mock despair and Wilson just shook his head. Alex sighed, but just had to smile; "Oh Owen, you can be a right twat sometimes." Owen scratched his head – unsmiling - "Now what the fuck have I done?" No-one bothered to answer that question. But Jericho pulled on his jacket and pointed towards the door; "Let's go people." and that was all he said.

4. THE CHURCH.

The van pulled up by the overgrown gate and the path that ran up to the church door, which was also overgrown. Jericho, who was sitting in the front passenger seat, stared at the derelict church and rubbed his chin; "Well. Someone has been here recently. The foliage around the church door has been pulled back and I would bet a dollar, that the door has been recently opened. So, who's been poking around a derelict church and more importantly: why?"

Wilson leaned over the steering wheel and pointed to the huge red and white sign hung on the church wall. "DANGER - DO NOT ENTER - VERY DANGEROUS STRUCTURE!" He grunted; "Some fuckers can't read then."

Jericho pushed open the van's door and smiled; "Neither can we." The team de-camped and Wilson struggled for a few seconds with the rusted gate. "No fuckers opened this in a while." He muttered and the team made their way up the path and arrived at the large broken door, which had been fixed shut by having large pieces of dark wood nailed across it. Everyone could see that the door had been opened from the inside and that had splintered the wood outwards. The undergrowth was all flattened towards the path. Someone had left the church; very forcibly. But how had they entered in the first place?

Leaving Alex watching the door, Jericho and Owen took the left side and Wilson the right. They battled through the undergrowth for some minutes and met together at the rear of the church; everything was boarded up and secure. Jericho rubbed his chin and stared at the churchyard - it looked like it had not been disturbed for years. "Well, someone got out the church, but how the hell did they get in?" He asked his colleagues, who just shrugged their shoulders. Owen pointed to the roof, which was partially covered with a thick, tar painted tarpaulin. "Through a hole in the bloody roof?" He ventured as an answer.

Wilson shook his head; "They would have needed ladders at least and that would have left marks in undergrowth, not to mention footprints all over the place and no-one has been walking around these walls in some time." Owen pointed to the overgrown south wall of the churchyard; "That's where that Ray fellow must have nicked the flowers; the road runs right next to it and look at those flowers growing there?" Wilson nodded; "Looks like the same flowers that appeared in Alex's shit smelling bouquet."

Jericho pulled the orb from his jacket pocket and held it up; the circumference was clear. He sighed - a little with relief - and started to walk back to the front door. "Well, whoever broke out of the church was probably human; but how did they get in to start with?" He muttered. They found Alex sitting on an old tombstone, reading her mirror.

"I take it you knew, that Ray Chapel has previous for exposing himself, peering through windows and was once caught masturbating outside a girls school?" Alex held up her mirror and added; "Quite an innocent little pervert compared to some we have met." Jericho just smiled and pointed to the door; "I think we can squeeze through there but be bloody careful; I don't want to call a Knight for a quick resurrection!" Everyone chuckled at that, and Wilson pulled the door open a couple of feet and little bits of masonry fell about their heads. "I now have bloody brick dust as dandruff." Owen cursed and the team squeezed into the old church.

Despite the summer heat, it was dark, damp, and gloomy inside. They used their mirrors to illuminate the semi darkness. "I can smell burnt..." Owen didn't finish his statement because their mirrors were all pointing to the middle of the church. There was a partially burnt bonfire piled three or four feet high. It appeared to have been constructed from the old pews, some crates and other bits of church furniture. There was a distinct smell of petrol and traces of some other pungent entity.

"Bit early for Guy Fawkes night." Wilson said and shone his mirror about. That's when he saw the dark shadow on the floor by the smashed alter. As he looked down, he could see the footprints in the debris and dust - all heading towards the door. – Away from the broken alter. "I bet this place has a crypt and I think I know where the entrance is." He called to the others and carefully made his way to the old alter.

They gathered around the hole in the floor and shone their mirrors down; a well-worn set of steps presented itself, twisting and turning downwards to a dark reflective pool of water. "Its fucking flooded." Cussed Owen and then sighed; "It must be deep because the crypt would have a vaulted ceiling; whatever is down there is under several feet of dirty stinking water." They all turned to Jericho who smiled; "We need someone who is slim and a good swimmer to take a look."

They all then turned to Alex and grinned.

Alex held up both hands and said firmly; "No bloody way am I diving into that filthy water!" and folded her arms; repeating loudly; "NO." Wilson chuckled; "I'm way too big, as Jericho says; it has to be someone who is slim and agile; that's certainly not me." Jericho nodded his agreement with that; "Sorry, it's you or Owen." He muttered and smiled - again. "How come you have discounted yourself?" Owen said openly and also folded his arms. Jericho shrugged his shoulders; "One simple little fact stops me from diving down there." Alex nodded; "Oh, I see, you can't swim." Jericho held up both hands; "No, I can swim really well." Owen, looking a little bemused had to ask; "Well, if you can swim, what's stopping you going down there?"

Jericho sighed; "The little fact that I'm the bloody Inspector."

Wilson laughed outright at that and agreed totally with his 'boss'. "Down to you two." He said with some real pleasure. Alex shook her head; "I can't strip down to my underwear because I'm only wearing a little pair of cotton panties. It must be Owen. I know my lovely colleagues wouldn't want me parading around in just little panties that will go see-through in water." She smiled and then saw the look on their faces. "Bloody perverts!" She muttered and Owen pulled a coin from his pockets; "Toss you for it?" He flipped the coin and shouted; "Heads!"

Unfortunately for him, Wilson caught the coin before he did and turned it around in his big fingers. The coin displayed 'heads' on both sides. They stared at Owen who simply groaned and stared at the dark water in mock despair.

"Off you go lad." Was all Jericho said between chuckles.

Owen descended the steps in just his underpants and vest, clutching his mirror. As he stepped into the water he yelped; "It's fucking freezing!" and disappeared from view. Jericho carefully watched his own mirror, with Wilson and a very happy Alex at his shoulders. "Record everything you can." He told Owen, whose teeth could be clearly heard chattering; everyone could make out a couple of things Owen said, and they weren't pleasant about his Temporal colleagues.

That's when the church seemed to move beneath them, there was a loud crashing noise and the trio dived to the floor, with Wilson throwing himself over Alex as bits of masonry fell about them. Part of the church's front had collapsed. They lay in darkness until Wilson rose to his knees, shaking bits of brick and mortar from his head and shoulders. "What the fuck just happened!" He shouted and shone his mirror to the front of the church - it was now just a pile of rubble - a bloody big pile of rubble.

Alex staggered up, coughing from the dust swirling around. Jericho was shouting into his mirror; there was no answer from Owen. Wilson and Alex were now yelling down the hole, but again; there was no answer from Owen. "Oh, fucking shit!" shouted Wilson with some real concern, pulling off his jacket and boots. But Jericho stopped him; "Your way too big." Was all he said and pulled his own jacket off, kicking his shoes away and pulling down his trousers. He was already stepping into the water when Alex joined him - just in her panties - That would have put a smile on Owens's face. They plunged into the darkness together.

Wilson knelt by the hole and shone his mirror down. Only a few minutes pasted - but it seemed like hours to the big man - Despite the cold, damp atmosphere; he was sweating, and his mouth was dry; "Come on, come the fuck on." He whispered and again shouted down the hole, then suddenly Alex's head popped up from the water, she was panting and clearly crying; "No bloody sign of the little twat...no bloody sign." She sobbed between chattering teeth. Wilson pulled her up with both hands and wrapped her in his discarded jacket. A very silent and grim-faced Jericho popped up and dragged himself up the steps.

They all sat around the hole and consoled Alex, who was weeping, gripping Wilson's jacket around her. Jericho finally muttered; "I'll see if I can get hold of James [a Knight of God] on the hurry up, but we must find Owen first. He can't do anything without the body." Wilson cuddled Alex and nodded; only James could recall Owen's soul from the darkness or the boy's soul would be lost - for good - he wasn't from this era.

Before Jericho could put the call into Control, his mirror buzzed with an incoming call - it was Owen! - Jericho grabbed up his mirror and shouted; "Are you fucking alright boy?" Owens's wet and smiling face appeared - with daylight around him - "Yeah, I'm fine, but you'll never guess where the fuck I am?"

Everyone sighed with huge relief and Alex brushed away her tears and took several deep breaths before saying; "You bloody little twerp, we thought you had bloody snuffed it!" Wilson couldn't hide his relief and finally said: "Where the fuck are you baby brother?"

Owen grinned and pointed his mirror around; they could see that he was at the excavations!

5. THE EXCAVATIONS.

Old Tom sat at the reception desk and watched with some amazement as the four 'Paranormal Investigators' trooped past him. Jericho was clearly wet from head to toe and clutching his clothes with both hands. Owen was next; again, just in his underpants and carrying his clothes over one arm. The big fella looked quite normal and had a huge grin on his face. Tom smiled to himself when he saw Alex; wrapped in the big man's jacket and nothing else; she was also very wet.

He rose from his chair and was about to ask what happened, when a grim Jericho simply said; "Don't even bloody ask." and they disappeared up the stairs. Tom watched closely and was rewarded with a quick glimpse of Alex's bare bum at the top of the stairs. "Not even wearing panties." He muttered and really did grin. That had made his day; well, if he was honest; it had made his bloody year actually!

He sat back down in reception and opened his paper. He was having quite a good day so far and chuckled to himself. He sipped his coffee and took a bite from his cheese and onion sandwich. He looked up to see the professor walking towards the hotel with a pile of papers tucked under his arm.

Tom pointed up the stairs and said with quite a smile; "The ghost busters are back and very wet." he chuckled at the puzzled look upon the professors face and shrugged his shoulders; "They said don't bloody ask - so I didn't."

Fielding just grunted and wondered where the hell they found somewhere to swim around here - the place was miles from the sea and no-one - well, anyone sane - would dive into the local river? He would wait until someone came down to reception. But Tom slapped the paper down and smiled; "The bar's open; if you fancy a drop of the good stuff." The professor didn't have to be asked twice.

The team came together in Jericho's room - after hot showers and a change of clothes - Owen slapped a bottle of brandy on the desk and they gathered around as he filled glasses. Jericho tapped the rough drawing that Owen had produced; "At the rear of the crypt, the builders constructed - for all intents and purposes - a fake door with angels and such things engraved on it. But the collapse pulled the top part down and behind lay a small tunnel." Owen was able to squeeze through and simply walk, quite crouched down, through it.

"You would have never made it big man; you would have been stuck like a pig in a poke." Owen chuckled and sipped his well-earned brandy. Wilson just grunted and rolled his glass in both hands, smiling; "If I was a skinny, weedy thing like you, I would never have witnessed our lovely colleague stripping down to her little white panties and diving into the water." He raised his glass, adding; "Being like a pig in a poke does have its advantages." Alex slapped his arm; but did smile a little.

Jericho continued unfazed by the banter; "The tunnel bought Owen out into the diggings from behind a concealed entrance. Now that's really interesting because someone had to conceal that entrance and they did it with bushes and thicket. Why? I believe the doorway was revealed by the builders when they first excavated the site. But it was hidden when the archaeologists turned up - again - why?" He took a long sip from his glass and smiled at his team, replacing the glass down for Owen to refill.

Owen scratched his nose; "I know this is bloody obvious; but they wanted to hide the secret tunnel that ran to and from the old church?" He said quietly. Jericho nodded; "But why?" He asked again. "So, they could use it when they liked without anyone else knowing about its existence." Alex muttered, then added; "But for what purpose?"

Jericho rubbed his hands together; "Spot on and if we discover that purpose, I think we may find out what happened to our vanishing hoteliers." Wilson accepted a refill from Owen and said; "What bothers me is the bonfire in the middle of the damn church; what was that for?" A knock at the door ended the discussions; for now. Alex pulled open the door and found detective Constable Sharon Smith standing there with a uniformed officer and old Tom at the rear. The detective didn't smile - which was quite usual for her – she stared at Alex and walked straight past her. She stood by the desk, looking down at the hand drawn map. She removed her thick, police issue spectacles and wiped them with a bright blue hankie. "I take it Mister Tibbs, that you know withholding vital evidence into a possible abduction and maybe murder, is a serious offence?" she replaced her spectacles and smiled; it certainly didn't suit her face or demeanour.

Jericho raised his arms and smiled; "Yes of course, we were on our way to your good selves, but we simply had to change from our wet clothes and get a quick brandy to steady our nerves. I'm so sorry for the delay, but your here now; how can we be of assistance?" Old Tom coughed; "That's correct Officer, I saw them return; they were drenched; from head to foot." The detective just grunted and scooped up the map. "When are you departing?" She asked, folding the drawing and pushing it into her oversized handbag.

"They paid for two nights Miss." Tom said and smiled at Jericho. The detective nodded and looked Jericho up and down - almost with contempt - "You know that the church has been sealed off by local council engineers and no-one is to go near it; you understand that?" Jericho nodded and picked up his glass. Owen offered the constable a brandy, which she refused. "Just stick to the hotel and the diggings in future, otherwise you might find yourselves down the station explaining to my Inspector; you do understand that?" Jericho nodded again.

"If I had my way, I would charge the lot of you with criminal damage to the church, but the engineers have informed my Inspector that it was subsidence. An act of God apparently – if you believe in such things - So he's decided to take no action"

She looked quite disappointed by that decision. She walked to the door and turned again to Jericho; "We've managed to locate the couple's next of kin and they will be flying in tomorrow. It's a certain Sean Murphy; a cousin of John Murphy and I have no doubt, from my telephone conversation with him, that you and your band of so-called Paranormal Investigators will be off site and not returning." Now she did smile at that.

The detective glanced at old Tom; "I understand that he's bringing his own staff with him, but that's his call. He'll have his accountant with him and really needs to look over the books."

She gestured to the uniform officer who had said nothing the whole time; "Let's go. Our business with these people is finished. For now." They both left and old Tom just sighed; "I didn't know Mr. Kent had a cousin." But smiled strangely, which Alex noticed as he turned away.

Owen refilled the glasses all round and gave one to Tom, who took it with some gratitude. "Now that's one police officer who has honed her people skills to perfection." Wilson muttered with real sarcasm in his voice. Everyone had to chuckle at that - including Tom - who knocked his drink back and left; he had the account books to find.

Jericho stood rubbing his chin - deep in thought - He finished his brandy and turned to Owen; "Find out all you can about this 'Sean Murphy' and while you're at it, check the history of our missing couple again. I have a bad feeling we've missed something bloody obvious about the pair." Owen nodded and the meeting broke up and the team headed for the excavations; again.

6. THE NECKLACE.

Professor Fielding was waiting for the team at the large pit; he had already heard about the police detectives visit. She had told the professor that the cousin was going to close the dig early; he wanted the place reinstated and was also considering cancelling the contract for the new extension. That really did make Jericho think. Sean Murphy had already contacted a solicitor about obtaining 'power of attorney' whilst the pair remained missing.

"He's certainly not hanging about getting his feet under the table." Alex said as they gathered around the hole.

The hole was about fifteen feet deep and four feet wide. The walls were brick and stone, and they could see that the top had been smoothed. The professor pointed out that the prisoners were lowered down on ropes and a metal grill would have been placed over the top and locked. "They didn't keep prisoners long, there was usually a quick trial, and they were released or executed; there were no real prisons for offenders. You could be hung for stealing bread in those days." He informed the team and added; "The necklace was found right at the bottom of the pit, where the floor had some brickwork left."

"Was it found before the couple disappeared?" Jericho asked, peering down into the hole. The professor nodded, then hesitated; "Actually, I think it was found on the very day they disappeared."

"Who discovered it?" Wilson asked and the professor pointed across the yard as Ray was walking towards them; "Ray did, he was the lead Archaeologist for this pit. He and a volunteer discovered it - a lad called Leon O'Connell - I think."

Ray joined the little group, and everyone realised at once, that he had been drinking; but said nothing. He stood by the edge but didn't look down. "I didn't put it there, if that's what your fucking thinking." He said quite loudly and staggered a little; Wilson grabbed his arm and pulled him back from the precipice. He pushed away Wilson's hand and snarled; "I don't need fucking help you black bastard, you stick to handling that white slut of yours!" He was drunker than anyone had realised.

The professor grabbed him with both hands and pushed him towards the caravan; "Go and bloody sleep it off you idiot." He spoke close to Ray's face, that suddenly smiled; "Yeah, sure." He muttered and pulled away from the professor's grip and staggered towards the caravan, muttering obscenities. The professor tried to apologise to Wilson and Alex, but they waved it away and appeared to treat it as a drunken joke - for the old professor's sake - He was clearly distraught and embarrassed by his colleague's actions.

"You best go after him Fielding." Jericho said quietly and patted the professor's arm. He nodded and went after Ray, who had pulled open the caravan's door and fallen through it. Everyone watched the old man hurry away. Owen tapped Wilson; "Jesus, you showed real restraint there big man. I would have thumped him for that." But Wilson just grunted; "I don't thump drunks; even foul-mouthed racist bastards." Jericho certainly appreciated Wilson's actions with the man and said so. The group returned to staring at the pit.

"No one had even suggested that he placed it down there; so why so quick to deny it?" Alex said softly; she had calmed down from the insult thrown at her. "That probably means the bastard did put it there." Owen said, then added; "Yet another bloody O'Connell; the lad with Ray when the necklace was found." He muttered and knelt down by the edge and tugged at the ladders that had been fixed to the wall of the pit. "They are well secure Jericho, should I go down and take a look?" Alex stepped forward; "No, I'll do this one; no swimming in crap required." She grinned and started to descend down the ladder, slowly and carefully.

"That's our girl." Jericho said with some pride. Then Owen gripped the ladder and swung onto it, when Alex had reached the bottom; "She didn't hesitate to go in after me." He smiled and made his way down. The pair wandered around the bottom and found nothing unusual. Alex pulled out her mirror and slowly moved it around in a full circle. She stopped suddenly and called quietly to Owen, who now stood by her shoulder - after a few minutes - Alex looked up to her colleagues and shouted; "There's a bloody half open time portal!" She gestured to the brickwork facing her. "It's linked to August 6th, 669AD." Owen called out and saw that Jericho and Wilson were already on their way down.

They gathered by the portal and Jericho nodded; "Well, let's take a trip back to ancient times and see what happens." Everyone agreed with that. But from above they could hear a heavy engine running and they stared up to see the bright yellow bucket of the small JCB [which had been left by the builders, pending their return] appear at the edge, pushing loose, damp soil down upon them.

"Into the portal!" Jericho yelled and the four disappeared into the brickwork, as large amounts of dirt started to fill the pit. This went on for some minutes until the pit was about half full; then the machine tipped over the edge and fell about eight feet onto the dirt and lay on its side; the engine now silent.

The forest was quite damp and cold, despite the warmth of the summer day and the team, in single file, quietly made their way through the thick undergrowth. Jericho was consulting his mirror as they walked. "I think we all know who was driving the bloody JCB." Owen turned and spoke to Alex who nodded. Wilson, who was at the rear muttered; "If we were living humans that bastard would have buried us alive, now that definitely deserves a thump."

Alex chuckled and pushed foliage from her face as the little group moved on, she spoke to Owen; "What better place to dump some unwanted people - without resorting to murder - than sending them back in time some fourteen hundred years!" Jericho waved for silence and the group hid behind some large overgrown rocks and stared down into the small clearing. There was thin grey smoke coming from the reed thatched roof of the mud build hut. The door was closed with nothing, but a large stick pushed between the frames. A wooden pitchfork lay against the wall and two scruffy goats were tethered a few feet away. There was a small patch of cultivated land next to the house - probably herbs and small vegetables - Owen whispered to the others.

Alex tapped Jericho's shoulder and pointed to the rope slung between two small trees; it had washing hanging there. "Since when did our Anglo-Saxon ancestors wear modern trousers?" She said quietly and then chuckled; "Isn't that a bloody large brassiere I can see?" She added. Everyone exchanged glances and Jericho rose and headed for the house with the others following. As he approached, He shouted [In 'Old English] "Hello in the house!"

The group waited outside, they could definitely see someone moving about inside and Jericho repeated his salutation. A woman appeared in the doorway, clutching her discoloured apron. She was probably in her late twenties but looked tired and well worn. Her dress and woolen blouse had clearly seen better times; she had no shoes. "One for me I think." Alex said and approached the woman with her hands clearly in view. "We're strangers here and we mean you no harm. We just need to speak to you." But the woman stood rigid and silent, staring at them, if they were monsters from some dark hell. Finally, she stepped forward a couple of feet and stopped again. She was crying and rubbed her face a few times. "Your clothes...that clothing...are you really from home?" She spoke quietly and started to sob openly and staggered a little, then held onto the water butt by the doorway. "Are you from home?" She whispered and fell to her knees and wept loudly.

Alex grabbed her and held her tight; "It's alright Anne, it's alright, your safe now." Owen turned to Wilson and muttered; "Mrs. Anne Murphy I presume?" Wilson nodded and consulted his mirror; "It sure is, but where's Kent Murphy?"

Alex managed to get the distraught woman to her feet and the group shuffled into the house - it was semi dark - the only light coming through the door and gap's in the roof. A small open fire, constrained by several large stones, was the centre piece of the house - there was no other furniture - apart from a wooden frame that had straw piled upon it. "That's the bloody bed." Owen said and watched the smoke disappearing through the roof. "I love the chimney." Muttered Wilson and coughed from the smoky atmosphere.

Anne gulped down some brandy from Alex's hip flask and hugged her tightly. Jericho quietly asked; "Where's Kent?" Anne took a couple of deep breaths and sobbed again, but quickly composed herself, she gestured towards the door; "They took him for questioning some days ago. We're strangers here and they want to know about us. We couldn't tell them what happened to us because they would treat us a demons or ghosts. They are really primitive and superstitious – savages - They have never heard of Jesus Christ; they're pagans!"

Owen whispered to Wilson; "If they were really that savage, they would have killed them immediately and not bother to ask any questions." Wilson had to agree with that, but he was a little puzzled; "Why didn't they take her as well?" Owen smiled; "She's a woman and no threat to them; it's their culture. They didn't even persecute witches." Wilson nodded; "Who are the real savages then?"

Everyone sat on the straw covered floor and listened to Anne's story

7. THE MURPHY'S.

"At first, we really couldn't believe what the builders had uncovered in the old gardens. Even the local historian - a Mr. Ted English - was completely taken back by its discovery. There were no records of it; none, no folklore or legends, nothing. That's when old Professor Larbert turned up with team from the local University. He's a lovely old man, but his assistant Ray is a real odd fellow - Kent and I really didn't take to him - which is unusual for us." Anne sipped Alex's hipflask and dried her face with her sleeve. Wilson grunted; "Odd is not the word I would use to describe the bastard." That made Owen chuckle. Anne continued; "Everything was fine at first, we were quite excited by it all and Kent said we should consider cancelling the extension - despite the money we would lose - and use the ruins as a tourist attraction. Kent believed we would draw more visitors and guests to the hotel if we left it alone. That seemed to make the old professor very happy. But then one night - a couple of months ago - we were just sitting down to dinner...." Jericho interrupted Anne; "Did you say this happened months ago?" Everyone looked at each other; it had only been a couple of weeks. Anne nodded and confirmed they had been in this terrible place for a couple of months.

Jericho shrugged his shoulders and asked Anne to continue, which she did; after taking another swig from the hipflask. "We were just sitting down to dinner - liver and bacon casserole - Kent's favourite. When old Tom appeared and said something was happening at the old church; we had just purchased it and the land that it stood on. That was another part of our plan to attract visitors." Wilson tapped Jericho and said quietly; "Didn't he say, that on the night they disappeared, he had come on duty at ten o'clock; as usual?" Jericho just nodded and waited for Anne to continue.

"Well, we just left dinner and Tom offered a lift in his car - it was already parked by the doors - so we all jumped in and drove up to the church. We could see smoke and little flames through the partially open door. Someone had got in and started a fire. We squeezed through the door and saw a bonfire burning in the middle of the bloody church!" She sighed and shook her head; "We had hurried out so quickly that Kent had left his mobile phone on the dinner table, so Tom said he would go outside and call the Fire Brigade. Kent and I started to look around for something to extinguish the flames, when suddenly; something in the middle of the bonfire just flashed and a green smoke filled the place. We really did start to choke and staggered towards the door, but never made it. We must have passed out."

Anne started to sob again and accepted Alex's hip flask. Wilson sighed; "I suspect that the green smoke was some kind of knockout gas; little wonder old Tom went outside." Owen checked his mirror and looked quite grim; "Thomas Edward O'Connell was born in 1694 and there's no record of his dispatch [death] - he's a missing soul - Should have been collected in 1753 - he obviously didn't turn up for that little party and guess where he spent most of his life?"

"Let me guess; Gallows Tree Manor House?" Alex sighed, and added: "He couldn't have dragged the Murphy's down that tunnel from the church to the pit on his own - he must have an accomplice - but who?" Wilson scratched his chin, thinking. "If old tom is from the original family that owned the house and land, then we need to look for other O'Connell's; maybe?"

Owen smiled; "The lad that found the necklace with Ray; he was an O'Connell."

"Did you say necklace? Someone stole my bloody necklace. It was around my neck the night we went to the church and was gone when I woke up in this shit hole. It was my Great-Grandmother's." Anne shouted and straightened up - now a little worse from the contents of Alex's flask - she hadn't drunk strong alcohol for some time, and it was showing- She didn't speak for a minute or so and then said; "When we came around, we were here...in this terrible place.... we couldn't believe what had happened and we just wandered around in shock, I suppose. Nothing was the same. After a few hours, we realised that something terrible had happened. We were lost in a forest with nothing - absolutely nothing except the clothes we were wearing." She slumped against Alex's shoulder and had passed out. She was sleeping; heavily.

Jericho and Wilson gently placed her upon the bed of straw and covered her with a thick, rough blanket. "Best let her sleep it off." Alex said, making the woman as comfortable as she could. The little group sat in silence for a few minutes. "The necklace was obviously dropped in the pit when Anne and her husband were pushed through the time portal, then not discovered until Ray and the boy went down the hole to finish clearing it." Wilson said softly but pulled a face; "That doesn't make sense, if Ray's part of this; why draw attention to the pit by telling everyone about finding the impossible necklace?"

"He didn't; because it dropped from Anne's neck as young O'Connell and his accomplice: old Tom O'Connell pushed the couple through the time portal. When they found it the next day; the boy didn't have time to hide it from Ray and so it became part of the mystery." Jericho folded his arms and sighed; "What the hell is the time travelling Tom after in this century? This young O'Connell must be a descendent of his?"

Owen stared through the doorway; "I think we have visitors." He said softly.

Jericho went to the doorway and watched as the half dozen men approached; everyone had a spear and shield, a couple carried swords at their hips. One had a bright two coloured tunic over his rough shirt and was wearing a silver helmet; that was the leader. Jericho raised his hand in welcome and greeted them in their own language; old English.

They seemed totally surprised that the stranger dressed in strange clothes could speak their tongue. Offa [the Chief] asked Jericho why he had come onto their lands and what the woman was to them. Jericho replied that the woman and her man belonged to his tribe, and they had come to collect them and return the pair home. Offa half-smiled; he wanted to know how he [Jericho] could speak the language, but the other strangers' couldn't. Jericho smiled and told Offa that the priesthood to which he belonged had taught him several tongues as a boy.

Offa asked where the woman was, and Jericho pointed to the sleeping Anne and explained that she wasn't well. The Chief nodded, he did not smile, but held up his spear and waved it twice. From the trees came two burly warriors carrying a litter; they laid it down in front of Offa. It was a body covered with a rough blanket. "I don't think this is good news." Wilson whispered to Alex, who glanced down at poor Anne and really did feel sorry for her.

Jericho and Alex pulled back the blanket and stared hard at the face looking up at them. Alex sighed and threw the blanket back over it. Jericho thanked the Chief for returning the body to his woman and didn't ask how he died. The Chief was a little puzzled that Jericho didn't ask about the man's death and so told him what had happened.

Whilst being questioned by the Chief and the local priest [pagan] John had simply keeled over and died. No violence had been used against him. So, they had returned him to his woman for burial; according to whatever customs the strangers followed. Their task completed, the Chief and his men disappeared into the forest. Alex sighed; "I best get the hip-flask ready." They all looked at the sleeping woman and felt sympathy for her, but most of that sympathy was kept for John Murphy; his soul was now lost because he had died outside his own era.

Wilson knelt by the body and consulted his mirror; "According to Human Records he was suffering from a weak heart for some years and was on really serious medication for it. The poor bastard had no access to such drugs here - it was a sudden death waiting to happen - no matter how well the local tribe treated him."

Owen scratched his head; "What amazed me was that they just accepted you - I mean - had they seen coloured people before? If this was early Christian times, they would have been quite frightened of people like you Wilson, because all the painting of devils and demons at the time was mostly red or black." Wilson grunted and rose up and pointed to the trees. "We have more visitors."

A group of village woman stood by the trees; they were carrying clay pots and flowers. The old lady who was in charge introduced herself; they were here to help Anne bury her man with decency and respect. She was accompanied by her two teenage sons - big strapping lads - who would dig the grave for Anne's man. She explained that if 'John' had been a member of the tribe; the men of the village would have buried him, as was the custom for these people.

Both the young men smiled constantly at Alex as they set about breaking open the hard earth by the trees. Hagga [the old lady] said he should be buried near the trees, home of the tree spirits that the tribe worshipped. She also informed Jericho that if Anne stayed, she would be treated with respect as a widow-woman widows - with or without children - would be looked after. Wilson

smiled and said quietly to Owen; "Real savages, aren't they?"
Owen just smiled and said nothing.

"I'll put a call into James [a Knight of God] and he can eradicate
Anne's memories of all this." Jericho muttered and discretely
operated his mirror, adding; "He can do nothing for Kent; he's
been dead too long. His soul has gone for good."

8. THE RETURN.

Wilson carefully laid Anne upon the old tomb stone and removed
the rough blanket: Alex had dressed her in the clothes they had
found hidden in the hut and she had been returned to the interior
of the derelict church. The team checked for the local council
engineers, returning to complete the shoring up of the building.
Soon as they appeared in Gallows Lane, Jericho operated his
mirror and the team disappeared.

They walked back to the hotel in relative silence, stopping only to
watch the professor hooking up his caravan to his old jeep; he
didn't look happy. They waved at him, and he walked over.
"What's going on Fielding?" Jericho asked and the professor who
shrugged his shoulders; "That Sean Murphy has arrived and the
first thing he did was to order me and Ray off site. He's
wandering around the hotel trying to find Tom O'Connell;
apparently the reception safe is wide open and empty. But Tom's
old mini is still in the car park." He pointed to the car, sitting at
the top of the car park.

"Where's Ray then?" Owen asked and could see that question
agitated the old professor. After a few seconds Fielding sighed;
"He gone. I can't find him anywhere. I think your case of 'Johnny
Walker' that you left in Reception has gone too." Jericho offered
the professor his hand and Fielding grabbed it and smiled; "I take
it there was no ghosts or demons to chase here then?" He smiled
when Jericho nodded; "Yeah, none had checked into the hotel."
Both men chuckled and Fielding jumped into his jeep and with a
little wave drove from the car park and turned into Gallows' Lane.
They watched him disappear as a police car turned into the lane.

The big man standing in the doorway of the hotel was on his
mobile phone; he also didn't look happy. The team walked up
and said hello; at first, he simply ignored them until his call was
finished. He stared at them and folded his arms; "Are you the so-

called Paranormal Investigators?" Jericho nodded and he snorted with undisguised contempt; "Well, sling your fucking hooks, your free loading days here are over. I want you out within the hour; Now piss off - I'm busy - I'm expecting my son to join me."

A restrained Jericho pulled out the receipt old Tom had given him and offered it to Mr. Murphy; "We paid for our stay here actually." He said quietly and didn't smile. Sean Murphy snatched the receipt and looked at it; he smiled. "Like I said you dumb morons; fuck off." He ripped the receipt up and allowed the pieces to flutter to the gravel. He pushed past Jericho and headed for the police car that had stopped some yards from them.

Wilson sighed; "He and that Detective Smith should get on like a house on fire." Everyone chuckled at that and headed for their van. Alex seemed troubled and said to Owen; "Doesn't that Murphy remind you of someone?" Owen nodded but screwed up his face; "No-one comes to mind; sorry."

Anything the temporal detectives had left in the hotel had already disappeared - there would be no trace of their occupancy anywhere - They eased into their van and watched Murphy talking with detective Smith. Alex actually laughed; "I don't think that he'll take Anne's survival and return too well. He's anticipated new fortune has just vanished."

Wilson leaned over the steering wheel and smiled broadly; "Could not have happened to a nicer man." Owen sat quietly in the back [with Alex] and consulted his mirror; he tapped Jericho on the shoulder; "Our Mr. Sean Murphy is a fake. His real name is Joseph O'Connell and he use to be an employee of John Murphy some years ago - when John ran a building company in Wexford - He has quite a bit of previous for fraud and theft. He's a con artist."

Owen looked at his mirror again; "He has two sons, one called Leon who's done time for fraud already, despite only being young. Where have we heard that name before?" Jericho rubbed his chin and turned to Owen; "Buzz human records and find out who Mr. Murphy was calling when we turned up."

"I have no doubt; Anne has told her rescuers that John didn't have a cousin called Sean." Jericho said quietly as they watched

'Sean Murphy' being pushed into the rear of the police car - still protesting his innocence - "I still feel a little sorry for Anne, she has lost her husband and will never know what happened to him, especially since James [a Knight of God] had removed all her memories about the last few weeks here." Alex said softly and took a sip of her hip-flask - she was disappointed; it was empty —so she borrowed Owens's - he didn't protest.

Jericho leaned back in his seat and stretched his legs - as best he could - and watched the police car pull away. "Let's go Wilson. We'll jump when we reach a quiet stretch of road." A police van pulled up and the police car stopped by it. Detective Smith jumped out the car and walked towards the teams van. They watched as Sean Murphy was transferred to the police van, which then departed.

She tapped on Jericho's window; he pressed the button and the window slid down. "I'm glad to see that you're not buried at the bottom of the pit, as that will save us some real trouble. We don't have to dig the bloody thing up." As usual she didn't smile. They all appeared to look quite bemused by what she said and Jericho held up his hands; "Someone tried to fill in one of the pits?" He asked with a 'surprised' expression. The detective just snorted; "That drunken idiot Ray Chapel called us; shouting about you and your so-called team being buried alive in the big pit."

Everyone exchanged glances of bewilderment and shrugged their shoulders. "Well, obviously he was mistaken." Alex said and made a show of swigging Owens's hip flask. She passed it to back to him and he took a swig; "I'll drink to not being buried alive!" He exclaimed and grinned. The detective just shook her head; "He claims that old Tom O'Connell buried you. He watched him do it, he was absolutely certain that all of you had gone down into the pit just moments before."

"Well, it's nonsense. We're all here; alive and well." Jericho said - so Ray wasn't a murdering bastard after all - just a drunken racist one. Detective Smith folded her arms; "The pit is half filled with a bloody small digger overturned on top of it. The building company is coming to retrieve its machine. We won't dig the bloody pit up then; since you're all sitting here."

"What will happen to Ray?" Owen asked and sipped his hipflask.

"He'll receive a Police caution for wasting our time - when he sobers up - My Inspector has already contacted that old professor to come and collect him." She turned to walk away, when Jericho asked about Tom O'Connell. She stopped and smiled; "He has simply vanished; we can't find any trace of him – nothing - that happens a lot around here; apparently." She returned to her car and the police vehicle pulled away. Wilson started the engine and followed it down Gallows' Lane.

Night was approaching fast, and Wilson switched the headlights on. Jericho spoke softly; "I get a mental picture of what probably happened, Tom O'Connell arrived in this century from wherever he had resided before, and found that his old home was now owned by someone else, the Murphy's. But he had descendants; Joseph O'Connell and his sons and they hatched a scheme to get the house and land back. The discovery of the ruins set the plan in motion, or I should say the re-discovery of the ruins. I think old Tom got a job here because he knew that the ruins were here and more importantly; the bloody time portal was here." Jericho accepted Wilson's hipflask and took a swig.

"So they hatched an audacious plan, firstly they would get rid of the Murphy's; a double murder would attract too much attention - from the police and the press - far better if the couple simply vanished and were never seen or heard of again. Then the 'next-of-kin' shows up. The Murphy's had no family or close friends that knew they had no other family. So, Joseph O'Connell [Sean Murphy] turns up and having worked with John Murphy for so many years, knows the man well. He easily passes himself off at Murphy's cousin with some good, false documents. There was no-one to say otherwise - the Murphy's were gone - But they didn't count on us turning up and retrieving Anne Murphy; it was an excellent plan and probably would have worked." Jericho concluded and smiled.

The van headed for the village. Detective Sharon Smith sat and watched the white van behind them, in the side mirror and then opened her large handbag. She pulled the scruffy notebook, still held by the big elastic band and tapped it gently with her fingers. Apparently, Tom had dropped his precious book as he fled from the scene with the digger. She turned to the uniform officer [who always said nothing] and smiled - maybe it was becoming a habit for her - she chuckled; "God works in bloody mysterious ways, don't he?"

Her colleague didn't answer - but did smile - He appeared really interested in the little notebook and watched, as Sharon pushed it into her bag.

9. AROUND THE TABLE.

Jericho told Wilson to stop the van outside 'McKay's Fish & Chip shop' in the village; everyone was practically starving. He pulled the brown envelope from his pocket that contained the money that supplies had given then for this mission; "Who fancies a fish supper?" Everybody said 'YES!' and Jericho, with Alex, disappeared into the busy shop.

Owen rubbed his hands together; "I could eat a fucking horse; dead or alive." He said to Wilson, who just chuckled; "You're always fucking hungry. I would swear that you had hollow legs or large worms." Wilson glanced into the side mirror; a police car had pulled in behind them and the uniform constable stepped out and headed for the chip shop. "Isn't that old misery guts' driver?" He asked Owen, who nodded. Wilson grunted; "Pull up his details for me."

Jericho and Alex returned carrying several packages, wrapped in white paper - the smell was gorgeous - as they climbed into the van. Owen and Wilson sat grinning. Alex handed out the packages and tins of juice to her colleagues who were smiling broadly; again. "What's up with you two?" She asked, examining her two battered sausages and chips, with loads of ketchup on. Jericho opened his Cod and chips, then also saw the look on Owen and Wilson's faces. "What have you found out?" He asked and opened his tin of Coke.

Owen had already stuffed half his steak pie down his throat - he also had a battered sausage to contend with after that - "That young policeman is called William O'Connell and his brother is called Leon - their father is a certain Joseph O'Connell - aka Sean Murphy. Now that's a real cracker, isn't it?"

Jericho sipped his coke before attacking his limp fish. "I see." was all he said and started eating his fish with a small wooden fork. Owen finished his pie; "The number Mr. Sean Murphy called on his mobile was the extension in...." He didn't finish because Jericho said quietly; "The extension in old Tom's room; am I right?" Owen nodded - he wasn't surprised - very little about Jericho surprised him these days. They all watched as the constable returned to his car; carrying three packets.

"Unless he's like our Owen; an empty vessel waiting to fill up with food. He's bought dinner for three people; I wonder who?" Wilson lowered his steak pie and smiled at Jericho. Alex suddenly yelped - that made Owen jump - and said quietly; "That bloody face. His face Jericho. Where have we seen it before?" Jericho dropped his wooden fork back into the chip paper; "Sweet bugger! He's a dead ringer for old Tom O'Connell!" Everyone watched the police car pull away and Jericho yelled at Owen; "Get control to trace his destination and I will bet that it's not the bloody police station." Wilson dumped his supper on the floor and started the van. Owen groaned about his dinner but operated his mirror; "I have him." he said quietly, and the van pulled away.

They found the police car parked outside the derelict church; empty and silent. "I can see torch light inside." Wilson said, as the team quietly left the van and made their way to the church. They crouched in the overgrown church yard and Jericho operated his mirror; "Three people inside; eating fish & chips." He whispered. "Who's with him?" Owen asked, still thinking - with some regret - about abandoning his dinner to a waste bin in the village high street. Jericho scratched his chin; "Constable O'Connell, his brother and Old Tom O'Connell."

Alex crouched down and leaned against an old tombstone; "I don't expect it's a happy family meal." She muttered and adjusted her jacket - the night was oddly cold - for a summer evening. Jericho sighed; "I should have noticed the similarity between Constable O'Connell and old Tom before this. I think they are definably his descendants; there were more O'Connell's involved in this than you could poke a bloody stick at." Wilson nodded; "He must have a time controller, the time portal in the pit was locked only to one location and the pit had been filled in for centuries."

"Well, let's get the damn thing and put an end to Tom's travels. I'LL offer him the opportunity to return to 1753, to be collected and move on." Jericho reasoned and the team headed for the church and a large opening in the North Wall, covered with a tarpaulin. "I still don't think Anne will ever be safe, whilst this mob is around." Alex commented and Wilson agreed with her; "There's so much money and property at stake, they're bound to try again to get their hands on it." They stood outside the new 'doorway' and Jericho pulled out his mirror and almost grinned; "I have an idea." was all he said and stopped time. They wandered into the church and found the three conspirators sitting around a small folding table on camping chairs. A fish supper lay before each, Owen immediately started to pinch chips from each until Alex gently slapped his hand. Wilson pulled the little, scruffy red notebook from William O'Connell's fingers; it appeared he was about to hand it back to his ancestor; Tom. Wilson grinned; "My mirror informs me that I'm a holding a time portal calling device." Jericho nodded; "Just don't recite anything written on page 7, otherwise you'll be somewhere else and at some other time." Wilson very carefully placed it in his jacket pocket.

"What have we here." Alex picked the map up from the table and smiled; "They deliberately flooded the crypt. This is a schematic showing the water values and drain points of the church's water system. It's Edwardian; old Tom must have picked it up from that time."

Jericho grunted; "They flooded the crypt after dragging the Murphy's thru the tunnel, to stop anyone finding it at the excavations. They also hid the tunnels exit at the dig with undergrowth. To give old Fielding his due, he kept worrying about the builders photo's of the site - they had gone too - because the big pile of bushes and branches were not on those original pictures. But were on the one's the archaeologists had taken. That would have been a dead giveaway that something was hidden there."

Jericho grinned and operated his mirror; time started again. Owen suddenly looked up; "There are cars pulling up outside; police cars." Jericho said quietly; "I think our miserable police colleague has finally realised there are too many O'Connell's in this story and it's not just a co-incidence."

The three at the table suddenly jumped up in unison and shouted at each other, they pushed past the temporal detectives and rushed to the tarpaulin covered hole; straight into the arms of living detectives.

Detective Sharon Smith smiled broadly at Jericho - it was certainly becoming a habit for the young woman - the temporal detectives stood to one side as the three were lead away by uniform officers. Detective Smith adjusted her glasses; "Now my happy little ghost busters, you are definitely going down the police station to help us with our enquiries and that actually makes me very happy. I have already thought of several charges I can press against you."

Jericho shrugged his shoulders and yelled; "The crypt!" The detective just sighed as they ran to the opening in floor and dived into the dirty black water. Wilson did actually fit quite easily down the stairs - that wouldn't make Owen or Alex so happy. But they would argue - sorry, discuss - that later, over dinner.

The uniform officer standing next to Sharon grunted; "There's only one exit out and our boys are waiting there; they can't go anywhere." But Sharon just grinned and whispered; "I wouldn't count on it."

The team walked back to the lighthouse - drenched from head to foot - They passed a very bemused Mr. Harris standing in the doorway. Jericho just looked at him; "Don't even ask Mr. Harris; please don't." was all he said.

THE END

EPILOGUE:

"With the recovery of Anne Murphy's soul, but the loss of John Kent Murphy's soul; the mission was not considered a total success. But Team 74 managed to close two dangerous 'Time Portals'."
SJW.

CHARACTERS:

Professor Fielding Larbert bailed his assistant Ray from the police station and the pair returned to their university. They continued to work together for some years until the professor's unexpected death in 2011 - he choked to death whilst drunk - His soul was collected and processed.

Ray Chapel was soon dismissed from the University after the professor's death, a little incident in the female student

accommodation sealed his fate. Wilson must possess the gift of prophecy; for Ray ended up working in electronics' shop in Cardiff high street - selling white goods - badly. He died in 2024 from cancer and his soul was collected and processed.
John Kent Murphy's body was never found, since he was buried some 1400 years before he was born! As a human who died out of his ordained time, his soul remains missing to this day.

Anne Murphy stayed loyal to her late husband's wishes and the ruins at the rear of her hotel became quite a tourist attraction: Gallows Tree Hotel prospered. She mourned the loss of her husband for the remainder of her life and never remarried. She died in 2009 whilst on a rare holiday in Turkey; Anne Murphy apparently walked in her sleep and fell from the hotel balcony. Prior to her death, many times, over the subsequent years, she had strange dreams about her and her husband living in savage times, in a mud hut - she never divulged those dreams to anyone - Her soul was collected and processed.

The police could not prove murder against the O'Connell's but secured abduction and kidnapping charge against them over the disappearance of Mrs. Anne Murphy. Joseph O'Connell - aka Sean Murphy - received a sentence of 17 years in prison; he served 12 and was released in 2011. He did various jobs over the years in Ireland and England. He died in a hospice at the grand old age of 97, surrounded by his grandchildren and great grandchildren. His soul was collected and processed.

Ex Police Officer William O'Connell was dismissed from the force in 2000, he escaped any prison sentence due to lack of evidence and returned to Ireland, where he worked on a farm for several years. He was killed in a ploughing accident in 2009. His soul was collected and processed.

Leon O'Connell served several years in prison and was never released; he died in 2006, in Wentworth prison, from a drugs overdose. How he obtained the lethal dose was investigated by authorities, but no charges were made against any inmates or prison officers. His soul was collected and processed.

Thomas Edward O'Connell was sentenced to 22 years in prison for his conspiracy to kidnap and murder the Murphy's. He was considered quite strange by social services and prison authorities because they could find no records concerning him; anywhere.

He died in Brixton prison in 2013 and because he was a human out of his time; no soul was collected, and it remains missing to this day.

Detective Constable Sharon Smith was promoted to Detective Sergeant over her successful conclusion to the Gallows Tree Hotel Mystery. But she left the police in 2004 and started her own company, investigating paranormal activity! It was highly successful and was actually a TV series at one point. She married a TV presenter and had three children. She died in 2025 from complications following surgery for hemorrhoids. [She had suffered with them for years. Maybe that's why she never smiled....] No soul was collected, and the case was investigated by Temporal Detective Inspector Wilson Franklyn and team 22. The case awaits resolution.

Ted English, the local Historian who attended the site for the Murphy's, wrote a book about the 'Gallows Tree Hotel Mystery' and actually mentioned the team of 'Ghost Busters' who helped solve the case. The fact that he could find no trace of them – anywhere - added to the mystery. Luckily, the book didn't sell too well. Old Ted died in 2020 during the flu-like epidemic that swept the world that year. His soul was collected and processed.

Gallows Tree Hotel changed hands several times over the years following Anne Murphy's death. Unfortunately, it suffered a disastrous fire in 2014 and lay in ruins for some years until it was finally demolished in 2021. There is now a car park and small visitors centre at its location, which services the Anglo-Saxon ruins, they have become quite a tourist attraction. There are many stories about the ruins, of paranormal activity, ghostly sightings and apparitions. The site has become a regular stop for paranormal detectives over the years.

The derelict church was completely demolished in 2001; after the major subsidence it couldn't be saved. Contractors working on site reported strange sights and sounds, when filling in the old crypt and it remains buried beneath the grassy mound that now stands there.

The Anglo-Saxon pagan temple, which lay below the crypt, was never found and the great Chieftain Offa remains undisturbed with all his gold and treasure to this day. He was buried with his beautiful young wife, Essa. She was much loved and respected and was often seen around the villages in her long flowing white dress, administering to the sick and poor. Her early death was greatly mourned, and Offa soon died after his wife, and she was interned with him. Legend says she still visits the area today in that white flowing dress; a strapping young woman with a 'Venus' like figure....

ILLUSTRATION CREDITS.

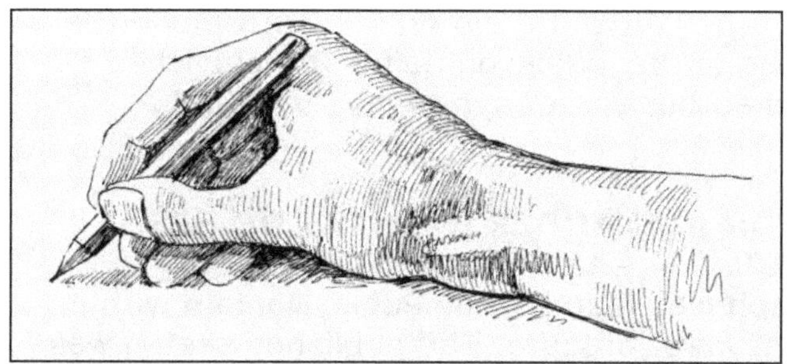

"ILLUSTRATION CREDITS FOR THE TEMPORAL DETECTIVES: SERIES 1. "

"All sketches as noted were created by the author and are copyright. The original images were found in the public domain with obscure or lapsed copyright accreditation. Should you claim current copyright to any please, contact the author immediately at:

stephen.williams24@btinternet.com

ALL original drawings, photographs or other images were found on various websites using 'Google Image Search'. They were found in the Public Domain with no artist details apparent [except where noted] and their copyright status was at the time; obscure or unknown. Where artist details are known; only images released into the Public Domain have been used for the sketches. All the published sketches were created by the author and are *Copyright © 2011-2023 Stephen Williams.*

EPISODE 1: "THE MAN WHO DIED IN THE FUTURE TO SAVE HIS PAST."
The original photograph was found in the Public Domain with its copyright status unknown or obscure. The published sketch was created by the author and *Copyright © 2011-2023 Stephen Williams.*

EPISODE 2: "THE DUNMORE WITCH TRIALS."
This image [a woodcut] of witches being burnt was found in the Public Domain with no current copyright owner.

EPISODE 3: "THE GHOSTS AND MISS JESSICA MARTIN."
This sketch created by the author from an original picture taken by photojournalist Herbert Mason from the rooftops of Carmelite Street, London during the Luftwaffe raid on 29th December 1940. The original was found in the 'public domain'. The published sketch created by the author and *Copyright © 2011-2023 Stephen Williams.*

EPISODE 4: "DOCTOR ALEXANDER HARRIS AND HIS BATTLE WITH GOD."
The original photograph was found in the Public Domain with its copyright status unknown or obscure. The published sketch was created by the author and *Copyright © 2011-2023 Stephen Williams.*

EPISODE 5: "THE IMPOSSIBLE FILMS OF MISS STOCKYARD CANNING."
The original photograph was found in the Public Domain with its copyright status unknown or obscure. The published sketch was created by the author and *Copyright © 2011-2023 Stephen Williams.*

EPISODE 6: "BETRAYAL AT GETTYSBURG."
The original photograph was found in the Public Domain with no photographer details and its copyright status is obscure. The published sketch was created by the author and *Copyright © 2011-2023 Stephen Williams.*

EPISODE 7: "HOBBS ABBEY AND THE DEVIL'S GRAVEYARD."
This sketch created by the author from an original photograph by Adrian Pingstone (2009) who released the picture into the Public Domain. The published sketch created by the author and *Copyright © 2011-2023 Stephen Williams.*

EPISODE 8: "CORDLESS, CORDLESS & FRASER (SOLICITORS)"
The original photograph was found in the Public Domain with no photographer details and its copyright status is obscure. The published sketch was created by the author and *Copyright © 2011-2023 Stephen Williams.*

EPISODE 9: "PHARAOH AMENHOTEP V AND THE MIRROR OF TIME."

The original photograph was found in the Public Domain with its copyright status unknown or obscure. The published sketch was created by the author and *Copyright © 2011-2023 Stephen Williams.*

EPISÓDE 10: "THE DEVIL'S CIRCUS."
An illustration taken from a website on Satanism showing no artist details and its copyright status unknown or obscure. The published sketch was created by the author and *Copyright © 2011-2023 Stephen Williams.*

EPISODE 11: "GHOSTS IN THE DEVIL'S GARDEN OF THE DAMNED."
The original photograph was found in the Public Domain with its copyright status unknown or obscure. The published sketch was created by the author and *Copyright © 2011-2023 Stephen Williams.*

EPISODE 12: "THE GALLOWS TREE HOTEL MYSERY."
This sketch created by the author from an original photograph which was discovered in the Public Domain. The published sketch created by the author and *Copyright © 2011-2023 Stephen Williams.*

OTHER IMAGES USED:

IMAGE USED ON PAGE 8.
The 'Crazy Writer sketch' was found in the Public Domain and is shown as 'Royalty' free and gave no copyright details.

IMAGE USED ON PAGE 403.
The 'pen and hand' drawing was found in the Public Domain and is shown as 'Royalty' free and gave no copyright details.